Josephine Moon's first novel, *The Tea Chest* (2014), delighted readers with its strong heroine and enchanting story and was a bestseller both in Australia and overseas. Her second novel, *The Chocolate Promise* (2015), was a love-story with a difference set in luscious Provence and rural Tasmania and was also a bestseller.

The Beekeeper's Secret, a novel of family and the happiness, guilt and grief that can lie within them, is her third novel.

Josephine lives with her husband, son and her horses, dogs, chickens, goats and cats on acreage in Queensland.

The
Beekeeper's
Secret

JOSEPHINE
MOON

ALLEN&UNWIN
SYDNEY · MELBOURNE · AUCKLAND · LONDON

Published by Allen & Unwin in 2016

Allen & Unwin
Sydney, Melbourne, Auckland, London

83 Alexander Street
Crows Nest NSW 2065
Australia
Phone: (61 2) 8425 0100
Fax: (61 2) 9906 2218
Email: info@allenandunwin.com
Web: www.allenandunwin.com

Cataloguing-in-Publication details are available
from the National Library of Australia
trove.nla.gov.au

ISBN 978 1 92526 613 9

Set in 12.4/17 pt Minion Pro by Bookhouse, Sydney
Printed and bound in Australia by Griffin Press

10 9 8 7 6 5 4 3 2 1

For my sister, Amanda, who in 1981 was adamant she
would wear a lolly-pink dress to her first Holy Communion,
rather than a white dress, thereby forever being the
pink sheep in the formal group photo.
I so love your individual spirit.

And for my nan, Marie Joan, who came to our house early
in the afternoon before I made my first Holy Communion
and stood with me outside the kitchen in the sun and
brushed my just-washed hair until it was dry.
Such a precious memory.

1

Fridays at Honeybee Haven were the busiest day of the week for Maria. Guests were usually checking in to or out of the six cabins on the property. It was also the day before the Yandina markets, and rain, hail or shine, the Haven had a stall there each week. Consequently, almost as soon as Maria had finished breakfast, her small kit home was overrun with preparations.

Wafting from the oven was the mouth-watering smell of roasting almonds. Maria had coated them in honey from her beehives beyond the vegetable garden. She'd have to get the nuts out of the oven soon or they'd burn. Then, after sprinkling them with sea salt, she would pack them into sterilised recycled jars and label them for sale. Not to waste a single minute, she was making throat lozenge lollipops at the same time. Her hand hovered over the pot of boiling honey, the sugar thermometer indicating that the molten gold was ready to be spooned over the tops of the lollipop sticks waiting on the lined baking tray. The lollipops were always great sellers at this time of year, as temperatures began to drop and people prepared for flu season.

With her nose monitoring the roasting almonds behind her, Maria spun the honey into well-shaped circles on the sticks and left them to cool and set, then pirouetted around (as deftly as a seventy-three-year-old could) in her tiny kitchen to open the oven, snatch up the pot holders and extract the tray just in time. The smell was intoxicating, and it was all she could do to stop herself from popping one in her mouth and letting the flavour overwhelm her tastebuds, evoking an indulgent fantasy of a cosy fireplace and warm honey mead.

But stop herself she did. These almonds, just like the honey lollipops to be wrapped in cellophane and tied with pretty strings, and just like the pyramids of jars near the window that were filled with raw honey and fresh-picked herbs, were not hers. Everything she did here was for the children. Honeybee Haven was owned by Michaela's Cambodian orphanage and was its prime source of income. Maria served here, just as she'd served during her years in the convent, right up until . . .

Stop.

She swatted away the memory like an annoying fly.

It wasn't exactly an *unwanted* memory; she deserved to remember it. But it was distracting, and there was no time today to be anything other than completely focused. There was no time to be drawn back into the past.

Maria's assistant, Petrice—employed through an agency that matched people with disabilities to jobs—had been here early this morning to make breakfast for the guests, allowing Maria to clock several industrious hours in her kitchen. Now, most of her market wares were ready to pack into the Haven's car to drive down the mountain in the dark tomorrow morning. She still had to whip some honey into a luxuriously thick cream spread, but for a brief change of scenery, she began the long walk down the steps to the letterbox at the gate of the property. She'd long ago made her peace with the one hundred and twenty-four handmade earth treads in the side of the hill. At first they'd been daunting; she wasn't young, after all. But as soon as she'd made the mental commitment to love each step, to love the burning in her thighs and the acceleration of her heart as she ascended them, to appreciate that these steps were keeping her fit and strong for the work she had to do and the service she could offer, they'd become her friends. Each one had its own story to share and wore down in different ways, and she kept a watchful eye over them, mending them as needed.

She paused at the wide, circular rest area halfway down, with the life-size statue of Saint Ambrose, patron saint of bees, in the centre. It was a nicely humble statue of Ambrose, who so often was depicted in his pompous gown and pointy bishop's hat. In this one he wore the simple robes of a monk and bees had settled on his shoulders and arms.

The statue had been a gift from a well-off Sydney gentleman who'd struck up a friendship with Maria over many visits over many years. He'd been taken with the multi-faith nature of Honeybee Haven. There were the obvious Buddhist influences, such as the six 'Tara' cabins, each named for a different form of the Buddhist deity Tara, their colours representing various virtues. Maria was particularly fond of Blue Tara, known for transmuting anger. Maria had had to do a lot of that in her life. The colour blue was also associated with Mary, whom Maria loved very much. She'd collected many small figurines of Mother Mary from the markets and contributed them to the Haven. Over the years, visitors had gifted their own symbols of faith and prayer—Hindu statues in the gardens, a copy of Sanskrit writings, a Jewish Menorah, prayer beads and other tokens of devotion. Honeybee Haven prided itself on inclusion.

Maria stopped before Saint Ambrose not so much because she needed a break, although of course it was good to check her pace and make sure she wasn't rushing—she'd be no use to anyone if she ended up in a heap at the bottom of the hill. She paused here simply because she appreciated the view. A mix of eucalyptus and rainforest trees sprawled out before her, cascading down towards the town of Eudlo at the foot of the mountain, and continuing all the way to the expanse of blue ocean on the horizon. It was silent here, except for the leaves rocking in the autumn breeze and the happy chitter-chatter of birds. Gazing out, she raised an age-spotted hand to shield her eyes from the late morning sun, and smiled. Honeybee Haven was as close to a home as she'd ever had.

Continuing down the hill, she listed in her head all the things she needed to do when she got back to the top. Firstly, she needed to check on the bees. It had been chilly this morning, so they would have slept in, but now that the day was warming up they'd be getting out and about and in a good mood. She had a hive to open today, and it was ill advised to do so if the weather was poor. Cold, grumpy bees did not take kindly to having their home taken apart. A couple of midweek visitors would be checking out of Red Tara. Petrice would be cleaning the cabin and washing the linen for the group arriving on Monday—a corporate team-bonding trip. Maria would have to do an inventory of the pantry and what was doing well in the garden to know what supplies to pick up tomorrow afternoon when she'd finished at the markets. Her handyman, Trav, was coming today to do a few odd jobs, so she'd also have to show him what needed doing.

On the last stretch of the steps now, she began to plan the next week's meals. She had requests for food that was gluten free, dairy free, paleo, vegetarian and vegan. Personally, she thought all of this fuss over food these days was rather indulgent, but if it kept customers happy and made the charity money, then so be it.

Finally reaching the letterbox, she flipped up the bright yellow backside of a large metal bumblebee and withdrew a fistful of envelopes. There was nothing unusual in that; Maria preferred paper correspondence. Of course she used email for work purposes, but only because she had to. When she'd left the convent, the world had been on the precipice of the great internet revolution. She'd hidden overseas for several years, working with non-government organisations in some of the poorest countries of the world. Then, twelve years ago, she'd come here.

Michaela had built up the business and then holidayed in Cambodia, seen the dire situation there, and decided to come back briefly to employ a manager for Honeybee Haven, renouncing everything that was easy about Australia in order to serve others, making it her life's work. Maria had liked her immediately. Michaela had been desperate for someone like Maria—someone with a broad skill set and no family commitments, and no desire to earn much money, motivated by service rather than status. It had been a win for them both.

These days, Maria used email to communicate with Michaela about the property. But she had never bothered to create a personal account—there was no one to write to. And whenever she had to fill in a form she just ignored the section that asked for an email address. She didn't have a mobile phone either. It just kept things a lot simpler. Most of her correspondence came via actual letters, which had the added benefit of keeping her at arm's length from the world. In any case, it was rare for anyone to write to her personally.

But today there were two envelopes in the bunch that caught her attention. One was a lovely pink with careful, obviously female handwriting on the front. It was addressed to her by name: *Maria Lindsey, Manager, Honeybee Haven.* The sender's name, written on the back, was Tansy Butterfield, from a unit in Noosa Heads. Only an hour away. Intrigued, Maria dug her ridged thumbnail under the flap and tore it open, pulling out a handwritten note on matching pink paper. A brightly coloured business card fluttered to the ground and she picked it up. It identified Tansy as a Children's Bedroom Decorator, and listed her contact details.

'What's this?' she asked the air around her. 'Someone canvassing for a job?'

But she began to read anyway, and to her astonishment, the woman introduced herself as her niece, twenty-nine years old and the second daughter of Maria's sister Enid.

Heavenly Father.

Maria hadn't seen Enid since the day their mother had dropped Maria, then sixteen years old, at the tall gates of the convent in the northern suburbs of Brisbane, a sprinkler spitting water across the green lawn. She could remember her younger sisters sitting in the back seat of the Holden, Enid's face dark and furious, while Florrie's was tear-stained, her bottom lip trembling.

Maria leaned back against a large boulder beside the letterbox. Tansy went on to explain that she'd managed to find Maria online as the manager at Honeybee Haven and had been delighted to discover that her aunt was living so close by.

Maria's heart gave a loud knock against her chest. Was she that easy to find? She'd thought she was hidden away up here on the mountain, able to tend to her work, make money to serve the children in Cambodia, and live out her days in relative peace and quiet. But now this Tansy girl had tracked her down and wanted to meet her.

Maria took a breath of the cool air and refolded the note, stuffing it back into its envelope along with the business card, and returned it to the pile of letters to be considered later.

To distract herself, she opened the other letter that had caught her attention. Also addressed to her by name, it looked official, marked with a special government crest.

She read it, then read it again.

Her mind went blank. She couldn't conjure a single thought. All she could do at that moment was stare straight ahead at the magpie sitting in a low branch of a tree, its head cocked to the side and its sharp beady eyes scanning the ground in search of prey. She felt coldness seep through to her bones from the boulder behind her. And she heard one of her girls buzzing somewhere nearby in search of pollen and nectar.

She managed to push herself away from the boulder, but there she stayed, her feet unwilling to move from the spot. She read the letter again.

Ian Tully.

Through concerted practice, she'd managed to edit him into the background, drape him in shadows.

Now it seemed that what they said was true, that the past would indeed always catch up with you—especially if you had something to hide.

And that no good deed ever went unpunished.

If Dougal hadn't thrown this huge announcement at her, Tansy might never have realised that her period was late. She was terribly forgetful for someone her age. Still in her twenties. But only just.

A whisker away from crossing over into the very-mature thirties. She still hadn't come to terms with that. It sounded so grown up. Like she should have it all together. Which she did, didn't she? A great husband, and a perfect home, their apartment overlooking Noosa National Park, the famous Main Beach (recently recognised as one of the world's most iconic surfing beaches, right up there with Waikiki and Malibu, thank you very much . . . not that it mattered to her, because she didn't swim in the ocean) and Hastings Street. To describe their postcode as enviable was an understatement of great magnitude. That was all evidence of having it together, surely?

Also, she had a career. Okay, maybe not a career, but a *business*. Definitely a business, as a children's bedroom decorator, a job she loved. Then again, if she was honest, which she did like to be (forgetful she might be, but dishonest she was not), as far as businesses went, it was more of a hobby, and could probably be legally classified as such by the tax office. But still, it was *her* hobby. All hers. One she'd worked hard to get off the ground, stubbornly refusing to take any advice or guidance from Dougal, who was well established in the corporate world. She liked to believe she was finally gaining some momentum here on the Sunshine Coast. And she probably would be if she remembered to organise some proper advertising in a glossy magazine or something.

And that brought her back to the forgetfulness and Dougal's big announcement.

Yesterday afternoon, her husband had told her he was taking her out to dinner in Hastings Street tonight, which wasn't unusual except that he'd said there was something important he wanted to talk to her about. She'd had a day to wonder what it might be and slowly but steadily decided that he'd changed his mind, after seven years of marriage, and decided that he did in fact want a baby. She was turning thirty, a number guaranteed to make people think about Time Running Out. Her best friend, Belle, and her husband, Raj, had a four-month-old baby and when they'd visited them two months ago Dougal had been clearly clucky.

His eyes had gone all soft and romantic like they did sometimes when he was feeling particularly in love with her. He'd been the only one who'd been able to settle Hamish that day, holding the baby on his nicely shaped chest in the baby carrier for nearly an hour, Hamish nuzzled in under his chin, snoozing away in his fluffy romper suit. Dougal was a total natural with babies, she'd discovered. She longed to zip back in time to when Dougal's grown son, Leo, had been a baby, just so she could see that look of tenderness on Dougal's face and absorb the misty, wafty, loving glow.

At the end of the visit, Tansy had had the creeping suspicion that she'd been wrong to make such a huge decision about her future in her early twenties, agreeing not to have children, a thought that was both alarming and mortifying. Her mother and sister had told her she'd regret it and she'd stubbornly ignored them.

'Why?' Tansy had argued, as only a naive twenty-something could. 'Because I'm a woman?'

'No,' her mother had countered. 'Because you are full of love to give.'

She'd mulled over her mother's words in the car on the way home from Belle and Raj's place that day; in the days following she kept the baby idea to herself, feeling foolish for even entertaining the thought when Dougal had been so clear from the start of their relationship that Leo would be his one and only child.

But since that visit, Tansy had shown Dougal some pictures of Hamish on her phone, and he'd smiled and puffed with pride that he'd been the baby whisperer above everyone else. And she'd let the little seed of hope sit in her navel, forgetting it was there until the day when he said he needed to talk to her.

Then it bloomed. *He feels the same.*

Excitedly, she'd held his hand as they walked down the hill to Hastings Street and into a fine restaurant, where a classical guitarist serenaded the patrons from a corner of the al fresco section. Big green leaves of a fairy-lit tree hovered behind them. They couldn't see the beach from where they were, but they could hear the waves crashing to the shore and feel the stickiness of the salt in the air on her skin.

And it was while she was sipping merlot, her silk shawl pulled around her shoulders, waiting for Dougal to admit that he'd been silly to make that decision about not having any more children, and now that she was nearly thirty, and having seen Hamish, and realising he wasn't getting any younger either, that he was wondering (he knew it would be a big ask, because she'd put so much thought into it in the first place, and he had explicitly said it was non-negotiable and she'd have to live with her decision forever, so she had to be *sure*) would she, *maybe*, consider having a baby, that she realised she couldn't remember when she'd last had her period. But no sooner had the question wandered into her mind than Dougal dropped his news, bringing all thoughts to a screeching halt.

'The company wants us to move to Canada for a year, maybe two.'

She'd quickly swallowed her wine. 'I'm sorry, what?'

'The company wants me to go to Toronto for the next year or two as part of the engineering design team for a new medical university they're building. It's a fantastic opportunity,' he'd said, as if knowing she wouldn't be on board with the idea straight away.

'Canada? As in snow and sub-freezing temperatures, on the other side of the world?'

Too cold for babies, surely.

The waiter returned with menus, placed them on the table and shook out the white linen napkins across their laps.

'I know it's a bit of a bombshell,' Dougal went on, indicating the garlic bread to start them off. 'And I know you'll want time to think about it.' He paused, as if hopeful she would cut him off and tell him that no, she didn't need any time at all, she'd love to go. Excitement hovered around him like a halo. Corporate success was the thing he'd clung to in order to prove himself to his family after his early setback.

'And what about Leo?' she said. 'Where will he go?' Leo attended the University of the Sunshine Coast. His mother, Rebecca, lived in Brisbane. Leo had moved up here three years ago, from his mum's place to his dad's, to be closer to the uni.

Dougal shrugged. 'I figure he can stay in the apartment and look after it for us. It's actually a lot easier for everyone if he does. We don't want to have to look at selling or renting it out or selling cars and all our furniture and all that, putting things in storage and the like. This way, we can simply pack up our bags and go. Leo can drive us to the airport and pick us up again in a year or two's time.' He smiled, stuffing a hunk of garlic bread into his mouth.

'Have you told him yet?' she asked.

'No. I wanted to talk to you first.' Dougal reached out and took her hand. 'We don't need to decide right now. Let's just enjoy a nice meal and go for a walk on the sand afterwards and then, when we get home . . .' He trailed off and gave her a suggestive wink.

'You're a rogue.' She laughed. 'You're quite frisky for your age, you know,' she teased. Her tone was light but her heart was not.

Now lying in bed, their evening completed, she knew she'd been wrong; Dougal didn't want a baby. And yet she might be pregnant.

2

It should have been the sounds of the markets that filled Maria's head: customers calling for half a kilo of prawns from the seafood van opposite; the delighted squeals of small children running across the grass with a bag full of bric-a-brac treasure; the sway and rustle of plastic shopping bags; dogs barking; and the squeaky wheels of wagons laden with potted plants. Instead, Fred Astaire's voice, in scratchy, bumpy, old-vinyl sound, floated in Maria's head as she wrapped up two jars of honey sugar body scrub—cheap as chips to make and a great little earner—in pink tissue paper and tied it with string.

'They Can't Take That Away From Me' was her parents' favourite song. Her mother, Elyse, told the girls that she and their father, Thomas, would play the song on their record player during the war, sometimes when they were frightened and it felt as though the whole world would collapse. They would play it to give themselves hope. And sometimes they played it when they

12

were upbeat and puffed up with national pride, perhaps after an exciting day when Pa had received a covert shipment of his carefully selected imported tea leaves, which he was employed to do on behalf of the tea control board. The tea had to make it through the trade routes infested by the Japanese navy in the Pacific, so it was cause for great national pride when it made it to the docks. Thomas would joke that the Germans and the Japs might be able to take a lot of things but they would never get their tea.

And then years later, after Pa had died suddenly on the docks one summer—heatstroke, they said—her bereft and weary mother would play it alone in the lounge once Maria and her sisters were in bed. Maria and Enid shared a double bed in the shadow of the tall, dark wardrobe with the key always in the lock (except for the day that Enid lost it and the girls were told they weren't allowed to leave the house until it was found again, which it was, thankfully, two days later, when all of them were ready to kill each other). The sisters would listen to Fred's optimistic voice and curse out into the darkness that 'they' *had* taken it away from them. Their beloved father was gone.

Now, Maria paused in her ruminations to say hello to a middle-aged couple who'd been hovering over some of the framed artwork at one end of her stall. Some months ago, she had picked up several books of old sheet music from an op shop and posted them to the orphanage for art projects. The children had screen-printed honeybees onto the paper, in various patterns and colours, and posted them back, and Trav had used some offcuts of wood from other jobs to build simple but sweet frames for them.

'These are handmade by the children in the orphanage,' Maria said helpfully, gesturing to the donation tin and the information leaflets.

'Oh, how adorable,' the woman said, quickly reaching for her purse to retrieve a five-dollar note and stuff it in the tin. Minutes later, they'd left with two matching bee artworks, some honey Dijon mustard and several of the lollipops Maria had made yesterday. Any sale from her stall was a gift that kept on giving, but Maria did especially love to see bee artworks get picked up. She hoped they would go on to inspire more people to think about bees, the work they did, and the crucial role they played in humanity's survival.

In her convent days, she'd been the head beekeeper. She had a way with the bees that no other sister had. Sister Frances was too heavy-footed, too impatient in her movements, too grumpy. The bees didn't like grumpy people and didn't trust anyone thumping around their homes. Frances was too much like a grizzly bear, Maria had often thought. Sister Celine was too timid. Such a mouse of a girl when she'd arrived on their doorstep, fleeing her troubled home. The convent was her refuge, but she had no confidence with the bees and would bolt if one landed on her.

Father Peter claimed he was allergic to them and would swell up like a puffer fish if stung. But hardly anyone was truly allergic to bees. Everyone swelled to some degree when they were stung; it didn't mean it was life-threatening. She suspected it was simply a ploy on his part to avoid work. It was typical—so much like the bees. The female bees did all the work. The male bees sat around eating honey, getting fat and waiting to copulate. That was it. Male bees didn't even build the wax house in which they lived. They didn't even groom themselves.

The sisters were the worker bees of the church, out there nursing, teaching, farming and whatever else they could do, donating their wages straight to the church. The only difference between the beehive and the church was that a queen sat at the top of the beehive and a man at the top of the church.

Maria liked bees much better.

She could never understand why people were afraid of them. A bee didn't want to sting anyone; it would die if it did. A bee would only ever sting if it was under extreme threat, or to save the hive from an intruder, like a foreign insect, which they would then wrap up in propolis to quarantine it and prevent any possible spread of infection. The girls—the worker bees—had one aim in life only, and that was to serve, nurture and protect. What wasn't to like about that? The bees were her inspiration. She'd lost a lot in her lifetime, and had accepted that life was far beyond her control, but if she could have one prayer answered it would be that the bees were the one thing that could never be taken away, not even after her secret was revealed.

She would go to Canada. How could she not? That was what you did when you were married, wasn't it? But uprooting herself from this life here on the coast was such an enormous concept that it didn't fit into her head properly yet. Besides which, this morning Tansy had some other mental tidying to do. Getting rid of any fantasies about babies was the first thing. She gave herself a stern talking-to in the mirror while simultaneously pulling her dark shoulder-length curls into a small, low pony and chewing on a toothbrush, toothpaste leaking out the corner of her mouth.

She'd just got caught up in the romance of seeing her husband in the role of a father, that was all. She and Dougal shared a wonderful love. It was surely natural to occasionally fantasise about expanding that love into something even greater than the two of them. In their early months of dating, in that heady, lust-filled time, it sometimes felt as though there was simply too much love just for the two of them. It seemed almost selfish to keep it all to themselves. That was the trap. It had to be. That was when people leapt recklessly into the world of baby making. But then reality struck, and there was no turning back. Look at her life now. It was beyond wonderful.

She spat the toothpaste into the sink and rinsed.

R u up?

Speaking of reality, here it was. Belle, up early as usual.

Yes, on my way out. How are you?

Belle and Raj lived two and a half hours away inland, an exhausting drive along a snaking one-lane highway through cattle country. For the past four months, since Hamish had arrived, texting had been Tansy's prime form of communication with her childhood best friend. There was just never a good time to call when someone had a newborn, let alone one with reflux who screamed incessantly. *Except when Dougal had him in the baby carrier, rubbing his downy head and whispering to him . . .*

Stop it, she told herself. *Or you'll have to eat Brussels sprouts.*

Eating Brussels sprouts was Tansy's way of punishing herself when she'd done something bad—like, in this case, coveting someone else's baby. And it was a valid punishment, because not only did Brussels sprouts taste disgusting but they gave her serious wind too, and that was never pleasant for anyone.

Tansy had made Belle promise to text regularly, even if she had nothing to say.

It was a complete schlock of a night, Hamish screaming for most of it. Belle, who had always sworn like a sailor, was now making a supreme effort to give up cursing in front of her baby. Schlock was her substitute for the other s-word (and happened to have almost the same meaning). *One and a half hours sleep last night. That is all.*

Sorry, lovely. I hear it gets better xxx

I hope so xxx

Tansy had been meaning to send Belle a care package for weeks now. She fished in her handbag for a pen and a petrol receipt and wrote a note to herself to do that. The other person she needed to make more of an effort with was Rose. Her sister had been MIA for months, barely coming to the surface for an occasional text. Tansy sent her a message now.

I'm heading out to go to church with the olds. Want to come? Would be great to see you xx

Then, tucking the receipt into her money purse, she picked up her keys and left Dougal and Leo sleeping, as she always did on her monthly Sunday trips to Brisbane.

The drive down the highway was smooth and swift and she arrived at her parents' home in the northern suburb of Alderley ahead of time. The two yapping poodles met her at the front door, which she opened with her key, and she pushed past their leaping front paws to the cool tiled interior.

'Hello?' she said to the empty lounge room.

'Tansy?' Enid called.

'Yes, it's me.' She knelt down to scruff the cinnamon-coloured dogs scrambling for affection. 'Hello, boys, how's the world treating you?'

Enid appeared from around the corner, dressed in tailored blush-pink pants and a white blouse, carrying a cardigan over her arm in case of a chill, and smelling of Chanel perfume, which always made Tansy's nose twitch. 'You're early,' she said observationally, coming to kiss and hug her daughter.

'Good run down. How are you?' Tansy asked, casting her eyes across to the kitchen, which was unusually neat and tidy for a Sunday morning, when bacon and eggs was the norm.

'Can't complain,' Enid said.

'Have you heard from Rose this morning?' Tansy asked, checking her phone to find no reply.

'No, why?'

'I sent her a message to see if she wanted to come, that's all.' Tansy shrugged, disappointed but not surprised. 'What's Dad doing?'

'I'm here,' Finlay said, his veiny legs showing beneath shorts, a tuft of white chest hair sprouting at the neck of his shirt. He certainly wasn't dressed for church. Gardening, more like it. Beside Tansy, Enid stiffened ever so slightly.

Tansy looked from one to the other, trying to read them. 'Are you both ready?'

'Your dad's not coming today,' Enid said, gathering her handbag and stuffing extra tissues inside.

'Got a headache, love,' he said, coming to greet Tansy properly. 'Think I'll take it easy today.'

'Is everything okay?' Tansy said, assessing the colour of his cheeks (as ruddy as ever) and the clarity of his hazel eyes (all good), holding onto his arm a little longer than necessary. For most of her life she'd had morbid thoughts of losing her parents. It was just what happened when you were born as a 'surprise' fourteen years after your sister, when your mum was forty-one and thought that she was done. By the time you were ten and could understand some medical terminology, it was easy to see that your parents were on the wrong side of the lifespan and you might lose them at a young age. Even her sister, at forty-four, seemed a generation ahead of her. She could never catch up to them, always that gap behind, racing to grasp what was already gone. Most likely, she would be living her life with her parents gone for more time than she'd had them.

It was one particular bout of melancholic navel-gazing along these lines that had prompted her to try to track down her estranged aunt before she died. Tansy wanted to know all of her family and thought her mother should reconnect with her sister before it was too late.

'Yes, yes, fine,' Finlay said. 'I just need a lie-in this morning. Old age catching up with me.'

'Could you please take out the rubbish before you go back to bed?' Enid asked him.

'No problem.'

Tansy was uncomfortably aware of the stiffness between them and the chilliness of the room, the silence of the street outside. They'd obviously had a fight, something that didn't happen often but was of course inevitable if you'd been married for nearly fifty years.

'Thank you,' Enid said. 'Okay, Tansy, let's go.'

St Columba's church in Wilston was a hundred-year-old brick building, in the traditional shape of pitched roof and high domed ceiling, with pillars, narrow stained-glass windows, big heavy wooden doors, a choir loft and amazing acoustics. There were hardly any of these old churches these days, but they had infinitely more spirit than any modern building. Tansy's family had been coming here for as long as she could remember and, now that she thought about it, probably longer than that. She'd never thought to ask. She loved to watch the light streaming through the high windows and down onto the marble flooring of the apse and altar, framed by the curved whitewashed sacristy at the rear.

The church still had wooden pews, with padded kneelers, and had a strong smell of wood polish and old dust about it, something else Tansy loved. She felt herself relax the moment she stepped inside. Today, Enid led the way to a pew on the right side of the aisle, under a station of the cross, and they took their seats with the soothing clunk and creak of wood as people shuffled around.

Tansy took the hymnbook her mother passed her and flicked through it, noting songs she knew well and songs she loved, as well as some that should long ago have been retired. She rubbed a thumb along the curved edge of the pew in front of her, appreciating its smoothly worn surface, and reflected on how much this building had been a part of her life.

She had been baptised here, and apparently 'screamed blue murder' when the priest poured water on her bald head, so much so that the congregation couldn't even hear the priest's next words and he'd had to take a break until she stopped crying and nestled, hiccupping, on her father's shoulder. At eight, she'd made her first Holy Communion, in her white dress and veil. After the mass, she'd received a gift of a framed picture of Jesus with the glowing Sacred Heart, and at home they'd had a family-sized block of Cadbury chocolate to share. The same year, she also made her first Reconciliation, where she'd fearfully confessed her sin of forgetting to feed the guinea pigs, forcing her mother to do it instead, and Father Dennis had been so kind and told her he was certain she hadn't meant to make more work for her mother and that if she would like to say a Hail Mary he was sure she would be just fine.

She'd made her Confirmation here at the age of twelve, professing to believe in the one true church of God, with lovely Aunt Florrie standing beside her supportively with her hand on her shoulder. And now she thought about that, it was generous of Florrie to be her sponsor, since her aunt was so different to Tansy's mother—it was part of what Tansy loved about her—and might not have actually believed in what she was saying there in front of that priest. She was all into yoga and meditation these days.

Gosh, this morning it seemed as though there was a lot of things she'd never considered about her family. Perhaps she should say an extra prayer after communion for help to put them at the forefront of her mind.

And then, of course, she and Dougal had been married here by funny, gentle Father Bryce. He was her favourite of all the priests she'd seen come and go. He'd been so kind and welcoming to Dougal, a divorced, lapsed Catholic, and she'd never forget how during the ceremony he had placed a hand on each of their shoulders, his voice booming around the church, and said that he married a lot of people but rarely did he see a couple with such faith and commitment not only to God but to each other. And somehow she'd felt the power of those words run through his hands into them both, and it seemed even more important than the words she and Dougal had spoken.

Their wedding had been such a happy day. Both their mothers had cried. Her father had walked her down the aisle, and she'd felt the pride coming from him with every step. Leo, right on the verge of manhood, had stood there in a suit slightly too large for him and passed the rings when asked, and later danced with Belle during the reception at a restaurant on the Brisbane River. Rose had been matron of honour; during the lead-up to the day, with the planning and the bridal shower and the hen's party, Tansy had felt closer to her older sister than she ever had when she was young and Rose had seemed so many leagues ahead of her, many more than the actual fourteen years' difference between them. It was as if Tansy had finally grown up and was now part of the same tribe. And of course Belle had been a bridesmaid, beaming in her pale pink strapless dress, with tan marks around her neck from her swimmers.

Now, with the first hymn playing, Father Bryce stepped up to the altar and knelt and genuflected to the cross, and Tansy took a deep breath, feeling great love for this church, and wondering what might have caused Maria to leave and abandon her vows.

She knew that her mother held great resentment towards Maria for not attending their mother's funeral. And she knew that her mother had actually wanted to become a nun and sometimes had moments of 'what if?' about that, though she was quick to assure the girls she had no regrets about following a different life of a wife and mother. Tansy had thought she'd picked up a whiff of jealousy, even, that Maria got to lead the life Enid had wanted. But there was more going on here, and she was determined to find out what it was.

'Did you know that a collection of sharks is called a shiver of sharks? Isn't that appropriate?' Tansy said. It was a tradition for her and her mother (and usually her father) to go out for morning tea after church to Riverbend Books in Bulimba. They usually sat on the deck to have a pot of tea and some cake before each choosing and buying a book to read over the following month and then chatting about it the next time they were here. Since Enid was unusually quiet today, Tansy had brought a few books to the table to peruse while they waited for their order to arrive, and had come across this fun fact. 'I certainly think I'd be shivering if I came across a group of sharks swimming my way,' she said.

'Except you're afraid of water and don't swim in the ocean,' Enid replied, flicking through an art book of Italian sculptures.

'And you can have a flamboyance of flamingos,' Tansy went on.

Enid looked up and nodded approvingly. 'I like that one.'

The tea and cakes arrived at their corner table, which was too close to another table with several rowdy children at it. Wordlessly, mother and daughter poured milk and shared the honey spoon.

'So,' Tansy began, sipping her vanilla tea. 'What's new in your world?' She was, in fact, itching to tell her mother both about Toronto and also that she had tracked down Maria, but—in view of her most recent resolution to put thoughts of her family to the forefront of her mind—she made a supreme effort to concentrate on her mother's accounts of the latest goings-on in their life of retirement, which consisted of a lot of medical appointments and standard screenings for all sorts of cancers and diseases, the new herb garden they were building, and the leaky pipe under the sink that her father was trying to fix while stubbornly refusing to call a plumber.

'Have you had any thoughts on what you're going to do for your birthday?' Enid then asked.

A rabble of butterflies began beating their wings in Tansy's tummy. 'Interesting you ask, actually. I was thinking of having a family gathering, with everyone there, maybe outdoors so Rose's kids can run amok and not trash anything.' This was the perfect opportunity to tell her about Maria and the great idea she had about inviting her to the party. It would be a reunion! It would be easier on Enid and Florrie to see Maria again after all these years if they were in a neutral location with lots of other relatives there to help dilute the tension from whatever had caused the separation in the first place.

'That sounds lovely,' Enid said, genuinely pleased. She clearly thought of Tansy as being older than she was, because she made no reference to that being an 'old woman' thing to do, as Tansy's husband had done when she'd mentioned it to him. He'd been teasing, of course, but the jibe made her wonder if she'd let the best years of her life pass her by with a man so much older than her. She could have spent the past eight years climbing the Himalayas with a Sherpa with a chipped tooth and dimples. Or dancing the rumba in the streets of some Latin country, a mojito in one hand and the other on her instructor's bare midriff while his pelvis thrust forwards into hers to the beat of the maracas.

There'd been Brussels sprouts for dinner that night after all that fantasising. And not even any white sauce to cover them.

'I'm glad you think so,' Tansy said now, replacing her china cup on the saucer. 'Because there's something I want to talk to you about.'

Enid, sensing an impending announcement, put down her own cup with extra care and leaned forward. Despite the noise coming from the kids nearby, including a tinny rendition of 'The Wonky Donkey' from a three-legged toy donkey and book set, and the accompanying squeals of delight from the boy who'd pressed the button, she dropped her voice. 'Are you *pregnant*?' She seemed almost giddy with delight at the possibility.

For the second time in a few days, Tansy was thrown. Her jaw loosened and she scrambled for something to say, suddenly remembering that she'd meant to go back through her diary to work out how long it had been since she'd had a period, but in the shock of Dougal's news she'd forgotten.

But all of that was a large and complicated amount of information to give to her mother, who was nearly salivating at the thought of another grandchild. She was the most excitable grandmother, which still managed to astound Tansy—even after four of the cherubs had come via Rose and Sam—because she had no real memories of Enid being that playful and carefree with herself as a child. Rather, she'd seemed tired and harried most of the time.

'Mum,' she began, edgy because this was cutting a bit close to the bone of the fantasies she'd had recently, but also annoyed that she was having this conversation with her mother yet again. 'You know Dougal doesn't want any more children. We all knew that before we got married. He was clear, right from the start. I made my peace with that.'

I thought.

24

'Yes, yes, I know. I just always thought he'd have changed his mind by now,' Enid said, exasperated, as though she'd been waiting daily for the news that Tansy was having a baby.

'Well, you know they say that's the greatest mistake women make, thinking they can change a man.' *Pretty good advice, Tans. Maybe you should have listened to that.* 'Anyway,' she said, keen to move the subject on, 'guess who I was thinking about this morning?'

'Who?'

'Maria.' Tansy said it tentatively, unsure how her mother would respond. Instantly, Enid shot her a brittle glare that made Tansy flinch. *A shatter of stares.*

'What on earth for?' Enid demanded.

'Just being in church, you know, because she was a nun . . .' Tansy let her words trail off, no longer feeling confident her mother would welcome the idea of Tansy contacting Maria, let alone her plan to bring her to the party.

'Pft. If she was a real nun she'd still be in the order, wouldn't she? She took holy vows to serve the church for the rest of her life, until death. But then she abandoned them, just like she abandoned our family right when we needed her the most.' Enid paused, her eyes focused somewhere in the distance, remembering. 'She didn't care what happened to us, and it was all for nothing, apparently, since she left the church anyway.'

'I'm sure she had her reasons,' Tansy ventured.

Enid shook her head. 'She was married to the church and she broke those vows. When we take the sacrament of marriage we take it for life. *For. Life.* There's no getting out of it when it doesn't suit you anymore.'

She had Tansy's attention now, as well as her concern. 'Is everything okay with you and Dad?'

Her mother's verbosity of the past couple of minutes dried up and she folded her arms. 'Fine.'

Tansy nodded slowly. She knew this stance. She knew that her mother had shut down the louvres over the window to her thoughts and the more Tansy tried to pry them open the tighter they'd close.

The piercing sting of sunburn drew her attention and she pulled a cotton shawl around her shoulders. Even in the last month of autumn you could still burn in Brisbane.

'But forget that,' Enid said, waving away the conversation. 'What was your news?' She was trying to sound interested, but the set of her mouth and the frost in her voice said she was still preoccupied with thoughts of Maria.

Oh dear. This well of bitterness was a lot deeper than Tansy had realised. 'I have a new client to meet this week,' she fudged, hoping that would be enough to keep her mother happy. She didn't feel like talking about Toronto now and she certainly wouldn't be sharing anything about Maria. She needed more time to discover why the sisters had had such a falling-out and to prepare Enid for Maria's arrival at the party. But that would have to wait until Enid was in a much better mood. And of course, Maria would have to agree to come. There was no point counting any chickens before they'd hatched. For now, she would just get on with planning what she hoped would be a wonderful reunion. And she'd try to talk to her father and find out what was going on at home. More than anything, this little chat today had convinced her one hundred per cent that she needed to pull her family together before she left the country.

3

Monday morning, Maria woke with a horrible kick to her chest at the memory of the official letter. But, nowadays well practised at dealing with huge emotions, she effectively slammed closed an iron door on those thoughts. Beginning her day just before dawn as she'd done for decades, she pulled one of her two op-shop-purchased cardigans around herself and went from her small bedroom into the adjoining office. She adjusted her glasses on the bridge of her nose, turned on the laptop and logged into the Haven's inbox. Michaela had emailed again from Cambodia, this time with a sad face in the subject line. Maria sucked in cool early morning air through her teeth and opened it.

Hi Maria, I hope you don't mind my writing again but I couldn't sleep and needed to talk to someone. It's too hot to sleep here anyway and the children are restless. The fans click interminably day and night, though I only notice them when I'm awake at night.

And there's the chanting from the monks. They've been here for the past week (did I tell you that?) giving special instruction to the children. I do love their chanting, though. It sounds so otherworldly, like it's coming from a galaxy far away.

Maria leaned back from the screen to take a moment to listen to her own surrounds. The kookaburras announced the first rays of light, the tin roof creaked slowly as it woke for another day, and there was the gentle whir of the laptop. But otherwise, all was quiet. It wouldn't stay that way, of course, not with a busload of corporate guests arriving in a couple of hours' time. They'd be as they always were—some yahooing men looking forward to the afternoon drinks, some women irritated to have to participate in juvenile games, some falsely jovial managers who were silently stroppy that their billable time sheets would be suffering from this waste of productivity, and a cheery human resources manager who lived for this one event a year.

She focused on the screen once more, feeling the pinch under her skin as she read the rest of Michaela's email. Michaela was still fretting about how to find the money for Sopheak's spinal fusion operation back here in Australia to correct her scoliosis. Sopheak's wheelchair was also getting on, and while not urgent, it would be wonderful to replace it so she could get around more easily to play with the other kids. Michaela always felt guilty that she couldn't do more.

Maria knew about guilt. It was a pervasive and toxic emotion, and incredibly difficult to shake.

She started to type a reply to Michaela, then deleted it. It was far too pragmatic and Michaela was all heart. She'd given up her life in Australia to serve orphans in a treacherous, often violent country, with nothing but faith. Maria understood that too.

She wanted to be a shoulder for Michaela to cry on. Clearly, Michaela wanted that too or she wouldn't unburden her soul to Maria so frequently. But Maria knew she just didn't have the words Michaela needed to hear. So she settled on a prayer—one of her favourites, from Saint Therese, the 'little flower' who didn't think herself capable of much at all but who inspired miracles around the world. *Little Therese, benefactress of the needy, pray for us.* And she told Michaela that she would say a decade of the rosary for her.

It had been years since she'd said the rosary each day, but she still liked to do it from time to time. After doing it her whole life, her body had a physical reaction to just holding the beads in her hands. They were prayer beads, essentially, not dissimilar to those used by the Buddhists in the Cambodian orphanage. Meditation beads. They brought her great peace.

Maria hit send, checked the time, decided to make a cuppa, and then returned to the laptop carrying a steaming mug of black tea with just a splash of milk.

The next email was from Tansy Butterfield. Her niece.

Another jolt zapped Maria's chest and she automatically placed the warm mug there, in an unconscious attempt at solace. Once again her sense of safety had been pierced. In the past, she could have hidden from the world. Now it seemed anyone from anywhere could track her down and invade her private space.

Hi Maria,

I hope you received my letter on Friday and have had the chance to consider it. (If you haven't, this email will be quite a bolt from the blue!) I was at mass yesterday (at St Columba's) and thinking about you. Look, in short, I'd like to meet you. I work for myself, so I have some flexibility in my days, and you're not that far away.

Maybe I could come up and help out with some chores? I've been reading about the orphanage in Cambodia—so horribly sad—and I'd love to help raise funds. It's clever of the orphanage to have a business here in Australia to create a steady supply of income. I think that's going to be the way of the future for charities, don't you? It's hard to just keep asking people for money for nothing but a good feeling in return. It's far more sensible to link it to a business. Maybe I could offer some help through my business. I'd love to chat to you about that too.

Gosh, I have raved on, haven't I? You see, we won't have any trouble filling the silences! So, what do you think? Would it be okay if I came up to see you?

Tansy xx

Maria didn't know whether to laugh or shake her fist at the screen. Part of her was intrigued by this young woman, with her rambling thoughts and her whimsical attitude to life and her belief that Maria would of course love to meet her too. Part of her was also drawn by Tansy's offer of assistance to the orphanage. Maria was focused on one thing only, raising funds for those children, and she never, ever turned down help, donations or publicity from anyone (although she was careful to keep herself out of the limelight as much as possible and refer interviews to Michaela). Part of her was outraged that Tansy was so pushy and had managed to break into her early morning solitude. And part of her was deeply saddened.

Tansy was her family, and family was something she'd long since let go of. Family was something she'd worked hard to forget. But sometimes a memory would float to the surface and she'd find herself watching it, like stepping into a room and finding a movie playing on the television.

There was the one about the hard years after her father's death, with her mother doing leatherwork to make a little money, staining the strands and weaving them into belts and handbags; sending her three daughters to school in second-hand uniforms the nuns found for them; and inventing a thousand different ways to use pumpkins.

Heavens, Maria hated pumpkins. For years, she could barely walk past one in the convent garden without gagging. Mother Veronica had made her pray to stop being so wasteful and ungrateful. But as far as she was concerned, the pumpkin's only virtues were that it was large and easy to grow, it multiplied faster than the loaves and the fishes in the Bible, and it was versatile. Actually, that was quite a lot in its favour. But there was only so much of the stuff anyone could eat in a lifetime. Now the ones she grew in the garden she could sell for money for the orphanage. For that, at least, she was grateful. But her dislike truly did verge on hatred.

She stopped herself; now she sounded like one of the fussy eaters who came to stay at the Haven.

Another memory arrived, this one the mini movie of the three of them—Maria, Enid and Florrie—playing in the creek one hot summer's day and disturbing a huge red-bellied black snake. Maria screamed, Enid wet herself, and Florrie fainted, and the two older sisters had to carry her back to the house, slowed down by her small frame flopping between them, terrified the snake was chasing them the whole way, waiting for the feel of its fangs in their ankles.

There was the day Maria grievously sinned, altering her own life forever, her mother's ashamed face by the light of the lamp in the corner of the lounge, telling Maria what she would need to do to atone.

And there was the day Mother Superior told Maria that her mother had died suddenly of a massive stroke. And Maria, then in her forties, had wept in the grotto with the convent beehives buzzing nearby.

A sliver of sunlight fell through the window onto Maria's hand and brought her back to the present. She checked the time. She needed to go and set up the trestle table in the dining area with tea and coffee things for the group's arrival and then start making ginger and honey scones for morning tea. (The vegans and the dairy- and gluten-free people would be having nuts and dried fruit while everyone else drooled over her delicious-smelling fluffy hot scones, topped with melting butter and honey.)

Outside, she shrugged into an anorak and stepped into boots. To the left of her little kit home were the shower blocks, and then the beginning of the arc of six Tara cabins (starting with Blue Tara), the dining hall, the small car park that doubled as an unloading bay and the meditation room to the right of her cabin completing the circle. Within the circle formed by the buildings was a lawn, with a wishing well for donations at the centre.

She headed across the dewy grass to the dining hall, basic in structure but filled with colourful artworks and photographs from Cambodia, many made by the children themselves, and some by the monks who regularly visited the orphanage to impart traditional cultural values.

Her breath misted in the air; she'd have to turn on the heaters in the hall today. But just as she stepped onto the first of two stairs (flanked, like the steps to the cabins, with pots of brightly swaying daisies, for the bees), she stopped, confused. On the top step sat a blank envelope.

She stared at it. It was nothing special, just an ordinary envelope with the four empty orange squares at the bottom right corner for a postcode. But there had been enough surprises in the past few days to make her hesitate. She looked around at the nine other buildings, but every one of them sat silent. There were no footprints in the dew other than hers, and the birds were barely stirring in the trees.

A chill ran down her spine. As far as she knew the envelope wasn't there before she went to bed and she'd been the only person here overnight, with no guests and Petrice not due to come back until the lunchtime rush today.

But someone had been here while she slept.

She stared at the envelope for so long that she got a cramp in her foot from the cold.

Should she call the police? No, that would only lead to questions she didn't want to answer. Questions like: *Is there anyone who would have cause to want to frighten you?*

Should she jump into the Haven's yellow Citroën and leave the place until the corporate group arrived? Should she lock herself in a cabin? Search all the cabins? Go and arm herself with the machete she used to clear lantana from the property?

She was being melodramatic. She deliberately straightened her shoulders and turned to face the open space, cleared her throat, took a deep breath and called out, 'Hello?'

She waited, but the only thing she heard in response was her pulse in her ears. She could feel the beats of the arteries in her neck.

Gathering more courage, she called again, louder this time, with more authority, 'Is anyone there?'

Still nothing.

Eventually, she bent down as quickly as she could to pick up the envelope. Perhaps it was from someone in need, she told herself. The Haven employed people down on their luck—homeless, low income, people with disabilities (like Petrice, with post-traumatic stress syndrome as a result of a violent childhood), ex-prisoners, refugees, non-English speakers. It went out of its way to exemplify the values of Michaela's Buddha and Maria's Christ. Working to serve that clientele brought challenges, but it also brought rewards and surprises. And the Haven was far enough up the mountain that anyone who wanted to get there had to be determined to do so. She hadn't heard a car groan up the steep access road to the temporary loading bay, so whoever had left the envelope must have come on foot, and that took some effort. It was most likely someone looking for help.

Talking sternly to herself, she tore open the envelope and pulled out a single sheet of lined paper, folded into three. She expected to read a plea for work, or a bed, or even a meal.

Instead, she found four words.

Silence is a virtue.

4

Tansy snapped off the elastic band that held her diary shut. She'd been meaning to check those dates for days. She flicked back, scanning the past month. Trying to remember.

A deeply tanned waitress with fluorescent pink hair interrupted her to deliver her order.

'Thanks,' Tansy said, pushing her diary aside to make room for it. A thick slice of toasted banana bread with butter, and an almond milk and honey chai latte were Tansy's lucky combination. She liked to bring her sketchpad, concept book and iPad here to Peregian Beach, to the Raw Energy cafe, one of her favourite places to sit and plan new designs. The warm banana bread was particularly yummy at this time of year when the mornings were fresh. And this little nook of Peregian, this humming little corner of life, was so much a part of what she and Dougal loved about living at the coast. It was so easy to be healthy here, with delicious, nourishing food on every street, beaches that cried out to be run on and oceans that begged to be swum in, all manner of water sports, a variety of walking trails, and fit swimwear-clad bodies at every turn. The weather was warm almost all year round, so there was simply no excuse not to live life outdoors.

Tansy hadn't always been like that; as a teenager she could wolf down an upsized Macca's meal with the best of them. It would only take a couple of friends to suggest a food hoedown and she'd be there. If you put a slab of chocolate in front of her—no matter how cheap it was—she'd eat it.

The thing was, though, that she'd somehow forgotten to maintain those friendships. Her only real friend left was Belle. Belle was family, really, in her life since primary school. But other than her? Tansy had only been at university for one semester and hadn't made any lifelong friends there. She'd had friends, usually colleagues, while working as a barista. But they'd drifted apart when she relocated to the coast, and fallen away over time, busy making babies and up to their ears in nappies, playgroups and mothers' groups.

And now Belle had joined the ranks, overwrought with a baby that screamed with reflux for hours each evening. Understandably, Belle was a big basket of weepy emotions herself. When Tansy and Dougal had visited her, Belle's hair was hanging all over the place, in need of a trim, and she kept getting cranky with it and pushing it away from her face, or plaiting it to keep it out of the way, only to have it loosen and dangle in her eyes again. Finally, she said, 'Do you have a hair elastic, by any chance? I can't find a single one.'

'Here, take mine,' Tansy said, pulling it free from her neat ponytail.

Belle's eyes welled with tears. 'You'd give me the elastic from your hair?'

36

Tansy laughed and hugged her. 'I'd give you anything. I'd give you my bra too. You know, if you needed somewhere to put your lipstick.'

That had cheered Belle up and she'd smiled. 'I'd give you my bra too. You know, if you needed sails for a boat or something.'

Tansy should put a packet of hair elastics in with that care package, when she got around to making it.

The almond milk in the chai had separated and she stirred it vigorously. Adding honey, she wondered: maybe she'd just adopted these healthy eating habits because of where she lived and the culture that surrounded her. Maybe, if she had close friends here who loved marshmallows dipped in chocolate sauce and covered with condensed milk and sprinkled with hundreds and thousands and then rolled in butter cream, that would be what she ate too.

She loved to sit in this cafe and watch the people come and go, or come and sit with their groodles, spoodles, moodles and shmoodles on leads under their chairs. Peregian as a whole was super dog-friendly, with buckets of water set out for thirsty canines to rehydrate.

Those without dogs came with their laptops and sat under the pandanus tree in the courtyard. The joggers and the cyclists in their Lycra, with their tanned muscles, stopped for beetroot juice. The beachgoers came up from the sand, draped in towels, or sometimes in nothing other than board shorts or bikinis, and ordered smoothies. The holidaymakers and loved-up couples, with their newspapers and sunglasses, soaked up the sun in companionable silence. The fashionably dressed women past their baby years came for the delights of the French patisserie next door. And the bleary-eyed mums, with prams and sleeping babes in arms, came for coffee and the buzz of cutlery and chatter and signs of life. No one ever seemed in a hurry on the coast. Nothing bad ever touched this part of the world.

She was immeasurably lucky.

In her notebook were her scribbles from the meeting yesterday with Genevieve and Isabelle at their home in the hinterland mountain town of Montville. Isabelle was the lucky recipient of a bedroom makeover to celebrate her birthday. She and her mother lived in an impressively large white Hamptons-style home, with topiaries and manicured lawns and a view from the curved balcony over the most breathtaking vista of green mountains, stretching all the way out to the ocean.

Soon after Tansy got there, a slender young girl had arrived on the balcony, wearing three-quarter pants and a pink singlet identical in hue to her mother's, her long hair in plaits. 'Hi,' she said, smiling.

'This is Isabelle, my daughter,' Genevieve said.

'Hello, Isabelle. It's lovely to meet you.' Tansy held out her hand for the girl to shake. 'Thanks for agreeing to talk to me.'

'That's okay,' Isabelle said, shrugging. She sat down on one of the lounge chairs and tucked her feet up.

Tansy pulled out her notebook. 'So, you're turning ten. Happy birthday.'

Isabelle smiled, a tooth missing from the bottom row. 'Thanks.'

'And your mum tells me you'd like a bedroom makeover. Do you have any ideas of what you'd like?'

Isabelle cast a look towards Genevieve, who nodded for her to speak. 'Well, I like Paris.'

'Paris?' This was new. Tansy hadn't had a Parisian request before. 'Paris the city or Paris Hilton?'

Isabelle giggled. 'The city. In France.'

Tansy made a great show of writing down *France* in her note-book. 'And what do you like about Paris?'

'I like the Eiffel Tower, and the river, and croissants, and the music, and Audrey Hepburn.'

'Audrey Hepburn?'

'She was in Paris in lots of her movies,' Genevieve explained.

Tansy wrote down Audrey's name, feeling a touch inferior that she had never seen a single Audrey Hepburn movie while this ten-year-old was an avid fan. She'd have to download some to watch. Maybe it would be a fun date night with Dougal.

'I like pink,' Isabelle continued. 'And poodles. And makeup and *Moulin Rouge*—the movie,' she added helpfully, pointing to Tansy's notebook so she would write it down.

'And if you had to choose between black and pink, or white and pink, which would you prefer?' Tansy asked, some images forming in her mind.

'Hmm . . .' Isabelle gave this due consideration. 'I think white and pink.'

'Good, you know what you like. That will help me a lot.'

They continued to talk for a while, then Tansy asked to see her room, and Isabelle took her up a spiral staircase to the last bedroom on the top floor. It was currently themed with princess and mermaid images.

'I've outgrown this.' Isabelle waved her hand dismissively at the passé decorations around her. 'It will all have to go.'

Tansy bit her lip to stop herself smiling and took out her tape measure to record the room's dimensions and the position of the two large windows and the power points.

'I think I've got everything I need for now,' she said, finishing up.

'Okay, I'll walk you to the door,' Isabelle had said. Then she'd bellowed, 'Mu-um! Tansy's going now,' undoing all the grown-up-ness she'd just been displaying. It had touched Tansy's heart. Isabelle was a little girl and a little woman all at once, standing in the doorway between two worlds.

Apart from loving to work here in this sun-filled courtyard, Tansy had come today because Dougal was working from home, busily making plans for their relocation to Canada in two months' time; if she'd stayed, she would have been constantly interrupted by his voice, raised a few decibels into the mobile phone. Leo had a late start this morning at the trendy surf-themed cafe in Hastings Street where he waited tables and washed dishes between uni lectures. Right now he'd be lifting weights, sweating to the soundtrack of whichever band he was into this week. Sometimes she felt quite old around Leo.

Although she and Leo were both in their twenties, there were moments when she felt as though she belonged to another generation—particularly when his grating music was playing. It made her wonder if marrying a man twelve years her senior had aged her faster than she should have. But she wasn't in Dougal's generation either. They were definitely different. He was born in 1974; Tansy, 1986. And Leo was born in 1994. Almost a decade between each of them. No wonder she felt marooned between them.

It was weird at first, dating 'Daddy Dougal', as Belle had once unkindly called him early in the piece. But Belle was going out with someone who was 'practically in nappies', Tansy had retorted, at which Belle had sheepishly changed the topic. With their ages ranging from twenty to mid-thirties the possibility of double dates was quickly dismissed. Dougal was well past the stage of getting drunk simply because it was a day ending in *y*, and Tansy, back then, found arts festivals and property discussions tedious in the extreme. Actually, she still wasn't a big fan of ballet, but whenever she had to decorate a little girl's bedroom in a ballet theme she somehow found the enthusiasm and lived and breathed tutus and toe-crippling pointe shoes. And pink. Always loads of pink.

Much as she was doing for Isabelle today. The key challenge was always to find some sort of balance in the colour wheel, a hue pink enough for the small client but not too garish to the larger client, whose home was undoubtedly tasteful and stylish and carefully decorated in its own right before it had been invaded by the small person with ideas all of her own.

Tansy searched the web for images, collecting ones she thought Isabelle might like. She would ask her to rate out of ten how much she loved each one. That would give Isabelle a sense of involvement in the process and at the same time provide Tansy with lots of useful feedback. She had also set Isabelle a project for the next two weeks of taking photos everywhere she went, capturing any item, toy, piece of furniture, picture, colour or pattern she loved, then printing off her absolute favourites and collating them into a collage, ready to hand over at their next meeting.

'You're great with kids,' Genevieve had said after Tansy had outlined the art project to Isabelle. 'Do you have any of your own?'

'No,' Tansy had said, smiling.

It was a question that she fielded frequently, asked by everyone from family members to perfect strangers. She was in her late twenties and married: it was assumed she would be reproducing. But saying that she didn't have any children created an awkward moment when Tansy didn't know what would follow. Some people said, 'Oh, I'm sorry,' and changed the subject immediately, likely imagining all sorts of devastating scenarios—miscarriage, infertility, infant death. Some people would ask outright, 'Why not?' Some told her that she'd 'better get cracking, tick tock and all that'. Others eyed her carefully, perhaps judging her for putting a career over a family. Some let the silence hang there, a space Tansy generally felt compelled to fill. 'My husband already had a son when we met,' she'd say breezily. 'He didn't want any more.' And she'd finish with a casual shrug and a wave of the hand to reassure the questioner that she was in fact okay. Some people tried to joke it off: 'That's a good thing—they cost too much and you never get a good night's sleep again.'

Whatever the response, it was never easy and always left Tansy feeling needled and uncomfortable.

Yesterday, Genevieve had said, 'Well, I'm sure you'd make a great mum if you wanted them.'

Tansy thought about that now, watching a pair of immaculately groomed golden retrievers come smiling and trotting into the courtyard as though they owned the place, taking their people for a walk rather than the other way around.

Did she want children?

As far as her marriage was concerned, it was a done-and-dusted debate. Dougal had been upfront with her right from the start and she'd been too young to care much at the time. And after a couple of years of being together she knew she could never end it with him. He was her person. Simple. If being with him for the rest of her life meant no children, then so be it. Nothing was perfect.

Finishing off the banana bread, she focused on her diary again. The thing was that she didn't keep track of her periods anymore. She'd been on the progesterone-only pill for years now and her periods were so light and unobtrusive that she didn't need to keep track of them as she used to, marking the expected date with an asterisk and planning her life around migraines and heavy bleeding. The pill had taken care of both, and life was much easier. So she looked back at events and appointments and tried to remember. But she was drawing a blank.

She went back further.

Ah, there. That night they'd had dinner at her cousin Jordan and his partner Katarina's place in Tewantin, with six-year-old Toby watching *Frozen* in the lounge room while they had canapés on the balcony, overlooking the river. (Jordan and Katarina counted as friends, surely. Okay, they were family, and she'd always thought of Jordan as more like a brother, being closer in age to her than she'd been to Rose, and she saw them at least once a week, but for now she would put them in the 'friends' column so she didn't feel so pathetic.) That night, definitely, she remembered.

But the date was two months ago. She must have had a period since then and just forgotten. Still, maybe she should buy a pregnancy test, just to be sure. Then again, any time she'd bought a pregnancy test in the past it had always been negative, she'd got her period one or two days later, and she'd blown the cost of half a cocktail.

She'd give it two days. Two more days and then she'd buy one.

Maria had Fred Astaire in her head again as she walked along the path in her bee suit and face netting to check on the bees. She'd been thinking about her parents a lot in the last few days—her parents, and other things from the past. She knew full well that anything could be taken away in an instant. Her life here, for example.

At the hives, she knelt and lit the dried grass inside the smoking can and puffed on it a few times to get the flames and smoke going. But then she put it aside; as always, she would only use it if she absolutely had to.

Then she lifted the lid of the white hive she'd come to see, the girls buzzing amicably around her.

'You're doing a wonderful job, girls,' she said, spraying water on the upturned lid to give them a drink, a far kinder and more sensible thing to do than to smoke them, which only made them panic and eat honey because they thought they were under threat from a bushfire and might have to fly away and start a new hive from scratch. Giving them a drink was a treat. They needed so much water to make honey and for cooling the hive. To lower the temperature if it got too hot, they would place lines of water and beat their wings to cause evaporation and cool the interior. Not that it would be a problem at this time of year, of course.

Some research had concluded that bees could recognise human faces, and though other scientists weren't convinced, the idea pleased Maria greatly. She loved her bees. She'd always known they loved her. And knowing they could recognise her face made her feel that much closer to them. It simply made sense to her. The doubters argued that because a worker bee had such a short lifespan of between six and twelve weeks it wasn't possible that they could learn their keeper's face in that time, and even if they did they would die shortly after. But bees communicated all sorts of things to each other, including the precise location of particular flowers kilometres away. It was as if the whole hive shared a single mind. Maria believed hives were actually the most powerful supercomputers on the planet, likely storing millions of years of knowledge in their collective consciousness.

Today their melodic humming soothed her and kept her—well, 'grounded' was the popular term these days. She had so much on her mind. There'd been another email from Tansy, a quick afterthought after the first one, inviting Maria to her thirtieth birthday party along with all her family (imagine!). She also suggested that she might just pop along one day and surprise her. Truly, she didn't even know where to begin with Tansy. There was the ongoing pressure of her busy schedule here, hosting the accommodation bookings and coordinating everything from food to washing to paying the insurance bill, managing the employees, her gardening and harvesting work, the weekly craft work for the markets, and then selling the products, knowing that she was the linchpin for the orphanage's sustainability. And then there was the anonymous delivery of that letter.

Silence is a virtue.

'Actually, I think buzzing is a virtue,' she said now to the bees, rejoicing in their company. She knew perfectly well where that mysterious letter the other morning had come from. It had come from Archbishop Tully.

Ian Tully, formerly Bishop Tully of the diocese west of Brisbane for the latter half of her time in the convent. He'd been such a young man for the role. Certainly he'd been too young for the responsibilities he'd needed to take on and had instead let them go, perhaps from lack of experience, perhaps from lack of understanding, confidence or strength, or perhaps from lack of moral fibre. She didn't know.

She wasn't surprised that he'd surfaced now. Somehow, deep down, she'd known this time would come. In part, she was grateful to be able to finally let it all go. And she could even accept the fate that awaited her, because she knew—she'd always known—that the knowledge she and Ian Tully shared would bring them to account, if not in this life then certainly in death when they faced their maker.

The easy thing to do would be to pick up the phone and call Investigating Officer George Harvey, named in the official government letter that had arrived the same day as Tansy's first letter. She could call him right now and make a time to go and tell him everything she knew. But, as Shakespeare would put it, there was the rub. Once she did that she would go to jail. And there were fifty-six children in Cambodia who were depending on her to provide the steady income that supplied all their needs. Sopheak needed surgery and a new wheelchair and money simply shouldn't be the thing standing in the way.

It wasn't that she was deluded enough to think that she was indispensable, but even a small delay in the flow of Australian money to that Cambodian orphanage would be devastating, because the place operated from one bank transfer to another.

Maria herself might be prepared to lose everything, but those children didn't deserve to be placed in danger because of her past. She'd spent almost all her life trying to make up for her actions. She wasn't going to stop now.

5

People often said that Investigating Officer George Harvey looked a lot like Dr Phil, and with the number of testimonies he'd taken from men and women reliving their childhood, he'd started to feel like a psychologist too. George was half a century old but felt at least a hundred. Maybe a hundred and fifty. Maybe three hundred.

'Don't be dramatic,' his wife, Hilda, chided gently, passing him a cup of tea with soggy yellow things floating in it.

He sniffed. 'Chamomile? I'm not a horse.'

'No caffeine,' she reminded him, her finger in the air, level with her turquoise-framed specs with the diamante flourishes like wings. 'You need to get your cortisol levels down.'

She selected a soothing soundtrack of ocean waves from the laptop that sat permanently on the kitchen bench, and lit a candle that was scented with something lemony.

'Lemongrass,' she said, as if reading his mind, and blew out the match. Then she sat on the leather footrest at the front of his lounge chair, pulled off his shoes, closed her eyes and began to rub his feet.

Voodoo, George called it. She was crazy if she thought rubbing the centre of his foot, just below the ball, would improve the flow of energy to his kidney. And he loathed her horrible herbal teas. But he took several deep breaths as she instructed, and, if he was totally honest, he *could* feel himself start to relax. He leaned his head back against the chair and closed his eyes, enjoying Hilda's fingers working his soles, touched by her ongoing concern to get his stress levels under control and keep him healthy. It must be hard for her, too, to have him so burdened and dispirited so much of the time. So . . . affected.

The police service's counsellor came by last week, a young lady named Anita, who'd said she was 'just doing the rounds' and 'touching base with everyone'. She spoke directly yet kindly, offering her card and assuring him that she was available at any time and it was all free of charge and completely confidential. 'We can talk about work,' she'd said, 'your cases, or anything else . . . your marriage, your kids, your friends. We can talk about exercise, alcohol, or even just have a chat about the weather.'

'Thanks,' he'd said, and pocketed her card with no intention of ever calling her. His marriage was wonderful; all five of the kids were doing well, and there were only two of them left at home now so that took out a lot of the chaos; he only had an occasional glass of wine; he didn't exercise enough, but that wasn't going to be solved by talking; and the only chat he needed to hear about the weather was the daily forecast to tell him whether or not to layer a singlet under his shirt.

But he knew what she was getting at: the evidence, the testimonials and statements. The grown men and women crying in his office, some of whom self-medicated just to get through it.

The images he had in his mind that no one should ever have to picture, let alone actually live through. Images he couldn't unburden onto anyone else, because that would just be spreading the misery further. No, it stopped with him.

Hilda thought he was carrying it all himself. And he was, for the most part. But—perhaps ironically—the person he'd found the most comfort in was Father Bryce, a man who'd heard more confessions and taken on more burdens than George ever would. A man who could still smile and care and listen to George as though he was the only person in the world and Father Bryce had nothing else to do but be there for him.

'You're doing God's work,' Father Bryce had assured him, stretching out his arthritic knee in his small office at the back of the church. 'And God's work will always bring challenges of faith and trust.'

'But how do you . . . aren't you . . . *ashamed* to be a part of the church?' George had asked, barely able to voice the question. George was a Catholic, an earnest, committed, believing Catholic, descended from a large herd of Catholics, and he was feeling it. The shame, the anger, the dissillusionment. The breach of trust. The challenge to faith.

'I am not ashamed of Catholicism,' Bryce said, steepling his fingers together at his chest. 'I am certainly ashamed of my peers who have acted immorally, indecently and illegally, and I welcome the efforts to bring those people to light and to account. But it doesn't change the fact that the number of good people in the church,' he reached out his hand and clasped George's arm, 'just like you, far outweighs the bad. Evil turns up every-where—in families, in schools, in churches, in the street and in the police force.'

George had nodded sadly. He knew that to be true. Time and again his investigations turned up the names of officers who had willingly covered up and ignored testimony and evidence. For this, George wasn't openly attacked or snubbed by his fellow officers, but there was tension every time he walked into a room.

'People should be glad when the corruption is discovered,' he'd raged to Hilda. 'No one wants to be working with a bunch of liars, creeps and perverts. But no one's thanking me for it. People shrink from me in the lunchroom.'

Hilda had held him until his breathing calmed. Then she'd sent him to the garden to dig and work off the anger, before nurturing him with chicken soup.

He would have loved to discuss it all with the parish leaders council, which met at the church once a month on a Tuesday night under Father Bryce's guidance. It was a diverse group of half a dozen parishioners, including a high school teacher, a youth worker, a grandmother, a nurse practitioner and a serving nun, who came together as an advisory board to Father Bryce and also to provide guidance to members of the parish who wanted to discuss issues in any area of their life. For the most part, George found the council members to be fair and reasonable and good problem solvers, and at least one parishioner each month booked an appointment with them to discuss anything from their drug-taking teenager to marriage problems and career crises. George would have loved to unburden himself in their presence, but the laws bound him to silence. Fortunately, confiding in his priest was a different matter.

'Have no doubt,' Father Bryce had said, 'God has called you to do this important and noble work. Stand strong, George. Have faith. We need you.'

And that was what kept him going through the hard days.

'Thank you, Father.'

'Would you like to pray with me?'

'Yes, I would.'

And together they'd lit candles in the quiet darkness of the church.

6

'Have you had any thoughts about whether you might want a housemate while we're gone?' Tansy asked as she and Leo ascended the side of the hill, the eucalyptus bush on their right and on their left the expansive blue ocean stretching all the way to the horizon.

They were walking the seven-kilometre beach-to-forest track through Noosa National Park, which began a short walk from their building. They alternated between jogging and walking, depending on their energy levels. Dougal never jogged, with a trick knee he'd had since his time as the high school rugby team's front row forward. He did still play social tennis with some of his work friends who either lived on the coast or came up for weekends. And he swam in the ocean, while Tansy walked the sand. But today she and Leo were walking the track up the hills, Leo a bit flat and moody, which was unlike him.

They'd shivered in the cool morning air, but only for a couple of minutes. The strengthening sun and their own exertions quickly chased any chill away. Their plan was to complete the track and end at the kiosk for coffee and muffins; Leo loved the triple chocolate ones and Tansy couldn't resist if he was having one.

See. Gosh, what a sheep she was when it came to food. Imagine what would happen when she hit the freezing temperatures of Canada. She might make new friends but they'd probably spend all their time trapped indoors, sitting by a fire and drinking hot chocolate and eating hot puddings. She'd come back a veritable blimp.

'Not much,' he said, answering her question.

'Do you think you'll be lonely on your own?'

'Maybe.'

'You could find someone from uni,' she suggested, and then thought that maybe that wasn't such a great idea. Leo was lovely, and he had a lot of nice friends, including many sensible young ladies, who were doing the same degree. But they were all still only a few years past teenagehood. She could well remember what she and Belle had been like at twenty-two. They were drunk at least fifty per cent of the time.

'Or maybe your mum knows someone?' She trailed off. Rebecca and Leo were close and spoke often, but he was well past the age of taking advice from his parents.

'I don't know if it would be a good idea to live with a friend,' he said. Their feet made gentle squeaking noises as the paved track gave way to soft sand. 'I've seen a lot of mates bust up over stupid things when sharing a house.'

'That's insightful,' she said, genuinely impressed.

'Do you ever regret not finishing uni?' he asked suddenly.

'Hell, no.' She laughed. 'I don't know what I was thinking enrolling in something as dull as commerce. I only lasted a semester and only then because my parents just about had a coronary when I said I wanted to leave after four weeks.'

'It all turned out okay for you, didn't it?' he said.

'Definitely. I loved working as a barista for those few years. There was great camaraderie in the coffee shop, we were always flat out so I was never bored, and I met so many interesting people and learned firsthand how to run a business. And of course I met your dad, so that was a bonus. When I finally worked out what I was genuinely interested in, I had the time and money to do the TAFE course in home styling, and life's been up and up ever since.'

One thing she loved about Dougal was that he had never once—despite his own driven work ethic and career ambitions— made her feel inferior, less educated or less worthy. Even when they'd first met, when she was a barista. Even when his two older brothers clearly dismissed her as some sort of passing fancy for Dougal, a time filler until he found a proper wife. Those brothers epitomised everything that was awful about the all-boys Catholic school they'd attended—the elitism, the sexism, the arrogance and self-interest—unlike Dougal, who seemed to have absorbed all the good things a privileged education had to offer: generosity, compassion, an enquiring mind and robust good nature. They hardly ever saw Dougal's brothers and their families anymore. She loved him for that, too.

She and Leo were silent then, walking comfortably in the gentle breeze, their footsteps in a natural rhythm together. A bush turkey scratched vigorously at detritus among the scrub and they could still hear the gentle roar of the ocean down below.

'Why do you ask?'

Leo waited a moment before saying, "Cause I was thinking of dropping out.'

Tansy stopped and grabbed his arm to bring him to a halt. 'What? Why?'

He shrugged, his eyes hidden behind sunglasses. 'I don't think it's for me.'

'Why not? Haven't you always wanted to be a writer?'

Leo had fought hard to convince his father that doing a degree in creative writing was a good thing. Such an impractical course of study had been difficult for Dougal to accept, his own motivations being to climb corporate ladders and build a secure financial future as quickly as possible.

'But what are you going to do at the end?' Dougal had objected.

'Write,' Leo said, confident, assured.

Dougal held up a newspaper in front of Leo and said, 'I don't see any job ads here for a writer. Not a single one.'

'The world's not the same place as when you were starting out,' Leo had said calmly, and Tansy had smothered a small smile. Leo was right; the world had changed significantly in the past twenty years.

Dougal and Rebecca had both been at uni and living in share houses when they met and fell in love, and they hadn't been together a year when Rebecca fell pregnant. Dougal's family had 'old money'—as old as money could be in Brisbane, anyway—and a large home in Hamilton near the river. His older brothers had both been school captain, had finished university and were excelling in the business world, and had a bevy of socially appropriate young women knocking on their doors. Now Dougal had to slink back home with his pregnant girlfriend in tow to live with his parents once more.

Nonetheless, he was expected to complete his undergraduate degree followed by a master's in business administration, while Rebecca had to drop out of university to care for Leo. They got married, of course, because it was the expected thing to do. Dougal's father had given him a speech about responsibilities and being a man. It was a toxic combination of circumstances, and the marriage foundered four years after it began. Tansy had met Rebecca many times since her own nuptials. She and Dougal had shared custody of Leo after their divorce with grace and consideration and surprising levels of good humour. Sometimes Tansy wondered if they'd been given a better start, if the cards had fallen differently, if their marriage would have survived.

Dougal's dream was to see Leo get a better and easier start in life than he'd had. And in his vision, creative writing was not that start. After extensive to-ing and fro-ing, though, Dougal had swallowed his doubts with great effort and left Leo to his dreams. Which were, it seemed, his dreams no longer.

'I can't see a future in it,' Leo said now, picking up a banksia cone and running his fingers along the alternating spiky hair and smooth seedpods that made it look like a human face.

Tansy's heart sank. 'But this semester is nearly finished and then you've only got six months left,' she said, increasing her pace to keep up as Leo's strides increased. They sidestepped two joggers coming the other direction.

'What difference does it make if I leave now?' he said. 'It won't change anything. You dropped out and you've got a great business that you love. Everything turned out well for you.'

Tansy was silent, trying to find the most helpful thing to say. 'Great business' wasn't a term she would necessarily apply to what she did. She loved it, sure; it brought her delight and fulfilment. But if he was thinking in terms of financial abundance, then the term wasn't appropriate. Not yet, anyway. One day she hoped it would be. But even if it never became financially rewarding she would still want to do it. Money certainly wasn't everything.

Then again, her lifestyle would be vastly different if they didn't have Dougal's salary coming in. Her nose twitched while she struggled with all of these thoughts and the emotions they brought up. Maybe she was selfish to pursue what she loved at the expense of their overall income. But that was crazy. It wasn't as though they didn't have enough—look at where they lived.

But what defined enough?

She felt herself frowning, appalled to think she could have—however innocently—encouraged Leo in any way to leave when he was so close to finishing his degree. Dougal would be furious. And most of all, she didn't understand. There'd been no warning that this was coming, as far as she could tell.

'Has something happened?' she asked. 'Has something, or someone, made you feel like this?'

Leo stopped, threw away the banksia pod, and raised his sunglasses to sit on top of his light brown curls. She stopped too, and removed her own sunglasses so that their eyes met. With his Rip Curl shirt, dark tan and fair hair, he looked like a surfer, although he wasn't. He'd tried surfing once, but said it wasn't for him. Still, he spent a lot of time at the beach, jogging, sunbaking and swimming, playing touch football with male and female friends.

'It's been coming since the end of last year. I do love to write, but not the sorts of things they're teaching. In some ways, I think it's taking me further away from my own style. I feel like there's something else out there for me and I need to free myself up to do it.'

'You *feel*?'

'Call it a hunch, a gut feeling, whatever you like.'

'Do you think you should speak to Rebecca about this? A student advisor?'

'I'm an adult and I can make up my own mind,' he said irritably.

'Of course you can,' she said. 'I didn't mean anything by that; I just don't understand and I'd like to.' She tried to sound as reasonable and interested as she could without letting her rising panic show. Leaving uni would be a mistake—a terrible mistake.

'Look,' she said, grasping for a compelling argument, 'you've got time before the end of the semester, so why don't you just think about it for a while longer? In fact, don't you even have some time into next semester to pull out or defer without penalty?'

Leo's face softened. 'Yes.'

'So, use that time, okay? Don't do anything right now. Just concentrate on getting to the end of this semester and do your best. You'll have a few weeks' holiday and you can reassess in that time.'

He nodded, not quite a nod of agreement, but at least she hoped that her suggestion might make him pause before he did something he'd regret.

After their walk, Leo went to uni, a bit reluctantly, but at least he'd gone. Heading to the shower, Tansy hoped that some sort of light bulb would go off in his head while he was there. As for her, she had things to do. At the top of the list was the reunion (cleverly disguised as her birthday party) she was planning for just over three weeks' time. She should have sent out invitations by now, but she'd been busy with Isabelle's bedroom and the many details to do with an impending move to Canada. Where were they going to live? What would they leave behind and what would they take with them?

The weather was completely different, so they'd need new heavy coats, gloves, woollen scarves, maybe boots. All the things they didn't have or need on the Sunshine Coast. She was building lists of things to buy, subscriptions and automatic debits to cancel—gym memberships, her subscriptions to home styling magazines, Dougal's wine club membership, their mobile phone plans. Health insurance? Would they need new health insurance over there? She supposed so. Then again, maybe they'd lose all their waiting periods and tax benefits. And maybe they wouldn't even stay there that long. If something went wrong and they wanted to come home again quite soon, it would be a real pain to set everything up again. She put a mental asterisk next to that one to remind herself to phone their current insurance company to talk about it.

Better yet, she would start a new list, this one of things to allocate to Dougal to take care of. It was only fair that they share all the stressful preparation for leaving.

Refreshed from the shower, she made herself a hot lemon tea and threw open the glass doors to the balcony, which overlooked the heavily treed hillside on which their unit complex nestled. She set up her laptop at the table and brought out an aromatic candle for ambience. It was fining up into a glorious warm autumn day, much more typical of the coastal weather than the cold snap they'd had the past few days. A kookaburra landed on the railing and cocked its head to the side, gazing down its lethally sharp beak at her to see if she had any breakfast scraps to throw.

'Not today, mate,' she said, holding out her hands to show they were empty. The kookaburra regarded her for a moment, as if assessing whether she was telling the truth, and then shot off again in a snap of wings against air, looking for snakes or grubs to eat instead.

Lighting the chai-scented candle, Tansy opened her laptop and began to type up her email invitation to family members. *It's my thirtieth birthday soon*, she began. *Please join me at Noosa River on . . .*

She filled in the important details, then explained that it was her wish to see them all together before she and Dougal left for Canada. Then she changed her mind and deleted that bit. It would be more fun to announce it on the day. She'd already sworn Leo to secrecy and he could keep a secret as well as any spy, so there was no chance of it getting out.

She'd decided on meeting at the barbecue sites along Noosa River. As a venue, it was relaxed (and that could only be a good thing, given that she was planning on introducing Maria into the fray) and always busy with people (which meant no one could kill anyone . . . only kidding . . . sort of) and had space for the children to run around. She put her own email address in the top line, CC'd the rest of the family, but BCC'd Maria. She wanted her aunt's arrival to be a great surprise too, and didn't want to give her mother any opportunity to back out of the meeting.

Speaking of which, she must call Enid and try to suss out what was going on between her and her father. She could call Finlay, of course, but he was impossible to read. He and Leo would both be great employees of the national security service.

She sent the email, stood up and stretched, and then went into her office, which also faced the glistening expanse of the ocean and so was drenched in warm morning sun.

Soon, though, serious doubts began to creep in. She'd sent the email with a dollop of giddy good intentions (she'd go down in genealogical history as the person who reunited their family!). But now she began to fret. What if no one came? What if they all came but then hated her for dropping them into a situation they didn't want to be in? What if the reason for Enid and Maria's falling-out wasn't just that Maria had abandoned the family . . . what if she'd done something really bad?

She sent a quick text to Rose. *Hiya, how are you? Do you have time to talk? I need a second opinion on something. PS I've just sent you an email about my birthday xx*

Time ticked on and after an hour with no response from her sister (as usual), Tansy decided that she should just bite the bullet and pay a visit to Maria. It was too late to go today; she still had too much work to do on Isabelle's room and a new email enquiry that she would have to answer promptly in order to pitch her services. And she had another new client to meet this afternoon—a young boy named Ernest, who, his mum said, loved rocks. That would be interesting.

But tomorrow. She would definitely go see Maria tomorrow. She'd bake a cake. Or, okay, maybe she'd buy one, because she wasn't much of a baker and it was the thought that counted, wasn't it? They could have tea and cake. The fact that Maria hadn't responded to her emails probably just meant she was shy and feeling awkward because Tansy was Enid's daughter and something had gone down between the sisters that made contact difficult.

Maria and Enid were two grown women in the autumn of their lives. They were family, for goodness' sake. This was how wars started and carried on through generations. Time went on and no one had a clue what anyone was fighting about anymore. It was crazy. It wasn't good enough. Tansy couldn't do anything about the wars around the world, but she could do this. She could help end the madness here in this family, once and for all.

And then they would all eat cake.

7

Tansy followed the grass pathway away from the cabins and dining hall where a group of barefoot women with yoga mats were drinking from mugs in the sun, past the vegetable garden and wandering chooks, and through the gradually thickening bush, just as the young woman, Petrice, had told her to do. The girl was short and stocky and probably around Leo's age, Tansy guessed, but with a lot less confidence. When Tansy had addressed her, asking where to find Maria, Petrice had stopped and leaned on her broom; Tansy noticed a large purple burn mark on the hand that gripped the shaft.

'She's checking the bees,' Petrice had said, talking to Tansy in an off-centre kind of way that made Tansy feel that she shouldn't make too much eye contact, as if Petrice was a formerly abused dog that remained wary of another kick coming its way. 'She'll be up there for a while.'

The hives—four multistorey sets of white boxes placed several metres apart—were situated in a rough clearing away from the tall trees and with an enviable view over the rolling hills below and out to the ocean.

And it was Maria, she assumed, there in among them, dressed like a space alien in head-to-toe white protective clothing, with thick yellow gloves, and a broad-brimmed hat with a black net falling over her face and well down her chest. She was bent over a hive with some sort of metal tool in her hand, gently prising off the lid of a hive box, a thick, tacky dark substance stretching apart as the lid yielded.

'Hello,' Tansy called cheerfully, fuelled by her high expectations for this first meeting.

Maria didn't seem to hear her, so Tansy swung around to approach from the side, not wanting to startle her by coming from behind. The bees' buzzing increased.

Suddenly, Maria straightened and spun around, her metal tool in one hand, the square lid of the hive in the other. 'Don't move,' she instructed, and Tansy froze to the spot.

Maria studied the young woman in front of her, wondering who she was. Was she part of the yoga retreat? The corporate group had left and the yoga women were not long here. She hadn't learned all their faces yet. At the same time, she was concerned about the increased noise from her girls. They were agitated. Maria deliberately took a deep breath to calm herself, and spoke soothingly. 'It's okay, it's okay. Just relax.'

'Oh, I'm not frightened,' the woman said, smiling a huge toothy smile.

'I wasn't talking to you,' Maria said. 'I was talking to the girls. Are you allergic to bee stings, by any chance?'

'Ah, I don't know. I've never been stung.'

Maria *tsk*ed. 'Wonderful.'

'Why?'

'You're too close. They don't know you. And you've come the wrong way. See?' She pointed to the line of bees coming and going from the hive. 'You're standing right in their flight path. When you approach a hive, you should come from the side or the back. They're very busy, very driven. They dislike having their work interrupted.'

'Oh, I'm sorry . . .' The woman went to step backwards.

'Just wait there,' Maria said. 'And don't swat, whatever you do. I'll not have one of my bees killed because you bumbled into their workspace. Just hold on.'

She gently replaced the lid of the super—the upper box of the hive. She'd have to leave that one until tomorrow. Her hand hovered over the smoker, wondering if it was warranted; the girls were obviously upset. But instead she picked up her spray bottle of water and spritzed the top of the hive and a nearby log with droplets to distract them, began to hum a gentle hymn, and walked slowly and diagonally away.

'Follow the way I'm going,' she directed the woman. 'Don't hurry. Don't let them think you're worried.'

'Well, I wasn't until you began to—'

'Probably best if you don't speak. And remember to breathe.'

Maria kept walking down the pathway, keeping a sideways backwards glance to make sure the woman was following, and stopped when they were a safe distance from the hive. Then she turned to face her surprise guest.

'I'm so sorry if I've caused you any trouble,' the woman began, raising her silver-braceleted arms to shade her eyes from the sun. 'I only wanted to let you know I was there, so I didn't startle you. I didn't realise I would upset the bees.'

Maria reached back behind her head and removed her hat and net to see the stranger more clearly. She had dark hair and a long nose. Long limbs. She was rather tall. She looked like an artist. Or a triathlete. And she also stirred something in Maria's chest, something from the past.

'I'm Tansy,' the woman said, holding out her slender hand. 'Your niece.'

And when Maria didn't respond, unable to speak over the lump that had suddenly formed in her throat, Tansy held up both her hands and shrugged with that toothy smile again. 'Surprise.'

To reach the stove, Maria had to move aside a host of materials she'd got out in preparation to begin work. With the markets on again tomorrow (gosh, they came around quickly each week), she was in full production mode today. Burn salves were at the top of her list, and chunks of rendered beeswax were waiting to be melted and whisked with raw honey, coconut oil, sea buckthorn oil and aloe vera gel before being poured into tins and left to cool and harden.

'Let me help you,' Tansy said, picking up various jars and tubs to move across the bench, ignoring Maria's demurral. 'What's sea buckthorn oil?'

'It comes from a shrub with tiny yellow berries and has healing properties for the skin.'

'Not from the sea, then?' Tansy grinned.

'No.'

'What are you doing with all this?'

'I'm making a balm that treats minor burns.'

'Oh, can I help?'

'Let's start with a cup of tea, shall we?'

That seemed to satisfy Tansy for the moment, and her niece carefully moved a box of pamphlets and bunting off a chair at the small kitchen table where Maria ate her meals, normally alone.

Maria lit the gas with a match. The stovetop had an automatic starter but she preferred not to use it. There was something about that moment when the head of the match cracked against the flint and there was a tiny pause, just a millisecond in time, before the flaring of the flame that brought Maria great solace. It reminded her that while she might have done things that had had a transformative effect on her life and on those around her, there was still in her past that millisecond in time, that tiny space of silence, after she'd set her intention but before she'd taken action, before everything changed, and she could revisit this moment whenever she wanted, just by striking a match.

'I hope you don't mind my dropping in unannounced?' Tansy said, her voice rising in evident hope that Maria would absolve her of any transgression. When Maria didn't respond, her niece busied herself opening a fruitcake she explained she'd picked up at the store on the way. It made Maria think about her own mother's fruitcake recipe, which she still knew off by heart, and that always resulted in a dry over-boiled lump with not enough fruit to warrant its name, but which she had always loved and returned to for second helpings.

'I guess you do mind,' Tansy said, her face falling, 'or you would have replied to my letter or emails.'

Maria cleared her throat and pulled out tea and honey. 'It's a bit of a shock,' she said truthfully.

Tansy seemed a fraction buoyed by Maria's having spoken at last. 'A shock that I found you? Or that I'm here?'

'Both.'

Tansy nodded.

Maria joined Tansy at the table and handed her a plate but didn't speak. 'Tell me about yourself,' she said, as a way of buying more time to allow her feelings to mellow, if nothing else.

'Gosh, where to start,' Tansy mused, slicing thick pieces of a moist-looking yellow cake with outrageously green and red jellied fruits inside. 'I'm a children's bedroom designer and I live in a unit just back from Hastings Street in Noosa, on a hill near the national park?' Her upward inflection signalled a query.

'It's lovely there,' Maria affirmed. 'I've been there a couple of times. The beach is so white.'

Tansy's mouth opened. 'Only a couple of times? But you live so close.'

Maria smiled a little. 'I don't leave here much; I have a lot of work to do running this place and trying to raise enough money for the orphanage to meet their daily needs, and hopefully to build an emergency fund as a safety net. But every day since the orphanage opened has been an emergency, so we're constantly running on empty.'

Tansy nodded. 'I only got to have a quick look at the website the other day, but I read a story about a mother who had to give up her daughters because she couldn't afford them and the only other alternative was to sell them into sex slavery. I'd love to help in any way I can.'

Maria got up to stop the kettle from whistling and poured the water into the teapot. 'Well, I never say no to an offer of help,' she said.

'Excellent. So you can't get rid of me,' Tansy said, picking off a piece of cake and nibbling at it.

'We'll see,' Maria said, feeling much better now that tea was in progress. 'But keep going. You were telling me about you.'

'Oh, okay. So I'm married to Dougal. He's forty-two and I'm twenty-nine—thirty in three weeks' time, which you know of course because you got my party invite, didn't you?' Maria nodded. 'Oh good. So, anyway, there's a bit of an age difference, and Dougal has a son from a previous relationship, Leo; he's twenty-two and living with us and going to uni. Dougal didn't want any more children so we don't have any ourselves.'

She paused and ate a chunk of cake. Maria poured the tea.

'Sometimes I wonder what life would be like, if things were different,' Tansy said.

'If you had a child?'

'Yes.' More cake. 'Oh, listen to me. We've only just met and I never say that to anyone. I'm sorry. God. The last thing you want is to hear me rave on.' Tansy's dark eyes widened. 'And now I've said "God". Sorry. That's probably offensive to you, being a nun—or an ex-nun, but probably still liking God—and I'm actually a Catholic and go to church, once a month, granted, but I go and I enjoy it. Do you still go?'

Maria couldn't help but laugh. 'It's all okay, Tansy.'

Tansy laughed too and waved her fingers at her face as if to cool down her cheeks, which had flushed red. 'Sorry.' Then, to Maria's great surprise, Tansy placed a hunk of cake on her fork and dunked it into her tea, let it soak, then slurped it into her mouth. Gosh. After first wanting to chide her, Maria grew warm and happy, and wished to hand her more cake to do it again.

'You don't seem anything like your mother,' she said, surprised herself at the feelings Tansy's presence roused in her.

'I'm going to take that as a compliment.'

'Oh, it is. Not that I'm saying anything about Enid, just . . .' Now it was Maria's turn to blush.

'This is awkward, isn't it?' Tansy said. 'Us, sitting here, skirting around the elephant in the room.'

'Enid?'

'Yes, Mum.'

'Hmm.'

'And Florrie, for that matter. You know, now you mention it, I think I'm a lot more like Florrie than Mum. She's married to someone much older too. Alastair's *twenty* years her senior. Do you think I could have my aunt's genetics rather than my mum's?'

'I can see Florrie in you, actually. You remind me of her when she was young. You have the same long limbs. We all come from the same pot of genetics, I guess,' Maria said.

'I suppose so.'

They were quiet for a moment, drinking tea and contemplating the small room, each other and the conversation.

'Look, Maria—can I call you Maria?'

'What else would you call me?'

'Sister Maria?'

'I'm not a sister anymore. I stopped being one a long time ago.'

'Yes, you did. And I guess that's what I want to know. Why you've kept away all this time. Why we've never met. Why you and Mum have *issues*. I know we've only just met and I don't expect to get those kinds of answers today. But I do want to get to know you. Whatever you and Mum and Florrie are to each other, you're *my* aunt, Maria. I want to have a connection with you. I want you in my life.'

Maria could feel her nostrils flare, breathing in to steady the torrent of emotions that this unexpected visitor had evoked. And she'd turned up now. Right when Maria had so many other difficulties to deal with thanks to ghosts of the past that were moaning at the back door.

God did have a tremendous sense of humour, laying this on her all at once.

But then, God was also wise and generous and knew more than she could ever hope to know. The decision she'd made in the past had been made contrary to God's will. If it was God's will that Tansy was here now, then, well, maybe she owed Him one.

Actually, she owed God about a million.

Tansy was still waiting for her to speak.

'I think that it would be nice to form a *connection* with you too,' Maria said slowly, not quite believing that the words were coming from her own mouth. The whole reason she loved it here at Honeybee Haven was that she could keep to herself and live her own life in peace. Connecting with Tansy was like striking a match.

She was sitting in that tiny pause now, she realised. Tansy had come with an intention and Maria had responded. This was the moment to turn back if she wanted to. The tiny slice of silence before it crackled and flared into new life and energy, casting light on everything around her.

'Maria, I'm so happy you've said that. Truly. I know we're going to be great friends.' And to Maria's astonishment, Tansy jumped out of her seat and hugged her. Her curly dark hair, smelling of sweetly scented shampoo, brushed Maria's nose and she knew that the moment had passed. The match was lit.

8

The Eumundi markets heaved with people, as they did every Saturday. Tansy and Dougal had slept in, then lazed in bed with Tansy's expertly made coffee and their iPads. Dougal had got home much later than usual last night, after a long meeting he couldn't get out of. By the time he'd arrived, he'd just wanted to eat takeaway Thai with a glass of wine and then go to bed.

This morning she'd filled him in on her visit to Maria and the bees, but Dougal had still seemed preoccupied, so Tansy had tempted him into the shower, conveniently accruing some incidental sexiness as their naked bodies bumped up against each other with bodywash and warm water. Then they'd headed into Eumundi.

Now she hoped the sounds of live drumming and didgeridoo music, the smells of Vietnamese street food, the vibrant colours of flags and crystals and pottery, and the general bustle would bring his mind back from wherever it was. She couldn't help but think of Maria, too, wondering how she was getting on selling

71

her wares at the Yandina markets, just fifteen minutes away. She briefly thought of taking Dougal there to meet her, but wanted him to be in a better mood first.

The markets were a useful place for Tansy to do research for her work, stay abreast of new trends, and pick up items for her bedrooms in progress. 'Not that I expect to find rocks here,' she said, reaching for Dougal's hand as they weaved their way through the throng.

'Could be a cheap job,' Dougal said. 'Plenty of rocks on the side of the road you could go and pick up.'

'Ernest doesn't need any more rocks.' She laughed. 'I think a big part of the job might just be finding pleasing ways to display them and keep them out of the road of the vacuum and out of his bed.'

Over the years Tansy had been doing this job, she'd come to realise that a significant part of the service she offered people was simply organisation. It amazed her that so many people lacked practical skills—unable even to use a drill to put up a shelf—and had no idea how to approach decluttering in a sensitive yet pragmatic way. At first she'd been frustrated with jobs like this, wishing for more challenging design jobs, free rein to totally gut and rebuild a room. But she'd come to accept that these types of 'organising jobs' she did for her clients were truly needed and deeply appreciated. And that was a great feeling.

'He sleeps with his rocks?' Dougal said, pausing to hand over a note for a freshly squeezed lime juice.

'Yes, sometimes. His mum is pretty tolerant, actually. She doesn't like them but she wants to support his obsession.'

'It makes a change from Thomas the Tank Engine.'

'Thankfully, yes.' She linked her arm through his, pleased he was lumbering out of his mental man shed.

They wandered through the maze of stalls for a while and she took in the regular offerings: original artworks, hammocks, children's tents, handbags, candles, crystals, soaps and woodcarvings. For the first time she noticed a few items decorated with bees, and wondered whether they'd always been there and she just hadn't been aware of them, or whether they were new.

She waved to a few artisans she'd bought items from in the past, some of them regular suppliers for her kids' bedrooms, and subtly navigated Dougal in the direction of the chemist. She ought to buy a pregnancy test today. 'Let's head this way,' she said. 'The wooden toys are down here; I might see something new.'

After passing the hot nuts, which smelled divine, and doughnuts, which smelled sickly, she decided to address Dougal's distracted mood head on. 'You're waking up,' she said cheerily.

'What do you mean?'

She shrugged. 'You've just been a bit quiet since last night. Did everything go okay in your meeting?'

He pulled her off the footpath, out of the way of walkers, and they stood underneath a huge shady tree on the edge of the stalls while he finished his lime juice. He tossed the cup in the bin, grimaced and thrust his hands in the pockets of his pants. 'The company wants me to leave earlier than originally planned.'

'Why?'

'Kenneth, the guy I was going to help over there, has quit. His wife's had a car accident—'

'Oh no.'

'—and she's had some spinal damage and it looks like the rehab will take quite a while. He needs to be there for her and their three children.'

'That's terrible.'

'Yes, it is. The upshot is that they need me there as soon as possible.'

'When?'

'Next week.'

'Next *week*?' Her voice squeaked.

'I'm afraid so. That's what the meeting was about last night.'

'But . . . but you can't.'

'Is there any reason we can't go next week?' He sounded genuinely curious.

'Because . . .' *I might be having a baby.* 'Because we're not ready.' She looked around for a seat to sit on. The closest one was in the playground, so they walked over there, Tansy's mind racing. All the seats were taken by families and couples eating burgers and baked potatoes. Tansy sat on a blue and yellow metal seesaw instead, near the fulcrum at the middle so she didn't tip to the ground, and stared up at her husband.

'I know this is sudden,' he said.

'Have you said yes?'

He scrunched up his nose and made some muttering noises, wiped a hand across his mouth and chin. 'No. But I didn't refuse either.'

Tansy stood again, a fraction taller than Dougal, her hands on her hips. 'Shit, Dougal.' She began to pace.

'But if you think about it, there's no reason we can't get on a plane next week. Because Leo is staying in the house, we don't have to do any major organisation, we can pretty much just leave. We don't have pets, infirm parents or young kids to take care of, no garden, no real commitments that would stand in the way.'

'What about my job?'

He nodded. 'There is that. But you can just cancel the clients you've currently got and give them back their deposits, can't you?'

A toddler in gumboots and overalls came running to the seesaw and clambered on one end, so they moved out of the way and headed to the playground's wooden train, where they leaned against the engine.

'Well, I *could* do that. But that's not the point, is it?'

Dougal scratched the back of his head and nodded. 'I know your work is important to you too.'

'It is.'

'And I think I've always been supportive of it, haven't I?'

'Yes,' she confirmed.

'So I don't want you to think I'm dismissing it, but this is an unusual situation. And we *had* agreed to go anyway.'

'In a couple of months' time, not next week.'

He nodded silently, giving her a few moments to get her thoughts together. 'I feel torn,' he admitted at last. 'I've been so excited about this new job. This will be the biggest, most complicated building I've worked on and I don't feel like I can leave the company in the lurch. No one saw this coming; it's just a freak accident that's changed the plans and everyone has to adjust. I'm sorry.'

She took a deep breath. 'It's not your fault, I know that.'

He blew out a breath of tension and looked up past the end of the park. 'Look, I need another coffee. You?'

'Yes please.' There were coffee stands and coffee shops every few metres. The smell was intoxicating.

'I'll go and order, give you a few minutes to catch your breath.'

She nodded, tears brimming. 'But what about the reunion? And my birthday?' If they left next week they'd be on the other side of the world for her birthday: there would be no reunion, her parents might still be fighting, and she'd have lost her chance to get to know Maria and certainly to get her mother and Maria talking again.

Dougal wrapped her in a big hug and held her tightly. 'Just think about it.'

Tansy nodded into his shoulder and then he headed off to get their coffees. She spun in circles for a bit, gazing at the main street of Eumundi that she knew so well—the hanging pots above the footpath; Berkelouw bookstore with its trendy cafe, people sitting out the front drinking coffee in the sun; the double-storey wooden pub; and the cute shops with clothes and knick-knacks. It was all so familiar. It was her home. And she could be leaving it all behind as soon as next week.

Her eyes focused on the chemist across the road. She pulled out her phone and texted Dougal to say she had a headache and was popping across to get some aspirin and would meet him back here.

It took her a while to find the pregnancy tests, and then longer than she'd intended to decide on which one to buy. In the end, she chose the most expensive one, which claimed it was capable of the earliest and most accurate detection. She was just handing it over to the smiling, perfectly made-up woman at the counter when several people appeared at her shoulder.

'Hi!'

She snapped back her hand, still holding the box, and dropped it to her side, trying to conceal the box against her thigh.

'Look who I found on the street,' Dougal said, smiling. 'We were just saying we should do dinner tonight.' With him were Tansy's cousin Jordan and his partner, Katarina, along with their son, Toby. Jordan and Katarina smiled, and went to hug her, and then looked down at her hand by her side, and Katarina tilted her head and opened her eyes wide, questioning, and the woman behind the counter was waiting with her hand outstretched. Dougal squinted down, confused. 'What's in your hand?'

Jordan at least seemed oblivious, his eyes now on Toby, who had wandered away and was picking up bubble bath off a shelf. Katarina, clearly totally aware of what was going on, plastered a huge smile on her face and said, 'Look, we'll keep going—give us a buzz later, Dougal, if you still want to do dinner tonight.' She deftly pecked Tansy on the cheek and shepherded her flock out of the shop, leaving Tansy standing with the box in her hand and Dougal staring at her.

'What's going on?'

'Did you want me to ring that one up for you?' the chemist assistant asked helpfully.

Tansy handed it over with a note.

'Tansy?' Dougal was still waiting for an answer.

'Can we talk about this outside?' Tansy said, taking the box and her change and leaving the building.

'Clearly, we have more to talk about than I first thought,' Dougal said, matching her stride. His tone was unreadable. 'Are you pregnant?' They threaded through the crowds on their way back to the car.

'I don't know,' Tansy said, irritated. 'That's why I bought a test.'

'But how could you be? You're on the pill, aren't you?'

'You see me take it every morning.'

The words caught in her chest. She *had* been taking it properly, hadn't she? She hadn't forgotten one or something?

'How could this happen?' Dougal asked.

'We don't even know if I am pregnant, so can we worry about this after we've got the results?' she snapped.

Dougal clicked the remote of the Audi. 'Yes, let's just get home.'

9

'Do they still exhume bodies at night?' Hilda asked.

'They do,' George said, closing his eyes while Hilda rubbed lavender oil into his temples.

'I suppose it would be awkward if you were there to bury Granny and the grave next door was being opened up. Not exactly comforting.'

'No.' He scratched at his moustache. The lavender smell had got up his nose and made him sneeze.

'Who's being exhumed?' Helen asked, eyes wide beneath the long trendy grey fringe (why on earth young people would want to dye their hair grey for fun was beyond him) that George wished she would cut. But you can't tell a sixteen-year-old girl what to do with her hair. She was foraging in the cupboard for a snack.

'No one,' George mumbled.

'It's the priest, isn't it?' Helen grinned, pulling out a packet cake mix.

'No,' he said, cranky that she knew as much as she did.

'Yes it is,' she said calmly, pulling out the mixer and a bowl and tearing open the cake mix. 'I think it's a great idea. The guy's got a lot to hide.'

Should he be concerned that she was so eager for a man's remains to be exhumed at night, like some scene from a horror movie, or proud that she had such an analytical mind? She was a lot like him, after all.

'How did you get the judge to order that?' she went on, cracking eggs.

Hilda's fingers were getting firmer and rougher at his temples, the pressure almost reaching painful levels; she clearly wished their daughter would drop the subject.

George gave up. They would both read about it in the paper eventually. 'It's not totally uncommon with murky cases like this,' he said. 'The man died in the seventies, before we had the level of forensic technology we have now. Today, we can do all sorts of tests on bones to get more information.'

Helen narrowed her eyes at him. 'Yes, but *why*?'

'Yes, why?' Hilda murmured behind him, caught up in the mystery.

'The death certificate says that he died from an accidental fall. But I have a hunch.'

'A hunch?' Helen said. 'I bet the judge loved that.'

'Don't you have homework to do?' Hilda said, snippier than usual, her hands now kneading his whole scalp as though it was a recalcitrant lump of dough that her life depended on wrangling into submission.

'It's Saturday,' Helen said, rolling her eyes.

'Oh, that's right.' Hilda's hands stopped kneading and began tugging at the short hairs behind his ears. 'Isn't there a bake sale on Monday to raise funds for Nepal?'

Their daughter shrugged. *So?*

'Good thing you found that packet mix; we'll need it for cakes.'

'But I wanna eat it now.'

'Well, make cupcakes; then you can have one and we'll send ten,' Hilda said, massaging George's shoulders now, which was a great relief, as there weren't that many hairs left on his head to lose to her determined fingers.

'Why not eleven?'

'Because that would look like we ate one.'

'We *are* eating one,' Helen countered.

'Technically, *you're* eating one,' Hilda said.

'And sending ten is better than sending eleven?'

'Yes. Clearly you don't understand the politics of bake sales. There are some frosted flower decorations in the cupboard so use them to make them pretty. They can charge an extra fifty cents that way.'

George couldn't quite fathom how they'd moved from discussing body exhumation to cupcakes in a matter of seconds.

His superior (in rank, not years), Prosecutor Blaine Campbell, hadn't been quite so jovial about it and had taken some convincing to submit the application.

'It's a waste of time,' he'd said, between a mouthful of burger, a slurp of coffee and a frantic cigarette, standing on the corner of Elizabeth and Edward streets in the middle of the day on his lunch break, which was the only time and place George could catch him in person. 'The priest did the crime but he's dead. We're after the other bad guy, the one that covered it up. He's still alive. We can get a conviction for him and send him to jail and win a lot of public goodwill in the process. What use is it to dig up the dead guy?'

'You've been reading the testimonials,' George said. 'I've seen firsthand the hatred and venom his victims have for the priest and the bishop. I don't buy that the priest fell down a well. Who falls down a well? That's nuts. I think there's a lot more going on here and it's our duty to find out what.'

'Probably a goose chase at taxpayers' expense.'

'Isn't it about time the force stopped cutting corners with this thing and ignoring potential evidence?' said George. 'That's exactly the attitude that got the royal commission going in the first place. The public support is there.'

'If you don't find anything, we'll look like tossers.'

'And if we do, they'll call us heroes.'

'Do you know how much it costs to exhume a body?' Campbell said, raising his voice over the growling engine and hissing brakes of a passing bus.

'Probably not as much as it has cost these people in lost wages, fractured marriages, health care and therapy.'

Campbell sniffed. As a prosecutor he wasn't motivated by personal stories, George knew, but by the thrill of winning a legal argument. He tossed the last of the burger in a bin, chucked the cigarette butt on the ground, swilled his coffee, wiped his mouth on a serviette and tossed that too, all the while playing a staring game with George, who held his eye and refused to be the first to look away.

'I'll talk to the judge,' Campbell relented. 'I'm meeting him tonight anyway so I'll bring it up, see what he thinks.'

George tried not to look too grateful. 'Thanks.'

'But no promises.'

'Fair enough.'

It was later that same night, as George was removing his reading glasses, putting away the latest Jeffrey Archer and easing into bed, that his mobile phone had beeped.

Polish your shovel. Court order on its way.

And for the first time that day, George had smiled.

10

It was God day. Even after all these years, Sundays still held a certain feeling like no other day of the week. Maria didn't go to church regularly anymore, but she liked to think about God on Sundays. Of course, she thought about God all the time, if thinking about God included having a clear focus and intention for your work, which she believed it did. But she still liked to honour her past relationship with the rituals of Sunday mass, and that deep fondness in her core for ceremony and quietude, by hitting the large brass gong near the dining hall three times at sunrise. The sound reverberated across the grounds of Honeybee Haven and down over the mountains below, out into the space beyond. It was something Buddhist nuns and monks did too. Such a simple, peaceful reminder to be still.

She would tend to the guests' needs, of course, but most checked out by mid-morning and then she was left to spend the rest of the day in peace, with just herself and her gardening and bees. It was as close as she came to bliss.

Now she was sitting on the ground, among the flowers, watching her bees work. She'd woken early this morning from a terrible nightmare, feeling sick, her heart pounding. In her dream, she'd come up here to check on her bees to find them all dead. Thousands lay lifeless across the grass, and her feet crunched over their bodies as she raced to the hive boxes. She frantically tore off the lid, the inner mat, the honey super, and pulled out all the frames, hoping to find some survivors, but hundreds of black and yellow bodies fluttered through her hands and blew away in the wind. She reached down to remove the queen excluder, but the queen was dead and the brood chamber empty. There was nothing left.

Troubled by the dream, as soon as she'd finished setting out the breakfast things for the yoga women she'd rushed up here, recalling all the stories she'd heard from America and Europe and New Zealand about colony collapse disorder, where a beekeeper went to check her hive, which the day before had been healthy and productive and heaving with bees, and all the bees were gone, simply vanished, with no explanation and no evidence as to why. Just an eerie silence instead.

But her bees were still here, buzzing away, industrious as ever, determined to make the most of the warm weather before winter set in. Autumn was an important time of year for the girls. They were busy filling the frames with as much honey as they could produce to feed the hive over winter and insulate the brood to a constant thirty-six degrees Celsius. Maria probably wouldn't be able to take much more honey before winter if they were to survive; and she certainly wasn't going to do what so many commercial bee farmers did and take all the honey and feed the bees with sugar water. How ridiculous. It made her livid with anger. How did they possibly expect to keep a strong and healthy hive when

they were replacing honey—an incredibly complex, living, enzyme-
and vitamin-rich food—with refined sugar? People could be so
breathtakingly short-sighted.

One of her girls landed on Maria's steel-capped boot. The
baskets on the backs of her legs were laden with dark orange
pollen and the sun shone on her tiger stripes. Maria smiled.

'Well, hello, dear. You've got a huge bounty there.' It wasn't usual
for a bee to stop on its way home to the hive—the phrase 'making
a beeline' meant exactly that. She should be headed straight home.
That precious pollen needed to get into the hive for the workers
inside to store to feed the brood. And her belly would be full of
nectar, which she needed to transfer tongue-to-tongue to other
workers and communicate where it came from and where they
should go to get more—a vital skill, given that bees had to make
one million visits to flowers to make just a kilo of honey.

'You should get home,' Maria said, shifting her boot gently.
'Your friends are waiting.'

The bee regarded her for a moment with its huge dark eyes,
vibrated its translucent veiny wings, and then alighted into the
air and disappeared into the melee of fellow workers focused on
their jobs.

A gentle breeze swayed the tops of the lettuce and coriander
that had recently flowered, the bees feasting on them almost as
much as on the native banksias, flooded gums and stringybarks,
which were their main source of food.

But in spite of the happy buzzing around her, the dream had
taken hold in Maria's psyche. Maybe it was time she talked to the
bees about what was going on.

She cleared her throat. 'Girls, I have something I need to tell you.'

But the words halted as she was struck by the memory of the day
Father Peter died—the last time she'd had to go and tell the bees.

'Telling the bees' was an old English custom and had been passed on to Maria by the head beekeeper before her, Sister Claire, who'd taught Maria everything she knew.

'It's crucial,' Claire had said in her heavy Irish accent, 'that the master of the house, or the head beekeeper, always politely and fully explains to the bees major changes in the house, especially deaths, marriages or comings and goings of members of the family. If you don't, the bees have a habit of dying, or simply leaving. One day you'll go out and they'll just be gone.'

Perhaps that was the cause of colony collapse disorder, Maria thought now. No one was talking to the bees anymore, just stealing their honey and feeding them lolly water instead.

'Especially deaths,' Claire had gone on, rubbing at her whiskery chin. 'You must invite them to the funeral.'

'The bees?' Maria had asked, still a novice at that time, only seventeen years old.

'Yes. Turn the hive to face the church, maybe even carry it to the churchyard or graveyard. Hang a black cloth near the entrance to the hive. Offer them wine and cake from the wake. Knock on the hive's top to get their attention before you make your announcement. Wait till they are listening.'

Maria had thought it all rather strange. But when Claire died just a few years later, she'd done exactly as she'd been taught to do. She took Claire's worn pocket Bible and placed it on top of the hive, rapped her knuckles on the lid three times, and waited until the bees came, which they did, hovering around her in a buzzing, attentive cloud.

'It's my sorrowful duty to inform you,' she said, her voice shaking with grief for the loss of her mentor, 'that our much-loved beekeeper, Sister Claire, has died.'

She paused, not knowing what to expect—perhaps the bees would swarm or attack her. But they seemed to quieten, many of them choosing to rest on the outside of the hive, as if shaken by the news. The noise of the buzzing dropped and she could hear the trickle of the creek nearby. Tears welled. It was as though the bees had wrapped her in an invisible comforting hug, saying how sorry they were.

'The funeral will be in two days' time,' she said, and attached a handwritten invitation to the side of the hive with a thumbtack. 'You're all invited. I'm sure Claire would love to have you there.'

A couple of bees hovered near the funeral notice.

'I'll be your new beekeeper now,' she said. 'I'll take good care of you.'

And when the funeral happened, two days later, a bevy of bees did indeed come to the gravesite, flying over the mourners and resting on the spiked metal fence nearby.

So years later, when Father Peter . . . Well, Maria knew she had to go tell the bees, just as she'd done for Claire, and for many similar events over the years. But this time it would be a speech like no other.

She'd approached the hives late in the afternoon, as the workers were returning home from the last trips of the day and settling in for the night. She rapped on the wooden lid and waited a few moments, while several guard bees came to the entrance to see what was happening and assess the situation.

'I have some news,' she began, and clasped her hands together because they were shaking so much. 'Father Peter died yesterday.' Her voice was quiet in the peacefulness of the afternoon, long shadows streaming across the vegetable gardens, and chooks clucking as they settled on perches for the night. Maria took a deep breath. And another. The bees watched her quietly.

'The funeral will be at the end of the week, and you are of course invited to attend.' She rushed through the words. And then she fell to her knees on the grass, the cool damp quickly soaking through her stockings.

'I ask your forgiveness.' Her eyes were downcast, focusing on the grass. 'I want you to know that what I did was for the greater good, because I had no other options. No one would listen. Father Peter was not a true servant of God,' she said, trying to keep her words measured and moderate. But a wave of anger and sickness washed over her and her fists balled. 'He was evil.'

She had looked into the bees' eyes and confessed her sin, the sin she then believed she would never tell anyone else.

That memory still had the power to evoke the exact same physical sensations as she'd felt on that day—the nausea, the shaking, the urge to cry. But time had trained her to process them faster, so Maria knew that within four or five breaths she would feel okay again.

Now, once she was ready, she addressed her bees. 'I need to tell you something important,' she said, and sure enough, a number of bees settled nearby to listen. They would go back and communicate with the rest of the hive. Just as they communicated the most complex information about the precise location of pollen and nectar by vibrating their wings in a waggle 'dance', any information she gave to even one bee would pass through the whole family like electricity.

'A long time ago I did something that I felt was the right thing to do in order to protect innocent young people from a man with power over them. But it was a grave sin.'

She gave the bees a moment to absorb that information, and absently flicked off a couple of ants that had crawled up her arm.

'The thing is that I've now been caught up in an inquiry, which seems like it has nothing to do with me, because it's quite rightly investigating a bishop—now an archbishop—who didn't do anything to stop the priest. I'll be made to give evidence, which, honestly, I'd quite like to do.

'But there's one problem.' The bees waited, cleaning their wings and storing the information she was giving, like little hard drives. 'Someone else knows what I did—Archbishop Ian Tully, the man under investigation. He saw me. And his silence buys my silence, and vice versa. But once I tell the police what I know, he will speak up too. So, I'm sorry to say, there is a good chance that I might have to leave here.'

She waited, tugging at a dandelion stalk in the grass next to her, giving them a moment to process what she'd told them. It was funny, the thought of leaving the bees made her sadder than anything else. She was devoted to the charity and its work, but these bees were her family, her clan.

'But I want you to know that I will make sure you are well looked after. I love you, my darling bees. I won't leave you untended, I promise, even if I'm going to jail.'

11

'Belle, I'm so glad you answered.'

Belle had obviously pulled over on the side of the road. Tansy could hear the indicator tick-tocking and the low hum of the car in neutral.

'What's happened? You sound teary,' Belle said, pulling on the handbrake with a sharp *scritch*.

Tansy took a shaky breath and gulped a few hiccupy, sniffly sobs.

'Has someone died?'

Tansy shook her head. 'It's Dougal . . .'

'Dougal died?'

'No, sorry. We had a fight. A big one. Can you talk? I so wish I could pop around.'

'I've just pulled over but don't worry about that. I spend half my life on the side of highways now that Hamish is in the world. I think he'll wake up any moment and need a bottle, but start talking and we'll see how we go. I can always call you back after that if I need to. What's happened? You two never fight.'

'It started yesterday, while we were at the markets.'

Tansy and Dougal hadn't talked much on the way home from the markets. They'd stopped in the kitchen, with the package from the chemist, still in its paper bag, lying on the bench between them.

'We should talk,' Tansy said.

Dougal's face was drawn but he didn't look angry, which was something at least. She was momentarily thrown by how handsome he was, which was a weird thing to be thinking at that time. But he was holding his age well. It wasn't like he was a model or anything, but he was pleasant looking. A kind face and smooth skin, plenty of thick dark hair, and a reasonably sized nose. Nice teeth. Teeth were important. She'd always thought his sideburns were a touch too long, but it wasn't as if they were Abraham Lincoln's or anything.

'What are you staring at?' he asked.

'Oh, sorry. I was just looking at your eyes. They're lovely.'

'Thanks,' he said, confused, guarded.

'You're welcome.'

There was a pause and Dougal pulled out a stool at the bench and hitched up his pants to sit down. He'd lost some weight, she realised. He *had* been working quite hard for some time now. Maybe he wasn't eating enough.

'It's probably a waste of time to speculate,' he said evenly. 'Why don't you just take the test and then we'll deal with this discussion if we have to.'

'*Deal* with it?'

'Tansy, please don't do this. Don't try to trap me with my own words. Not right now. Please just do the test. I think it's better if we don't say things now that we might regret later.'

'Regret?'

'Tansy, please.'

She raised her chin in defiance, something that was unconscious but she noticed as it happened. Her defences rose, ready to do battle if necessary. But she tried to rein them in. He was right, of course. Whatever conversation they had now would be a total waste of time if there was nothing to talk about.

Or would it be? Even if she wasn't pregnant, was having a baby something they should be reconsidering? Just over a week ago she'd convinced herself that this was something Dougal wanted, and she'd found herself elated at the prospect. Then she let it go, convinced she'd been caught up in the idea, spurred on by her falling fertility. But maybe it wasn't just a passing 'moment'. Maybe it *was* what she wanted.

Without another word, she took the paper bag from the bench and retreated to the black-and-white-tiled bathroom to pee on the stick. When she was done, she clipped the cap back on, put it on the edge of the vanity and studied herself in the mirror, illuminated by the row of warm bulbs across the top edge as though in a makeup studio. And it was while she was looking into her own eyes that she knew, without a shadow of a doubt, with every flicker of her nervous heartbeat, that she wanted this test to be positive. She wanted a baby.

'And?' Belle asked frantically. In the background, Tansy heard a truck roar past and could almost feel Belle's car rock in its wake. 'Was it? Are you pregnant?'

Tansy left the test in the bathroom, without waiting for a result, and returned to the kitchen.

Dougal jumped up from the stool. 'Well? What did it say?'

'It's not ready yet,' she said. 'But I think we should talk.'

Dougal let his head fall back on his neck to look up at the ceiling for a moment before rocking forward to look at her and sigh.

'I know,' she began, speaking as slowly and reasonably as her emotions would let her, 'that we discussed children right from the start.'

'We did,' he said.

'And I knew how you felt then, and I think I know how you feel now.'

'You *think*?'

She bit her lip. 'But I think my feelings have changed. And I'm wondering if you . . . would you consider . . . is it possible . . . ?'

He cocked his head to the side, his fingers gripping the back of the stool. 'What? Want a baby?' He seemed horrified.

Her heart plummeted. Then anger rose. 'I know it's not fair,' she said. 'I didn't set out to feel this way. I didn't try to make this happen; this is as much of a surprise to me as it is to you. I want you to know that.'

'Okay.'

'You believe that, right?'

'Yes.'

'Good. Because I want that test to be positive.'

Dougal's countenance crumpled and he ran both hands through his hair and linked his fingers behind his head, flapping his elbows like a bird as he paced the room.

She waited for him to stop pacing, which he did, placing both hands on the edge of the sink to gaze across the island bench at her, his jaw working and his chest rising noticeably.

'Well?' she prompted.

'I don't think we should talk about this until we've seen the result of the test,' he said.

'Well, I do.'

'Why do you have to push?' he groaned.

This was not the first time she'd heard this lament from her husband. Usually it was in response to her attempts to hustle him into taking Latin dance lessons with her, or hassling him about taking extra fibre each day because bowel cancer killed more people each year than breast or prostate cancer. No, it wasn't a pleasant thing to think about—no one wanted to think about their poop—but it could save his life. Why wouldn't he just take the damn psyllium? It wasn't that big a deal, surely. He was being such a baby.

'I need to hear your thoughts,' she said now. He wasn't getting out of this. She needed him to open that man cave of a brain and share.

He looked to the ceiling again, wrestling with his emotions. She waited. 'We're leaving for Canada next week,' he said.

'We might need to review that if the test is positive.'

'But I need to go now,' he said, straightening again.

'Well, I don't think babies like external schedules and rules. They tend to do what they want when they want.'

'I love that you're a dreamer, but you only ever dream of good things and happy endings. I'm past this. I did this when I was young, and my life was on hold for years and I was financially ruined for so long. Now Leo's nearly out of uni. I should be preparing to be a grandparent in the next five years, not changing nappies and drowning in sleep deprivation. This is *not* what I want and you knew that. That was part of the deal.'

'Deal? I didn't realise this was a business transaction!' she shouted. She was in full flight now, a mother lion protecting her cub and nothing and no one was going to stand in her way. She didn't even know the result of that test, but some kind of raw, primal fierceness had risen up inside her at the mere suggestion that there was a baby.

Dougal swallowed. 'That's not what I meant. This wasn't the conversation I was expecting to have today, or ever. Because we'd decided. Years ago. And now you're saying you've changed your mind. What am I supposed to do with that?'

'Things change. Life throws curveballs. I'd accepted that agreement, but I was young. Maybe too young.' Her voice wobbled. Dougal's eyes flashed fear as he suddenly realised that this could be a Very Large Problem. 'I'm nearly thirty. Time isn't on my side anymore. Things seem clearer. I want a baby.'

'And what if I still don't?' he all but whispered. 'I get no say in it. Just like last time.'

'"Last time" had nothing to do with me. This is an entirely different situation. I'm not Rebecca.'

She burst into tears then, went back to the bathroom, locked the door and sobbed, sitting on the edge of the spa bath.

There was silence from outside the door. She had no idea if Dougal was even still in the house.

Then, abruptly, she stopped crying and wiped her nose, stood up and picked up the test stick. There was one pink line.

She wasn't pregnant.

'Schlock.' Belle let out a long slow breath on the other end of the phone. 'What happened then?'

'I waited a while, took some deep breaths. Then I went out to the lounge, where I found Dougal distracting himself with a glass of scotch, handed him the stick, told him I didn't want to talk about it and that I was going to Jordan and Katarina's for the night.

'He tried to grab my hand but I shook it away and left. I'm still here. They clearly know what's going on but they're not asking questions. Katarina just said they were there if I wanted to talk, otherwise they'd just feed me and make me tea till I was ready to go home.'

'What are you going to do?'

'I don't know,' Tansy whimpered, barely holding back tears.

Belle *ummed* and murmured sympathy for a few moments. Then she said, 'Can I make a suggestion?'

'Yes, please do.'

'I know you're hurting right now and everything seems awful, but this could be a good thing in the long run. It's not ideal, the way this came up, and if I was going to offer some tough love here it would be that, maybe, pushing him to have that discussion while a pregnancy test was ticking away in the next room wasn't the best time.'

Tansy didn't say anything, embarrassed and annoyed to acknowledge that she'd let her feelings override Dougal's. Belle was right, but she couldn't admit it out loud.

'I think you're going to need to give him some time to come to terms with this. Maybe some space today is exactly what you both need. Let things settle. Try to get some clarity on your feelings.'

Hamish began to mew in the background. 'Oh, he's awake, I've got to go. But you'll be okay, I promise. It will all work out in the end. Text me when you've gone home and talked to Dougal so I know you're okay.'

'Okay.'

'Love you.'

'Love you too.'

'It's too good a day to spend inside moping,' Katarina declared in her mother-cum-teacher voice. 'Let's head to the marina.'

By mid-morning, Dougal still hadn't texted or called and Tansy was worried and stroppy. They'd never had a fight like that before. Never. And on the odd occasion that she'd left the house to go for a drive to cool off, he'd always texted her minutes after she'd left, assuring her he loved her and he was sorry. She hadn't texted either, of course, but she was old-fashioned like that and deep down felt it was *his* job to chase her.

But he wasn't chasing. And the silence was deeply disturbing. Maybe Belle was right and they both needed some space.

The marina was festively busy, with a small collection of market stalls lining the wide boardwalk on the river, the cruise boat hooting as it left the dock, the sky as blue and the sun as bright and warm as they could be.

Toby led the way to Chocol'Arte, tucked in between a clothes shop and a florist, and they all took up residence on small wooden stools at the table where they could gaze through the glass at the handmade chocolates and the cakes and biscuits in their jars.

'Hot chocolate all round?' Katarina suggested, getting up to order. They all agreed and she waved away Tansy's money.

Jordan—a theatre nurse at Noosa's small private hospital— worked rotating shifts but had today off. He was unshaven but still handsome, his blue eyes the same colour as the water outside. He'd always been a heartbreaker as a teen, living life on the coast with Florrie and Alastair as an only child. He'd been a member of the surf lifesaving 'nippers' club from a small boy, and weekends spent in the sand, training hard, had given him a permanent golden glow, along with salty, sun-bleached hair and toned muscles that kept the girls interested. He was two years older than Tansy, which had served her well once boys had made it onto her agenda, Jordan's friends bringing a constant supply of new dating opportunities. As for him, he'd met Katarina at a uni soccer weekend and she'd quickly become a permanent fixture in Tansy's visits to the coast. Luckily, they'd hit it off from the beginning and if Jordan was the brother she'd never had, Katarina had been the other sister. Which was a wonderful thing at this moment when she needed their support.

But not in the mood to chat just yet, Tansy gazed out through the doors to the white pop-up tents of the stalls and the tall masts of sailing boats beyond, and a squadron of pelicans flying in a straight line high in the sky. Toby wandered around the gift section of the store, picking up brightly painted wooden eggs, patchwork owl doorstops and a porcelain teapot shaped like a chook before Jordan called him back and directed his attention to the game of Jenga stacked on the bench where they were seated. He was showing Toby how to play the game when Katarina returned, sliding her purse into her handbag.

She sat down next to Tansy, tucked her blond bob behind her ears and adjusted her green-framed glasses on her nose. 'I got us a gingerbread man each too,' she said, reaching for the sugar sticks in preparation to add extra to her hot chocolate when it arrived. Tansy must have looked surprised, because Katarina said, 'I tried starting the day with your kale juice and wheatgrass and I was as green as the ingredients. I need coffee in my life. And chocolate. And sugar.'

Tansy smiled and held up her hands. 'I'm right there with you. You couldn't keep me away from it today if you tried.'

'Do you want to talk about it?' Jordan said, extracting a piece of Jenga from the stack while Toby bounced up and down in his seat waiting for it to fall.

'No,' Katarina intervened. 'She's here for chocolate, not to be interrogated.'

'It's fine,' Tansy said. She paused while their beverages arrived, big deep mugs of frothing hot milk with a wooden stick weighed down with Belgian chocolate.

'Yum,' Toby said, pulling out his stick of chocolate and sucking on it.

'You're meant to stir it in,' Katarina said. 'Otherwise you'll eat it and just be left with hot milk.'

Toby studied the stick for a moment but clearly decided it was worth it. He shrugged his shoulders and shoved the stick with the huge lump of chocolate into his mouth.

'Thattaboy,' Jordan said. 'You enjoy it any way you like.'

Katarina watched her son, a small amused smile on her lips, then enjoyed sharing the moment via eye contact with Jordan. Tansy felt a tug of longing, watching them mist up over something so little, something that their small person could do that could enchant them so much.

Katarina still worked a part-time arrangement with a fellow teacher, job-sharing a Year Five class of students, a position she'd secured when Toby was small. Even though he was at school now, she felt that teaching full time took too much out of her and didn't leave enough left over for her own child. 'He'll be a man before I blink,' she'd often say, already sad for the day when she was no longer the centre of his world.

The gingerbread men arrived and Toby dunked his into his hot milk and sucked it dry, giggling as milk ran down his chin.

'I thought I was pregnant,' Tansy said.

Katarina nodded, waiting for her to go on. Jordan looked surprised and cast a glance at Katarina, but didn't say anything, instead taking a serviette and wiping up Toby's spilled milk on the bench.

'But I'm not. And Dougal and I had a nasty fight about it.'

'About you *not* being pregnant?' Jordan asked.

Tansy gave a weak smile. 'No. Because before I took the test I told him I wanted it to be positive, and that I'd changed my mind and I wanted a baby.'

Jordan let out a low whistle, and husband and wife exchanged another glance while they absorbed this news.

'And he didn't take it well?' Katarina asked, sipping her drink.

'You could say that.' Tansy gulped down her drink. Even though it was dark chocolate, it was incredibly sweet, and she felt the sugar rush to her blood instantly.

'So, just to be clear, Dougal doesn't want any more kids, is that right?' Katarina said.

'Correct,' Tansy said.

'And that's definitely non-negotiable?' Jordan asked.

Tansy shrugged. What she'd hoped was that she would announce her feelings and he would have a swift turn-around and come on board. Part of her still believed it was possible.

'Well,' Katarina said, 'just to play devil's advocate, it's not exactly something you can negotiate, is it? I mean, you either have them or not, there's no halfway, is there? You both need to be in sync for something as life-changing as that. It's a huge, gigantic commitment. You just never know what you're going to get on the other side. You need to be a totally united team.' She spoke decisively, as many parents did, about the rigours of commitment to child rearing.

'That's probably not what she wants to hear right now,' Jordan said.

'No, it's okay. It's what I *need* to hear,' Tansy said, before her eyes spilled over and tears fell down her cheeks. 'I did go into this marriage knowing that was how he felt. It's not exactly fair to him.'

But is it fair to me?

Katarina rubbed her arm for a few moments as the pan flutes of the Andean music in the shop filled the silence.

'So what are you going to do?' Toby asked, a gorgeous milk moustache on his upper lip as he looked up at Tansy. She hadn't even thought he'd been listening or comprehending.

'Well, I don't know yet,' she said to him.

'Mum says when you have a fight you should say sorry.'

'Your mum's wise,' Tansy said.

'You know you're welcome to stay with us for as long as you need to,' Jordan said.

'Thank you.'

'But one of you has to make the first move,' Katarina said.

'I'm just not ready,' Tansy said. Tears threatened once more and she made her apologies and hastily picked up her bag to escape to the boardwalk and the fresh air. She headed down past the day spa and kept going towards the end of the marina. It was quiet here; the open water stretched out in front of her and she watched black birds bobbing up and down on the floating pontoons, and could even see an iridescent blue jellyfish blobbing against a barnacle-encrusted pylon.

Katarina was right, of course. One of them had to make the first move. But stupid, injured pride meant she didn't want it to be her. She wasn't ready to accept that, just possibly, neither of them was in the wrong here. And neither of them was right. They were at a stalemate.

She leaned on the metal railing at the end of the wharf and let the breeze dry her tears. And at last, there came a text from Dougal. She tapped it open, her heart in her throat, hoping for a tremendous apology and gushing pleas for her to come home and talk. Maybe even an admission that he secretly wanted a baby too.

Instead, it said, *I know we still need to talk about yesterday, but you'd better come home now. Your mother's here and she's brought suitcases.*

12

When Tansy arrived home, Enid was already unpacking in the guest room, carrying her toiletries into the ensuite, and hanging up clothes.

'Mum,' Tansy said, a little breathless from taking the stairs two at a time. She'd opened the front door cautiously, not knowing what to expect, and found Leo in the kitchen making vegemite and banana sandwiches (his favourite ever since he was a child). He'd waved cheerily as though nothing was wrong and said, 'Your mum's down the hall,' through a mouthful of food, heading out to eat on the balcony.

'Thanks.'

She went straight to her mother.

'Hello, darling,' Enid said, spinning her suitcase around so she could better access the shoes stuffed into the pocket under the lid.

'Hi. What's going on?' Tansy reached for her and hugged her. Shoes still clutched in her hands, Enid didn't say anything, so Tansy let her go and stared at her, waiting for a response.

'I'm having a break,' Enid began, carefully.

'Okay.'

'From your father,' Enid clarified, sighing and dropping the shoes into the bottom of the walk-in wardrobe.

Tansy perched on the end of the bed. 'Why?'

'We've been arguing. A lot.' Enid shrugged, as though this was an embarrassing thing to admit to her daughter. 'And we came to the conclusion this morning that we needed a bit of time apart.'

Them too? 'So, you're separating?' *And coming to live with me?*

'No, no. We just need some space to clear our heads, see if we can sort things out without being so much in each other's faces.'

'Could you sit down for a moment? You're making me dizzy.'

'Oh, sorry.' Enid flipped the suitcase lid closed and joined Tansy on the bed.

She could feel the heat coming from her mother's body. Smell her Chanel. 'What have you been fighting about?' she asked, then sneezed as the perfume tickled her nose.

Her mother adjusted her weight distribution over her buttocks and kicked off her navy-blue Mary Jane shoes. 'Church. Your father has decided that . . .'—her voice caught in her chest and she coughed lightly as though she'd breathed in a speck of dust—'. . . he doesn't want to go to church anymore.'

Tansy kept waiting for more, but nothing came. 'Is that it?'

Enid looked at her sharply. 'Isn't that enough?'

Tansy wasn't sure what to say. After what she'd just been through with Dougal, it seemed laughable. But she knew she needed to tread lightly, so she sprang off the bed and busied herself fussing with linen in the wardrobe, pulling out plush towels and bathmats and an extra sham for the bed as the nights had been getting cooler.

'It's not just that he doesn't want to go to church,' Enid went on, 'though that's upsetting enough. He says he's lost faith.' She whispered the last sentence as though it was a scandalous revelation.

'Does he still believe in God?' Tansy called from the ensuite, laying out guest soap on the basin.

'He says he does.'

Tansy brightened and returned to the bedroom. 'Well, there you go. It's not all bad. It's not like he's renounced everything.'

'You sound just like him,' Enid said with dismay. 'And I'm a member of the parish leaders council, for goodness' sake, hand-chosen by Father Bryce himself. It's beyond humiliating.'

Not knowing how best to be supportive at this time, Tansy decided to change the topic. She rubbed her mother's upper back. 'Has anyone made you a cuppa?'

Enid shook her head, biting back tears, all her resolve suddenly vanished, looking like an older woman than she was. Looking, well, *frail* wasn't the word—her mother was far too stout for that—but beaten down, like well-travelled luggage.

'Come out to the kitchen and I'll put the kettle on,' Tansy said, pulling gently on her mother's arm to ease her off the bed. But Enid pulled back, halting Tansy and making her look at her.

'Is it . . . I hope it's okay for me to just drop in like this,' she said with sudden vulnerability. Tansy felt a twang of fear and sadness.

'Of course it is.'

'It's just that I didn't want to ask Rose and Sam, they don't have the space with all their lot. I think they've been somewhat stressed lately in the run-up to the school holidays. They've been obviously tetchy with each other, and last time I spoke to Rose she sounded awfully distracted and like everything was getting on top of her. You know how much she puts into the kids and their schooling, helping out in the classroom and doing tuckshop duty and after-school activities—'

'Yes, I know,' Tansy said, cutting her mother off. She'd tried to call Rose three times in the past two weeks and her sister hadn't even bothered to reply with a text. Tansy wanted to be understanding—four children must be a lot of work—but it was irritating.

This time last year, she and Rose had been having a regular lunch date up here on the coast once a month. With her three older children at school and just Amy in tow—who was a dream to take out to cafes, happy with a colouring book and an iPad—Rose was free for the first time in Tansy's adult life to be a true friend. (Did her sister count as a friend?) They'd talked about all sorts of things they'd never had time to discuss before, covering everything from fashion, movies and addictive television to Australia's future and the ethics of stem cell research. But then the lunches had stopped, with no explanation as to why.

'Anyway, I thought putting some distance between Finlay and me might do us good,' her mother said, picking up the thread of her thoughts again. 'And I knew you had the room, but if it's too much—'

'Stop. It's fine. You're always welcome. Come on; let's get you a cuppa and get you settled. This will all work itself out soon enough,' Tansy said, sounding far more certain than she felt. It was odd having a parent run away from home and land on your doorstep. It was supposed to be the other way around, wasn't it? Your parents were always supposed to be there as the safety backup plan for when you screwed up your life and needed to start again, when you lost your job or were getting divorced.

Divorced. The idea made her dizzy.

She had no idea what would happen when she next spoke to Dougal. She might well need to flee back to Jordan and Katarina's herself.

'Where is Dougal?' she asked, ushering Enid to the cream lounge suite, then rummaging in the kitchen.

'He said he needed to pop out for a few things and that he'd pick up something for tonight's dinner while he was out. That was a while ago. I'd say he'll be back soon.'

Leo came in from the balcony, put his plate in the dishwasher and went to sit on the lounge chair opposite Enid's.

'We haven't even had a chance to talk yet,' Enid said to him, smiling. 'How's uni? Do you have a girlfriend? A job? You're not into drugs, are you?'

Tansy rolled her eyes from above the jiggling teabag. But Leo just laughed. 'I've missed you, Enid. It's been too long since we've caught up,' he said. 'I might well ask you the same questions.'

Enid tittered. 'Okay, but you go first.'

'Uni is tedious. I'm thinking of leaving, actually.'

'No, no, he's not,' Tansy jumped in, waving her arms. 'He's working towards his exams right now and then he's having a holiday at the end of semester, and he'll see how he feels after that. It's plenty of time to think things through.'

So many people taking time to think things through. It was as if life had hit the pause button and was waiting for each of them to choose the next scene to go to.

'Aren't you nearly finished?' Enid asked him, taking her tea from Tansy.

'Yes,' Tansy said, taking a seat next to Enid, glaring at Leo and willing him to stop talking. The last thing she needed was for her mother to blurt all this out to Dougal tonight.

'I don't see the point in spending a moment longer than I have to in the wrong place. All that's doing is treading water and delaying starting my real life.'

Enid looked from Leo to Tansy's stony face. 'Oh.' That was an unusually restrained response from her mother.

'If I wanted to, I could travel the whole world in the six months I would spend slowing dying in that final semester.'

Tansy couldn't help herself. 'Dying? Leo, you've loved that course. You've wanted to write since you were small. Be reasonable. Finish your degree and then go and do whatever you want to. Travel the world for two years, or twenty years, it doesn't matter. But six months is nothing in the grand scheme of life.'

'I can attest to that,' Enid said. 'Here I am at seventy-one and it's all gone by so fast. Six months is a blip.'

'Do you have regrets?' Leo asked. 'Things you'd do differently?'

Tansy expected her mother to fold her arms and close the blinds on the conversation. But she gazed off into the middle distance. 'Yes,' she conceded.

'Like what?' Tansy asked, genuinely fascinated.

'Well, I think we all have regrets,' Enid said evasively. 'You wouldn't be human if you didn't. No one's perfect and you can't lead a perfect life, unfortunately, no matter how hard you try.'

Then she leaned forward and pointed her finger at Leo in a gesture that only senior people could get away with. 'But finishing uni, if I'd been given the chance, that wouldn't be one of them,' she said sternly. 'It simply wasn't an option. I had to work, then I got married, spent my time building a home and raising Rose.'

Tansy arched a brow, registering that she hadn't even existed for so much of her family's history. Leo listened politely, but she could tell he wasn't applying any of Enid's advice to his own situation.

'I couldn't leave my husband and child to fend for themselves,' Enid said.

Tansy sipped, thinking how much times had changed, how many more opportunities were open to women now. Still, the difficulties of child rearing persisted and did in fact continue to stop women doing what they wanted. 'What would you have studied?' she asked, her curiosity piqued.

'History,' Enid said, raising one shoulder sheepishly, embarrassed by her confession. 'The Dark Ages especially.'

Tansy smiled. 'I never knew that.'

But Enid turned the focus back to Leo. 'So, next question. Do you have a girlfriend?'

'No.'

'Why not? Look at you. You're a good-looking young man, kind and smart. I'd imagine you'd have girls falling at your feet.'

Leo shifted in his seat and tucked a foot up under the other thigh. Tansy waited, eager to hear his response. As his stepmother (and therefore not a friend), she always worried about asking him questions like that so directly, lest she be branded interfering or prying. But trust the step-grandmother to get straight to the point.

'There was someone I liked. But she liked someone else.'

'Oh, shame,' Enid said, with genuine sympathy.

'And is she together with that someone else now?' Tansy asked.

'No.' Leo laughed. 'Because he likes someone else.'

'That sounds complicated,' Enid said. 'Okay then, what about drugs?'

'No drugs. You?'

Enid squealed with joy. 'No.'

'Me neither,' Tansy said. She checked the time—nearly midday. 'The best we can do is scotch or a glass of wine.'

'I'll get the glasses,' Leo said, jumping to his feet.

'White, please,' Enid said, looking far more jolly than she had in the bedroom earlier.

'Me too,' Tansy said. A glass of wine was exactly what was needed to quell the stress of the past twenty-four hours.

Ten minutes ago, Maria had been enjoying herself.

As well as her bees and the daily tending to the garden, her clutch of a dozen chooks provided much opportunity for peaceful meditation in motion. They were a motley crew of black Australorps, Rhode Island reds, a couple of ditzy-looking silkies and another couple of striking black and white Dorkings. She didn't have a rooster, though. She delighted in their strutting and crowing, and thought they were handsome, but she didn't appreciate their incessant hassling of the girls, and neither did she fancy eating fertilised eggs. It just didn't seem right. Only a couple of cells in the egg, sure, but still it was a life just beginning, only to be fried or boiled.

She had a bucket of scraps for them today, crusts of toast, lettuce and silver beet, and quite a few mung beans that she'd sprouted herself, which the girls snatched up with glee. They ran to her the second they saw her coming, their tough, scaly feet making lovely swishing sounds across the green grass, murmuring and gibbering with excitement. Reddish-brown Poppy, with one top of a toe missing, always sounded offended, even when things were going her way. She stood on Maria's boots and looked at her sideways, groaning as though in pain, which she wasn't; it was just how she spoke. It always made Maria laugh.

But that was ten minutes ago. Because it was at that moment, when she was savouring the chooks' company and relishing what a beautiful day it was, that the tranquil atmosphere split open as though heaven itself was being torn in half, with a wrenching, ear-splitting sound. Maria dropped the bucket of scraps and reflexively covered her head with both her hands, spinning at the same time to find the source of the commotion.

An enormous eucalypt was falling from the sky. It was the one that had stood behind White Tara and provided such lovely shade from the western sun. But not anymore. Now, it gathered momentum and paused not even a second as it smashed through the cabin, the earth trembling as it hit the ground.

Maria felt the blow in her body, and stumbled backwards as though winded.

The wooden boards of the cabin shattered as though they were nothing more than kindling and sprayed up in the air before raining down around the trunk. The upper branches extended into the centre of the clearing, knocking over the wishing well, its grey stones clattering as they fell.

The chooks scattered in terrified squawking zigzags. Maria clutched at the shirt on her chest, her mouth opening and closing, her heart pounding like a galloping mob of brumbies.

The sharp scent of eucalyptus flooded the air. The tree lay there, far bigger than it had ever looked while standing, a fallen giant who'd never get up again.

An entire hut had been destroyed in a matter of seconds, and the wishing well too, and the Haven was fully booked with guests for tomorrow. She couldn't cancel them: the orphanage needed the money. It was Sunday; she was unlikely to be able to find anyone to come and remove the tree today. And even if she did, it wouldn't solve the accommodation problem. Or the mess of the wishing well or the smashed hut.

Thank God that no one was in the hut.

She crept towards the tree and stood near it, gazing along the length of its body, touching its green leaves. How could this happen? How could a tree just suddenly fall from the sky?

Emotion overcame her and she knelt down to wait for it to pass. It was the fright; it had to be. Of course, she was in shock.

As much as Maria loved to be independent and self-sufficient, it was clear as day that this was too much to do on her own, even if she pulled in extra help from Petrice to manage the bookings. And Trav, great handyman that he was, wouldn't be able to deal with this alone.

She rose to her feet and half walked and half ran back to the office, knowing she had to call someone. But who?

Tansy.

The thought came to her as though whispered by a friend standing nearby. Tansy—her energetic, enthusiastic niece who'd been offering to help in any way she could.

She flipped open her diary to the place at the back where she'd written down Tansy's mobile phone number, and dialled it immediately. And as it rang, she had the new but not unpleasant sensation that she wasn't alone in the world anymore.

13

Tansy took Maria's phone call and excused herself, leaving Enid and Leo to continue catching up. She stepped out onto the balcony, closed the doors behind her, and leaned as far over the railings as possible to avoid being overheard.

'I hope I'm not interrupting.' Maria's voice sounded shaky. 'If it's a bad time . . .'

'No, no, please, go on. It's been an eventful couple of days, culminating in my mother's unannounced arrival. She's here now.'

'Oh.' Maria was clearly taken aback.

'It's okay. I've stepped outside. I'm so pleased you've called,' Tansy said, surprised but delighted to hear from her aunt. Now that she had Maria in her life, however tenuously, she wanted to keep her there. 'You sound worried, or something. Is everything alright?'

Maria told her about the fallen tree, the smashed cabin and the twenty-four people arriving tomorrow morning for three days, a mix of adult carers and children with special needs coming on their first camp. Her voice wobbled as she stressed that she couldn't let them down. 'It's so important for the parents to have this respite, and it's important for the children that everything is calm and runs smoothly. I can't cancel them. And the orphanage needs the booking fees. I just don't know what to do.'

'How many people did the white cabin hold?' Tansy asked, an idea already forming in her mind.

'Only two. Thank goodness it wasn't one of the ones that hold six. But still, I simply don't have any other beds. I could give up mine, of course, but there'd still be one short . . .'

'You won't need to do that. I have a plan,' Tansy said, smiling. 'You do?'

'Yes. Just hold tight; I'm coming up there and I'll be bringing reinforcements. We'll sort out the accommodation and get rid of the tree and have it looking good again for tomorrow. Maybe not as perfect as it was, but it will be good enough, I promise.'

On the end of the line, Maria was silent for a moment, and Tansy could hear her making small swallowing and breathing noises.

'We'll be there as fast as we can.'

'Thank you. I'm so grateful.'

Back inside, Tansy had only a split second to decide what to do. She always told the truth, but this? This news would be too much to drop on her mother all at once right now, just after she'd left her husband.

So—for the greater good—she concocted an elaborate lie, declaring that she had an emergency decorating job she needed to go to this afternoon. She told Leo firmly that she needed him for some muscle work, not giving him any option to back out. Not that he would. He was generous to a fault.

'What kind of emergency?' Enid asked, incredulous. 'On a Sunday afternoon?'

'It's a respite centre here on the coast,' Tansy said, trying to hold eye contact with her mother as best she could while her brain searched for a convincing story. 'They've had some . . . water damage. A pipe burst and has flooded the place.'

'Oh, that's no good,' Enid said, sitting up straight. 'Sounds like they need a clean-up crew, not a decorator.'

'The clean-up's largely underway,' Tansy said confidently. 'But they need help to get the place feeling calm and homely again by tomorrow and asked me to do a bit of styling and the like. I don't mind. I like to help and it's good networking.'

'I'll come too,' Enid said, rising from the couch.

'No! No, Mum. I couldn't let you do that on your first day here. Please stay and rest. If there's more work to do tomorrow you could help then,' Tansy said, her heart thudding.

'But you know I like to help out in the community,' Enid protested. 'Honestly, it would give me something to do to keep my mind off things.'

Tansy was momentarily lost for words, imagining the family crisis that would erupt if she told her mother the truth about going to Maria's place. Besides, she'd enjoyed their cup of tea the other day and was chuffed that Maria had called her now and didn't want to lose this opportunity.

'Cake,' she suddenly said, snapping her fingers. 'You know, I bet the hospice would love some baked goods, to help lift their spirits and all. Why don't you stay here and bake and I'll drop the goods down to them tomorrow?'

Enid considered this. 'I guess I could do that.'

'Your honey bread's a winner. Why don't you do that?' Tansy said, nodding and smiling as though it was the best idea in the world.

Her mother's eyes slid from Tansy's to Leo's. Leo looked completely unconcerned; he had already put on his shoes and was waiting to go.

'Okay,' Enid said. 'It has been a big day. Perhaps it would be best if I stay and bake. If you think that would help?'

'Absolutely. I'm positively sure it's the best thing you could do right now.'

'So let me get this straight,' Leo said, sitting beside her in her white Barina, rather more modest than Dougal's sleek dark Audi, as she drove the winding roads past horse properties and crop farms, heading towards Eudlo. He'd been listening to the many phone calls she'd made while driving, talking on the hands-free, ordering Leo to look up numbers for her. And now that she'd finally fallen silent, he wanted answers. Her fingers tightened around the wheel.

'We've just lied to Enid and sent her on a wild bake chase, hired two chainsaws, and roped in Jordan, Katarina and Toby in an elaborate plot to help your aunt, a woman you've only just met, who used to be a nun and for some reason hasn't spoken to your mum or Florrie in more than fifty years, and who runs a business that serves an orphanage and has had a tree fall through a cabin. Yes?'

'That's about it, yes.'

'And what does Dad think about all this?'

They passed an unmanned stall on the road selling avocados with an honesty tin near the bags of fruit.

'That's a good question,' Tansy murmured.

'He doesn't know?'

'Not about this. He knows I've been planning a family reunion and that I wanted Maria there as a surprise. He was supposed to be helping me organise it, but I guess the Canada thing's got in the way.'

'But you're not leaving for ages yet.'

Tansy shot him a quick sideways glance. 'Ah, I forgot you didn't know. There've been some changes and it looks like Dougal's going next week—*this* week, actually. He only told me yesterday. I'm sorry you didn't know yet.'

'Oh.' Leo took a few moments to absorb that information. Then, 'And what about you? Are you going this week too?'

She tapped the wheel as she slowed for a particularly sharp bend. 'That's also a good question. I should be, I guess. But now I'm not sure.'

'Is this why you stayed away last night?'

'I was at Jordan and Katarina's,' she said, without elaborating.

Leo seemed to sense that he should leave it alone and didn't say any more. They passed through the tiny town of Eudlo and headed up the mountain to Honeybee Haven. Shortly afterwards, Tansy spied Jordan and Katarina's blue HiLux coming into the rear-view mirror. Picking up the chainsaws had slowed Tansy and Leo down, which meant both cars were now on track to arrive at the same time. Leo turned around in the seat and waved to them.

The main parking lot for Honeybee Haven was at the bottom of the hill, but Tansy had learned (after walking up all those steps the first time) that there was a tradie's track up to a temporary parking and loading bay next to the dining hall, and she led the blue HiLux up there now.

Maria felt better the moment she saw the vehicles pull up and Tansy step out of her car, smiling her wide smile, her sunglasses perched on her wayward dark curls. She'd have thought the arrival of so

many people—all of them related to her, or so Tansy had warned her on the phone—would have been something to fret about. And maybe two hours ago it would have been. But instead she felt almost giddy. The weight of silence and loneliness of the past two hours, waiting here on her own, feeling vulnerable and helpless, flew off, like a kite snatched up by the wind and buffeted away.

She embraced Tansy gratefully, then stood back and shook Leo's outstretched hand, gazing at this man, her step-grandnephew, arriving on her door with his tanned skin and easygoing movements. And then tumbling out of the HiLux came a small boy—Toby—another grandnephew, this one barrelling towards her and talking to her before he was properly in earshot. She shook his hand too, and placed her own on his head, emotion—glorious emotion—welling thick in her chest. And there was Jordan, her nephew, Florrie's boy, and his partner, Katarina. All five of them stood before her and she could barely speak for the whirling in her heart and mind.

'I'm so happy and grateful to have you all here,' she managed. 'And I'm so pleased to meet you all, finally.' She bit her lip and Tansy squeezed her to her side, supporting her.

'It's our honour,' Jordan said. 'You've been missing from our family for too long.'

Maria laughed. 'The black sheep.'

'Not anymore,' Tansy said. 'But we'll have plenty of time to talk through all of this. Right now, we have a lot of work to do.' She gazed at the huge tree that stabbed across the lawn. Its branches, even lying down, were much taller than any of them.

'We've brought chainsaws,' Leo said, opening the boot and pulling out the treacherous-looking orange and black weapons. 'We'll stack up all the wood and you can use it yourself if you've got a fireplace, or sell it to make money for the charity.' He placed the chainsaws on the ground and returned to the boot for the jerry cans of petrol.

'We don't have a fireplace, sadly, but that's a wonderful idea to sell the wood. I can get our handyman to take loads down the mountain in his ute. He should be here soon and can help stack them up. It'll be a great seller coming into winter. Thank you.'

'Let's get moving,' Tansy said. 'We have to get it all cleared before Tulip arrives in the morning.'

'Tulip?' Maria said. 'Another family member?'

'No. She's a friend of mine. She's a children's party host and she has a fairy-themed caravan that she takes around to parties. It's painted bright pink, fully kitted out inside as a magical garden and fairy land, and also has a double bed and two single beds, all with beautiful netting and fairy lights that twinkle from the ceiling. We cross each other's path from time to time, just by virtue of working in the same circles, and we get along well. I phoned her and called in a favour.'

'I don't understand.'

'She's bringing her caravan up here for your guests to stay in instead of the poor old cabin over there.' Tansy gestured to the splintered boards beneath the fallen tree.

Maria tried to visualise a pink van in the midst of the other cabins.

'I know it's not in keeping with your theme . . .' Tansy said, looking suddenly worried.

'It's perfect,' Maria said quietly, taking Tansy's hand. 'The kids will love it. They'll probably fight over it, actually.'

'She'll also be doing a show for all the kids, free of charge.'

'I can't believe this,' Maria said. 'I can't believe it. You've done so much.'

Tansy laughed. 'We haven't even started yet.'

'Come on, boys, time to flex your muscles,' Katarina said, taking charge and moving them towards the tree. 'Now, Toby, you aren't to touch the chainsaws under *any* circumstance. Do you understand?' she pressed, pointing at the tools as Leo and Jordan started pouring petrol into the tanks.

Toby looked longingly at the chainsaws, their metal teeth being unsheathed in readiness to take on the tree. But he nodded obediently.

'Good boy. You're going to help me,' Katarina went on.

Jordan straightened and looked at Katarina. 'Make sure you leave anything heavy to us,' he instructed. 'Don't overdo it, okay? You can give orders instead.'

'Okay.' She nodded, sounding a little exasperated. 'We talked about this on the way up. I promise not to do anything silly.'

'What are we doing?' Toby asked his mum.

Katarina turned to Maria. 'Do you have a wheelbarrow?'

'Yes, of course. It's in the garden shed, up near the chook house. I'll take you up there.'

So the three women, plus Toby, took the short walk across the lawn, past the shower block and the raised garden beds over-flowing with bright red capsicums, yellow chillis, purple eggplants, and virtual forests of spinach, silver beet and spring onions. Jolly bees hovered and darted in among the flowers. Maria yanked open the rickety wooden shed door. They filed in and collected gardening gloves, bags, rakes, shovels, long-handled secateurs, hammers, screwdrivers and buckets. They loaded most of it into the wheelbarrow, looked at each other for a moment as if only now realising what a huge job lay before them, and then smiled, put their heads down and started hauling the items back towards the sound of the chainsaws ripping into the silence and the tree.

An hour later, two more cars arrived. A person emerged from each, and Tansy recognised one as timid Petrice, but she didn't know the other.

'You made it!' Maria cried, her hands clasped around Petrice's biceps.

'I'd do anything for you,' Petrice said shyly, the toe of her shoe digging into the dirt and her fingers tucking her purple-streaked hair behind her triple-studded ear.

'I know you would. You're my right-hand-girl,' Maria said gently.

Tansy was touched; Maria had obviously played an important role in this young woman's life and recovery.

The man shook hands with everyone and introduced himself as Trav, the dogsbody.

'Stop it, you are not,' Maria chided. 'You are our skilled and generous handyman.'

Trav was white-haired, with huge dark eyes, a thick Scottish accent and a gentle demeanour. He wasn't especially tall, but seemed sturdy. 'Wow,' he said, viewing the tree, already being broken down into logs and rounds. He ran his hand across the back of his neck. 'That's nowt something you see every day, Sister, hey?' He turned to Maria and gave her a sympathetic raise of his bushy brows.

'Certainly isn't,' she agreed.

Tansy's phone buzzed and she dug it out from a deep pocket in her cargo pants. It was a text from Dougal.

I'm sorry we didn't get a chance to talk before you had to leave. I hope everything is going okay at the hospice. What time do you think you'll be home?

She'd have to clear up that little lie with Dougal tonight. She wouldn't be able to keep track of all these stories soon.

Up here on the mountain, in this surreal situation and surrounded by these people, with the afternoon sun still warm and a gentle breeze in the trees, the memory of the argument with Dougal lost its heat. He'd made an effort to be nice in his text, which meant quite a lot, actually. It was more than she'd done, she acknowledged.

She looked at the massive task in front of them and at all the busy hands moving, stacking, dragging, carting, raking and hauling. There was noise and industry all around—the roar of the chainsaws, the scraping of branches and leaves across the grass. The crunch of gravel as the remains of the hut were dragged to the loading bay, and the smashing and clashing as wood, bricks and metal were stacked in readiness for the skip bin—the biggest one she could get—that she'd organised to be delivered at six tomorrow morning.

She quickly texted back. *After dark, I'd say. Can you make sure Mum gets something to eat?* She paused before adding, *I'm sorry too. I love you.*

He replied immediately. *I love you too.*

The sun began to fall off in the distance behind Yellow Tara, which was next to where White Tara had been, flooding their work area with a burst of intense heat and glaring rays. To Maria, it felt cleansing. They weren't that far from finishing. She'd never have thought it possible when the tree first fell, but it was incredible what eight hard-working individuals could do when they set their minds to it. And it was all because of Tansy.

She stood with a tray full of sandwiches and cups of water, and watched her niece take one end of a sheet of corrugated iron from the roof of White Tara and her nephew—her *nephew*—Jordan take the other and together, laughing, carry it across the lawn towards the rubbish pile that now extended into the loading bay. Katarina, Toby and Petrice had put themselves in charge of the wood; they had stacked it in attractive pyramids behind the dining hall as there was no more space in the loading bay. Over time, Trav would load the wood into his ute and deliver it to customers.

Trav's and Leo's shirts were stained with sweat patches, and Leo had pulled his shoulder-length hair back into a tiny ponytail to keep it off his neck while he worked. They were now considering the wishing well, and were moving stones here and there, assessing what they needed to do to fix it.

'Let it go to the skip,' she ordered. *Good riddance.* In all honesty, she was glad to see it go; she could do without any reminders of wells lying around. Later on, she'd put a beautiful birdbath there instead.

Maria was filled with a rush of achievement and a glow of gratitude. Then she realised she'd been standing and staring, grinning like a fool, while the worker bees in front of her needed sustenance. She set about taking the tray around to everyone, somehow feeling light despite the chaos of the afternoon. Today, a lot had been lost; but so much had been found.

14

Returning to Honeybee Haven on Monday morning, Tansy and Leo alighted into a hive of activity. Maria seemed to have recovered her fortitude, if the fact that she was shouting into a megaphone was anything to go by. Trav cleaned up debris from the wishing well, dug out the remnants of the concrete and patched the earth. Tansy wondered why Maria would want to get rid of something as feel-good as a wishing well, particularly one which actually collected coins for the orphanage. Petrice was loading rubble into the ginormous skip bin with metallic bangs and clangs. She staggered under the weight of a large plank, and Leo leapt to her aid, catching the end of it before it swung around and knocked her over.

'Are you okay?' he asked, steadying the weight.

Petrice gaped at him and nodded rapidly, her neck flushing with colour.

Leo laughed. 'Come on, let me help you.' He led the way to the bin, whistling the dwarves' 'Hi Ho' song, while the colour rushed further up Petrice's neck.

Maria jumped in surprise when Tansy reached her side. 'Oh, Tansy.' She beamed. 'What have you got there?'

'Honey bread. Six loaves of it, actually.'

Maria lowered her megaphone and sniffed the bread through the cling wrap. 'That reminds me of childhood,' she said softly, straightening.

'That might be because my mother made them,' Tansy said.

'Goodness.' Maria inhaled the aroma again. 'She must have got Mum's recipe before she died.' Her voice was low and wistful. Tansy had the urge to hug her aunt but knew that Maria needed to keep it together today. There'd be plenty of time for sentiment once this crisis had passed.

'I had to keep her occupied while I came up here.' Tansy squirmed. 'I'm afraid I told a few lies. Sorry. I'm not normally so deceptive.'

Maria's nose twitched and several thoughts seemed to flicker behind her eyes. 'Sometimes you just have to do what you need to do,' she said, then raised the megaphone to shout, 'Make sure you check the other trees too,' at a man in a long-sleeved khaki shirt who was bent over inspecting the remains of the trunk and roots of the eucalyptus tree. He nodded and looked around at the other trees nearby.

'I've got the arborist out to investigate what went wrong with the tree,' Maria told Tansy, nodding towards the man in the khaki shirt. 'We can't have that happening again. And these other men are the electricians, securing the site.' A couple of men in orange high-viz vests squatted at the plot where White Tara had stood just this time yesterday.

'Remember to put in an external power point for the caravan,' Maria shouted at them. One of the men raised his hand in acknowledgement.

As if on cue, a slow rumble of an engine alerted them to the arrival of Tulip's four-wheel-drive, towing her wondrous pink caravan up the hill.

'Here she comes,' Tansy said, and waved her hand high above her head to get Tulip's attention; in reply, Tulip's four-wheel-drive flashed its lights. The paintwork of the fifties-style beetle-shaped van glittered in the morning sun. Tulip was a bona fide friend, Tansy realised. Well, maybe a work friend, outer-circle type, good acquaintance. But in the realm of friendship, certainly.

'What time do the kids arrive?' she asked.

Maria checked her watch, a simple silver band with a small face, which Tansy found endearing—hardly anyone had a proper watch these days, instead forever checking their phones or Fitbits. 'They're due at ten. It's eight thirty now so that should give us a whisker of time to get it set up in place.'

The caravan was artfully embellished with toadstools and secret doorways, trees, lanterns, rainbows, small furry animals, fairies, bridges and wood folk.

'We've never had a pink Tara cabin,' Maria said quietly, her eyes bright.

Tulip pulled up in the driveway and Tansy and Maria met her at the driver's door. Tansy put her bounty of honey bread down on the ground and hugged Tulip, who was a slight elfin-like creature herself, with a modern pixie haircut and even slightly pointy ears. She was dressed in a chocolate-brown miniskirt with rainbow-striped opaque tights and green felt shoes with bells, which matched her green felt vest.

'You look wonderful,' Maria said, holding out her hand to Tulip. But Tulip wrapped her in a hug instead. 'Oh, goodness, you're a strong little thing.'

Tulip's laugh tinkled. 'It's such a pleasure to be here. I'd heard about this place and wished I could do something to help. Now here's my chance. I'm one lucky fairy.'

'That's incredibly good-spirited of you,' Maria said.

'I'm just sorry the universe had to throw a tree on your cabin to organise it,' Tulip said, her voice tinkling again. 'Now, where would you like me to park the van?'

'I'm just waiting for the electricians to finish up over there,' Maria said, waving towards the cleared space. 'But as soon as they're done, it can go there.'

'Okay,' Tulip said. 'In the meantime, come in and have a look.'

She led them inside to a nest of gauze drapes pinned back with colourful silk butterflies; there were cushions and throw rugs, cupboards with arched doors, gilded mirrors, lanterns, fairy lights, vines and flowers. The beds were set against the walls, with toadstool lampshades and netting; on the pillows were books about enchanted woods.

Maria held a hand to her cheek, seemingly speechless.

'I love this job,' Tulip said, picking up a snow dome of a forest with white horses and giving it a shake to set the flakes whirling about.

'The children are going to love this,' Maria said. 'But I don't know how they'll work out who gets to sleep in here.'

'There'll be a riot,' Tansy agreed, grinning.

'Well, if they're desperate, you can fit four in here in total. There are two roll-out trolleys under those beds,' Tulip said, indicating with a pointed toe, the gold bell at the tip ringing with the movement.

And in the end, that was exactly what happened. The bus arrived with the twenty-four campers—sixteen primary-school-aged children and eight carers—and more than half of the children wanted to sleep in the fairy van. There were some tears from those who missed out, but three girls and one boy got their wish and beds in the Pink Tara caravan.

Maria, Tulip, Tansy, Leo, Petrice and Trav all worked until well after the kids were settled and had finished morning tea. Then Trav left with his first load of firewood. Tulip began her fairy show out on the lawn, surrounded by whooping and clapping children, playing her fiddle and flute, teaching them songs, blowing bubbles, sprinkling fairy dust and handing out fairy wings, which they pulled on like backpacks. She brought out face paint and adorned each of their faces in turn while they had a picnic lunch on the lawn. Petrice and Leo disappeared into the kitchen to take care of the washing-up and preparations for afternoon tea. And Tansy convinced Maria that the world wouldn't end if she slipped off to her own cabin to have a slice of honey bread and a cup of tea.

'I'm fine,' she protested, but not too much, Tansy noticed.

Maria agreed to put her feet up on a chair while Tansy fussed around with a tray of tea things, but swiftly knocked back any idea of a rug over her knees. 'I'm only two years older than your mother,' Maria scoffed.

'Of course,' Tansy said, a little chastened. 'And you're probably in much better physical condition, actually. Sorry.' She was trying too hard. It was far easier to worry about her aunt than about her own life.

'They want me on a plane on Saturday,' Dougal had said this morning in the kitchen. 'Can I tell them to book you a ticket too?'

They both knew there was still a lot to work through after the pregnancy test, but by the time they managed to talk alone last night it had been too late. They'd agreed to raincheck the conversation for a better time. But Tansy wasn't ready to jump on a plane with so much unfinished business between them.

'I don't know,' she'd finally said, her words shaky.

'I'd like you to,' he'd said. 'I want you with me. I know things got out of hand the other day. That's why I didn't want to talk about it.'

He'd stopped short of blaming her for backing him into a corner, but she still felt the sting of his words. What had she expected? That he'd suddenly capitulate after all these years? Be eager in an instant?

'I'm sorry,' he'd said. 'I don't ever want to hurt you. I love you.'

She'd bitten her lip and nodded, mumbling, 'I love you too.'

'Will you come? Please.'

'I think it's all a bit rushed,' she'd said. 'I need more time.'

His nose had pinched upwards. 'How long?'

'I don't know.'

Now Maria broke off a piece of the honey cake and popped it in her mouth, closing her eyes. 'Oh my. That's so good. And so much like Mum's.'

Tansy sat down in the chair facing her. 'Does that make you sad?'

Maria considered this. 'No, I don't think so. But maybe a little homesick.'

'What for?'

'I left home when I was sixteen and never went back. I thought I'd let go of all that. Well, I had to let go of it; by the time I left the convent it was all gone. Mum had died, the house had been sold. There wasn't anything left.'

'But what about your sisters? Why didn't you contact them or go see them? They were still there. They're still there today. And all within an easy drive.' Tansy felt herself getting snappy with Maria then. Her mother was at Tansy's place, alone, going through some sort of marital crisis and probably watching daytime television, and all the while Maria, the sister she hadn't seen for more than three-quarters of her life, was right here. And worse than that, Tansy had connected with Maria behind her back and was lying about it.

Maria sipped her tea but didn't say anything for several moments, so many that Tansy began to think she'd never speak again.

Then, 'It worked both ways,' she said evenly.

Tansy conceded that that was true enough. Hadn't she recently witnessed for herself the intensity of Enid's grudge against Maria? 'What happened between you?'

Outside the window, there was a great cheer and squeals, and a flurry of children circling in a game of musical chairs.

'It's all so long ago now.'

'Exactly,' Tansy said, tapping the table lightly. 'Doesn't that seem like the perfect reason to let it all go? To be frank, none of you are getting any younger.'

Maria raised an amused grey eyebrow. 'Well, you have your mother in you after all,' she said, a smile skirting around her mouth. 'She was always good at getting straight to the point too.'

'Sorry.'

They watched the kids outside for a while and Maria chuckled at their merriment. 'Kids have it so much better these days,' she said. 'And that's how it should be. Each generation should be trying to do it better than the last. I hear a lot of people my age complain about children today and say that all *they* needed to be happy at that age was a ball of string and a stick, but they're wrong. They're so wrong. The rights of the child—the right to play and be happy and *be* a child—are so much better defined these days. It makes

130

me glad that I can do something like this'—she motioned around the grounds of Honeybee Haven—'and be a part of that change.'

'Well, I'm glad I can be part of it too,' Tansy said. She meant it. For so many reasons, she was grateful to be here right now.

Maria placed her cool hand on top of Tansy's. 'I can't tell you what a gift it's been to have you turn up in my life, especially with everything else that's going on right now.'

'What's going on right now?'

'Oh, nothing of concern, just some loose ends I have to deal with. But I think I needed you, and by the grace of God you turned up exactly when it would help the most.' She squeezed Tansy's hand and smiled, loose skin corrugating at the corners of her eyes. 'And I don't know what I would have done yesterday if I hadn't had you to turn to and you hadn't organised all of this.' She again gestured outside, where Tulip had the children following her through the gardens while she played her flute, like the Pied Piper. 'What can I do to repay you?'

'Nothing. You don't need to repay me,' said Tansy. 'It's been my pleasure.'

'I know I don't need to, but if there's anything I can do . . .' Maria trailed off.

Tansy seized her chance. 'Well, I would love to learn about bees,' she said.

Maria's eyes shone. 'Honestly?'

'Definitely.'

'I'd like that. I haven't had anyone to teach for many years.'

'And one other thing,' Tansy said slyly.

'Ah . . . here it comes,' Maria said, folding her hands on her lap as if she knew what Tansy was about to say.

'I want you to help me mend the family. I want to know what happened between you and my mum and Aunt Florrie, why you're all not speaking, and I want you to come to my birthday party. I know I have to work on Mum from my end, but that will only get me so far if you're not coming to the party, literally, from your end.'

Maria had pursed her lips and closed her eyes as though she was being given a court ruling she didn't want to hear.

Tansy waited, allowing Maria to absorb what she'd said, then added, cheekily, 'You did say *anything*,' with an appeasing smile in her voice.

'Yes, more fool me,' Maria said, opening her eyes.

'So what do you say?'

Maria inhaled deeply and rubbed her forehead with her fingertips. 'I say you're opening an enormous can of worms.'

'I love worms.'

'You might not like these ones; they have teeth.'

'All the better.'

'Okay then. I suppose everyone will know everything soon enough,' Maria murmured, gazing out the window.

'What?'

'Nothing. Come back tomorrow and we'll begin.'

15

When Tansy got home, she found her mother installed in the kitchen and laughing heartily with another small, stocky short-haired woman with long lines on her face. (Goodness, she was practically a clone of Enid.) Muffins of different flavours—blueberry, chocolate and banana, by the looks of them—sat cooling on racks, and another batch was baking in the oven. Her mother had a bowl of batter in front of her on the bench and the unfamiliar woman was just placing a hot tray down on the stovetop.

'Hello?'

'Tansy, you're back. How was your day?' her mother said, as though fifteen years had vanished and Tansy had just come home from school.

'Fine, thanks.' She turned her attention to the stranger in her kitchen, wearing Tansy's red paisley oven mitts and matching apron and smiling like a friendly aunt. 'Hello,' Tansy said.

'This is my new friend, Paula. I was so inspired by baking for the hospice yesterday that I popped down to the parish office at Tewantin today to see if there was anything I could do for them while I'm staying here. I might as well make myself useful. And as it turns out, Paula is coordinating the parish's first ever twilight fete for this weekend coming, a fundraiser for the church and its mission in Malawi.'

'The organising committee thought a night fete, with music and food stalls and coloured lights, would attract a more youthful crowd—people like you,' Paula added, her tone of voice seeking something from Tansy.

'They needed some extra hands. So we've been baking all day,' Enid finished happily.

'Lucky you,' Tansy said, ignoring Paula's suggestive encouragement.

Her mother had made a new friend in a single day.

'Did the hospice appreciate the honey bread?' Enid asked hopefully.

'Oh, yes, very much. They asked me to pass on their thanks and tell you how much it lifted their spirits,' Tansy said, marvelling at the ease with which these lies now fell from her lips.

'Your mother was telling me about the flooding,' Paula said, shaking her head. 'Dreadful business. Which hospice is it? Enid wasn't sure, but I know most of them on the coast.'

'Oh, it's way down the south end of the coast,' Tansy said evasively. 'It's all better now. Everything's fine.'

Paula frowned as if still trying to place the hospice; just as her mouth opened to ask more questions, Tansy jumped in to deflect them. 'I've got work to do for some clients, so I might just lock myself away in the office while you two finish up here,' she said.

'Oh, and I dropped Leo down at the beach but he'll be back in time for dinner.'

'Of course, darling, don't let us get in your way,' Enid said.

'I bet the hospice was grateful for a young man's labour,' the baking intruder said, and Tansy tried to tell herself that the note of suspicion she heard in Paula's voice was nothing but the workings of her own guilty conscience.

At this rate, she'd need to buy a Brussels sprout farm.

Finally, Tansy and Dougal saw the opportunity to have a proper conversation about the pregnancy test—one where they could take their time and find some common ground, without any need to whisper or hide their issues from Enid or Leo.

'We're leaving you with a takeaway menu,' Tansy said, passing it and the phone to Enid, who had her slippered feet up on an ottoman, tired from the day of baking. 'We've been invited to dinner at one of Dougal's business associate's and we just can't get out of it.'

All this subterfuge was becoming exhausting.

'It's a kind of going-away get-together,' Dougal said, trying to be helpful.

Tansy froze. She hadn't told Enid about Canada, not even the original plan of leaving in a couple of months' time.

'Going away? Where?' Enid asked, a sharp edge to her words.

'You haven't told her?' Dougal turned to Tansy.

'No, I haven't yet.'

'Why not?' he said.

Tansy moaned and dropped down on the couch. 'If you remember, it was supposed to be announced at the party,' she said tersely. 'And then the plans changed quite suddenly and it's only been two days since you told *me* about it and there's been quite a lot going on, don't you think?'

Dougal fidgeted.

'What on earth *is* going on?' Enid said, leaning forward, alarmed.

'Dougal's going to Canada,' Tansy said. 'On Saturday.'

'Saturday? Why? For how long?'

Tansy worried at a fingernail and indicated for him to fill Enid in.

'For work. I've been recruited to Canada for a year or so to work on the design and construction of a university. It will be huge. We were supposed to leave in a couple of months, but the situation has changed and I have to go sooner.'

'You were both going?' Enid said, her expression crestfallen.

'Originally,' Tansy said. 'But I'm not going on Friday,' she reassured her mother. 'I need more time.'

'Canada. That's so far away.'

'Yes, it is,' Tansy agreed. She was fractious and moody again, her optimism that an evening with Dougal would mend their rift gone. Still, she pulled herself up off the couch with as much brisk efficiency as she could muster. 'I'm sorry, Mum, but we'll have to talk about this later or we'll be late for dinner.' She kissed Enid on the cheek and left, Dougal a couple of paces behind. They went down the hill and turned left, then veered right up Hastings Street. They walked in silence side by side until they reached 'their' bar.

'Are you going to tell your mother about the pregnancy test?' Dougal asked once a vodka on ice was in front of him.

They sat opposite each other in the big white lounge chairs of the bar, adjacent to the footpath of Hastings Street, the concertina windows pushed open and the Monday night sounds drifting in. Pedestrians passed by about a metre below the windows, licking ice creams, walking dogs on leads, or with sleepy children clinging to their daddy's neck, sand plastered to their bare legs.

'That's a tough question,' she said, sipping her white wine. 'I don't know. I'm more interested in where we're at.'

The lighting was dim in the bar, big round woven lampshades hanging from the raked ceiling high above, the colourful liqueur bottles lit up behind the counter. It somehow encouraged Tansy to speak more freely, as though the softness of the lighting would also soften their words. Of course, the wine was likely taking the edge off too.

'What are we going to do?' she said, feeling quite helpless. 'I don't want to talk about the fight. It was terrible and we said awful things.'

'I wish you had told me how you felt sooner,' Dougal said. 'Or later. Any time other than while we were waiting for results.'

'I know,' she agreed, angry with herself. 'I'm sorry for putting my feelings first; it wasn't fair. But what are we going to do?' Tears leaked from the corners of her eyes and she brushed them away, gazing out the windows at the fairy lights in the trees that lined the street. It was like Christmas every night of the year here. They should be happy.

Dougal thought in silence for a few moments and Tansy waited. 'Rebecca and I had had a good run before Leo came along,' he said. 'I know we hadn't been together long when she fell pregnant, and I know we were young, but everything changed once Leo arrived. We fought all the time. The sleep deprivation, the crying, the stress, the pressure on me to achieve at uni, go out and find work and make money, the crushing responsibility of creating a life for him . . .' He trailed off. 'We resented each other. Lost interest in each other.'

'But you were so young,' Tansy said. 'You were only twenty when he was born, virtually a teenager. Anyone would struggle.'

He shrugged a shoulder. 'Maybe.'

'And now you'd have a totally different experience. It could be wonderful,' she said, a glimmer of hope in her voice, romantic visions of shared parenthood floating around her mind. But he looked unconvinced.

'Do you remember when we first talked about this, early on in our relationship, when I said I didn't want more children? That time we were in the car on the way to the movies?'

She shook her head. 'Vaguely.'

'You said that it was one of the great things about living in a country like ours, that you could make whatever choices you wanted and it was perfectly acceptable.'

'Yes, I do remember that.'

'And you said that there was no point putting the cart before the horse, that you needed a man before you could have a baby and it wouldn't work the other way around.'

She nodded. 'That's true.'

'I told you that you'd have to make a clear choice.'

'And I did.'

'So can you explain to me what's changed?' His voice was soft, wanting to understand.

'*I've* changed. I was younger then. What was important to me then is different to now. I'm the youngest person in my family. Everyone is older than me. I want some young blood; I want to know that life will continue after me.'

'Your sister has children. Doesn't that count?'

'I get the feeling I'm not particularly important in Rose's life anymore, let alone her kids' lives.'

'Then change that, and maybe it would be enough,' he tried.

She shook her head. 'The simple fact is that I made a choice then but now I want to make a different choice.'

They sat in silence for a few moments, looking at each other sadly and sipping their drinks carefully.

'Where does this leave us?' he asked. 'Are you saying . . .' He swallowed and his face crumpled up the way it had when he'd told her his father had died. 'Are you saying you want out of this relationship?' His voice cracked on the last word and she reached out to take his hand, fighting off a wave of panic herself.

'No. But at the same time I just don't know what to do,' she said. 'It's an impossible situation.'

They clung to each other for a while, desperate for some miracle answer, then they let go. Tansy pulled tissues from her purse and blew her nose. 'You know what? We don't need to do anything right now. Let's just give it some time, okay? You're leaving in a few days and I'm emotional and confused. Maybe the space will help us see things more clearly. Let's not rush anything.'

Dougal nodded and threw back the rest of his drink. 'Promise me you'll come to Canada,' he said, his eyebrows low over his dark eyes. 'At some point, whenever you're ready. But promise me this isn't it. This isn't the end.'

'It's not,' she said, the tears slipping down her face again. 'It's not the end. I promise I'll come to Canada.'

16

The truck that lumbered up the slope to Richer Street on the western boundary of Toowong cemetery was loud enough, but the clanking and booming necessary to unload the massive excavator from its back and ease it to the road was something else. The noise was appalling, and George cringed with every scrape and heave of an engine and bang of the tilt tray. Already, a cluster of residents living across the road had gathered on the footpath to watch the commotion, probably connecting the dots pretty quickly as to what was going on at this time of night in the cemetery.

Floodlights illuminated the section of mildewed graves and tombstones leading towards the priest's final resting place. There were two police cars and several men in uniform overseeing the action and keeping people at bay, two journalists, a stray jogger and a dog walker, and a court official carrying loads of paperwork, his mobile phone clutched like a weapon, ready to pull the trigger and call for the judge at the slightest hint of trouble.

'Why do you have to go?' Hilda had asked, pouring chai tea into a thermos for him, a compromise they'd made on coffee.

'I don't, actually,' he admitted.

She looked at him, stricken. 'Then why on earth would you go voluntarily?'

He shrugged. He wasn't sure himself except that it just felt right. He was shepherding this case. He'd called for the exhumation, based on a scrap of evidence and a lot of instinct. His reputation was on the line, as was his pride. But so too was his sense of duty to all the people he was trying to help via this investigation.

He leaned against his car and looked up at the stars—faint, due to the light pollution created by the bustling madness of the city just a stone's throw away, but still visible, still there. Looking down on everything. Distant, but accessible if you knew how to look. Like God.

His fingers fished in the pocket of his trousers for an antacid, but all he found were the remains of the wrapper. He must have gone through a whole roll today. Again. Perhaps he should see his doctor and get a script for something stronger.

The excavator lumbered awkwardly between the graves, the boom and arm top-heavy in front of the driver's cab, and pitched and swayed as it rumbled over uneven ground, like some monstrous, drunken praying mantis. It screeched and clanged and roared. Its handlers on the ground shouted and waved. The driver braked suddenly as the arm narrowly avoided knocking a tall marble cross off an elaborate headstone. George grimaced. They could certainly do without complaints of damage.

A low branch of an overhanging fig tree was ripped from the trunk and crashed to the ground as the blue digger adjusted its path, and he heard the audience on the footpath yell out at the vulgarity of it all.

But finally the beast came to a halt at the foot of a long concrete-topped grave. The driver shifted the gears and the engine noise dropped to an idling rumble. George took a deep, relieved inhalation and raised himself off his car, began to pick his way carefully up to the site. The court official was there, checking his paperwork, cross-checking with one of the officers, checking and double-checking that they had the right plot. George stopped a few metres away, puffing from the climb, and waited.

At last everyone was satisfied. They stepped back, and the court official raised two fingers to his forehead and then flicked them straight out in a salute to the excavator driver, and rapidly repeated the gesture to give him the go-ahead.

The beast revved its huge engine. Now, free of the need to climb hills or tiptoe through graves, its true mechanical beauty shone through. Its arm and bucket effortlessly plucked off the grave's concrete top and placed it gently to the side. Then its strong claws pierced the ground and carved up the earth in a matter of minutes.

George's blood pressure rose and he wiped at sweat around his neck.

Another pause while three men in high-viz shirts and hard hats attached chains to the arm before climbing down into the open grave, disappearing below the ground, harnessing the exposed coffin.

A helicopter flew overhead, the noise offering some distraction from the wait. A few of the residents from the street began to inch forward, and one of the blue-shirted officers moved towards them, hands raised, signalling them back again.

Eventually, the men hauled themselves out of the grave and stepped clear of the excavator. With another roar of the engine, the chains pulled taut and the coffin came bumping and swaying up from below, rising into the air, clods of dirt falling from it.

And George felt a strange sense of calm to know that, finally, all the truth would come out.

17

'Hello?' Rose's voice was uncertain, distant due to the car's microphone, and fragmented, fighting to be heard over her children's chatter. The school run, Tansy realised, checking the time on her own car's dashboard.

'Hello,' Tansy said, genuinely happy to hear from her sister. 'How are you?'

'Yeah, you know,' Rose said. 'Another day, another marathon.'

'What's going on?' Tansy's voice was loud in her own ears. She hated talking on hands-free. It was always so stilted and functional, not relaxed and intimate, especially with an audience listening. 'Hi, everyone,' she called. A mishmash of hellos and babble answered her.

'I'm just dropping the kids off but was hoping you might be around today. I thought I might come up with Amy and we could have lunch or something.' Rose sounded down and anxious; Tansy sensed she had something she needed to talk about.

Rats. She was already on her way to see Maria as they'd planned. And with their relationship so new, and with Maria on the verge of confiding in her, she didn't want to cancel their meeting today.

'I'd love to but I've got an appointment I can't get out of.' She didn't want to start lying to Rose as well, but now was clearly not the moment to tell her sister about Maria, over squabbling children—there was some sort of argument going on about a cheese sandwich—and reception that stuttered in and out. 'Can we do it tomorrow?'

'No, sorry. I'm due at the school for a reading assistance program.' Rose sounded disappointed.

There was a moment's silence as Tansy struggled to know what was best to do, while simultaneously exiting the highway at the turnoff to Eudlo.

'Look, it doesn't matter,' Rose said, forcefully cheerful.

'I'm truly so sorry,' Tansy said. 'It's been too long. I've got lots to tell you about.'

'Yes, me too.'

'Is everything okay? You've been a bit off the radar lately.'

'There's a lot going on,' Rose admitted, and Tansy knew for sure there was something important her sister needed to discuss.

'Can you call me tonight? We could have a good chat then?'

'Um, yeah, okay,' Rose said unconvincingly.

'But just quickly, before you go, I need to tell you that Dougal is leaving for Canada on Saturday.'

'Why?'

'For work, and it looks like he'll be needed there for up to two years. I'll be going too,' Tansy added, though it didn't seem real.

'Wow. How do you feel about that?'

Tansy sighed. 'It's complicated. I'd like to tell you all about it tonight if we can. We told Mum last night and I didn't want you to find out from anyone else.'

'Yes, of course,' Rose said. 'Okay, I'll try and call you tonight. Clearly we have a lot to catch up on.'

'Excellent, looking forward to it.'

Maria took the white box from her niece. 'Fortune cookies?'

'Dougal and I were at a bar last night and they were handing them out. Things have been unsettled lately so I didn't want to tempt fate and open any myself. I could do without dire predictions of hair loss or planes falling from the sky right now.'

Maria cracked open the brittle, puckered pastry of a cookie and pulled out the slip of paper from inside. In pale blue writing, her fortune was cast. *It is very possible that you will achieve greatness in your lifetime.*

'Well, that's a good one to get,' Tansy said.

Maria pondered the prediction. It seemed highly unlikely, given her past. Still, at this moment, there was a part of her that wanted the fortune cookie to be right so much that she was willing to believe in miracles. She put down the cookie crumbs and paper and resumed preparing her bits and bobs to make soap. Soap making wasn't particularly difficult, but it was fiddly and you had to get the timing just so. It was best to have all the pieces of the puzzle laid out before you began.

'What do you mean, things have been unsettled?' she asked Tansy. And actually, now that she looked at her, her niece's eyes held the look of someone who'd just received bad news.

'Dougal's leaving for Canada this Saturday.'

'For how long?' Maria lined up her bottles of essential oils—today she'd chosen rose, lemon and sandalwood—and the other ingredients to go with each one: cochineal and rose petals to go with the rose, freshly grated lemon zest with the lemon oil, and honey, nutmeg and cinnamon with the sandalwood.

'We're not sure. It's a work relocation for up to two years. I was supposed to be going with him in a couple of months' time. But the timing was suddenly brought forward and he only got a week's notice. Now he'll be gone for my birthday and the reunion, and to top it off we had a huge, ugly fight.'

'Do you want to talk about it?'

'I want a baby and Dougal doesn't,' Tansy said flatly.

'I see.'

Tansy filled her in on their situation and Maria listened and sympathised but really wasn't sure what to say that could help, though she was touched that Tansy trusted her enough to share such personal feelings.

'And now my mother's come to stay because her marriage is in trouble,' Tansy concluded.

Maria chose her words carefully. 'I'm sorry to hear that.'

'Yes. She's fretting today because she's supposed to be at the parish leaders council tonight. She seems to get a lot of esteem from her role there. I think she feels like she's a bigger part of the church than just an everyday parishioner.' Tansy took a deep breath, waved a hand and adjusted the dusk-pink-coloured scarf at her neck. 'You know what? You are the perfect excuse for me to get away from all that right now. I've got no in-home appointments for the next three days, and if Dougal is busy elsewhere then I intend to spend my time here, listening to your stories. We have a lot to catch up on and I don't want to lose another moment.

I can deal with what's going on at home when I get home. Right now, I just want you to tell me everything.'

So, the time had come. Maria had agreed to tell Tansy everything, and now she had to go through with it. She laid out the two-kilogram slab of white goat's-milk soap on the chopping board and chose her sharpest carving knife. Making soap from a base product was something she once thought of as indulgent. It was far more expensive to make soap this way—not that she ever kept her beautiful creations. But making soap from scratch was a time-consuming and potentially dangerous activity.

She suspected few people realised that soap was made by mixing lye—a caustic solution that would burn holes through a tea towel and burn your skin—with water to create a heating, fuming chemical concoction. You had to warm up your vegetable oils (or, in the old days, whale blubber), while watching for the lye mixture to cool down to the same temperature, and mix them when they had reached equilibrium. Then you added all your other mixers, like herbs and colours, and after that it had to cure for weeks. No, as much as she liked the idea of being able to do everything on her own, this was one thing on which she conceded.

The knife carved slowly through the soap block under her firm pressure. And when she placed the pieces into the stainless-steel bowl and popped it over the saucepan of water on the stove, it struck her, as it always did, how similar the process was to making chocolate—melt, add ingredients, stir, pour, allow to set, pop out of moulds, and wrap up in pretty packaging.

She straightened the silicone moulds—a blessed invention that made it infinitely easier to get the soap out—on the bench, biding her time before she had to face Tansy's questions. 'What do you want to know?'

'Of course I'm dying to know why you no longer speak to my mother and Aunt Florrie. But I suspect that would be a difficult place to start.'

Maria didn't say anything, thinking that it was probably the least difficult place to start.

'So let's start at the convent,' Tansy said, actually rubbing her hands together. 'I bet you have so many stories and so many memories. But let's begin with something random. Tell me what Christmas in the convent was like.'

This was going to be a long conversation. The rest of the soap making would have to wait until it had her undivided attention. Once the soap base had melted, it needed focus and swift handling. 'I'll put the kettle on,' Maria said, removing the soap from the stovetop. 'I think better with a cup of tea in my hand.'

Christmas time in the convent was one of the harder things for Maria to get used to. When she'd lived at home, and especially before her father died, the house had been awash with the smell of baking for what seemed like a whole month before the actual day. Her mother had been a prolific baker. She'd lived through the depression, of course, and had once confessed to Maria that one of the worst things about it was the sugar rationing; she had a terrible sweet tooth. She liked to soak the dried fruit in rum for weeks before baking. She relished the chance to make gingerbread men dusted with icing sugar, rolling out the dough and letting the girls eat the raw offcuts. The butter came from their neighbour's cow's milk, hand-churned by Elyse, and it gave the batter a warm yellow hue. Butter had never tasted as good since then. Store-bought butter today was like solid fat, but handmade butter had such a rich luxury to it.

The lead-up to Christmas Day always involved many visitors—neighbours, church members, family and her father's work colleagues. New tins of tea would arrive, in festive designs. And the house would be alive with moving whispers and secrets of gifts that had been bought or made for other members of the family, who weren't supposed to know of them but inevitably found out through the secret conversations the sisters held in bed in the dark.

Maria especially loved the Christmas Eve dinner they shared just as a family of five. Her dad would kill one of the geese, and her mother would roast it with spuds and turnips. They ate by candlelight and sang carols at the piano. The next day, visitors came all day long. They would sit around the twenty-seater table (which was actually two separate tables pushed together with three tablecloths on top), eating hot chicken sandwiches and playing cards. It was always loud, with lots of laughter and often an argument—frequently started by Enid, it had to be said—which was quickly settled by their mother.

In the convent, by contrast, Christmas celebrations were chastely observed, secretly enjoyed but publicly moderated. They had a special dinner, certainly. But the length of the prayers said beforehand meant that the food was always cold when they finally started to eat. With their slim pantry budget, special treats had to be made from cheap ingredients; apples dipped in toffee syrup and left to dry on racks were an annual tradition. Decorations were frowned upon. The only festive spirits were found among the girls who boarded at the school, whose excitement at finishing another year and being allowed to return home drove them to make paper crafts and daisy chains. Mother Superior chose to overlook these small reminders of the season.

'That all sounds rather sad,' Tansy said, swirling the last of her tea in her cup.

'It was certainly an adjustment. But it wasn't all bad: it brought new traditions too. My tastes have changed over the years and I have less of the sweet tooth my mother instilled in me. And until I went to the convent at age sixteen, I'd never eaten an olive. I've been making up for that ever since.'

'What was it like living with the other nuns? Were they mean?'

Maria hesitated. This was heading into trickier territory. To begin talking about the other sisters would lead to the priest . . . and that day. The day her life changed.

'Is something wrong?' Tansy asked.

'Oh.' Maria cleared her throat and forced a smile. 'Nothing. It's just old age,' she said lightly.

'Pft. Nonsense.'

'Well, I'll start at the top then, with Mother Superior.'

Mother Veronica was quite young compared to most in her position, not much younger than Maria's own mother. Originally from Ireland, she had been imported into Australia by the church in the fifties and established in the Brisbane convent specifically with the intention that she would take over from the previous mother, who was ailing and not expected to live much longer. This caused quite a stir in the convent, so Maria had intuited, because Sister Pauline had been expected to take the top job. As a result, Veronica had spent a good deal of time asserting her authority through lengthy and arduous punishments for minor indiscretions. But there was more to Veronica than discipline.

Not long after Maria had first walked through those tall iron gates and into the draughty halls of the convent, she'd fallen ill. Confined to her narrow bed, she had been utterly miserable, missing her mother terribly, imagining possible ways to escape this place in which she'd found herself. One late afternoon when Maria was alone and crying, Mother Veronica had visited her.

Feeling like a silly child, Maria confessed that she was yearning for her mother.

'And what would your mother do for you?' Veronica had asked in her southern Irish brogue, the gold cross at her neck reflecting the setting sun's light filtering through the tall window by the bed.

'She'd bring me cheese and vegemite sandwiches on white bread,' said Maria, sniffing into a handkerchief.

Veronica didn't answer but said some prayers over Maria, then pulled the cotton cover up around her shoulders and tucked it in tightly with swift, strong moves. But later that evening, Sister Felicia brought a plate of fluffy white triangles, with a double layer of cheese and salty vegemite spread right to the edges of the bread.

There were lots of sisters, many that came and didn't last, and there was the natural cycle of new sisters arriving and the aged passing on. But sisters were also moved around from time to time, depending on what was going on in their life. Sometimes, it was to avoid a scandal. Sisters were women, and they fell in love. It happened between sisters and laity, between sisters and priests, and sometimes, though rarely, between sisters. It was always the sisters who were moved on, never the men. Men had different urges and needs, they said. It was the woman's holy responsibility to guard her body and to protect the man from his own desires.

'Crikey,' Tansy said. 'What bloody hypocrites. So, you were right at the bottom of the church hierarchy, but somehow you were supposed to be more responsible than the ones at the top?'

Maria bit down fury. 'Yes. More than that, though, sisters weren't even considered part of the church hierarchy. We were merely members of the laity who had taken special orders. We hovered in an uncertain space where we weren't exactly part of the general faithful but we weren't part of the church proper either. We took our orders from Rome, but it was only our complete devotion to our faith that kept us there in the mother house, believing we were doing the work of God, serving the established order of the community.'

'Like the bees,' Tansy said.

'Yes, just like the bees.'

'Who was your favourite fellow worker bee?'

Of course, Sarah was her true favourite, but Sarah's story was still coming. If she had to pick one for now, it would have been Sister Celine, who'd come to the convent at eighteen years of age, much later than Maria, by a good fifteen years if her memory served her correctly. Celine was like a breath of fresh air, and it was well known—though now that she thought about it she couldn't quite remember *how* it was known—that Celine had sought refuge in the convent to escape a 'troubled home', which in those days was a euphemism for sordid behaviours covered up by shame and silence. Probably because of this background, Celine's often not-quite-right demeanour was tacitly accepted by the other sisters.

'You eat pineapple, right?' Celine said the first time Maria met her. The younger woman was then a postulant, not yet a nun, and Maria had found her in the garden, among the pineapples, touching their saw-toothed edges reverently. 'Pineapples are everything to me.'

That's what she said to Maria, completely out of nowhere. It was such a strange declaration that Maria simply said yes, she ate pineapples, before Celine continued with another obscure statement, about mice. She hated them, apparently, unlike her beloved pineapples.

At first Celine had been assigned to help in the kitchen. But she only knew how to make one dish—salmon mousse, set in an enormous fish shape. Nobody liked it. It tasted like emulsified canned salmon, which it was. But given the innocent joy it brought the fragile girl to create it, no one was game to say so. She was relocated to the garden instead, but she lacked focus and neglected most things in favour of showering love on the spiky pineapples.

Eventually, she was given the responsibility of polishing the chapel organs and tending to the felt and leather details. She was fiercely protective of them, like an alsatian, and wouldn't let anyone else touch them, other than the organ player and the professional tuner. She also paid ardent attention to pest control, seeking ways to destroy and deter moths, woodworms and mice, all of which could damage the precious instruments of God. Her only other job was to serve tea to visitors. She could boil water to make tea easily enough, and place some biscuits or slices of cake on a plate.

'What happened to her?' Tansy asked, leaning forward to rest her chin on her hand.

'I'm not sure, actually. She was still there when I left the order, and I never looked back. I never talked to any of them again.'

'Why?'

It was a natural question. She should just answer it outright. But today wasn't the day. Maria stood up, straightened her knees and stretched her back. She checked the time. They'd been sitting here now for an hour. She had to get moving; she had lunch to prepare for the guests and this soap wasn't going to make itself. She liked to give it a few days' curing time before the markets, if the weather was fine, longer if it was raining outside. It wasn't an exact science and she needed some leeway to be responsive to how well the soap was setting.

'I think we might have run out of time,' she said, looking out the window and watching the kids tumbling on the lawn and the carers kicking balloons in a gentle form of soccer. 'I need to go and help Petrice get lunch ready.'

Tansy groaned with disappointment and checked the time on her phone. 'I suppose I should get going too. I do have work to do myself. But talking with you has been delightful, thank you.' She considered her next words before continuing. 'I know you've put a lot of effort into living a life largely unconnected with other people. So I appreciate your letting me in, just a bit. Your life is fascinating, Maria.'

Fascinating? Treacherous, perhaps.

'Can I come back tomorrow?' Tansy asked, wrapping her in a hug.

'I don't think I could stop you if I wanted to,' Maria said affectionately. Tansy was relentless, but rather like a funny Staffordshire bull-terrier intent on sitting on your lap: all teeth and smiles and promises of friendship. She was hard to resist. Maria would tell her everything, bit by bit, and maybe—maybe—her niece would understand.

She pulled away and pointed to the fortune cookies. 'Do you want to try your luck now and see what you get?'

'Oh, what the hell. It's only a fortune cookie.'

Tansy reached into the box, waved her hand over the contents as if trying to feel which one would give her a positive result, and picked the one in the furthest corner. She bit into it to crack it open, loudly crunching the pieces, and pulled out the prediction inside.

The road ahead is bumpy.

'Great,' she lamented.

On the way home, Tansy pulled over on the wide grass verge, checked to make sure she had reception, and then called her father.

She needed to tell him about Dougal's impending departure but also to find out what he was thinking and feeling with Enid staying at her house.

'Hello?'

Tansy was surprised he answered; he almost never had his phone on him. 'Hi, Papa Bear. Where are you?'

'Hello, Daughter Number Two. I'm at Bunnings getting supplies for the leaking pipe under the sink.' He sounded rather cheery and not at all as she'd expected him to sound. Then again, he was always a doer and never one for moping.

'Oh. Do you have a few minutes to talk about what's going on with you and Mum?'

'Just a minute.' There were some rattling sounds, and then some swishy-swashy noises she assumed were the mobile phone rubbing against his clothes, and then he was back. 'Okay, I'm in a quiet aisle now.'

'Good. So, you know Mum is staying with me, don't you?'

'Yes.'

'Sorry I didn't call on Sunday. A work emergency came up and I've been run off my feet.'

'It's okay.'

'No, it's not. Mum says she's left you.'

'Has she?'

'Well . . .' Tansy thought back over the conversations they'd had so far. 'Actually, no. She said you were on a break.'

Her father paused a moment and Tansy could hear a salesman's voice in the background directing someone to aisle twenty-three.

'Are you going to be able to work things out?' she asked. 'Or is this it?'

'From my perspective, I think we should be alright.'

'And from Mum's perspective?'

'Enid's her own person,' he said gently. 'I can't make her change her mind. She needs to decide what's more important to her— being married to me or going to church with me even if I hate it.'

His words baffled Tansy. 'You *hate* it?'

'I do.'

'How long have you felt like this?'

'About fifteen years. I came to the conclusion a long time ago that there's more to the story than what religion and the Bible say. It's not the end of knowledge, just one part.' His voice took on the energy of passionate debate. 'And look at all the abuse stories in the news. All this time they were feeding us a pack of lies. And I think that at seventy-two I'm old enough to make up my own mind about whether or not I want to be fed lies and whether or not I want to go to church.' He finished decisively, and Tansy suspected that this was a well-worn speech he'd delivered to Enid on more than one occasion.

She took a deep breath. Her parents were at a stalemate, just like her and Dougal. 'So how do you move forward from here?' she asked, hopeful that her dad might have the answer to her own problem, too.

'Well, I might not have faith in the church anymore,' he said, his words slightly muffled as if he was rubbing his hand across his chin, as he often did when thinking. 'But I still have faith in my marriage. So I'm holding onto that.'

Tansy made one more stop on the way home, pulling over at Kunara, the huge organic superstore at Forest Glen, to buy Dougal some things to take on the plane with him. He wasn't a good traveller, getting dizzy, nauseous, sweaty and pale in anything beyond a car. So she stocked up on a 'travel blend' of bush flower essences, some acupressure wristbands, ginger tablets and peppermint lollies. Dougal would scoff and say they were all useless in practicality, but she knew he'd also be touched and would use them once he was in the air, just like he had when they'd gone to New Zealand. He hadn't wasted any time breaking them out when the sweating began on the runway.

The gifts were for him, but also for her. She wanted to feel as though she was nurturing him, particularly after their rift. The last thing she wanted was for him to leave the country feeling unloved. Because he wasn't. He was very, very loved.

Tears pricked her eyes. She still had faith in her marriage too.

She got a power protein smoothie while she was there and then resumed her trip home, ready to start anew with her husband, at least a little bit. At least for today.

She found Dougal in their bedroom, supposedly working from home today but instead pulling out clothes and making lists in the notes application on his phone. He began asking her questions the second she came into the room, wanting to know where his favourite wool jumper was and why he only seemed to have five pairs of socks to his name.

She ignored all of that, shut the bedroom door, closed the blinds. He looked up, caught the look in her eye, returned her smile. And they found peace in each other once more.

As they held each other in the falling light, Dougal stroking her hair, he said, 'I got you a present today.'

'Did you?' she asked, surprised that he'd had time and touched by the gesture.

He rolled over and reached under the bed. She pulled herself up on her side and leaned over his body as he withdrew something from a small paper bag. 'I saw these and thought of you,' he said.

They were black and yellow earbuds in the shape of bumblebees.

'They're so cute.'

'They just jumped out at me. You've got bees on my mind with your visits to your aunt. I thought you might like them for when you're jogging.'

'I love them,' she said, and kissed him, then kissed him some more.

And while she was busy kissing her husband, she missed the phone calls from Rose, who rang twice but didn't leave a message either time.

18

The group of kids and their carers was leaving this afternoon, and there was much whooping and yelling and even some crying around the campsite as bags were packed and lost items located. Tulip had been to collect the beautiful fairy caravan; the children had waved goodbye as it rumbled down the hill, watching till it disappeared from view.

Maria wanted to be outside where she could keep a rough eye on what was going on, so she'd asked Tansy to help her change the water in the birdbaths and clean the marbles.

'Why are there marbles in the water?' Tansy asked, pouring out the green water from a large round terracotta bowl, the marbles thudding onto the grass.

'The bees can rest on them while they drink so they don't drown,' Maria said, scrubbing scum off the base of an aged concrete trough.

'What a fantastic idea.' Tansy picked up another scrubbing brush and began to do the same.

'It makes it safe for other insects too, like butterflies, and for birds. There's nothing sadder than finding a bird drowned in a water trough,' Maria said bitterly. 'It's just tragic.'

'I never even considered that bees need to drink water,' Tansy said thoughtfully.

'They need quite a lot. They'll drink pool water but the chlorine's bad for them and will end up in the honey too. You can also use floating corks in the water,' Maria added as an afterthought.

'Dougal and I could help with that. We open a bottle of wine most nights and we still buy a few brands with corks in them.'

'What's he doing today?' Maria asked, turning her scrubbing brush to the marbles themselves. An errant pink balloon drifted past, and she snatched it and tied it down to dispose of later.

'He's in Brisbane in meetings. No rest for the wicked. They're going to get as much flesh out of him as they can before he leaves. He's only got a few days left.'

Tansy's voice was flat. It seemed as good a time as any for Maria to resume her storytelling. But to confide in Tansy with the whole truth, she had to go back even further in time, to her early days in the convent and to her friendship with fellow postulant Sarah.

Sarah had come from the hot inland Queensland town of Roma to the cooler, leafier Brisbane convent at the age of eighteen. She'd always wanted to be a teacher and had prayed since she was a small girl to be able to do so as part of an order of sisters. Sarah's mother, herself originally from the city before she'd married and moved hundreds of kilometres west with her husband, wanted a different life for her daughter. So, she bought Sarah's placement in the Brisbane convent with a large donation from the family's successful cattle station.

Maria and Sarah got on from the first moment they met, at the dinner table. Sarah was a strapping farm girl, with strong muscles from riding horses and wrangling cattle, and golden skin from the endless sunshine. She liked to eat, and her enthusiasm for food was frowned on by the nuns but brought indescribable glee to Maria, who'd remained melancholy since arriving at the convent. Sarah was like a big gust of jasmine-scented spring air in the echoing halls of St Lucy's.

'Nothing in the Bible says you can't have fun,' Sarah said to Maria later that first week. She was perched in the limbs of a mulberry tree at the back of the convent's orchard, picking and eating the mulberries until her mouth and fingers were stained purple.

Maria sat beneath the tree, afraid of getting into trouble, nervously looking over her shoulder for the black and white habits of the sisters.

'Here. Catch.' Sarah's legs swung from the branch as she threw Maria a handful of berries. Maria had to drop her books to catch them, and a few exploded on impact, the juice spraying her in the face. Sarah hooted with laughter, her voice still farm-loud, not yet convent-quiet.

Their friendship continued over the next two years, through a shared bedroom, secret looks and quick elbow jabs in mass. Every day was a good day with Sarah nearby.

But then she was sent away. Deemed too wild to ever be truly tamed by the habit she too easily wore, she was sent back out west, even further than her home town, perhaps in an effort to break her spirit—though the nuns would have called it 'encouraging her humility'. They sent her all the way to Longreach, to the only school, where she remained as the sole teacher and later head teacher for decades. Maria had never seen her since.

'That's so sad,' Tansy sighed, her hand on her heart, squinting into the sun. 'You were like Anne Shirley and Diana Barry from *Anne of Green Gables*—kindred spirits—and they tore you apart.'

Maria laughed. 'Where *do* you get this romantic streak from? I don't think it's from your mother, unless she's miraculously undergone a transformation since her younger days. I always think of her as so pragmatic and sensible.'

'She is.'

'Your father then? Finlay?'

Tansy tilted her head to the side, thinking. 'I wouldn't normally say so, but he surprised me yesterday with something he said about his marriage to Mum. He's a *believer*.' She waved a fly away from her face. 'But let's get back to the story. Did you ever hear anything from Sarah again?'

For her sins, Maria *had* kept in touch with Sarah, defying direct orders from her superiors that she break off all contact—Sarah was seen as a bad influence. Maria wrote letters to her friend, then hid them in her habit and posted them when she was in town on errands. Sarah, alone in Longreach and in sole charge of her affairs on a day-to-day basis, was able to receive them. Maria, on the other hand, lived with more than a dozen other sisters, and all their correspondence went through Mother Superior, who could, and would, open any letter, even if it was privately addressed.

So Maria had to be crafty in order to stay in contact with Sarah. It was a sin, she knew; the sisters in her order were supposed to renounce everything, including their own family. She'd asked a mature, trustworthy senior student called Lauren Hanley, who was close in age to Maria and Sarah, to act as go-between. A good Catholic girl, Lauren held all the sisters in high regard. But she was also smart and an independent thinker, considering the teachings and doctrine for herself. After school she was set to attend the University of Queensland and become a scholar. She too had a best friend and couldn't imagine life without her, and was only too happy to help Maria.

A day student, Lauren lived near the convent and was a frequent visitor outside of school hours, bringing the sisters flowers from her family's garden, surplus eggs from their chickens and ducks, and preserves that her mother had made. So it was not unusual to see her walking around the grounds and stopping to talk to Maria, at which point she would surreptitiously pass on Sarah's letters.

'So cloak and dagger,' Tansy said, pouring clean marbles back into her birdbath.

Maria stared into the middle distance. 'I lost a lot of sleep about that, for so long.' Then her eyes snapped back to Tansy, alert. 'But the day came, after seventeen years, when I knew without doubt we'd been right to keep up our secret correspondence.'

'What happened?'

Maria inhaled deeply as everything came back—the doubt, the frustration, the injustice, the rage. Her out breath was unsteady, but still it calmed her, gave her the strength to finally tell someone, other than her precious bees, the whole story.

Sarah's most important letter had arrived on a scorching hot November day, with the jacarandas in purple bloom and full of busy bees, and the senior students studying for exams. Lauren Hanley was by now in her mid thirties, a university lecturer, a wife and mother of two children, still a good Catholic woman, and the volunteer provider of floral arrangements for the church altar. And she still delivered letters to Maria, having never once questioned her role despite her full knowledge that she was participating in a deceit of almost two decades.

Maria was now a seasoned teacher of English and geography in the senior school and a much-loved class teacher in the primary school. She was stern but not unkind, and her students often brought her gifts of posies or fruit or handmade cards.

She read Sarah's letter in the classroom after school, the students all gone, the afternoon sun beating down on the buildings. Piles of English assignments sat beside her, waiting to be marked. But the yellow-lined notepad paper on which Sarah's letter was written was far more enticing.

My dear friend and sister, Maria,

I hope this letter finds you well. If you're anything like me you'll be both dreading and longing for the final weeks of school to pass so you can have a brief reprieve before beginning the planning again for first term. After all this time, it still amazes me how quickly it goes.

Alas, I'll have to keep the pleasantries and news updates to a minimum. It is with a heavy heart, and after considerable meditation and prayer, that I write to you today. I am sure you will understand the gravity of what I'm about to reveal, both in its content and what it means in the context of my vow of obedience to our church superiors. It is therefore a sin for me to tell you this.

Our parish priest, Father Peter Cunningham, of whom I have spoken a little in the past, has received his transfer orders and will be joining your parish. I know you've always spoken fondly of Father Brian and will be sad to hear he is leaving, but you will be sadder still when you learn of Father Peter's character.

My dear, there is simply no easy or polite way to say this. Two of my students, whom I will not name here (two young girls, of twelve and eleven), confessed the most horrible things

to me, things done to them by the very priest in question.
Appallingly, these things were done as part of their 'penance'
after their confession of sins to him, and by the time they came
to me it had been going on for two years.

I feel sick, Maria. These girls were in my care.

I reported it, of course, to Bishop Tully, but he told me in no
uncertain terms that these matters were dealt with internally
in accordance with established church policy, in absolute
secrecy, and to go against that was to go against the Vatican,
and surely I, a mere sister, didn't believe I knew better than the
wisdom of the Pope. He advised me that to lose faith in our
religious superiors—men chosen by God and filled with God's
authority—was a sin against God and I must pray for more faith.
I was instructed to never speak of it again on pain of immediate
excommunication.

His answer to the problem I presented him was to relocate
Father Peter to your parish.

Maria, I don't know what to do. This letter alone is grounds
for my excommunication. That is my deepest fear, because I feel
I still have much work to do here for these students and to serve
God. My life is here, not out in the wider world. I'm needed in
this town, in this school and in this community. I couldn't do
the work I do without the church.

My hands are tied. But I had to warn you.

Please, I beg of you, burn this letter the second you have
read it.

Yours in Christ,

Sarah

Maria had sat frozen, the letter clenched in her hands. Her
body began to shake, firstly from the inside, deep within her

bones, then spreading outwards until the paper rustled in her fingers. A fallen priest was on his way to her parish, to listen to her confessions, to listen to her students' confessions, to offer the holy sacraments and be the guiding light in the faithful's moral life, and he was hiding the most grievous of sins.

'I don't know what to say,' Tansy said, her hands at her face. 'That is ghastly. I mean, you hear it in the news all the time these days, but to hear it from you, having lived through that era.' She shook her head. 'It's just dreadful.'

Maria walked with Tansy to the tap, each of them carrying buckets to fill with water. 'Yes, it was.'

'And you burned the letter?' Tansy was clearly dismayed.

'Yes. In the incinerator—it was the done thing to burn anything in an incinerator in Brisbane in the seventies. And lawn sprinklers would be going day and night. Those were the days—pollute the air and use endless water without a second thought. It's so different now, isn't it? I guess people did a lot of things in those days with far less conscience than they do now.

'Back then, the Vatican itself ordered complete secrecy around these types of matters. The initial intention *may* have been to protect everyone until a final verdict was reached—I can't say for sure—but in my experience, any such intention was twisted and misused and in practice came to mean that all testimony and evidence was sealed and anyone who talked of it—including the victims—would be excommunicated.'

'So, basically, the victims were punished for speaking up.'

'Yes, and from what I've read of the trials both here and overseas, speaking up could lead to more of the same treatment the victims had already experienced as a way of further terrifying them into silence.'

Tansy was white.

Maria turned on the tap and water gushed into the bucket. 'Perhaps we should stop talking about this now. It's upsetting. I've had a lot of years to process this. It must be difficult for you to hear it for the first time.'

Tansy took the full bucket and passed Maria an empty one to fill. 'Of course. But just before we finish, was that why you left the church? Because of this Father Peter character?'

Maria gave a rueful smile. 'In part, yes. It was a lot more complicated than that. I stayed for another twenty years. But we'll talk about it another time.'

'I do have to go,' Tansy said. 'I've so many things to do.' She smacked her palm to her forehead. 'So much washing for Dougal.'

'I hope everything goes well in the next few days,' Maria said, her heart aching for Tansy. It must be a terrible weight on her niece's shoulders right now.

19

It was Thursday, and Dougal's departure was barrelling towards them. Only two days to go. Tansy could feel each hour slipping away. He was still going to work in Brisbane, much to Tansy's disgust. Without him here at home to distract her, her mind rattled with everything Maria had told her. Her stomach was in knots.

Enid, meanwhile, had Paula over, *again*, taking over the kitchen, *again*, making such a mess that no one else could find a clean spot on the bench to make even a sandwich. And she had begun to order them around whenever they so much as stepped into the kitchen.

'What are you looking for?' Enid would ask across the benchtop.

'Um, the muesli,' Leo muttered, afraid to enter the women's space.

'Here.' Enid plucked it expertly from the cupboard and passed it over, along with a bowl and spoon. 'And I've changed your milk to zero fat,' she said, pulling the carton from the fridge. 'So much healthier.'

Leo had shot Tansy a beseeching look but she simply didn't have the focus to deal with her mother right now. She needed to phone the doctor's surgery to see if she could get Dougal an appointment late this afternoon when he got back. He'd decided that although her gift of hippie travel-sickness medicine was lovely, he'd also like some bona fide drugs.

With the appointment made and Leo heading to uni, and Enid and Paula cackling in the kitchen, Tansy needed to escape from the pressure cooker her unit had become. She left the building and strode down to the fresh air and sunshine of the boardwalk, gazing out at the cobalt ocean and the surfers bobbing up and down on their boards, waiting for the perfect wave. Taking cleansing breaths, she phoned Maria, and was grateful to catch her inside and not out working in the garden.

'I can't stop thinking about what you told me yesterday,' Tansy said, 'and I keep pacing the house with anxiety over Dougal's departure. Talk to me, please, tell me what happened after Father Peter transferred to the convent.'

Maria paused, perhaps wondering if she should tell Tansy more. Then, 'Okay, let me just get settled.'

Father Peter, like Maria, was in his mid-thirties when he arrived at St Lucy's College for the morning tea the sisters had organised to welcome him to the parish. Maria had built him up in her mind to be such a monstrous figure that she stopped dead in the doorway of the dining hall when she first saw the ordinariness of him. Holding a cup of tea in one hand, he was smiling, and wore round John Lennon–style spectacles. His hair wasn't exactly long, as so many men of that era had begun to wear it; it *was* still above his collar, but it was also certainly fuller than she'd come to expect in a man of the cloth.

He was holding court to Mother Veronica, who was eating a scone with jam and cream, her tongue working its way around her teeth as she went, and Sister Margaret O'Shea, who had also recently transferred to the Brisbane college from a position up north, and was detailing her gratitude at leaving behind a sweltering north Queensland summer.

Maria hovered in the doorway, her stomach churning, her palms sweaty. Her legs were prickling beneath her thick stockings. She didn't want to meet the new priest—the wolf in sheep's clothing.

Worse, actually: the wolf in shepherd's clothing.

The room was full of sisters eating cake and talking. Everyone was relaxed, perched on the edge of chairs or standing in little clusters in corners with small plates. More than a decade after the Vatican II council, which modernised the church, the sisters had long moved on from the black and white 'penguin' habit, and they all wore conservative short-sleeved white dresses, with a crucifix on their lapels and sensible brown shoes. The only person in the room who looked even the slightest bit unnerved, other than Maria, was young Celine. Wearing a patchwork apron over her white dress, Celine scurried to and fro with slices of fruitcake and shortbread, her eyes downcast. Her fingers were stained, Maria noted, probably from her work on the chapel organs, which were undergoing their yearly servicing at this time.

Celine cast a wide berth around Father Peter; she met Maria's eye briefly, her green irises haunted beneath lowered brows. And—did Maria imagine it?—Celine shook her head, ever so slightly. Then she was gone, back through the swing door and into the kitchenette to begin the washing-up.

Maria's senses tingled.

Celine was a strange, unpredictable nun at best. Some days she was overcome with a nervousness and skittishness that defied explanation, jumping at the smallest sounds and rushing out of the room. On these occasions the other sisters generally left her to herself; she would spend a day, sometimes two, in prayer in the chapel, and return to her duties more settled. No one ever pressed her for answers, which they knew would only ever be riddles anyway.

But was it possible, Maria thought, that somehow Celine knew? Could this frail bird of a child, with her damaged psyche from God only knew what experiences in her home, who'd fled to the nuns for protection, who walked in the spaces between the earthbound reality and the invisible mysteries of a broken mind, somehow sense something in Father Peter that made her aware of what he was?

Or—more than likely—was Maria just seeing what she wanted to see because she didn't want to be the only person in this convent and college who bore the burden of such knowledge? Was she so desperate and selfish that she longed to share her own pain with someone else, in whom she could confide without fear of excommunication?

'Sister Maria.' Mother Veronica was waving at her from the other side of the room, smiling. 'Come join us.'

Maria took a breath, folded her hands together at her abdomen to keep them from trembling, and stepped towards the man who had committed unspeakable crimes and sins against innocent children, and who now turned to her and smiled, imbued with the power of Christ and the trust of the faithful; the man in whom she was now supposed to place her trust for her own spiritual guidance.

She stood beside him.

'Greetings, Sister Maria,' he said, and reached out his hand to take hers.

She hesitated for just a moment, but in that moment she saw clearly what she must do. Father Peter might have been sent to this place to be their leader but the look on Celine's face had marked Maria's soul and she could not turn away. If she'd ever had any doubts as to the reason she was here in this place, ever wished she hadn't agreed to her mother's plan, ever had any thoughts of walking away from the convent, they were gone.

This was why she was here. This was why God had put her on this path. She'd been chosen from among the many to be the one who could and would stand up.

She steeled her nerves and took the outstretched hand of the devil, feeling a sharp, sickening wave of disgust as their skin connected.

His fingers . . . fingers that have . . .

She quickly retracted her hand and placed it behind her back with the other one, then deliberately straightened her shoulders.

'Good morning, Father,' she said, locking eyes with him. 'I'll do everything in my power to watch over you while you're here.'

Every morning and every night, Maria prayed for strength to be in the presence of Father Peter Cunningham, knowing that if she was to fulfil God's calling to watch over him and intercede wherever it was needed, she would have to stay close to him.

Of course, it wasn't possible to be around him all the time: he had his own lodgings away from the convent and was not a teacher and therefore didn't need to be on the grounds throughout the day unless there were circumstances that called for it. It was still an age when priests were in demand. From the outside, for all appearances, he acted like any other priest in his position.

He baptised babies on Sundays, cleansing them of original sin. He married young couples in the chapel on Saturdays. He led the community in mass most days of the week. He was invited into the homes of the faithful for dinners. He gave last rites to the dying and then conducted their funerals. He took appointments in his lodgings with the laity, advising them and counselling them.

There was nothing Maria could do about any of this. But not long after the day when she'd first met Father Peter, she approached Mother Veronica to discuss taking on more work in the school for the coming year.

'I welcome your enthusiasm,' Veronica said, directing Maria to the chair on the other side of her polished desk. Her office was filled with final assignments, Christmas cards, report cards, and student awards to be presented at a forthcoming mass. 'But as the dust hasn't yet settled on this final term of teaching, I'm pressed to ask if there is something specific that has brought this about.' Veronica sat up straight in her chair, her hands folded neatly in front of her. She was middle-aged now, with a loosening of the skin on her face, sunspots on the backs of her hands, and reading glasses hanging on a chain around her neck.

Maria paused. Here was a chance to talk about the letter she'd received from Sarah. A chance to warn Veronica. But no faster did the thought cross her mind than she knew with utter certainty that what Sarah had said was true. Even if they spoke the truth and even if they were believed, they would both be excommunicated—because the Vatican had the final word, always. And the final word was silence. Nothing would be solved.

Instead, she smiled brightly. 'I know Sister Agatha felt the strain this year, alongside her stomach issues and the tests she went through, and I thought it would be an early Christmas gift to offer her some relief.'

Veronica nodded and smiled. 'That's charitable of you. What were you thinking?'

'I'm wondering if I might take over the coordination of the religious education programs for both junior and senior classes.'

Maria's heart beat faster as she spoke. The position of religious education coordinator added a considerable load to a teacher's work, but it also meant she would have frequent, close contact with Father Peter, who, ultimately, approved the program and assisted in its delivery. Father Peter would be called upon to instruct the young girls in preparation for their sacraments. He would oversee altar boys from the neighbouring boys school. He would hear confession from every student. As much as possible, Maria wanted to be there, watching.

'The position of religious coordinator is a considerable commitment professionally, personally and spiritually,' Veronica said. 'The coordinator liaises closely with the families and church community; as Sister Agatha knows only too well, it's a role that can attract conflict and judgement and requires sensitive, tactful communication.'

'Are you saying . . . Forgive me, Veronica, but what are you saying?'

Veronica studied Maria for a few moments. 'I don't often get people coming to me and asking to take on such an onerous task. But I think you would be a wonderful coordinator.'

'Thank you.'

'I will discuss it with Agatha and get back to you. But what about your role in the garden, Maria? We rely on your expertise with the vegetables and the bees for so much of our nourishment. Won't these extra duties have an impact there?'

Maria hesitated. Her garden and her bees gave her great sustenance and were her gift to this community. She would hate to lose them. But if that was what it came down to, she would do it. Right now, she was needed elsewhere. She would simply have to find a way.

'Could we just see how I go?' she said, sadness pulling at her heart at the thought of possibly handing over a role she'd come to think of as her own. But a nun should not become attached to anything other than God and the church. She knew that.

Veronica stood, signalling the end of their conversation. 'Leave it with me for now. We'll talk again once I've worked this through with Agatha.'

'Did you get the job?' Tansy asked.

'Yes.'

'So you had to work with him every day?'

'Not every day, but I certainly saw him a lot.'

'How did you cope?'

'Some days were excruciating and it was all I could do not to scream at him. Other days, it all felt very normal. *He* seemed normal, even decent. On those days I doubted myself. I doubted Sarah. I even wondered if I had dreamed the whole letter incident, or if I had simply interpreted it incorrectly or remembered it inaccurately.'

'Did you write back to Sarah and ask her, talk about what was going on at all?'

'Yes. I regret that now, of course, putting her in such a dreadful position, putting her at risk. But she never turned away my letters, never asked me not to write. She must have read them all, and it must have taken quite a toll, though she never spoke of the subject in her letters back to me. I burdened her with silence.' Maria paused, considering how that time must have been for Sarah, isolated in the bush and disconnected from the events Maria was describing. 'It must have been very disturbing and lonely and certainly unfair. Peter was the only one who should pay for what he'd done, no one else.

'It weighed heavily on my mind too,' she said. 'I couldn't tell anyone else. And the one person in whom I *should* have been able to confide with total confidence of secrecy and seek the comfort of advice during the sacrament of confession was the very last person I could turn to.'

'Oh, Maria. There are so many layers to the anguish you must have felt,' Tansy said. 'You had to keep going to confession, though, didn't you?'

'Yes, at least weekly. It was expected. And I certainly couldn't stop going if I wanted to keep my role as the religious education coordinator. I had to act as normally as possible.'

'So what did you confess?'

Maria chuckled and then tut-tutted as if scolding herself for her levity. 'I couldn't stand the idea of making a truthful confession to him, so I did the only thing I thought I could do without losing my mind or blowing my cover: I made things up. It was a total farce to expect my soul to be cleansed by the man who was the conduit to God when he was leading the life of the devil. I made the decision at that time that I no longer needed priests. I could communicate directly with God if I wanted to, and God would sort me out.'

'That doesn't sound too radical.'

'Oh, it was, believe me. That's precisely the belief that keeps all the men in the church in their jobs. Imagine empowering you to believe you didn't need them? The whole structure of the church would collapse.'

'Now I'm confused, because you stayed in the church for another twenty years. Why?'

'Ah.' Maria looked to the sky. 'That part of the story is still coming.'

Tansy groaned. 'You're killing me with the suspense.'

'I continued going to confession, but I confessed silly things. Nonsense things.' Maria snorted. 'I wasn't going to share a single serious thought or emotion with him. So I told him I dreamed of swimming in a pool of melted chocolate.'

Tansy laughed.

'Chocolate was a hotly debated item in the convent. Some sisters believed it was a temptation sent by the devil to distract us from our pure thoughts. Many thought it lowered our consciousness to focus too much on earthly pleasure.'

'I eat some form of chocolate every day,' Tansy admitted.

'I can't remember the last time I ate chocolate. A homemade apple crumble with honey and yoghurt is my only occasional treat. I'm not sure I can even remember what chocolate tastes like.'

'Well, we must fix that as soon as possible. I'll bring you some. Now, what else did you confess?'

'I confessed that I was feeling strung out one day and helped myself to some of Mother Veronica's medicinal brandy.'

'Ha! You didn't.'

'I did. That one got him hot under the collar, actually, and had the unfortunate consequence of his making me confess to Veronica for something I didn't actually do.'

'Oh dear.'

'Mm. She was none too pleased, either. Served me right, I suppose, for lying in the confessional. I also told him I left breadcrumbs under the organ to encourage the mice in order to give Sister Celine a sense of purpose in her job of defending the instruments.'

'Was that one true?'

'No. But I did think about it.'

'Celine still worried you.'

Maria nodded. 'She was so vulnerable.'

'Did she continue to avoid Father Peter?'

'You know what? She stopped going to confession with him. She outright refused, and nothing Mother Veronica said would make her go. Veronica threatened her, counselled her that her soul was in danger, even tried to bargain with her. But Celine wouldn't go.'

'She knew,' Tansy said, definitively.

'Honestly, I'm not sure. If she did, she never said anything to anyone directly that I know of. Then again, with all the secrecy involved, I wouldn't know. But sometimes I felt she might have had a sixth sense about some things. She certainly disliked him enough to cause tremendous waves in the convent. Her behaviour divided her fellow sisters. Veronica eventually allowed Celine to go to another parish for confession once a month in return for being responsible for serving Peter afternoon tea once a week.'

'Why?'

'I think she thought that Celine's irrational dislike of Father Peter would be gradually broken down if she spent a little time with him. So at half past three on Friday afternoons, Celine had to prepare tea and some sort of sweet for him. It also gave Celine an opportunity to practise her baking and develop a few more skills in the kitchen. Veronica was good like that; she wanted to help prepare Celine for a time when, for whatever reason, the other nuns might not be around to look after her. She wanted to give her life skills.'

'Did it work? Did she lose her fear of him?'

'I used to pop my head into the sitting room from time to time, where afternoon tea was served, and try to catch a glimpse of what was going on. And, truly, I was nervous for her, with his reputation, and her history. But I never saw them so much as exchange a sentence. She seemed resigned to presenting him with the tray of food and washing up afterwards in return for not having to go to confession, and that's the way it stayed.'

'Did you ever think, while you were in confession, that you might somehow let him know that you knew what he'd done?'

'I did consider telling him directly about the letter but, once again, I had Sarah to think of. And there was also the risk that he would have me removed from the position of religious education coordinator for some confected reason, or have me transferred entirely, and then I would lose my opportunity to observe him around the children.'

'That makes sense.'

'But one day I told him that I'd been confided in by a fellow sister on a grave matter involving church leaders and she had then sworn me to secrecy. But, I went on, the problem was that I wanted to share the secret, because I felt it was the right thing to do.'

'What did he say?'

'He said that I should honour my word to keep the secret. And then he said, "Silence is a virtue."'

20

It was Dougal's last day, and he was spending it in the office, again. Tansy was so sad that she forgot to eat breakfast and only realised her error when her hands began to shake from lack of food.

Tomorrow Dougal would leave and she had no idea how long it would be before she saw him again. She'd promised she'd go to Canada. But when? A week, a month, six months? She honestly had no idea.

Enid and Paula were bustling in the kitchen when Tansy went for a bowl of cereal to stop the shakes. They were covered in flour and chocolate icing and giggling like schoolgirls. They asked Tansy if she had time to help them, but she made a show of taking her bowl and packing up her notebook and laptop and saying she had appointments to go to. Enid sighed audibly, a sign of exasperation with Tansy's avoidance, she could tell. Paula sniffed and squinted, disapproving.

Ashamed, Tansy conceded to herself that she should be spending time with her mother. She still hadn't told her about the pregnancy kerfuffle and the deep fissure it had caused in her otherwise peaceful life and marriage. And she wasn't about to go into it with Paula hovering around.

Today, she just wanted to escape. And Honeybee Haven was the place she wanted to be. There, she found Maria in full market-day preparation again, this time hard at work on something fluffy, creamy and yellow. She could see the honey pot, smell garlic powder and freshly squeezed lemon juice, and there was some kind of dark paste in an unlabelled jar.

'What's that?' she asked.

'Taste this,' Maria said, passing over the stainless-steel bowl.

Tansy dipped in a teaspoon and sucked, then smacked her lips with pleasure. 'Oh, wow, that's great.' She smiled. 'Sweet and sharp and tangy all at the same time.'

'That's a relief; I thought I'd put in too much garlic powder,' Maria said, picking up another spoon and tasting it. 'It's honey mustard.'

Tansy picked up a tub of Greek yoghurt. 'Is this in it too?'

'Yes, it makes a lighter and healthier version than using cream.'

'Can I buy some from you? I'd love to make a special dinner for Dougal tonight, and I think this would go well with oven-baked chicken breast, stuffed with soft cheese and dressed with prosciutto.'

'That sounds wonderful,' Maria said, her voice tinged with emotion—longing, perhaps—and Tansy wondered how long it had been since anyone had made dinner for Maria, or cooked her soup when she was sick.

'You'll have to come down and visit and I'll make it for you too,' she said, and meant it.

Maria passed her some empty jars and motioned with her hand for Tansy to fill them with the mustard dressing. 'Yes,' she said, but she still sounded sad.

Tansy almost asked Maria what was wrong, but stopped herself; she knew she'd been peppering her aunt with a lot of questions in a short period of time, and her regret over being so pushy with Dougal was still fresh in her mind. Maria had been gracious in sharing her stories—the last thing Tansy wanted was to push her too far. Together they filled the jars in silence until they were all done. Tansy was handing over the last when she spoke again. 'Are you going to see the bees today?' she asked instead.

'I am. I just need to get these labelled and into the fridge, and then whip up a batch of honey bath bombs.'

'That sounds like fun. Can I help?'

Maria smiled and passed her a glass measuring cup and a packet of baking soda. 'I won't say no. Two cups of that, please.'

An hour later, Tansy sweated beneath the white protective suiting Maria was making her wear for her first official visit to the bees.

'Why do I have so many more layers than you?' she asked, zipping the veiled hat onto the outer jacket so that no bees could crawl down her neck and under her clothes. 'I look like an alien.'

'The last thing I want is for you to get stung, especially since we don't know if you're allergic. I'd rather spend more time kitting you out now than resuscitating you later.'

'Fair enough.' Tansy tucked the long cotton legs of the suit deep into her gumboots, and Maria ran masking tape around the tops so bees couldn't crawl down and sting her feet.

She struggled with a heavy elbow-length glove. The first one had been okay, but trying to pull on the second one was harder, since the fingers of the first hand were so thickly covered that she couldn't actually feel what she was doing.

Maria, on the other hand, simply wore long pants, ankle boots, a light zip-up jacket, yellow rubber kitchen gloves, and a hat with a net that didn't even connect to the top of the jacket.

'Don't you worry about getting stung?'

'My main concern is a happy hive. I keep my girls calm. Bees don't actually want to sting you; if they do, they die. If you work in with the girls, they'll respect you.'

'Then why am I so well padded?'

'Because they don't know you yet.'

Maria packed a bucket with a J-shaped metal tool, a metal smoking tin with bellows on one side, a barbecue lighter and some dry grass, and three wooden frames, each strung with three strands of wire and a sheet of human-made wax for the bees to build their honeycomb on.

'They can build honeycomb without it, of course,' Maria explained. 'They'll build off a tree limb if it suits them. A premade template just speeds up the process.'

Tansy offered to carry the bucket for Maria, and followed her aunt up the path to where the hives sat. There were four of them, spaced about a metre apart, fanning in a gentle arc. Each one was composed of a stack of three white boxes.

'I check one hive every few days, so I get all four done in a fortnight and then start again.'

'Why can't you check all four in one day?'

'I could, but if I'm harvesting honey I'd have to deal with all of it at once, and it's heavy work. Each frame can hold more than three kilos of honey, and a super—these boxes sitting on top of the brood box at the bottom are called supers—might have ten frames, so just one super could weigh more than thirty kilograms.

Harvesting is time-consuming and messy and you don't want to rush it. This way, I can spend as much time on each hive as it needs.'

They reached the hive furthest to the right and Tansy put down the bucket of gear, amazed at how hot she was already, and it was autumn. She couldn't imagine how hot it would be to do this in summer.

The bees buzzed in a pleasant, busy kind of way. She and Maria had approached from behind the hive, so as not to cross their flight path, and now stood quietly to the side watching them come and go through the small opening at the bottom of the lowest box. A few hovered there at the entrance. Others took off at a great rate, zipping up into the sky and hurtling over the edge of the mountain, out into the dense forest below.

Through her face net, Tansy watched Maria's face soften into an affectionate smile. 'Busy girls today,' she said. 'There must be some good food out there.' She pointed to the bottom box. 'That's the brood box. That's where the queen is and where she's busy laying fifteen hundred eggs every day.'

'Fifteen *hundred*?'

'Every day of her life for as long as she lives, which is two to three years. She only mates once in her whole life. She leaves the box at around three weeks of age and flies kilometres up into the sky and circles around until the drones from other hives, not her own, come to find her. She keeps flying while the weaker drones drop from exhaustion and then she mates with the strongest ones.' Maria paused, saving the best for last. 'Then she rips off their penises and keeps them inside her for the rest of her life.'

Tansy blanched. 'Jeez, that's brutal.'

Maria nodded. 'A bee's life *is* brutal. The workers literally work themselves to death, falling to the ground when their wings are shredded from overuse. The drones—the boys—are there solely for the chance to mate, and a queen only mates once in her lifetime. So the vast majority of drones never do a single thing. The worker bees will regularly toss them out of the hive, after first stripping them of their wings so they can't come back home. They starve to death on the ground or are taken by predators.'

Tansy was disturbed. Here she was thinking bees just pottered about in flowers and made delightful honey, when in reality they were kamikaze warriors with no qualms about their own fate or about killing their own kind to preserve the hive.

Maria lifted a large square of wood from the roof of the hive, which sheltered it from rain and sun. Then she continued her grisly account. 'The potential queen babies kill each other, until there's only one left, and when the ruling queen's too old and the hive thinks she's not fertile enough they'll toss her out too so they can raise a new one. A worker bee lives just a couple of months, will make thousands of visits to flowers, will clean and feed and nurture and communicate and defend, and make just a couple of drops of honey before she dies.'

'That's depressing.'

'They work to serve, sacrificing everything, including themselves, in the process.'

'Like nuns,' Tansy observed.

Maria grunted. 'There are a lot of similarities.' She pulled out the smoke tin and stuffed the dry grass down into the bottom, picked up the long barbecue lighter and clicked the button a few times until a flame appeared at the tip, then dipped it into the middle of the nest of grass until it caught. Smoke curled up out of the top before she flipped on the lid, puffed the bellows a few times to get it going, and let it smoulder.

She worked the edge of her J-knife under the lid of the upper box, cracking through a dark brown glue-like substance. 'That's propolis,' she explained. 'The bees use it to seal their home, fortifying it against pests and attack. If any intruders die inside the hive, the bees encase them in propolis because it prevents the decomposition of bodies, which might contaminate the hive. It's tremendously good for you, full of antibiotics, and heals wounds and ulcers. It can turn hard as cement, though, and make it difficult to access the hive.'

'I've always wondered why they don't use honey more in hospitals,' Tansy said.

'Politics, no doubt. Honey is the only food in the world that never goes off, because it is packed full of antibiotics and living enzymes. Manuka honey is sold for such a high price these days because of its medicinal value.'

'Sounds like we should be stockpiling it,' Tansy said. 'Maybe we should all be building cellars and storing it like valuable wine, if it never goes off.'

'In case of apocalypse, after all the bees are gone,' Maria puffed, working hard to prise the lid off the top of the hive. 'I've thought about it.'

'Have you?'

'Briefly. Though it's too sad a thought to dwell on for long. New Zealand has fallen victim to varroa mite and the results have been catastrophic for the bees. Australia can't be far behind.'

The lid cracked open and sticky brown propolis stretched between the edges as Maria worked them apart. Inside the hive, Tansy could see ten wooden rows—the edges of the frames. Two black metal trays lay between a couple of the frames. Bees moved everywhere, crawling over the wood, up from the hidden depths of the box, diving down between the frames, taking off for flight, and scurrying around in concern at the disturbance to their home.

Maria took the smoker and puffed the bellows once or twice so smoke billowed over the box and the bees. 'I don't normally use much smoke,' she said. 'It makes the bees think a bushfire is coming and causes them to panic eat. It keeps them busy, not calm, as many people think. I don't think it's fair to keep stressing and tricking them.'

'Crying wolf,' Tansy said.

'Exactly. And it makes the honey taste slightly smoky too. Sometimes I start with a little bit of smoke and then follow up with a spray of water later to distract them. But since you're here today, I don't want to take any chances.'

Maria took each end of one rectangular frame and lifted it up into the light to examine the ready-made wax template. Around half of the sheet's hexagonal units had been filled. Maria pointed out the cells containing red, orange and brown pollen, which had been stored for future use. Other cells had a solid amber-coloured surface. That was the capped honey, waiting for harvest.

'What are those for?' Tansy asked, pointing to the metal trays lying between the frames.

'They're traps for small hive beetle,' Maria said, disgust in her voice. 'It's an introduced pest—it's been in Australia for about fifteen years—and it can wipe out a hive. We didn't have them when I first started beekeeping but we're stuck with them now. The bees have no defences against them. But all hives have them now, so it's a matter of managing them.' She lifted up the long metal grille of the trap to reveal a similarly long tube beneath it, like a pit into which the beetles fell, filled with liquid. 'We put vegetable oil in there to entice them in and they drown. It's one of the maintenance things we have to do and why we have to keep checking the hives.'

Just then, Tansy spied a small black beetle running on the outside of the hive. 'Is that one?' She pointed to it.

'Sadly, yes.' Maria, one hand holding the frame, used the other to squash the beetle with the J-knife. 'This is a good, healthy frame but it's not ready to harvest,' she said. 'We don't take a frame until it's full of honey.' She lowered it back into the box and lifted out another frame, which had even less honey in it. 'Let's check the next box down.'

She put the lid back on the first box, heaved it up with a small grunt, and placed it on the ground. The box underneath was also crawling with active bees, far too interested in their work to be wondering what Maria and Tansy were doing. This box was topped with a metal grille.

'What's that?'

'That's a queen excluder. It makes sure the queen stays down below. That way, when we're moving boxes around to harvest frames and honey, we won't accidentally squash and kill her. The spaces in the grate are big enough for the other bees to move through, so they can go anywhere in the three layers of the hive, but the queen is bigger and can't fit through. Most beekeepers put their queen excluder on the bottom box, trapping her in that one, but I'm interested in keeping a happy hive so I let her move through two boxes. I think if she's got more room to move she's more content, and a happy queen means a happy hive.

'You'll know when a hive's unhappy. The buzzing will change from a gentle, soothing drone to a louder, angrier noise. They'll start dive-bombing you and climbing all over you.' She pointed at Tansy's suit. 'Not a single one has touched you yet.'

'No, I feel quite safe,' Tansy said.

Maria removed the queen excluder and pulled out a frame from within. This one had two long amber-coloured extensions hanging off an edge, somewhat like a wrinkly peanut shell.

'They're queen cells,' Maria said, excited. 'And look, that one's hatched.' The end of the cell had been chewed open. 'This other one's not far off.'

'So what happens to the queens?'

'They will fight it out, leaving just one.'

'Poor things.'

Maria replaced that frame and began to work her knife under the propolis to lift another, but the bees' noise escalated, their calm flight paths beginning to fracture into shorter, sharper turns.

'It's okay,' Maria said, clucking to them. 'I just want to have a look.' There was little honey on that frame either, so Maria put it back and replaced the queen excluder on top of the box. 'I think we'll leave this hive for today. There's not enough honey for us to harvest—in general, I like to leave at least four full frames of honey for them, because it's their food, keeping them alive, and the bees are busy stockpiling for winter right now. But we know the hive is healthy and busy. We'll check this one again in two weeks' time to see what's going on. Sometimes we have a late flush of flowers and a windfall of honey at this time of year. And then I'll refill those beetle traps and make sure everything is as it should be. It's not worth upsetting them further now.'

Tansy helped Maria pick up the top box, surprised at its weight even without full frames of honey, and they gently put the whole hive back together again. The bees calmed down, their buzzing lowering to an amiable working hum once more.

The women retraced their steps, leaving the small clearing and the bees in peace, and wandered in comfortable silence back through the vegetable garden and past the many rows of lavender, low on flowers at this time of year.

'Bees just love lavender,' Maria said, pulling off a rubber glove and picking a sprig to crush and smell. 'In general, they'll go for flowers that are purple and deep blue and bright yellow before they go to others.'

'So they'd love sunflowers then,' Tansy said.

'They certainly do. We need everyone to grow lavender and sunflowers to help support the bees.'

'I love sunflowers too. I can't even think of them without smiling. They just radiate hope. Do you know they used them to help clean up radioactive waste in Japan after the Fukushima disaster?' Tansy said, excited.

'No, I didn't.'

'Sunflowers transform some of the contaminants in the soil by taking it up into their bodies, and then the people harvest them and dispose of them.'

Maria shook her head, marvelling. 'I never stop learning about nature. Just when I think it can't get more amazing, it does.'

A couple of black chooks scooted past them in a spray of clucking and flapping, chasing some sort of moth on the breeze. Outside her cabin, Maria turned around. 'Are there any bees on my back?' she asked.

'No. Me?' Tansy did the same, holding out her arms for inspection as she twirled.

'No, you're clear.'

They took off their protective gear, Maria escaping from hers much faster than Tansy, who had at least twice as many layers to remove. It was a relief to be free of the heavy, hot material, the sweat on her skin evaporating as soon as it was uncovered. Maria's face was red from the effort.

'How do you do that in summer?' Tansy asked.

'I guess I'm used to it. Probably helps that I joined the convent before the Vatican II council and therefore spent years in the full-length heavy robes before the changes came in. You just learn to live with it. Learn to ignore it. If there's one thing the convent teaches you it's how to develop mental toughness.' Maria ran her hand roughly through her short curly grey hair, which had been flattened by the bee hat. She folded up the white suits, jackets, hats, nets and gloves and tucked them under her arm. 'Right, then. We better put the kettle on.'

Inside the dark, cool cabin, the honey bath bombs cluttered the bench. The women had pulled apart clear Christmas baubles to use as moulds, poured in the mixture, and then taped them together while the bombs set. Nearby lay strands of pre-cut red and white twine ready to truss the bombs once they were removed from the moulds.

Maria moved past them but froze at the stove. 'What is it?' Tansy said, flopping into a chair. She watched as Maria reached out a hand, slowly, and picked up a white envelope that was sitting on the stovetop.

Keeping her back to Tansy, Maria turned over the envelope. She cleared her throat. 'It's blank,' she said, her voice faint. And there was something in the way she was standing, holding that envelope stiffly, that shot a bolt of fear through Tansy's heart.

She stood and went to her aunt's side. 'Are you going to open it?' Maria didn't answer her.

'Do you know who it's from?'

Maria passed the envelope to Tansy, her face white. 'You do it. You open it,' she said. Then she began to pace the room. 'Tell me what it says.'

Tansy felt nauseous suddenly, infected by the waves of anxiety emanating from Maria. She slid her finger under the corner of the envelope and ripped it open. Inside was a single sheet of lined paper with just one handwritten word. She read the word to herself. And read it again. And looked up at Maria, staring at her, her tongue stuck to the roof of her mouth.

Maria stopped her pacing but kept wringing her hands. 'Well? What does it say?'

Silently, Tansy held the paper out to her.

Murderer.

21

'Where did this come from?' Tansy asked nervously, looking over her shoulder and peering out the windows. 'What's going on?'

'It's okay,' Maria said calmly. Too calmly, she realised. Like a person who'd just looked down to see that they'd stepped in a steel-jaw trap and had blood gushing from the wound. 'It's fine.'

'It's clearly *not* fine,' Tansy said, an edge of hysteria creeping into her voice. 'We had a cup of tea right here before we left and this envelope wasn't there. Someone's been here.' Her eyes widened. 'They could still be here,' she whispered, grabbing Maria's arm.

Maria's own fear had passed and she was back in control. 'Stay calm,' she said.

But a well-placed footstep on the linoleum floor made them both jump and spin around. Maria yelped. Tansy whimpered.

A tall, broad man stalked out from the hallway, moving straight towards them. Maria staggered back and fell, hitting her right buttock hard on the floor. The man took three confident strides and towered over her.

He was dressed head to toe in black, save for a small white square showing at his neck. He wore glasses. His hair was grey and receding. And his cheeks were papery, like the ageing man he was. 'I'm afraid you caught me taking a snoop around your little dwelling,' he said, oozing disdain.

It had taken her only a split second to recognise him. 'You,' she said, from her position on the floor.

'Maria,' he said evenly, his gaze unwavering, steady. Cold.

Tansy crept forward to help Maria to her feet, her eyes on the intruder. Maria clambered up with some difficulty, her legs wobbly, but straightened herself as best she could, while Tansy steadied her from behind. She tilted her head back to look up into the man's speckled green eyes.

'Long time no see.' She continued to face him, but turned her head slightly to speak over her shoulder to Tansy. 'Would you wait outside?' she said.

There was silence from behind her. Ian's eyes were still focused on Maria, not even deigning to register Tansy's presence, and Maria didn't take her gaze off him either. 'Tansy? Did you hear me?'

'Yes,' Tansy replied weakly. 'I heard you.' But instead of leaving, she stepped forward to stand at Maria's shoulder. Maria could sense the trembling in her niece's body. She knew she should order her to leave; but she couldn't. Tansy's presence, standing side by side with her in this moment, filled her with such a surge of confidence, and something else . . . what was it?

Peace. That was it. Tansy being there gave her peace.

Maria spread her hands out in front of her in a cocky gesture to let Ian know that he had them both to deal with now.

'I don't care about her,' he said, still looking at Maria.

Maria barked out frustrated, angry laughter. 'Of course you don't care. You didn't care then, why would you care now?'

They eyed each other silently for a moment.

'Actually,' Maria went on, 'I have no interest in talking to you. I've no interest in anything you have to say. Your two little messages, your pathetic attempts to scare me into submission once again, were wasted.' She looked him up and down, taking in the formal black robes—clearly he intended to remind her of the past, to intimidate her, to establish his authority over her once more.

She shot him her most withering look. 'I demand that you leave my house, right now.'

His turn to cast her a contemptuous glance. 'Your house?' He raised a bushy eyebrow and took in the meagreness of the pint-sized building she called home, with its few humble pieces of furniture. 'But it's not your house, is it?' he went on. 'In fact, you don't have anything to call your own. You left your family, your order, the church and God.'

'I never left God.'

'No? I doubt God would see it that way,' he said quietly, with deafening menace.

'What's going on?' Tansy said, her hand reaching for the mobile phone in her pocket. 'Should I call the police?' she whispered.

Archbishop Ian Tully turned his gaze to her then, so swiftly and fiercely that Tansy stepped backwards, clutching her phone to her chest. 'The police? Now that would be interesting, wouldn't it, Maria?' He slid his eyes back to her.

'I have no problem with that,' she said, pleased her voice remained steady and didn't betray her; while she *was* prepared to live with the consequences of her actions, Michaela's charity needed her, and she didn't want to let them down. But she couldn't allow him to know where her weakness lay. 'In fact,' she said, turning to Tansy, 'yes, do call the police. Let's have them come and meet the man who's been threatening me.'

'Threatening? I've done nothing of the sort,' he said, with great dollops of childlike innocence and well-practised sincerity. 'My visits have simply been a way to remind you of the special bond we share. And the only person who'd lose if the police were to visit would be you.' He turned to Tansy. 'Yes, dear, please do call the police and have them come up. I can give my statement immediately, detailing exactly what I witnessed your . . .' He halted, a hand to his chin. A scholar's expression. 'I'm sorry, I didn't catch exactly how you two are connected?' He waited.

'Maria's my aunt,' Tansy said uncertainly.

His face broke into a wide smile. 'A niece? Maria, how wonderful for you. I'm sure you're relishing reconnecting with your family at this time of your life. And I'm equally sure you'd be sad to lose them again.'

'Who *are* you?' Tansy said, gathering some defences now. 'What are you doing breaking into Maria's home and leaving a horrid note—'

'Two notes,' Maria corrected her.

'*Two* horrid notes,' Tansy repeated. 'And why are you dressed like—' Her voice faltered. She clapped a hand across her mouth and gasped from behind her fingers. 'I know who you are.'

Ian beamed. 'Always a pleasure to meet a member of the faithful,' he said, bowing his head condescendingly.

'Archbishop Ian Tully,' Maria confirmed. 'You've likely seen his picture.'

'I've seen you preach,' Tansy said, her voice laden with confusion and dismay.

'I do hope it was one of my better sermons,' Ian said.

'Oh, cut it out,' Maria said. 'Get to the point. What do you want?'

'You know what I want,' he said. His presence loomed large in her small home. The austere black frock seemed to drain all the light from the room. He radiated arrogance and fearlessness. But he couldn't be entirely fearless, she reflected, or he wouldn't be here. 'You want silence,' Maria said sadly. 'You want it now like you wanted it then. I was a fly in your ointment then and I still am.'

'Very good,' he said, with a small nod of acknowledgement. 'But you and I both know this isn't a one-way street. Is it? You want something from me in return. You wanted it then and, as you say, you still want it now.'

'What's he talking about?' Tansy said.

'I'm sure spending the rest of your days in jail was never in your life plan,' he said, still addressing Maria.

'I had no life plan other than to serve God and the people who needed me. You, on the other hand, were corrupted by the power bestowed on you by—' Maria almost said 'God', because that was what she'd been trained to believe. She lowered her voice. 'Did you ever care about your people?'

He flicked a finger to the scar above his eye, faded now after many decades but still visible. 'You know I did.' His voice betrayed genuine hurt at the suggestion that he was only a calculating yes-man and never a servant of God. He had been one once, she had to admit. The homeless were his particular passion, which was how he got that scar, attacked once with a broken bottle in the streets of Fortitude Valley in the early hours of the morning.

Somewhere deep inside herself she could even admit that he had, in all likelihood, entered the priesthood for the right reasons. But somehow those reasons had long been forgotten in favour of politics, power and notoriety. And those original intentions didn't make up for everything he'd done since.

Maria looked to the heavens and took a breath. Beside her, Tansy was still standing with the mobile phone clutched in her hand, seemingly struck dumb by the sight of the archbishop here in front of her. Maria spoke quietly but sternly. 'I'm still serving the people of this world who cannot defend themselves. The most vulnerable, the poorest, the ones others have given up on. Are you?'

He lifted his chin to peer down his nose at her, but said nothing.

'If it's in God's plan for me to go to jail, well, of course I'm only human and I'll feel . . .' She trailed off. *Devastated* was the word that came to mind. 'But I'll also know that I've been called there to serve my fellow inmates, because that's what Jesus would do. Can you say the same?'

'This isn't over,' he said quietly.

Maria went to the screen door and opened it wide, stepping out to direct Ian out of her house. He glided out of the room in a sweep of long black robes. He stopped briefly in front of Maria and opened his mouth to speak, but she got in first.

'I'm prepared to live with my actions,' she said. 'The question is, are you?'

Without a reply, he turned and left, his hands clasped behind his back, making his way along the little worn grass path that led to the car park and loading dock. It was only when she heard his car jump throatily to life and the wheels crunch over the stones and begin the long descent down the hill to wherever he had come from that Maria began to shake.

She had to make some big decisions.

But right now, she just let herself melt into the warm, firm embrace of Tansy, who'd come to her side once more and wrapped her arms around her.

'Oh, Maria, what have you done?'

22

The sun was recently up, but was still gathering its strength. Tansy, Dougal, Leo and Enid stood in a circle in the lounge room. Tansy clutched the car keys in her hand, biting her lip.

'Well.' Dougal smiled, addressing Leo and Enid. His bulging suitcase rested near his leg. 'This is it. I'm off.' He slid one hand across the other, nervous.

Leo cleared his throat. He still looked sleepy, and his shoulders were slightly hunched. 'I could come,' he said. 'I can get a friend to take notes in today's lectures and I could see you off properly.' His mouth twisted into a cheeky smile. 'I could wave flags and hold up a banner and everything, my nose pressed to the glass.'

Dougal inhaled and clasped his hand around the back of Leo's neck and rubbed it vigorously. 'Not a chance. You should be at uni. I'm so proud of you,' he said, his voice threatening to crack.

'Oh, come on.' Leo placed the heel of his hand to the side of his head, not knowing what to do with the emotions so obviously just below the surface.

'I mean it,' Dougal said, giving him an *I'm serious* face. 'I can't wait to get the photos from the graduation ceremony. I'm only sorry I won't be here.'

'It's okay.' Leo shot Tansy a quick glance and she raised her eyebrows in return. None of them had told Dougal that Leo was thinking of quitting.

Do lies of omission count?

'You've turned into such a fine young man,' Dougal said, as if he couldn't quite believe it himself. And he pulled Leo to him for a strong, manly hug. They patted each other on the back and then stepped back, neither daring to look at the other in case they broke down.

'I hope the flight will be safe,' Enid said. She'd spent much of last night expressing her concerns about the safety of airlines these days, discussing the likelihood of planes being hijacked or shot down from the skies or disappearing over oceans.

'It'll be fine, Mum,' Tansy said, a little prickly. The last thing she needed was to imagine horrible things like that. 'It's Qantas.' She didn't know why that was supposed to make it all better, but it felt good to say it.

Enid pressed three straight fingers to her lips and drummed them there as though she wasn't convinced but was trying to restrain herself.

'Oh, wait, I have this, too,' Leo said, composed once more. He pulled two long straps of woven leather from his pocket. 'Hold out your arm,' he instructed, and Dougal did as he was told. Leo fastened one strap around Dougal's wrist as he explained, 'I got them at the uni market day this week. They're locally made and stamped with starfish. See?' He turned over his father's wrist and they all leaned forward to peer at the workmanship.

'So it is,' Enid murmured.

Leo then fastened the other leather strap around his own wrist. 'I thought it would be funky if we both had one, each wearing it on the other side of the world. And you'd be reminded of the beach, with the starfish.' Even as he spoke, Leo's face had begun to colour with a wave of doubt. 'Of course, if you don't like it, that's okay too . . .' he trailed off.

'I love it,' Dougal said, and pulled his son into his arms for a final goodbye. 'I won't take it off, I promise.'

Tansy eased her nerves by relaying facts about Canada as she drove.

'Did you know that Canada is the second-largest country in the world? Russia's the first.'

'No, I didn't,' Dougal said, sipping from his takeaway coffee cup. 'Mmm, that's good coffee. I'm going to miss Australian coffee. One thing I don't know is what Canadian coffee is like, but if it's anything like American coffee I'm in a lot of trouble.'

'I should have made you one,' Tansy said, her nose pinching with threatening tears. 'Like I used to when I first met you.'

Dougal put his hand on her leg. 'You'll always be my barista babe,' he said. 'No one could ever make a coffee anywhere near as well as you.'

They both got a little giggly then, as though everything that had happened between them in the past week had simply vanished. A pressure valve had been released and they were suddenly Tansy and Dougal again—best mates, lovers, a perfect pair. Returned to a time before there was any suggestion of children or any alarming thoughts about where their future was going. When it was as simple as that she loved him and he loved her.

She slid him a sneaky sideways glance as she finished overtaking a car on the highway and set the Audi to cruise control once more. 'Do you think it's going to rain today?' She spoke breathily, to alert him to what she was doing. She was going back to the time when he would drop into her cafe in a busy Brisbane street each morning. For weeks, they'd played a game of cat and mouse, and it always began with her asking him if he thought it would rain.

Beside her, Dougal smiled. 'Not possible,' he said seriously, playing along.

'Why not?' she said.

'Because of that smile of yours—it's so full of sunshine it would dry up all the tears in heaven.'

'That's quite a line you've got there,' she said, playfully admonishing him.

'Is it working?' he asked innocently.

'Come back tomorrow and we'll see.'

At this point, she would always hand him his coffee and wave goodbye. And each day they enacted this exchange again, until the day when she asked him if he thought it was going to rain and he said, 'I don't care.'

She'd been taken by surprise, and turned off the steam in the milk so as not to burn herself. She'd peeked over the coffee cups at him. 'What do you mean?'

'I don't care if it rains, because I'm prepared for anything. I've got an umbrella, snow boots, sunscreen, gumboots, a beach towel, you name it. And come rain, hail, shine or heatwave, I'm going to take you to dinner.'

And so he did, to a classy, softly lit restaurant on the river, the lights of the Story Bridge in the distance and party boats floating on the water. And then she'd gone home with him, on the first date—something she'd never done before. But it felt so easy and natural and she couldn't keep her hands off him.

Weeks later, Dougal confessed that he'd fallen in love with her that night, the instant she dunked a piece of garlic bread in her red wine. Who did that? When he mentioned it to her, she had no recollection of having done it and was searingly embarrassed. 'It was totally endearing,' he said. Then he told her he'd spent most of the years since breaking up with Rebecca alone. He focused on work and his time with Leo, determined to do the best he possibly could in each. It meant he had largely given up on a social life and leisure time, but he was committed to getting at least one thing right. The shame of a failed marriage, broken hearts and upturned lives, was a wound he was constantly healing. Until he met her and unexpectedly felt worthy again.

'I'm so glad you didn't turn out to be a cad,' she said now, exiting the highway towards the Gateway Motorway and Brisbane international airport.

'I'm so glad you married me,' he replied.

'Me too,' she said.

'I guess you'll be doing this drive again soon,' he said, stretching his arms up and over the back of the headrest. 'Do you have any idea yet when you might be coming over to join me?' His voice was tentative, but he still sounded upbeat. Ninety-nine per cent confident she would keep her word and join him. 'No pressure, of course—I know you've still got stuff to work through here with your family and all.'

'I'm not sure yet. And you're right. I'm worried about Maria, actually.' She told him about what had happened yesterday with Archbishop Tully in Maria's home.

'This is unbelievable,' Dougal said, shocked. 'This story should be on an investigative journalist's desk. This is *not* normal.'

'Yeah, I know. It's beyond crazy. I asked Maria to tell me what she'd done but she said it was a long story and it would have to wait until I could next get up there.'

Dougal nodded. 'And when will that be?'

Tansy laughed. 'This afternoon, I'd say. Could you leave a mystery like that hanging?'

'No.'

'Besides, I'm going to need a distraction after letting you go at the airport, something to stop me from falling apart.'

He reached his hand over and she dropped her left hand off the steering wheel to hold it. She waited until the tightness in her chest eased. 'And the fete's this evening, so Mum's got the last bake-athon happening today with her new BFF, Paula. They'll be taking over the house again.'

They'd reached the turn-off to the airport now, slowed down by traffic but still moving steadily forward. Tansy's belly began to swirl. 'Nearly there,' she said, pulling a sad face.

Dougal began to hum.

'What are you . . . ? Stop that.'

He was humming John Denver's 'Leaving On A Jet Plane'.

'You know that song always makes me cry,' she said, slapping him on the thigh.

He laughed and held up his hands in surrender. 'Okay, okay. Sorry.'

All too soon, they were entering the winding laneways of the entry to the international airport, with planes taking off overhead, multistorey car parks, taxis, rental cars, buses, and the train line above them.

Tansy found a park and they unloaded Dougal's cases and put them on a trolley from a nearby rack. They stood on the bitumen and looked at each other, the wind buffeting Tansy's hair, roaring jumbo jet engines on the other side of the terminal. People rushing. Children crying. Trees gusting in the wind.

'So this is it,' Tansy said, tears falling now.

'Not for long,' Dougal said, pulling her to him. 'I'll see you again soon. And I'll call you as soon as I can.'

She nodded, not trusting herself to speak.

'You coming in?' he murmured into her ear.

She nodded again.

'Okay. Let's get this show on the road.'

He took her hand and together they walked into the terminal.

This morning's markets had been business as usual for Maria—a standard amount of money went into the collection tin, sales were decent, people were generally in a good mood. She'd packed up and gotten home easily by early afternoon. And now, she was waiting for Tansy to arrive.

The time had come at last. This afternoon, she would take Tansy to the prettiest spot on the hill, with servings of her homemade mead, and she would confess for the first time—to a human being—what she had done. She needed the practice; it wouldn't be long before she would be telling her story to the investigating officer—George something, if her memory served, though she'd tried hard to forget.

Maria made one batch of mead a year, and kept a small supply on hand at all times, deep in the back of the pantry in her kitchen. The proceeds of everything she produced went to the children in Cambodia, so taking honey for mead did seem extravagant. It took four kilos of fresh honey to make a batch, so she only liked to do it once each spring when the honey was flowing like sparkling rivers of gold. She followed as closely as she could the way the monks had traditionally made it, as far as she knew. She blessed the rainwater from the tanks before adding it, and fed the yeast raw sugar and crushed sultanas to get it going. She loved watching the mead move through its different stages, bubbling as the carbon dioxide rose to the surface. She would strain off the sediment from the dead yeast, add more honey and water and brew again. Strain again. Then bottle and seal with cork and hot wax stamped with the Honeybee Haven logo, a bee on a sunflower.

All things changed. Mead was a living product that started as one thing and ended as something totally different, just by putting those separate things in contact with one another. Just like humans. The people and circumstances that touched us changed us all.

She decanted some mead into a glass jug. Rich amber in colour, it had the consistency of port and smelled a little the same, but with more floral overtones. She swirled it around the jug and watched it cling to the sides as a good wine should. She resisted sipping some now and instead added more honey, stirred it with a spoon and placed it in the fridge. She checked the time—about two hours before Tansy arrived, the perfect length of time to chill the mead.

Maria greeted Tansy out in the car park with her basket in hand. 'How are you?' she asked, genuinely concerned. Tansy looked pale and her eyes red. She couldn't imagine how hard it would have been for her to say goodbye to Dougal.

Tansy got out of her car and took a deep breath of the cool mountain air. 'I'm okay,' she said. 'Not ready to party or anything, but okay.' She smiled heavily.

Maria flicked back the red-and-white-checked tea towel on top of the basket. 'Maybe this will help?'

Tansy's eyes brightened. 'I dare say it would.'

'Come on,' Maria said, poking out her elbow like a wing for Tansy to link with. 'We're taking a small walk and then we'll have our picnic.'

Tansy pressed the locking device on the key ring and the car blinked its orange lights and chirped cheerfully. Together they walked in silence that was filled with seriousness, but also with solidarity.

'I wish I'd met Dougal before he left,' Maria said once they'd passed the Yellow Tara and Green Tara cabins to find the beginning of a dirt path.

'He would have liked that,' Tansy said.

Maria wondered if she'd get to meet him at all now. An uncomfortable prickling sensation inched its way up her spine as she wondered, for the first time, if her newfound relatives would visit her in jail.

They began the ascent up the steep hill and passed a middle-aged German couple who were backpacking around the world and had booked in for the weekend. They greeted them with *guten Tag* and kept going.

'Why haven't I been up here yet?' Tansy asked.

'I'm not sure,' Maria said. 'I think I've been up here so often that now I tend to leave it for the visitors to experience. And I'm always so busy in the garden or with the bees, or preparing for the markets, or doing bookings and so on.'

The path became steeper, and here logs had been set in the ground to create steps. They adjusted their pace to accommodate these new footholds. The tall trees gave way to open space. Soon they'd reached the top, with a view to the horizon in all directions. There was a narrow bench and a small curved viewing platform with a safety rail and mud map of the area, hand-drawn before

Maria's time here, laminated and mounted on a post. The map identified a tall gum tree on the northern side, its head sticking far above the others around it, the oldest known tree in the area. It also showed the position of a waterfall off to the west, in a natural gully at the base of one of the hills. A creek system, wending and looping through the forest. Caves. Camping grounds. Small towns. Populated beach areas. The ocean.

'Wow!' Tansy rested with her hands on her hips, barely puffing, unlike Maria, whose heart thumped in her chest.

'Special, isn't it?' Maria said. She cast her eyes over the map, checking to see if it was still accurate or if developments had encroached or land had been cleared. Or if trees had grown, obscuring what was once visible. But it all looked in order.

'Which direction is Noosa?' Tansy asked, getting her bearings.

'That way.' Maria pointed.

Tansy talked through the process of identifying landmarks and estimating where Hastings Street and her unit might be. Finally satisfied she'd roughly found it, she shook her head. 'It's so beautiful. We live in the most gorgeous part of the world. I can't imagine leaving here,' she said. 'I just can't imagine myself in Canada.'

Maria didn't say anything, instead thinking that she couldn't imagine leaving here either. In a few foolish, romantic moments, she'd dreamed of her life ending here, amid her garden and her bees. But now? Now it would likely end behind bars.

She waited a moment and then sat down on the bench, her back resting against the railing, and uncovered her basket of goodies. 'Can I interest you in a glass of mead and some cheese and crackers?'

'Absolutely.' Tansy sat down and Maria handed her a glass and poured them each a small drink.

'Cheers.' They toasted and sipped.

Tansy coughed and her eyes watered. 'Whoa. Is this stuff legal?'

Maria widened her eyes. 'Perhaps a little too long on the brewing,' she said, but sipped more nonetheless.

Tansy went back for another sip and took a larger amount this time. 'I always wanted hair on my chest,' she said.

They both chuckled.

And then Maria began her story.

23

It was hard to know where to start, of course. Where was the beginning of this tale, exactly? When had Maria's moment of absolute certainty of the path she must take finally crystallised into a clear plan?

Perhaps a good place to start would be with Michelle Karakas, a once bright, bubbly, engaged fourteen-year-old who, seemingly overnight, turned quiet and sullen and withdrew from her friends. Who dragged her feet into confession as she stepped across the threshold and closed the door, alone inside with Father Peter Cunningham. Who came out with her eyes downcast and her hands trembling. Who refused to look at Maria when she'd asked if there was anything wrong, if there was anything troubling her, if there was anything she could help with. Who only ever shook her head and said, 'No, Sister.'

Once a popular, friendly girl, she became a victim of bullying. The other girls taunted her and Maria overheard a couple of them call her a slut. After that incident, Maria followed Michelle to the girls toilets and found her sobbing uncontrollably on the ground, pulling at her hair.

And that was when Michelle had broken down and told her the truth. She had gone to confession one day, wanting to relieve herself of her burden and be forgiven for her sinful behaviour. She'd found a special spot on her body that felt good to touch. She'd not known it was there but had come across it in the shower one day. For some reason, she knew she couldn't tell anyone else about it. But she could tell the one person who was there to save her soul.

Father Peter told her that she was a dirty, sinful girl. He told her she would go to hell if she didn't do what he asked of her. He was the voice of God. He was filled with the Holy Spirit and was the mouthpiece of Jesus, Son of God. Only he, Father Peter, could absolve her of her sins.

And so he insisted that she see him regularly and allow him to touch her, all the while telling her how awful she was, how dirty, how wicked and evil. What a grave disappointment she was to her parents. That she was no longer pure. He caused her pain in that special spot, and when she cried he told her that was good—her pain and her tears would cleanse her soul.

And while doling out her penance, he informed her that they weren't finished. She must also touch him, to see what a real man was like, a worthy man, so she would know what to do if she ever found a husband—one who could forgive her for being ruined. Then, at least, she could serve him properly and keep him satisfied so he wouldn't need to look elsewhere outside of their marriage to have his needs met.

It went on for months.

Of course, Maria went to Mother Veronica.

While Maria spoke, Veronica pursed her lips and folded her arms. Then she said, 'Leave it with me.'

Maria left, feeling sick but also relieved that Veronica knew. Now someone would do something.

But a day went by. A week. A month. And nothing happened. Veronica never mentioned the matter again. Never called Maria to her office. Michelle Karakas started coming to school less and less.

Finally, Maria went to Michelle's house to visit her and talk to her parents. When Mr Karakas saw Maria coming, he rolled his eyes. 'Is this because her grades are falling?' he called from the front door when Maria was only halfway down the footpath.

She stopped. 'No.'

'Because she's already been punished. We'll handle it from here. I'm sure you've got plenty to do, Sister,' he said, and closed the door.

Maria went cold all over.

She went back to see Veronica and demanded her help. Why hadn't anything been done? It was unacceptable. Illegal. Immoral.

'Silence,' Veronica said, and then reminded Maria of the church's edict on internal secrecy. They were all bound to silence—the Vatican had decreed it and they could not question it. They had to trust that their superiors were handling it; it was not a concern of the nuns.

That afternoon, Maria wept in the garden with her bees.

Then she went to the police station. She committed a grave sin, breaking the most important of all her vows: obedience. She was bound by absolute obedience to the church and to her superiors. Breaking that vow felt like a physical tearing of her body as she walked out through the front gates of the convent. Part of her left the church for good that day.

Unfortunately, the officer she saw was Michael O'Grady—the perfect Irish Catholic. He too knew of the church's policy. He would not take her testimony and he warned her that no one else there would either; it was a matter for the church to deal with.

Maria was stunned. This monster was going to continue to do this for the rest of his life and no one would stop him, he was untouchable. Shakily, she left the station, knowing that life as she knew it was over.

Over the next few days, she was constantly angry, stewing in her own bitterness, disgust and devastation. She couldn't sleep. She couldn't eat. She went through the motions in the classroom, demanding silence from the girls; there were too many thoughts in her head to deal with their chatter too. The only thing that gave her solace was her garden and her bees, which, thankfully, she'd managed to keep hold of despite her extra duties.

Then one Friday, after all the students had left, the opportunity arrived for her to do something to help. She was in the garden, digging a trench to lay seed potatoes, panting and sweating from the exertion. The weather was fine and warm and the bees were happily humming about, industriously working to maintain their society's order. One of her girls landed on Maria's bare forearm and she stood up. She took off her gloves and picked up the bee with her bare hand. She wasn't afraid of being stung.

She smiled. 'Hello there, darling girl.' And her heart swelled with joy. The little bee wiped her wings with her back legs and then took a few steps along Maria's arm, probably attracted to her sweat. Maria marvelled at the way the sun shone through her fine wings and all the veins turned iridescent purples and blues. There was still good in the world.

But the happy moment burst with the smarmy sound of Peter Cunningham's voice. Maria jumped and spun around.

'Good afternoon, Sister.' He smirked. 'Sorry to frighten you.' He stood rocking on his heels, a small prayer book clasped between his folded hands.

She couldn't speak. Couldn't even look him in the eye. Instead, she gently brushed off the worker bee and got her flying again.

Peter's face dropped. 'Oh, I didn't realise you were working with the bees.' He stepped backwards, trampling spinach seedlings and bumping into the old disused well. He ducked nervously and swatted at air as a bee flew in his vicinity. 'I'm just on my way to afternoon tea with Sister Celine,' he said abruptly. Then the lovely bee who had just been on Maria's arm landed on his shoulder. He froze. At the sight of him paralysed by fear, Maria smiled.

But then his hand shot up, lightning fast, and crushed the bee with the prayer book.

Her smile was dashed. She heard her own sharp intake of breath.

He had killed one of her hive.

She watched as he flicked the dead bee to the ground in disgust. Screwing up his nose, he put the toe of his shoe over its body and ground it into the dirt for good measure.

Maria stared at the remains of her dutiful worker bee, lost for words that anyone could so carelessly destroy something so beautiful and innocent. Then something inside her snapped—that was precisely what he'd been doing to children for years.

'Good day, Sister.' He strode off towards the sitting room for his afternoon tea.

Maria turned back to the garden, filled with waves of bone-penetrating distress. Her knees folded beneath her. Her ears buzzed. She felt sick.

Then her mind cleared.

It was simple. She was a servant of God. God did not condone what Peter Cunningham did to children, of that she was certain, and she didn't need the Vatican to tell her if she was right.

Someone had to stop Peter, and if no one else would do it, she would have to.

It was the strangest thing, but as she knelt on the ground that day she felt a strong, comforting warmth all around her. She felt the presence of Mother Mary and of Jesus too, standing at her side. She would never again let an institution stop her from doing what was right.

Another bee came and landed on her. A beautiful, innocent furry bee. She watched its eyes watching her. Bees had five eyes— two huge compound eyes on the sides, with almost seven thousand lenses in each, and three more on the top of their head. They saw infinitely more than human eyes. She wondered what the world looked like to a bee. Were there more colours than humans could detect? Could they see the goodness of a person just by looking at them? Could they see angels, saints and spirits? With eyes on the top of their heads, they were always looking to the heavens.

Maria and the bee held each other's gaze.

Take me.

It was a whisper, but still perfectly clear, a message from the small insect, herself a master of esoteric communication of the highest order.

Take me.

Peter claimed he was allergic to bees; that was why he hated them. If that was true—though she still suspected it wasn't—then a perfectly placed sting to his throat, around his airway, could kill him in minutes. *If* it was true.

Her eyes drifted to a paper bag on the ground that had held seed potatoes. With calm hands, as though watching herself do it, she opened it and held it near the bee. Without hesitation, the bee walked inside.

Maria lightly scrunched down the top to keep it contained and safe. And then she waited until Peter had finished his meal of whatever food Celine might have prepared for him. His last meal. *If* the allergy claim was true. She prayed that it was.

Tansy had stopped eating and drinking a while ago, though Maria wasn't entirely sure when. But the sun had begun its afternoon descent and the shadows were extending; and her buttocks were aching on the hard bench, which reminded her of her fall yesterday when Ian had invaded her home. She stood up to stretch and Tansy watched her wide-eyed. If she'd been pale when she arrived, she was ghostly white now.

'And did you do it? Did you make the bee sting him?' Tansy squeaked.

Maria looked out at the expanse of undulating land rolling ever downwards to the sea. 'Yes.' A great silence yawned out across the gully below. She knew Tansy wanted to know if Peter had died but was afraid to ask. 'The only people who know about this are you and Ian Tully. And the bees, of course.' Maria managed a small smile of affection for her bees—they'd been there beside her through everything, then and now, the only constant in her life since the day she'd joined the convent.

'Why are you telling me this?' Tansy asked.

Turning to face her, Maria took a deep breath and let it out heavily. 'I guess because you were here when Ian turned up yesterday.'

Tansy's face had now regained some colour, and at the reminder of the man in black who'd scared them both, she set her jaw. 'Tell me about that. Why was he here? What's he got to do with it all?'

There was a protective note in her voice. She'd moved quickly from horror to something else. If Maria was hearing it correctly—and she hoped she was—it was camaraderie.

'He wants an unblemished record in his run towards the position of cardinal. He has a lot to lose, and I could destroy everything for him.'

Tansy shook her head. 'How?'

Maria sat down and resumed her story.

Peter Cunningham had taken his blessed time having afternoon tea. Or maybe it had just seemed extraordinarily long because Maria was waiting to kill him. That would make time slow down, surely. A hysterical giggle erupted at one point—she was plotting to murder a priest. It was ludicrous.

The giggles ceased.

Had she lost her mind?

Her hands began to shake then, and sweat poured from her armpits. She nearly opened the bag and let the bee escape. But all she had to do was think of what that man had done to Michelle Karakas, and to Sarah's two students, and God knew how many others, and the trembling stopped.

At last Peter emerged from the doorway of the sitting room, wiping his brow with a handkerchief and loosening the top button at his neck with the other hand, so full and bloated he was from gorging on the offerings of his stupid, obedient, obeisant nuns. She hated them all in that moment. Hated herself for buying into this elaborate lie.

Her feet began to move, almost as though she had no control over them. She could hear them treading lightly across the grass. Everything was vivid. The blossoming wattle flowers were more intensely yellow than anything she'd ever seen before. A young magpie hopped across the ground and screeched while its mother collected food and neatly deposited it in its mouth. The sun blazed in her eyes. Children's laughter, from somewhere out on the street, sent chills down her spine. As did the sight of Father Peter, walking down the small path, his feet crunching on the stones.

He stopped suddenly, noticing her making straight for him. He must have registered something odd in her face, because he looked wary. 'Sister?'

She stood in front of him. Her heart felt as though it might jump right out of her chest. She stared him straight in the eye. 'Father,' she said, amazed at how even her voice was.

He looked down at the paper bag in her hand. 'Can I help you?' he said uneasily, then covered his mouth as a belch escaped. 'Forgive me.' He wiped his mouth with his hanky. 'I'm afraid I let Sister Celine talk me into one of her new creations today.' His eyes widened. 'She tries hard but she isn't the best cook. But she seemed so pleased with herself I didn't feel I could refuse.'

A pinprick of resistance then. A softening of her resolve. The man had, after all, some sort of heart, some sense of compassion. She felt her mind spin. This was her final moment to back out of the plan she'd hatched while he was eating that last meal—which, as it turned out, had been rather unpleasant, a thought that made Maria both glad and sad at the same time.

'She is known for her unusual creations,' she heard her own voice say, making small talk. 'We stopped allowing her to cook main meals not long after she arrived. But more fool us, we thought she was okay with biscuits and cakes and that sort of thing.'

She had to stop chattering. Her conscience was playing tricks on her, trying to get her to change her mind. With great effort, she regained her focus. 'I wonder if you'd help me with something,' she said, smiling.

Again he looked at the paper bag, but said nothing about it. 'I'm afraid I'm running late for a meeting. Bishop Tully should be arriving here any moment and we have important business to discuss with Mother Veronica. I need to brief Veronica first, so I must press on,' he said, attempting to walk around her.

Maria took a step towards him, to block his way. 'It will only take a moment.' She continued to smile.

He gave in and dipped his head in agreement.

'Thank you. I've been having difficulty with the well,' she said, holding her arm out towards it.

'The well? It's not in use anymore, is it?'

'No, but I've been trying to find a way to restore it; extra water in times of drought never goes astray. But I can't pull up that rope. See there?' She pointed to a long rope that hung from a rafter down into the depths of the well. There was a heavy weight on it of some sort. 'I'm afraid it needs some muscle behind it,' she said, deliberately appealing to his ego. 'Would you mind having a go?'

Peter peered down into the darkness, his hands resting on the edge of the short brick wall—a wall that served more as a visual barrier rather than a safety one by today's standards—then pushed himself back quickly, coughing. 'Ah, there's a strong smell in there,' he said, turning green. 'I think something's died.'

'Oh?' Maria was genuinely surprised.

Peter, grimacing as he steeled himself against the smell, rolled up the sleeves of his cloak and leaned over the edge of the well to grab the rope and test the weight. Here was her chance. She had no idea how she would explain herself if this didn't work. These thoughts were so clear, so calm. And even as she thought them, her hands got to work.

She swiftly opened the top of the bag and plucked out her sacrificial bee, sending out silent gratitude to her. While Peter grunted and murmured to himself about what could possibly be down the well, Maria placed the bee on the back of his neck, holding her lightly by the body to delay her sting. Here, Maria hesitated for a fraction of a second, taking in the bee's dazed circling on his skin as she tried to gather her wits for what she was about to do. Then she applied pressure to the bee's back—not enough to squash her, but enough to annoy and threaten her. And the bee did exactly as Maria wanted.

Peter felt the sting immediately and jumped up, smacking his head on the rafter of the well, his hand slapping at the back of his neck. 'What was that? Was that a bee?' He spun in circles, looking for the offending creature, which Maria thought she'd seen fall down into the loosened neck of his shirt.

'What was what?' her voice said, again as if of its own accord. Her hands were so firmly clenched that she suddenly felt piercing pain in her fingers.

Then Peter began to wheeze, as if having an asthma attack.

She was flooded simultaneously with alarm and fascination, anguish and relief. It was actually working.

Through the revulsion, her conscience shrieked at her. She should help him, get an ambulance, call for help. *Something*.

'Maria,' he gasped, clutching at his neck. His face was turning red with the effort of breathing. 'Help me,' he managed, before leaning his weight against the edge of the well for support.

She stood with him, bearing witness. 'Just try to stay calm,' she said. 'Just try to take slow breaths. It will be over soon.'

He gawked at her sideways, his face now blue, swirling with ugly purples and reds. *He knew*. He knew she wasn't going to help him but was going to watch him die. One of her hands reflexively reached towards him. 'Peter,' she whispered.

Then, from out of nowhere, Bishop Tully ran towards them. 'Peter!' He shook the priest as he slumped further to the side, his mouth open, his tongue visibly swelling. He let go of him and turned on Maria. 'Go and get help.'

But just then, Peter took a huge, violent gasp and fell backwards into the well.

In genuine shock, Maria screamed. And that alerted others and they began running, seemingly from all over. Ian Tully was shouting orders, telling sisters to call an ambulance, to get a ladder, to *do something*. All Maria could do was stand in horror, her hand over her mouth, and stare down into the dark well, knowing that Peter Cunningham was dead in there and it was all because of her.

He'd been right; he was allergic to bees after all.

And she had killed him.

Maria sat with her hands in prayer position, her fingertips just under her nose, staring at nothing in particular on the ground, her mind lost to the past, to that day, to the enormity of what she'd done.

Then Tansy's voice, small and cracking with worry, asked, 'Wasn't anyone suspicious? Didn't anyone see anything?'

Maria cleared her throat and pulled her focus back to the present. The sun had dropped further now, and the chill of the coming night had begun to seep into her back where she sat.

'Ian Tully saw it all,' she said.

'Was he still alive?' Tansy all but whispered.

'No. An ambulance officer was lowered down into the well in a harness, a miner's light on his hat, but called up quickly that Peter was dead. It became a retrieval for the body instead. It was around then that Ian took me away from the scene, gripping me painfully by the arm.

"'I saw you!" he hissed. "I saw you put the bee on Peter's neck. Everyone knows he's allergic to bees. You killed him!"

'Then I told him what I knew—everything Peter had done to Michelle Karakas. I couldn't let him know outright what Sarah had told me. But I had to say enough to keep him quiet.

"'You *had* to have known!" I challenged him. "You're supposed to be the all-seeing all-knowing shepherd of your flock. You are in charge of your priests. This couldn't have slipped by unnoticed." And the look of fear in his eye at that moment sealed his fate to silence too. I told him I wouldn't stop telling people about this until he, the exalted bishop of the diocese, as well as Mother Veronica and anyone else who'd covered up these crimes was in jail alongside me.'

'And he backed down?' Tansy asked, standing now and pacing, pulling her jacket on around her shoulders.

'Of course. He was a shrewd man; he still is. He knew what that kind of publicity could do to his career aspirations, and Peter's "accident" was a clean way for the problem to go away. So he told the police he'd seen Peter lean over the well and lose his balance—which was true, in a way. And no one would have questioned him. I, of course, said the same thing. I told a version of the truth—that I'd asked Peter to help me unblock the well and he fell. The final doctor's report came out, but Peter's body was so broken up . . .' Here, Maria lost the rhythm of her speech for a moment. Her niece came to sit beside her and put her arm around her shoulders. Maria lifted her hand and patted Tansy's gratefully.

'There was so much trauma to his neck from the fall,' she said. 'I guess it had all happened so quickly, and the neck injuries, along with Ian's testimony, and mine, both of us so respected .. well, it was the natural conclusion.'

'And you've both been silent ever since,' Tansy said.

Maria nodded.

'But why has Ian turned up now? What's changed?'

'There's an investigation. We've both been called to give evidence. The truth is going to come out.' A sob jerked out of Maria's chest and she buried her head in her hands.

'It will be okay. It will,' Tansy said, pulling Maria into her arms and rocking her like a child.

Maria shook her head vehemently. 'No, it won't. It can't be.' She clutched at her sister's daughter's arms, overwhelmed by gratitude to have Tansy here, and disbelief that she hadn't yet run screaming from the Haven with this new knowledge. Maria had deliberately cut herself off from the world, but she didn't want to be alone anymore. She wanted to be part of a family. 'Please help me.'

'Of course I'll help you.'

24

Tansy had no idea how she was going to help Maria. She was still reeling from what her aunt had told her, and even though she had the utmost sympathy for the situation Maria had been in, and disgust for Peter Cunningham and the church of which she was a practising member, it was still life-altering information. She knew a murderer. Not only did she know one; she was related to one. Had hugged one. Had loved one almost immediately. It was simply inconceivable.

She'd helped Maria walk back down the path to her little house, shaky on her feet from the confession (and maybe from too much mead). She'd made her a cup of tea and stayed with her until she was certain Maria would be okay and not do something silly, like accidentally leave the stove on. *Or, you know, plot another murder.* Ian Tully would be a good candidate for a second murder.

She had to stop it. Thinking like that wasn't helping anyone. But she'd never been in this situation before. There were no rules about how to process something like this. And to top it off, her mother—Maria's sister—was in her kitchen right now, humming along to Perry Como and wearing Chanel perfume while making scones with Paula and another woman.

'Tansy, this is Christine,' Enid said, waving a flour-covered hand between the two of them in introduction.

'Hi,' Tansy said, confused. 'Wasn't the fete last night?'

'Yes, all done and dusted, but we met Christine there, who was volunteering on the stall, and we all agreed we'd had such fun that we should just continue on as we had been and keep baking. Someone somewhere always needs baked goods,' Enid finished in a flurry, her eyes bright, clearly chuffed at making another new friend and finding a hobby to keep her busy here in Tansy's home while she hid from her husband. Christine plugged in the beaters and poured cream into the mixing bowl, ready to whip.

Tansy felt as though she'd stepped through invisible walls into a parallel universe. These women had no idea whose house they'd entered. It was the house of . . . an accessory after the fact? Was that what she was now? A stone plummeted through her abdomen. Her hands were shaking, she realised, holding them out in front of her, and she hadn't even had too much coffee.

'Tansy, come and help us knead the dough, would you?' Enid asked. 'We've overestimated how much our arthritic fingers can handle.' All three of them laughed at this, as though it was a wonderful joke.

'I was just about to go for a jog,' she said. It was impossible to stay here.

'Oh, to have the energy of the young,' Paula said, snidely.

Tansy chuckled uneasily and left the room. In the bedroom, she pulled on her exercise pants, racer-back bra and singlet, tied her shoelaces extra tight, popped in her bumblebee earbuds, touched again by Dougal's thoughtfulness, secured her phone to her bicep with a velcro strap and turned up the volume on Katy Perry. She ran down the stairwell, out through the chrome and glass security door and down the hill to the road, where she turned right and joined the throng of walkers, surfers and joggers on the boardwalk leading up to the national park.

Sunday was always a busy day on the tracks and she kept her head down, passing barefoot surfers with wetsuits undone to the waist, carrying their long boards under one arm as they jogged lightly up the hill. Families with their kids in sun-smart rashies, caps and sunglasses. Lone joggers, sweat patches seeping down their backs. Pretty European girls in flip-flops and skimpy dresses with their shoulders burned red, chatting excitedly in their native languages. She sidestepped them all easily, an expert now at nego-tiating this track and the hills and the sometimes-too-distracted tourists and loved-up couples who stopped for selfies with the huge blue ocean in the background. She'd been running these tracks for years. It was one of the things that had lured her and Dougal here.

She pushed on up the hills, her muscles churning out lactic acid in protest, the other joggers and walkers thinning now as the paved track ended, becoming bumpy, rocky and sandy footings. She let all thoughts of Maria slip to the background for the moment, giving her mind a break from trying to work out what she could possibly do to help. The eucalyptus and rainforest trees gave way to papery, narrow-leafed coastal scrub. It was more exposed here, a hot and sunny stretch on the way to Hell's Gates. It wasn't unusual to come across a large snake sunning itself on this section of the path, and she kept her eyes peeled for any fellow travellers of the slithery kind.

It felt quieter here, the waves smashing into the cliffs either with less gusto or simply with less surround sound. Not that she could hear much of anything today with Katy Perry singing in her ears. She slowed her pace to cast her eyes across the endless deep blue sea to her left. There were fewer boats out there on the open water. It was prime dolphin-spotting scenery, but she didn't slow down for long. It was endorphins she was after. That glorious runner's high where everything felt easy and painless and the world was reduced to just her and the track, her and her breath, her and her blood pumping to keep her alive.

Finally, she reached Hell's Gates, a massive rocky outcrop that plunged scores of metres straight down into the crashing, roiling sea. The waves rushed in through an opening between rock towers, swirled and spat and sucked and shot out again. She stood well back from the edge, even though others around her ventured close to the precipice, feeling daring, laughing in the face of life's risks. She had been out there, but the drop was dizzying and she felt no need to do it again. Instead she stood with her hands on her hips, sweating and puffing and staring out to the horizon. She plucked the earbuds away and let Katy's voice be replaced by the awesome crashing of water hurling itself at immovable rock.

Was that what she was doing with Dougal? Hurling herself at him in the futile effort to make him move on his position?

She lowered herself to sit on a rock warmed by the sun. Did she *really* want a baby? Or had she simply fallen in love with the fantasy? She'd seen Dougal's tenderness with Hamish and her heart had swelled. She was turning thirty, she was the youngest in her family and in her marriage, and she was afraid of losing everyone and being alone. She'd briefly thought she was pregnant and had convinced herself that this was some sort of sign, that she'd made a terrible mistake, and that she had to do something now before it was too late.

But maybe none of that was true at all. Up until two months ago, when they'd been to see baby Hamish, she'd been totally happy. She hadn't questioned the decision she'd made seven years ago. In the intervening years she hadn't felt as though she was missing out on something vital. The list of benefits for not having children was long. She'd recited it many times. She'd just been spooked, that was all.

She'd made a promise to Dougal and she'd broken it and now she might have damaged their relationship. Nobody's life was perfect, but hers was damn near close enough. What a fool she'd been. Well, no more. She would tell Dougal she'd been wrong and fix this problem before it got out of hand.

She checked her phone. Due to an unfortunately long stopover in Los Angelos, it was still six hours until her husband—her lovely, kind husband—would be in Toronto. She couldn't wait to speak to him and tell him what she'd realised. He'd be so relieved and happy.

Back in her unit and freshly showered, she settled herself in her office to work. The upheavals of the past week had put her behind on the two jobs she currently had going. Isabelle's image project was due tomorrow, and Tansy had an appointment with her after school to talk about it. And Ernest and his rocks were still needing her attention. His mother had sent an email, gently wondering how things were going.

Tansy still felt that the best way to approach Ernest's room was to do what she called ODD—organise, declutter and display. She opened files of previous jobs she'd done that had involved ODD and reviewed the systems that had worked then. She'd successfully modified rooms for intense enthusiasts of dinosaurs, Lego and model planes. This should be no different.

Her mother interrupted. 'The girls are just helping to clean up the kitchen and will be on their way soon. Would you like some tea?' she asked, poking her head into the office.

Tansy turned to face Enid, who was wearing a pinstriped apron. She must have bought that from somewhere around here, Tansy realised. She'd been shopping on her own, or maybe with her new friends, instead of with her daughter. Enid had been here a week now and Tansy hadn't been out with her once; she'd been too busy rushing to help or simply visit Maria, and preoccupied with Dougal's departure.

'Yes, actually, that would be lovely,' she said. Her mother knew exactly how she liked her tea—milky with one sugar and the teabag left in to steep. Her mother and Dougal were the only two people in the world who could make her tea *exactly* as she liked it.

'And I have a fresh ginger sponge on its way out of the oven. Shall I bring you a piece of that too?'

Tansy smiled. 'Okay. Thanks.'

Enid disappeared from the doorway and Tansy returned to pulling together pictures from previous jobs and laying them out on her desk, moving them around in a rudimentary plan for Ernest's bedroom. She checked her notes about the dimensions of the space and slowly a design began to take shape in her mind, though she was struggling to muster much enthusiasm for this job. She felt zapped of passion today.

Her mother returned with a teacup and saucer and a matching plate with a piece of warm ginger cake.

'Smells wonderful,' Tansy said, as Enid placed them carefully on her desk. 'Thank you.'

'My pleasure. You've had so much going on this week, with work and volunteering at the hospice after the flood, and with Dougal's leaving. It's been difficult, hasn't it?' she said, her hand on Tansy's shoulder. 'I hope I haven't been in the way. I've tried to give you your space and occupy myself so you didn't feel you had to entertain me, but I can see what a toll this week's taken on you. Perhaps it would have been better if I wasn't here.'

'No, not at all,' Tansy said strenuously. 'I was only just thinking that it would be lovely, now that things have settled a bit, for you and me to spend some time together. Maybe we could head out tomorrow morning and potter about? I've got an appointment in the afternoon with a girl and her mother—I'm designing a Paris-themed bedroom for Isabelle . . .'

One of Enid's eyebrows arched slightly. She'd never come to terms with the idea of children having bedroom stylists.

'So maybe you could come up the mountains to Montville with me and we could spend some time wandering the shops, then have a long late lunch, and I could leave you somewhere for an hour or so while I meet with Isabelle?'

Enid was clearly thrilled with the idea but was making an effort not to appear too keen. 'That sounds good,' she said, giving Tansy's shoulder a final squeeze before leaving the room.

Tansy worked for most of the afternoon, preparing enough for both Ernest and her meeting with Isabelle tomorrow that she felt competent and efficient once more. And then finally, at nine o'clock that night, Dougal phoned.

'How are you? How was your flight?' she asked, taking the home phone into the bedroom and sitting cross-legged, leaning against the bedhead. She couldn't wait to blurt out her news, to tell him she'd been an idiot and that it would all be okay.

'I'm alright,' he said, sounding weary. 'It's only six in the morning here and I was doped up for most of the flight so I'm totally out of it. But I'm here now, and I've got the rest of the day to hang out in the hotel and sleep, or take a walk around the city.'

'I can't believe you have to turn up at work tomorrow. You need a few days off to get your bearings.'

'I feel like crap right now, but it could be a different story in twenty-four hours, I suppose.' His voice was flat. He didn't sound as though he wanted to talk at all. She was crushingly disappointed but reminded herself that putting her need to talk before Dougal's needs was what had got them into a mess in the first place. So she held onto her news about her change of heart.

'I miss you already,' she said, clutching a pillow to her body.

'You too.' And then he yawned, a big bear yawn.

She was also dying to tell him about Maria's confession, but it clearly wasn't the right time for any news from her end. It would all have to wait. 'Well, I'll let you go and sleep now. But I'm so glad you're there and safe, and I can't wait to talk to you again when you're more with it.'

'Yes, me too. There's so much we have to talk about,' he said, his voice heavy and slow.

'There certainly is. But we've got lots of time.' *The rest of our lives.*

'I love you,' he said.

'I love you too.'

25

George had had a great weekend. His old mate Bart had invited him and Hilda over after church; Bart's wife, Gina, had cooked up a big Sunday roast and the four of them had indulged and shared red wine and laughed and talked and he hadn't once thought about the cases he was working on. Even when Gina had politely enquired as to how it was going, he'd just said it was going as well as could be expected and Gina had left it there and presented a huge pavlova topped with lashings of cream and strawberries. Then they'd brewed coffee and unearthed the Trivial Pursuit board and had a raucous afternoon ending with George and Hilda snatching the final piece of pie to win.

He'd woken this morning thinking—no, *feeling*—that life was pretty good. And as if it couldn't get any better, Hilda had surprised him in the shower wearing nothing but a grin.

He was whistling a tune as he stepped out of the elevator in the big police headquarters in Roma Street. He was humming a ditty as he made his way through the open-plan cubicles on his floor. And he practically sang 'Hello' when he reached his office and picked up his ringing phone, kicking the door closed behind him, bursting with energy.

When the receiver reached George's ear, Blaine Campbell was already in full flow, obviously having forgone any of the introductory pleasantries.

'What? Hang on, slow down,' George said.

'I said check your email straight away. The results on your dead priest came in over the weekend.'

And with that, the line went dead.

George's heart rate kicked up a notch. What had the results shown? He thought about ringing Campbell back and getting him to tell him so he didn't have to wait for the computer; but then again, if Campbell was angry that they'd wasted their time he'd rather read it himself first. While his computer was booting up, he went to make a coffee in the kitchenette, exchanged a quick word with another officer over the sugar bowl, and strode back to his office.

He craned forward in his chair and read the report as fast as he could.

And then he smiled.

He leaned back with his hand on his head, amazed. He'd had a hunch, but he'd never expected this. He read the report again. Then smacked his hand on the desk in victory.

Father Peter Cunningham did *not* die from falling into a well.

Not entirely, anyway.

He pulled out his mobile phone and tapped out a message to Campbell. He couldn't help himself.

Told you so.

And then he poked out his tongue and blew a raspberry at the phone. Boy, this day was just getting better and better.

26

It was a pleasant country drive to Montville, turning off the road before they got to Maleny and passing Spicers Retreat on the left. Spicers. Maybe that was what her parents needed, Tansy mused. Maybe they just needed to get away and reconnect—spice things up a bit? Not that she wanted to spend too much time thinking about that. She manoeuvred the car into a space on the flat dirt behind the cuckoo clock shop, and they started their browsing there.

Inside, whole walls were covered in imported clocks with intricate designs hand-carved into the dark wood, their small pieces whirring and bobbing, little figurines dancing. The clocks ranged in size and price, some costing several thousands. German wooden toys, classical beer steins and cellophane-wrapped ginger-bread filled shelves and nooks.

Enid shook her head sadly. 'We've never even been outside of Australia,' she said. 'We never had the money and it never seemed important. But now? I don't know. It feels like we've missed out. It's too late now.'

'But why?' Tansy asked, studying a miniature cuckoo clock that also functioned as a thermometer.

'We're not young anymore,' Enid said, shifting the weight of her vast handbag higher up her shoulder.

'No, but neither of you has any drastic health issues. If you wanted something more relaxed, you could take a bus tour so you don't have to worry about much more than setting the alarm in the morning and then turning up for dinner on time. It might be just what the doctor ordered for you and Dad.'

Enid shook her head, dismissing the idea quickly. 'Come on, there's lots more to see.'

In the chocolate shop, Tansy bought treats for Maria (if anyone in the world needed chocolate right now it was her) and Belle (Tansy would absolutely finish that care package today). From there, they stopped at a toyshop and Enid bought something for each of Rose's four kids. Tansy followed suit. She and Rose still hadn't spoken since the day last week when Rose had called her in the car. She should take Dougal's advice and invest more time and effort into healing that relationship. If Rose wouldn't come to her then she'd just have to redouble her own efforts. She'd do the same thing she'd done to Maria and simply turn up on Rose's doorstep unannounced, carrying a fruitcake, as well as toys for the kids.

They spent ages in a gorgeous, fussy knick-knack shop, flicking through diaries and notebooks, smelling soaps, testing hand creams, trying on scarves and hats, admiring jewellery and shaking out throw rugs. Enid turned up her nose at the esoteric shop with its tarot cards and statues of Kuan Yin, Buddha, fairies and dragons, so they continued to climb the hill, Enid's breathing becoming laboured, and popped into a clothing store to have a break and try on clothes, with Enid buying a beach coverall. 'Just in case I'm here for a while,' she said.

'Have you spoken to Dad yet?'

Enid set her jaw. 'I don't have anything to say than hasn't already been said.'

'Maybe he has.'

'Then he'd have called, wouldn't he?' she said, and turned away to march on to the next store.

In and out of shops they went until their rumbling bellies called them for lunch. They stopped at Wild Rocket, propping themselves up on the verandah and gulping down the bottle of water the waiter brought to the table. Enid ordered bangers and mash and a cappuccino, and Tansy chose a vegetarian pizza and jasmine tea. The courtyard behind them, near the bar, was busy, especially for a Monday. And the traffic up and down the hill was relentless. Two women walked past with three girls between them and Tansy wondered why they weren't in school. Homeschoolers, perhaps? There were a lot of those on the Sunshine Coast. One girl dragged her feet, looking bored. Another carried an expensive-looking SLR camera around her neck, her eyes scanning the overhanging trees above her head as she walked. The third, probably around eleven, Tansy guessed, blew bubbles through a bubble maker; they rolled out in front of her, shiny baubles reflecting tiny rainbows as they spun in the light.

The bangers came out on a bed of whipped mash, with gravy and an assortment of green vegetables and carrot sticks.

'I always loved bangers and mash as a kid,' Enid said, cutting through the thick sausage. 'Back then we ate it because it was cheap. Now you can order it as a gourmet meal. Times certainly have changed.'

Tansy thought about her mother eating sausages as a young girl and tried to picture her sitting around the dinner table with her two sisters. Maybe now was a good time to talk to her about Maria. Then again, what would she say? That she'd secretly tracked down her mother's sister, had been lying about where she'd been going this past week, had roped Leo into the lie, along with Jordan, Katarina and Toby (and Dougal), and oh yes, had discovered that Maria was a murderer?

Sure. That would go down a treat.

The time was coming, of course. She'd have to confess all of that. If nothing else, she couldn't expect the secret to stay that way for long now that she'd involved Florrie's family. But today, she decided, she would instead tell her mother about the pregnancy test and what was happening between her and Dougal.

Enid listened, exclaimed, sipped on her coffee with a furrowed brow, asked questions, gasped, and finally fell silent as Tansy reached the end of the story. Then she lined up her knife and fork on her plate to signal to the waiter that she was finished, leaned back in her chair and said, 'Tansy, has your period actually arrived yet?'

Tansy smiled thinly. 'Yes, this morning, actually.'

'Oh.' Enid's face fell. 'I just thought maybe . . . it could all have been made simple, the choice made for you both, if you *had* been pregnant after all. God's plan and all that.'

'Yes.' Tansy wasn't sure that would have made things simpler at all, but she could see where her mother was coming from.

'What are you going to do? How will you work this out?' Enid sounded worried.

'Well, we *were* at a stalemate.'

'Like your father and me.' Her mother pursed her lips.

'Yes, interesting, isn't it? We've both been having to examine our values in life and in our marriage. It's not easy. It's not something I'd ever thought I'd have to do. Dougal and I were—are—so compatible, but then everything changed, literally in a single day. The foundations of our relationship, which I thought were so solid, actually began to falter.'

Her mother humphed.

'Dad told me a little about his reasons for not wanting to go to church,' Tansy went on. 'Because of the abuse and the inquiries. How do you feel about that?'

Enid pushed her plate away and sighed, looking uncomfortable both physically and mentally. 'Honestly?'

'Yes, please,' Tansy encouraged.

'I find the whole thing . . .' she struggled for a word, then settled on 'embarrassing'.

'But you don't think people are making all this up, do you?'

'No, no, of course not,' her mother said hastily, lowering her voice and casting her eyes around as if this was a terribly impolite conversation. 'But I wish it would all go away. I just wish we could all go back to normal.'

'Normal? Just believing everything the priest says, you mean?'

Enid shrugged and waved her hands. 'I just wish it hadn't happened at all,' she said, finalising her thoughts.

'Yes, I can understand that.'

Enid reached over and took Tansy's hand, clearly wishing to move on from that topic. 'I'm sorry to hear what's happening with you and Dougal. You know I want you to have a baby. I'd love nothing more, for me or for you, and for Dougal too. But it's not simple once you've pledged to love someone for the rest of your life. I can't just tell you to leave him and find someone else. You've taken vows. That means something.'

'It does,' Tansy said definitively. 'Thank you. You've confirmed what I've decided, and that is that I was wrong. I was momentarily swept away with fantasies and dreams, but the reality is that I love Dougal and he loves me and our future is together, just as we'd always intended it to be. Once I tell him that, all will be well and we can get on with our lives.'

'I suppose,' Enid said, but she sounded unconvinced. She was silent for a long time, watching the cars lining the street and parents leaning on the school fence, waiting for the bell. Finally, she said, 'I think this is a test for you and Dougal. I don't know why, but I have faith you'll get through it and you'll come out stronger at the end.'

Tansy smiled. 'Faith, hey?'

'Yes, why?'

'I spoke to Dad the other day and he said something similar. He said he had faith in your marriage and believed it would be okay.'

Enid let go of Tansy's hand and sat up straighter. 'Did he? He actually used the word faith?'

'Yep.'

'Goodness.'

'I think there's hope for you both as well.'

Not long after, the school bell rang and children began to pour from the buildings into the arms of their parents, car doors opened and closed, and four-wheel drives clogged the narrow road.

'I better get going,' Tansy said. 'I can walk to Isabelle's house from here. Are you right to entertain yourself for an hour?'

'Of course. We haven't even touched the other side of the road yet,' Enid said, signalling the waiter for another coffee. 'I'll knock over the shops there just as soon as the school mayhem has passed.'

'Okay. I'll text you when I'm done,' Tansy said, and leaned down to kiss Enid on the cheek.

Tansy's meeting with Genevieve and Isabelle didn't go as she'd expected. She'd been looking forward to receiving Isabelle's collage of the pictures she'd taken and collected in the past two weeks and seeing the ratings out of ten that she'd given the pictures Tansy had emailed through to her. This was when the real fun usually began.

Tansy slowed her pace as she approached the line of spear-shaped trees on the neat lawn, caught off guard by the emotionally charged argument that appeared to be going on between Genevieve and her daughter, who were standing just inside the garage next to the car, Isabelle's school bag still on her shoulder.

'Hello?' Tansy said cautiously, still walking towards them, concerned now.

Her clients stopped talking instantly and turned to face her. Genevieve's face was red. Isabelle's eyes were bloodshot and her cheeks tear-stained.

'Is everything alright?' Tansy asked.

Isabelle looked back at her mother and then ran into the house, slamming the door to the garage.

Genevieve stepped gingerly towards Tansy. 'I'm so sorry you had to see that,' she said, her face drawn down. She smoothed her hands down her shirt.

'Don't be silly. Are you okay? Can I help?'

Genevieve pressed her hands together. 'I'm afraid we've hit a roadblock. Isabelle's best friend, Skye, has told her that Paris is boring and "so last season".'

'I see,' Tansy said, a tug at the corner of her lips.

'Apparently, New York is the latest thing and anyone who's anyone in the schoolyard is doing New York themes. Isabelle is crushed.'

'Oh, the poor darling.' Tansy was genuinely hurt for Isabelle. Why couldn't children just be children? Why was there so much pressure? Why couldn't someone just want what they wanted without judgement from others? 'Would you like me to start again, working to that theme?'

'No, I'm so sorry to say that we've wasted your time. Of course I will pay you for everything you've done so far,' Genevieve hastened to add. 'But right now she's saying she doesn't want to do her bedroom anymore. All the fun has been taken out of it thanks to Skye's silly words. And to think this is only going to get worse as she heads into the teenage years. I just didn't see this coming at all.'

Tansy had no words of wisdom for Genevieve, nothing that might ease the pain she knew this mother was feeling for her daughter, but she wrapped her in a hug just the same. Genevieve stiffened at first and then hugged her back.

'Thank you for your kindness,' she said, when Tansy stepped away. 'Send me your bill when you're ready.'

As Tansy walked back down the hill to go and find her mother, she pulled out her phone to call Maria. She felt bad that she hadn't called her yesterday. Maria probably thought she despised her now after what she'd confessed. Tansy had meant to phone, but she'd felt so out of sorts yesterday and then got distracted with work and simply forgot. And, also, she might have been a bit nervous to call Maria after her aunt's revelation. How do you carry on a conversation after that?

She pressed Maria's name and the phone rang at her aunt's end, in the cabin at Honeybee Haven. But it rang and rang until, finally, it went to the old-school answering machine.

'Hi, Maria, it's Tansy,' she said after the tone. 'I'm sorry I've missed you. I just wanted to check you're okay. I got caught up with work yesterday and I didn't want you thinking that I . . .'

She fumbled for words. That she judged Maria? That she thought less of her? The truth was that she didn't know how she felt about what her aunt had revealed. But she did know that she still wanted Maria in her life.

'I didn't want you thinking I'd forgotten about you,' she said, smiling, hoping the smile travelled along the phone line to Maria's answering machine. 'I'd like to come up tomorrow, if that's okay? If not, let me know. Otherwise, I'll see you then.'

Tansy answered the door with her toothbrush in her mouth. She'd always been a social flosser and brusher, wandering the house, watching television or carrying on a conversation while attending to her teeth. It still made Dougal laugh after all these years. This morning, she'd been pulling on her sneakers with one hand while the other held the brush when there was a knock at the door.

She flicked the bolts open. Standing there was none other than her father.

'Dad,' she mumbled, and wrapped her spare arm around his neck. 'Come in, come in, I'll just get rid of this,' she said, moving her mouth less and less as toothpaste began to dribble over the edges. She left him to close the door, ran to the bathroom (with her laces still undone), spat and rinsed and was back again just as her mother emerged from the guest bedroom.

'Hello, dear,' Finlay said, scratching the back of his neck. Enid's posture was stiff.

'Come and have a seat, Dad,' Tansy intervened. 'Would you like a cuppa?'

'Coffee, thanks,' Finlay said, easing himself into the soft lounge chair.

Leo appeared then and greeted Finlay, stooping to where he sat and hugging him. 'Good to see you,' he said. 'We've been enjoying

the company of your lovely wife. Thanks for lending her to us.'
He was trying to be charming, Tansy assumed, but it didn't quite
hit the mark. Clearly neither Finlay nor Enid knew what to say.

'Mum, would you like a cuppa too?' Tansy asked, motioning
to Leo to join her in the kitchen.

'Alright,' Enid said, sitting on the lounge opposite Finlay.

Leo retrieved cups from the drawer near Tansy and leaned
towards her, his voice low. 'Are you heading to the Haven today?'
he whispered.

Tansy shot him an alarmed look to tell him to be quiet, but
nodded once.

'Can I come too?' he mouthed.

She nodded automatically, with no time to think about how his
presence might affect her time with Maria. For now, she was just
hoping to keep her parents amicably in the same room together,
not yelling at each other, and no one storming off.

The cups rattled on the tray as she carried them to the coffee
table. Then back in the kitchen, she tamped down coffee into
the filter basket, striving as always for perfectly even resistance
in the grinds—one of the key technical processes in produ-
cing first-class coffee—and turned on the machine. The water
drizzled through the grinds and the tantalising scent of espresso
wafted around the room. Leo nabbed the first cup and excused
himself to have a shower. Tansy repeated the process twice more
then joined her parents, presenting the rest of the coffees, along
with milk and sugar, and took the opportunity to tie her laces.

'What brings you up here?' Enid asked Finlay, taking a coffee.

'I missed my wife and I'm not too proud to admit it,' Finlay
said, his eyes holding Enid's while her cheeks flushed pink.

Tansy wasn't sure where to look; the moment seemed so
intimate. She heard her mother swallow, then watched as Enid

replaced her cup on the table, and took another cup for Finlay and added milk and sugar just as he liked it, stirred it briefly and passed it to him without a word.

'Are you up here for the day?' Tansy asked, touching her dad's arm.

Finlay kept looking at Enid. 'Not sure yet,' he said.

Tansy nodded, accepting that this visit had nothing to do with her and that her presence was neither wanted nor required at this moment. She cleared her throat. 'Well, I have a client to visit today so I'll be off. Leo's coming with me, because he . . . um, well, he's offered to assist,' she stammered, wanting to get through this lie as quickly as possible, 'so we'll both be out of your hair. Dad, you're welcome to stay as long as you like. There's plenty of room.'

Her father looked at her then and gave her a grateful smile. 'Thank you, love.'

Leaving them to it, Tansy knocked on the bathroom door and yelled at Leo to meet her downstairs at the car. He arrived a short time later (men truly didn't need much time in the bathroom, she marvelled), with wet hair and smelling faintly of aftershave. She wondered who'd taught him to do that, to put on just the right amount of aftershave so it wasn't suffocating. Dougal, probably. Then again, maybe it was his mother, Rebecca.

'So why are you coming?' she asked, pulling out onto the road and stopping for a couple of surfers weighed down by boards balanced on their heads.

'No lectures. And I liked your aunt.'

'Is that all?'

He paused a moment. 'And Petrice will be there. I like her too.'

Tansy was surprised, but took a moment to check herself before she spoke. 'How do you know Petrice will be there?'

'We swapped numbers when I was last up there. We've texted a few times.' He smiled then. 'She's quite funny, actually. Her messages make me laugh.'

Tansy was totally perplexed, trying to imagine how that shy, petrified-looking young woman could possibly be funny, even via text.

But then, she'd never have guessed Maria was a murderer, either.

She wondered if she should tell Leo what she knew before they got there. No, it wasn't her story to tell. 'What do you talk about?' she asked instead.

'Books, movies, politics,' he said. 'Writing as well. She writes short stories.'

Interesting.

'So . . . she's a friend?' she asked, trying not to sound too excited but privately thrilled that he'd made a new connection with someone else who was a writer; her mind leapt to the hope that Petrice might convince him to stay at uni until he finished his course (of which there was only six months to go, for God's sake . . . anyone with half a brain could see it would be stupid for him to pull out now).

'Yeah,' he said, a little guarded. 'I'd call her a friend.'

'That's great,' she said, and genuinely meant it. 'You can never have too many friends in life.'

They cruised down the highway for about half an hour, then turned off into the long and winding green flats, where Tansy stopped to choose a bunch of yellow and pink flowers from a bucket on the side of the road, leaving five dollars in the honesty box chained to the wooden shelter, then continued up the steepening slopes to Honeybee Haven.

27

Maria saw the white car pull into the car park and greeted them there. 'I'm glad you're here,' she said, striding to the driver's door. Tansy's face fell as she stepped out of the car, clearly taken aback by Maria's brusqueness. Then Maria noticed Leo in the car too. 'Oh, hello, Leo.'

'What's the matter?' Tansy asked, thrusting a bunch of flowers and a box of chocolate at her. 'You seem upset.'

Maria took the flowers and chocolate, considered them briefly and said thanks, and even she could tell she was being too perfunctory. She needed to slow down. 'The flowers are lovely. And the chocolate will be quite a treat, I'm sure. So many years since I've tasted it.' She brought the package to her nose and inhaled, closing her eyes. 'Oh my.' Her words elicited a smile from Tansy. 'Please, don't mind me, I just have lots I want to show you today,' Maria said.

Tansy brightened. 'Bee things?'

'Yes. It's not overly common for this time of year, but one of my hives has been particularly busy and I have to extract honey. I want to show you how to do it.'

'That sounds like fun,' Tansy said, locking the car and following Maria across the lawn. Leo came too. 'Leo's come along hoping to see Petrice. Is she here today?'

'She was,' Maria said, 'but she's gone home.'

'Oh, why?' Tansy said.

Leo looked towards the dining hall as if hoping Petrice might still emerge. 'I'm sorry, Leo. Sometimes things just get too much for her and she needs to retreat. It can hit her quite suddenly.'

'It's okay,' he said, a small smile betraying at least a hint of disappointment. 'I'm sure you could use my help.'

'Would you like to work with the bees too?' she offered. Everyone liked to feel useful.

His smile brightened. 'Yeah, that sounds great.'

She considered Leo's face. It was such a gentle face. Not unmanly. But kind, yes, that was the word. He had a kind face. She didn't know why, but that observation made her feel sentimental, but for what she wasn't sure. Her father, maybe. He'd had a kind face.

She mentally pulled herself together. Over the past couple of days she'd experienced an endless flow of emotions. It wasn't just that she'd made her confession to Tansy, though obviously that was big enough. It was because she was 'getting her affairs in order'—preparing to leave this place. And that was why it was important to teach someone else as much as she could. Once she left here, Michaela would need to find a new manager. She'd briefly thought that Petrice might be able to step up. But realistically, and certainly after today, Maria knew that wouldn't be the case.

Petrice had been listening to the radio in the car on her way up to the Haven this morning. The hourly news had come on, something she'd learned to avoid in case of random triggers that could affect her mood. But she'd been distracted and forgot to turn it off in time. The lead story was about a man who'd burnt down his house with his children inside. Petrice had snapped off the radio, but it was too late. She'd managed to get to work but hadn't lasted long. Fortunately, Maria had phoned her psychiatrist and been able to secure an appointment for her for later today.

Still, she wouldn't give up on her altogether. Petrice had come a long way since she started here three years ago and Maria felt great pride that she'd played a part in that. Petrice trusted her, a bold and brave step for someone who'd been so mistreated. Maria wanted Petrice to have a job even after Maria herself was gone, but she wasn't ready for a management role.

She'd then entertained the idea that Tansy might be able to slip into the role. It was ridiculous, of course. For one thing, Tansy was leaving for Canada. And she already had a career; she didn't need another. But the thought had persisted, helping to quell her anxiety about leaving this place and her precious bees; she needed to believe that she'd be handing it all over to someone she trusted.

She glanced at Leo again, and wondered.

'Are you sure you're alright?' Tansy asked quietly, out of earshot of Leo, putting her hand on Maria's arm. 'I know that what we talked about on Saturday would have brought up a lot of *stuff* for you.' She was biting her lower lip and frowning.

Poor Tansy. What a load she must be carrying now. Her elderly aunt was a murderer. What a mad world it was.

'Come on, let's go see the bees,' Maria said.

At her house, she kitted Leo and Tansy out in layers of protective gear. Tansy shrugged into her full beekeeping suit with much more ease this time, Maria noticed. She walked more confidently towards the hives too. Leo carried the big food-grade bucket with the new empty frames inside. The wooden frames knocked against the side of the bucket as they walked. Maria carried the smoker, the bee brush and the J-knife, and led the way to the hive with a heavy sense of occasion. How many more times would she get to do this?

'Do you collect the wax as well?' Leo asked.

'I do. I use it to make candles, lip balms and hand cream, and body butters. The body butters are particularly rewarding, and good sellers. You whip them up with an electric beater and they're so fluffy.' Maria felt a small pang, a yearning, actually, to use those beautiful body butters on her own dry, ageing skin. 'You can use the wax to waterproof your shoes, too,' she added.

Tansy held up a frame with preformed hexagonal wax cells, studying them. 'Each cell is identical,' she marvelled.

'Well, they're done by machine, but the bees can do it too. They're master mathematicians, making absolutely perfect honeycomb.'

'That's wild. I couldn't do that with a ruler and set square,' Leo said, eyes wide, impressed.

Maria smiled, pleased with his wonderment. If only more people understood how utterly priceless bees were, and how inexpressibly clever. Instructed by God. They had to be. They lived such short lives and yet they seemed to hold all the knowledge in the world and conquer the equivalent of mountains in that time. What a gift they were.

When they got to the hives, Maria showed Tansy and Leo how to pull out the heavy frames full of honey, removing them slowly so as not to squash a single bee in the process. She showed them how to hold the frame with the cells facing downwards and watch to see if any honey fell out, which would indicate it wasn't yet ready to be harvested. How to gently brush the crawling bees off the frame, moving the wet bristles in an upward motion so that any busy bees with their backsides in the air and their heads inside the cells would be brushed out, rather than forced down and squashed.

'You must never kill a bee,' Maria said. 'It is of the utmost importance that not a single bee is killed.' She faced Tansy, her eyes drilling into hers through their face nets.

'Yes, of course,' Tansy agreed. 'I would never—'

'Every one of these bees is precious. Every one. And it is the beekeeper's duty to honour their lives. It is not a duty to be taken lightly. Do you understand?'

Both Tansy and Leo nodded vigorously.

Maria nodded too, satisfied, and went back to her task of imparting knowledge. She showed them how to replace the full frame with a new, empty one, ready for honey to be laid straight away. She checked the other frames, partly filled and capped, and again explained the importance of ensuring there was enough honey to keep the bees going if the great weather they'd had suddenly turned and the bees had to bunker down and look after themselves instead of foraging. As she worked, to her pleasure Maria managed to fall into the state she had come to think of as bee meditation—a timeless zone of bliss.

On the way back, Tansy and Leo carried the bucket between them, weighed down by three full frames of honey, totalling over ten kilograms. Some bees followed them, smelling the honey, or maybe wanting to protect it. But they left the bees behind at the front door of the cabin, painstakingly removing individuals from their bee suits, from the bucket and frames and then closing the screen door behind them. A few persistent girls hung around the door, buzzing gently.

'I extract honey the old-fashioned way,' Maria said. 'I like to be as hands-on as I can be, and it's also the cheapest way to get the honey, rather than spending money on equipment that makes life easier but just makes people lazy, I think.' They hauled the bucket into the middle of the kitchen floor and left it there while Maria pulled out more food buckets of the same size, a large metal spoon, bowls, knife and a large metal strainer. 'The trick is to get it as soon as possible once you've taken it from the hive, because it will still be warm and runny, at almost human body temperature.'

Maria placed one of the frames inside a big stainless-steel bowl holding it vertically, and worked a sharp knife down over the surface, the wax caps falling into the dish, releasing the honey. Her heart rate increased with the effort, her biceps complaining a touch with the resistance from the wax. You had to work hard to win the prize—bees had a lot of defence systems to get through. Then she placed the strainer over the bucket and rested the frame on them, and with her spoon began to scrape down the remaining wax and honey into a big, sticky orange mess.

'Gravity is our friend here,' she said, puffing slightly. 'We'll leave the honey to strain into the bucket overnight and tomorrow there will be clean wax on top,' she touched the strainer, 'and beautiful honey in the bottom.'

'What about those?' Tansy asked, pointing to the heap of caps in the first bowl.

'These we wrap in some muslin cloth and hang over another bucket and wait for the honey to drip out.' Maria smiled. 'And then we bottle it all and take it to market to sell for the Cambodian children.'

'It's gorgeous,' Tansy said.

Leo took a turn then, carefully lifting the second frame and repeating what Maria had shown them while she made subtle adjustments to his technique. He listened closely to her instructions and asked thoughtful questions. She liked him even more.

'It's been so nice having you here,' she said suddenly. 'Both of you. I've taken great pleasure in passing on my bee knowledge to you. I regret now that I haven't done more of that, run workshops and so on. People could have come and stayed here for a weekend and I could have taught them how to start a hive. The bees are running out of time.'

'You still could,' Tansy said, leaning against the kitchen bench, leaving Leo to do the muscle work. 'There's a growing bee awareness out there. Everywhere I look now, I see bees. It would be a great time to start and a way to raise even more money for the orphanage.'

Maria shook her head and washed her hands under the tap, the honey dissolving and disappearing down the drain. 'I'll be going away soon,' she said quietly.

'What do you mean?' Tansy passed her the knife and spoon to wash too.

'I have to confess to the police what I've done.'

Leo turned to face them then, confused. Tansy flicked a quick look his way but waved a hand at him to tell him not to get involved.

'What? No, you don't. Why would you do that?' Tansy said, her voice high-pitched.

Maria wasn't bothered by Leo's presence. Everyone would know soon enough. 'I need to give evidence against Ian Tully and he's made it perfectly clear that if I speak against him he'll turn on me. It's better if it comes from me first. Besides, my name is already on the list of people they're interested in. They'll be calling for me any day now.' She turned off the tap and faced Tansy, wiping her hands on a tea towel. 'The time has come.'

'No, it hasn't.' Tansy grabbed Maria's hands and took the tea towel off her, tossing it to the bench. 'Maria, you had no choice. I can see that plain as day. You did the only thing you could do given the circumstances you were in.'

Maria shook her head. 'There are always other options. Always. I made my choice and, yes, I could justify it at the time, but I can't anymore. I took a human life. Only God has the right to do that, never one of us. It's time I faced up to what I did and let justice take its course.'

Leo stood stock-still. Tansy paced, her jaw working. Maria was touched that in the short time they'd known each other, she and her niece had formed such a strong bond.

'I can see you're a determined woman,' Tansy said carefully.

Maria smiled. 'That's true.'

'Please, at least get some legal advice before you do anything. If money's an issue I can help. Let me help you.' Tansy stopped speaking and looked around the cabin, noted the piles of books, the boxes with knick-knacks ready to go to a charity bin, the bucket of cleaning products. Comprehension registered on her face. 'You're getting ready to leave,' she said.

'It's inevitable. I'll be going to jail,' Maria said, surprised at her own calmness. This morning she'd felt panicky and unable to concentrate. But now the steps leading to the final moments of her life as she knew it felt laid out. She only had to put one foot in front of the other and soon it would be over.

Tansy held up her hand sternly. 'Stop. Stop this. Right now.' She pulled out her mobile phone.

'What are you doing?'

'I'm finding you a lawyer, before this goes too far.' Tansy's hand hovered over the screen as she read something. 'Oh, shit.'

'What?'

'Toby, your great-nephew? Jordan and Katarina's son?'

'Yes,' Maria said, irritated. It wasn't as if she was going to forget the only family she'd had contact with since she'd joined the convent.

'He's off school, sick today, and staying with his grandmother— Florrie, your sister . . .'

'I know who my sister is, Tansy.'

'. . . and he told her that he met you. Florrie phoned Jordan, who had an early shift at the hospital today, furious, and he was forced to confess everything. And now Florrie is on her way to my house with Toby, looking for answers.'

Maria lifted her chin and took a deep breath. 'Well.'

'Yes.'

Maria wasn't sure how she felt at that moment. There was a fleeting impulse to tell Tansy that she would go home with her, to see her sisters before it was too late. There was a curious numbness towards this woman, Florrie, someone she didn't even know; all she knew of her was what she'd been like as a child. And there was anger and hurt on her own behalf, that even the mere fact of Maria's existence was somehow enough to enrage her two sisters.

Tansy rubbed her forehead. 'Look, I'm going to have to go and deal with this. Can you please just not do anything while I'm gone? Let me help you sort this out calmly and rationally.'

Maria didn't say anything.

'And stop packing,' Tansy ordered, hugging her goodbye. 'Leo, we're going.'

'Sure,' he said, looking from one woman to the other but not saying anything else. Maria liked him more by the minute.

Then Tansy kissed Maria on the cheek and left. Leo raised a hand in parting and followed her, leaving Maria alone with her prized honey and a single-minded determination to go through with exactly what she needed to do.

Tansy had no idea what to expect when she walked in the door, but from the number of cars in the visitors' spaces—cars she recognised as belonging to her family members—she anticipated conflict. She paused at the front door of her apartment; she could hear lots of voices inside. Next to her, Leo put a steadying hand on her shoulder. She'd given him a plot summary of Maria's story while they drove. He'd listened quietly, and then said, 'I know I shouldn't be, but I'm kind of impressed. Not that she killed someone, exactly; obviously that's wrong and I'd never condone murder. But, I don't know, it seems courageous, somehow.'

'I think I know what you mean. I certainly don't want to see her go to jail. But I'm sorry for getting you into this mess,' she said to him now, grateful that he was there beside her. There was something about standing next to a tall, strong young man that made her feel instantly better prepared to face the onslaught to come.

'It's okay.' He shrugged, dropping his hand. 'I don't actually think it's as big a deal as you think it is. This part, anyway, dealing with your family. The murder?' He wobbled a hand and grimaced. 'That one I'm not so sure about.'

Tansy let out a small laugh at the ludicrousness of it all.

Down the short hallway and into the lounge, it was instantly clear that the gathered relatives did in fact think it was a big deal. There were eight people in her lounge room (she was momentarily happy to see Rose there too), ranging from eighty-nine-year-old

Uncle Alastair down to her three-year-old niece, Amy. Even Jordan was there, having finished his shift, apparently, and still in his light purple nurse's uniform. Katarina was the only one missing, by the looks of it; she was at school today. Enid and Florrie were bickering, with tears from Enid. As Tansy and Leo entered, they all stopped and stared at her.

'Hi,' she said, forcing a smile. 'What a lovely surprise.' She allowed a hint of sarcasm and a lacing of irritation to infuse her words. Leo was right: this wasn't a national emergency that required a council of war.

Then again, she *had* wanted a family reunion. Seemed she might be getting it now.

Enid thrust herself to the front of the scrum, a tissue in her hand and her face stony with anger. She looked from Tansy to Leo, her eyes flashing betrayal, and peered past them down the hallway, searching for Maria, Tansy assumed. The room was silent, except for Toby's *broom-broom* noises as he pushed a Lego truck across the rug on the floor. The atmosphere was heavy with anxiety, outrage and anticipation.

Her mother worked her mouth for a few seconds before she hissed, 'Where have you been? Have you been with *her*? Have you been with her all this time, lying to me?'

Tansy bit her lip; she wasn't ashamed of tracking down Maria and getting to know her, but she was ashamed of the lying. She dropped her eyes to the floor and her voice was quiet as she admitted the unpalatable truth of her deception. 'Yes.'

Enid slapped her. The assault was so swift that Tansy was left speechless. She covered her cheek where the blow had struck. But the physical sting was nothing compared to the feelings of injustice and humiliation that quickly followed.

Several voices of protest were raised in Tansy's defence.

Leo stepped in front of Tansy protectively.

Enid's hands flew to her face in shock and she spun around to lean into her husband's chest.

And Tansy burst into tears.

28

As it turned out, Maria hadn't had the chance to make her confession yesterday after all, because she simply ran out of time. Today, a big booking was coming through for an African drumming camp, staying for five days. So after Tansy and Leo had left, she'd launched herself into work. Every bed in the place was booked, as well as many tent sites. And since Petrice had left early, Maria had to play catch-up with her offsider's unfinished chores, including the food prep, and then spent this morning rapidly making up beds and sweeping cabin floors. Trav was here today with his ride-on mower, tidying up the tent sites and trimming the central grassed area where the group would meet to form their drumming circle.

The group had stayed here before and Maria had enjoyed it, mostly. The members were friendly, earth-loving people, with dreadlocks and fisherman pants and leather straps tied at their necks. The camp was run by a couple in their forties who'd been drumming their whole lives and played professionally. And they always brought along a master drummer from Ghana to lead the group. Throughout the day there was music, raucous and energising, and you simply couldn't help but feel happy as the circles played. The group always wanted vegetarian food, and that was okay with her. She had a lot of vegetables in the garden she could use, and it saved money on meat.

The only thing she didn't like about them was the marijuana. Even though she had a no-drugs policy, she knew they brought it out late at night; the sweet smell floating on the air was unmistakable. But she turned a blind eye, because they were good customers and the orphanage's needs came first. As she finalised the menus, she thought how much she would miss them. This would be the last time she would be favoured with their vibrancy.

As soon as she was finished with her preparations, she told herself, she would dig out the number for George Harvey. But before ringing him she would email Michaela in Cambodia and explain everything. She wanted to do it now, when she had the time to do it properly, in case she was whisked away after her chat with Inspector Harvey. She was leaving Michaela in a terrible position, and at the very least Michaela deserved to hear the story from Maria first. She decided that she would give Michaela a day to absorb the news and get back to her with any questions or, indeed, with her horror, and then she would get this confession to the police over and done with.

The ocean breeze caressed Tansy's cheek, still tender from her mother's slap. She'd come here to the beach in an attempt to improve her foul mood. She'd already tried to distract herself from yesterday's family circus by finishing off her proposal for the rock boy's bedroom design and emailing it through to his mum. But she was still morose.

Slipping off her beach shoes and burying her toes in the soft white sand, she ached for Dougal's company. He never tried to talk her into getting into the water, even though she knew her fears were irrational and it was pretty crazy since they had deliberately bought an apartment right on the beach. He simply accepted that she loved the ocean as much as he did, but from the safety of the sand. His only disappointment, he said, was that he didn't get to see his hot wife in a bikini more often.

She spread out her towel on Main Beach in the shade of a large pandanus tree close to the boardwalk, the resorts at her back, and sat looking out at the azure water. Slowly, her feelings of anger, sadness and frustration eased. The ocean exhaled waves and white water onto the shore, and inhaled the water back out to sea. The sand was blindingly clean and white on the other side of her sunglasses. A few sticks of driftwood lay around her and she picked one up and began doodling in the soft grains at her feet, squishing her blue-painted toenails through it.

The apartment sat empty. Leo had left before Tansy got out of bed—she didn't know where he'd gone—and Enid had left with Finlay yesterday after the family's intervention into Tansy's behaviour. Her fingers touched her cheek and a new surge of anger rose up. How dare her mother hit her! As though they were in an episode of *The Bold and the Beautiful*. And in front of everyone, as if Tansy was a toddler in need of discipline. Except she'd never been hit at all, not even as a small child. Her mother had always been vehemently anti-smacking.

Immediately after the slap, Aunt Florrie had urged everyone to calm down and find a seat so they could talk things through rationally. Clearly ashamed, Enid had mumbled an apology to

Tansy, but held herself stiff behind crossed arms. Florrie had tried to mediate, but her own hurt at what she'd learned, not from her son but from the mouth of her grandson, showed in the deep creases on her face. As usual, she was wearing loose yoga pants and a tight-fitting top that showed off the remarkably toned and strong upper body that made twenty-somethings envious, let alone other women in their late sixties. Her twenty years as a yoga teacher had clearly done wonders for her physical health.

'I don't understand how this has all come about,' she began, addressing Tansy evenly. 'Can you explain it to us?'

Tansy explained that she'd tracked down Maria easily enough by searching online, and sent her a letter. She knew the family didn't talk to Maria but she wanted to get to know her on her own terms, without other people's opinions muddying the waters.

Florrie had nodded, but her calm veneer quickly started to slip. 'But why didn't you tell me that Maria was living not far from us, and . . .' She began to take emotion-charged breaths. 'How could you put my son in the position of keeping that secret from his own mother? I feel deeply betrayed, Tansy, I don't mind you knowing.' She gave a long, slow exhalation then—a yoga relaxation breath—and closed her eyes for a moment while her husband rubbed her back.

'Don't blame Tansy,' Jordan said reasonably, rubbing his eyes, likely tired from his morning shift. 'She was obviously going to tell you all and was just waiting for the right time, weren't you?' he finished, turning to Tansy.

'Of course,' Tansy said shortly, a little exasperated by the telling-off and still mortified by her mother's slap.

Jordan, concerned about the fighting going on in the room in front of his son, on a number of occasions signalled to people to quieten down and take a breath, and eventually pulled out his phone, loaded up a movie and relocated Toby to another room to watch it, away from the hullabaloo.

Florrie's husband spoke up in Tansy's defence. Alastair, twenty years Florrie's senior and equally impressive in his qi gong outfit of long white cotton pants and shirt, was more pragmatic than his wife. 'All things happen for a reason,' he said to Florrie. 'It's good this has come to light. You'll get past this moment and something beneficial will come of it, you'll see.' Florrie looked irritated; it must be difficult to maintain inner peace all the time, Tansy thought.

Meanwhile, Rose was running around after Amy, who wanted to explore the apartment. Her sister looked awful, actually. Her dark green pants were baggy around her hips and she had fastened a belt tightly around her waist to keep them from slipping down. Her long hair was flat and lank and there were dark circles under her eyes. What had happened to her? She chimed in from time to time as the child's wandering allowed.

'People do what they think is best at any given time,' she said quietly, fishing a small notebook and a sheet of fairy stickers out of her handbag to encourage Amy to sit still and entertain herself. 'I'm sure no one set out to hurt anyone.'

'Thank you,' Tansy said, sending her a grateful look. Rose smiled at her, but her face didn't light up. Tansy was just about to ask her if she was okay when Enid gasped theatrically.

'You were going to spring Maria on us at your birthday party, weren't you?'

Tansy hesitated a second, but the time for lying or delaying the truth had well and truly passed. 'Yes.'

'Unbelievable.' Enid shook her head. 'Disgraceful behaviour.' Her diatribe was cut short by Finlay's hand on her arm. He was trying to stay on the fence between his wife and daughter as much as possible.

They were all annoying Tansy now. She tried to explain. 'You see, the reason I wanted to have a party was because Dougal had the transfer to Canada, and we were going to—'

She was halted again by cries of outrage from Florrie, who was further offended that she had no idea that Dougal had left the country.

'Oh, I thought I told you,' Enid said vaguely, frowning.

'How many more secrets are you keeping?' Florrie asked Tansy. Then, glaring at Jordan, 'Did you know about this too?'

Jordan squirmed on the stool at the breakfast bar. 'Yes.'

'Jordan,' Florrie said, as calmly as she could manage, 'is there anything else you'd like me to know? Anything else you haven't seen fit to tell me?'

Jordan's jaw unhinged as he glanced around the room, and he grunted a few noises as though trying to hold back words.

Florrie arched a beautiful, menacing white eyebrow. 'Well?'

He half covered his mouth as he said, 'Katarina's pregnant. She's four months along. We hadn't told anyone yet because—'

'Oh, for fuck's sake.' Florrie threw up her hands dramatically, all pretence of yogi mindfulness gone. 'Anyone else? Come on, we're all here, let's get it out in the open.'

'Mum!' Jordan said, trying to get Florrie's attention, cranky she'd cut him off with his baby news.

'I've filled out the forms to defer from uni,' Leo said.

'Leo!' Tansy slapped the cushion beside her. 'Why would you do that? Have you told Dougal?'

'No. I don't need his permission,' Leo said mildly.

Tansy groaned. 'Perfect.'

'I don't want to be Catholic anymore,' Finlay confessed, scratching under his chin.

'Shh!' said Enid. 'We haven't decided on that yet.'

'Well, it's not for you to decide. It's *my* choice,' Finlay bit back. 'And the parish leaders council was actually very supportive.'

'You went to the council, aired all our dirty laundry, and you did it while I was away?'

Tansy rolled her eyes.

'Well, I could hardly go and ask their advice while you were there, could I?' Finlay argued.

'But isn't this why you're here? For us to sort it out?' Enid said, looking stricken now, her hand at her chest. Tansy almost felt sorry for her mother, despite the slap. Enid's world was falling apart.

Little Amy tugged on Rose's arm. 'Mummy, I've done a poopie in my pants,' she said.

Rose let her head drop backwards. 'Not again,' she said wearily. And four children down, Tansy reflected, Rose would be entitled to feel tired.

'That's a coincidence,' Alastair smiled. 'I have too.'

The room went still, staring at Alastair's serene, elderly face.

'Yes, my husband has faecal incontinence,' Florrie said sourly, adding her confession to the list. 'And we don't have sex anymore either, just in case you're wondering.'

'Bathroom's that way,' Tansy said, pointing across the room.

'Mum.' Jordan, standing now, demanded that Florrie focus on him.

'Do you want to come with me?' Alastair asked Amy, holding out his hand.

'Okay,' she said, and they tottered off together to take care of the situation in their pants.

There was a pause then and collective deep breathing as everyone corralled their emotions. Rose sniffed and wiped her nose.

'What's the matter, Rose?' Tansy asked, feeling some pressure lift off her now that the focus had been shifted to the others as well.

'I have a confession too,' Rose said, tears welling up now. She sat gingerly on the padded armrest near Enid. 'Sam wants a divorce,' she whispered.

'Why?' Enid screeched. 'He can't. You've been married in a Catholic church.'

'Because I had an affair,' Rose said, and then broke down into sobs.

'Oh, Rose. How could you?' Enid scolded.

'Is this why you've been avoiding me?' Tansy asked.

Rose pinched the top of her nose and shrugged, deflated, while Enid continued to chastise her.

'The *reason* we haven't told anyone about the baby yet,' Jordan shouted, his hands clenched at his sides as he attempted to cut through the clamour. Florrie was now actively performing 'lion's breath' yoga exhalations, making roaring noises as she stretched up high then flopped to the floor. But Jordan was determined to get his mother's attention, and continued loudly, 'We had the early genetic tests done and it looks like the baby might have Down syndrome.'

Florrie snapped up tall where she was standing near the wall. 'What?'

'We didn't want to do the amnio due to the risk of miscarriage, and'—Jordan's voice wavered—'we didn't want anyone to try to talk us into ending the pregnancy.'

Tansy gaped at him, and she wasn't the only one. Naturally, the room erupted into questions and expressions of sympathy and tea making, and all of the waves Tansy had made in her family's little pond were forgotten for the rest of the afternoon, along with everyone else's personal dramas. Still, Enid had left that evening with Finlay, clearly happier to be in the company of her Catholic ship–jumping husband than her lying and scheming daughter.

Now, Tansy wiped her sandy hands and pulled out her phone to check the time. Toronto was thirteen hours behind, making it ten o'clock at night for Dougal. She missed him fiercely; wondering if he was still awake, she tapped out a quick text to see if he would answer. But after a few minutes of waiting, with no response, she gave up.

Dancing across on the wind came the ubiquitous 'Greensleeves' music of an ice-cream truck as it rumbled into the reserved space next to the beach, just a short walk from where she sat. After everything that had happened yesterday, and with all the lingering uncertainty about what was to come, today suddenly seemed like a good day to indulge in an ice cream—a double chocolate-dipped cone, with sprinkles, nuts, whipped cream and extra chocolate on top.

29

Sitting at his desk, George drew bubbles around names on his notepad and joined them with dots, soft lines or hard lines, each one indicating a degree of connection.

It had been three days since he had received the results of the tests on the dead priest, and he'd barely slept since. His mind whirred with possibilities, and the excitement of uncovering a new layer of mystery kept a constant flow of energy through his belly.

Hilda wasn't entirely impressed with his ebullience. 'It's macabre,' she'd said, squinting behind her turquoise-framed glasses. 'I mean, do you necessarily *want* to uncover more evils in the past?'

Initially, George had been taken aback by her response. For so long now he'd been slogging away on these cases with no real light at the end of any tunnels; rather, it was like chasing shadows in the dark and slamming face first into brick walls. There was rarely any actual evidence other than testimonies, and many of those were shaky. To have real, hard evidence in his hand? It was delicious, actually. He had even developed a sliver of respect for Blaine Campbell, a man he'd thought vulgar with his hunt-to-kill attitude.

Still, he could see where Hilda was coming from, and he toned it down in front of her and especially if he thought the kids might overhear. He did pause to wonder if he was beginning to lose his humanity in this quest. He didn't actually want to end up like Campbell, desensitised and clinical, forgetting why he had joined the force in the first place—to serve people, not processes. At least, that was why George had joined up; he couldn't speak for Campbell.

But it was hard to contain his excitement, especially given the new leads he'd uncovered since Monday. Well, they weren't *new*, exactly; they were names that had cropped up in some of the many testimonies he'd taken from people who'd claimed the dead priest had abused them. Some of the claims came from as far away as Longreach. A few weeks ago he'd sent out letters to all of the people named, just covering his bases in case he needed to call on them. And now he was drawing connections, webs that held the whole story together, with Father Peter Cunningham hanging like the black spider in the centre of it all.

The names were of nuns, sisters who had been serving at the time of Cunningham's employment in the church. Just yesterday he'd flown to Roma, which was a five-hour drive west of Brisbane, to see Sister Sarah Townsend, now in her mid-seventies and living with her extended family in a sprawling homestead on a cattle property the size of a small country. Two women who had provided testimonies had said they'd told their teacher at the time, Sister Sarah. She was officially retired from teaching but was still a member of her order and served in her community, still tending to the poor and disadvantaged, assisting them with job placements and food drives, and was a loud advocate for women's rights and protection in isolated rural towns. She went out with the flying doctor once a month, offering counselling and support, and was a guest teacher with the School of the Air.

Sarah Townsend was a spry woman, with a sun-weathered face that had seen a good deal of skin cancer treatment, given the amount of discoloration and white and brown spots he could see in the shade cast by her Akubra. But she walked confidently, strongly. A woman of the land through and through. When he arrived she was standing on the wide verandah of the homestead, a mug of tea in her hand, dressed in trousers, a long-sleeved shirt and classically Australian stockyard boots. The cattle were being mustered today, and from the other side of the square green oasis that surrounded the stately, immaculately kept old building came the sounds of stockmen whooping and dogs yapping. Red dust swirled in the air, along with the scent of dried cow manure.

She'd greeted him with a firm handshake and introduced him to a few family members, including her older sister, who was president of the local branch of the Country Women's Association, and a grandniece with a baby in her arms, moving slowly in a rocking chair and swatting at flies that circled the babe's head. Then she'd ushered him inside to the air-conditioned office, all dark wood and high-backed chairs.

'I've been waiting for you,' she said, sitting opposite him. A tall bookcase rose behind her, groaning under a collection of books covering topics from cow handling to needlepoint and rural accountancy. He flicked his eyes over them, longing to browse the titles, but he had no time to waste; he was flying home that afternoon and they had a lot to get through. Sarah sat tall and straight, no sign of arthritis or weakness of any kind. No sign of slowing down at all.

'Thank you for seeing me at such short notice,' he said, taking out his notebook and clicking his pen, then setting his phone to record.

'Not at all. I'm pleased you're here. We should have spoken a long time ago.' Her voice faltered just a fraction as she gazed out the window and off into the distance, her eyes taking on the same lost look he'd seen on so many of his subjects' faces.

He waited a beat, allowing her to summon up the memories she needed. And when she was ready—a moment signified by a breath in and a direct gaze—he began. 'Tell me everything you can about your time in the church during the years that Father Peter Cunningham served.'

And she did. She skipped around a little, from her early days in the convent and her expulsion—her word—out to Longreach, before describing the grievous time she spent serving alongside the corrupt priest. She conveyed her extreme distress at being bound by the policy of silence, explaining her terror of excommunication and her agony over having to keep the secret, and the searing guilt that would follow her to the grave.

George listened, nodding, trying not to judge her, trying not to condemn her. They were different times. And from what he'd heard from so many others, even those who'd tried to do the right thing had been shut down and silenced. There was no reason to believe that she would have had any more success.

'Tell me about the different nuns you served with, the priests, the bishops, the altar boys, the . . .' he swallowed, 'the victims.'

There were tears. There were always tears. George couldn't say he was used to them, but on his good days he felt some sort of peace with this process—the letting go. And tears were inevitable.

Over the years, George's understanding of this whole sordid, tragic mess had changed. The original brief for this investigation was to bring to light everyone who had covered up these crimes. And he'd been prepared to rage against them all. But he now knew it was so much more complicated than that. What he'd come to understand was that there were so many victims in this horrid web of crimes, beyond those directly abused. There seemed to be an endless line of secondary and tertiary victims. And Sarah was one of them, bullied, harassed and threatened into silence. Forced to bear the cruel weight of her secrets because the power of the patriarchal institution in which she was employed, and of the patriarchal society in which she'd lived, which had offered her little protection outside the walls of the church, was simply too great.

He passed her a box of tissues that was sitting on the desk, then popped out of the room to politely enquire if someone might bring them tea. The friendly grandniece came shortly afterwards with a tray bearing a full matching set of teapot and cups and saucers as well as fresh scones and cream.

After a few sips of tea, colour returned to Sarah's face and the slight shaking in her hands subsided. She sniffed away the last vestiges of emotion.

And that was when she began to talk about the letters. The years and years of letters between her and Sister Maria Lindsey of the Brisbane convent. George leaned forward in his chair, his heart nearly bursting out of his chest, almost afraid to ask.

'Do you by any chance still have these letters?' he said, his throat turned sandpapery with anxiety and anticipation.

She waited a moment as if considering. 'Yes. I do.'

Now here he was at his desk, the letters beside him in the tattered grey shoebox where Sarah had stored them for so long, and a notepad in front of him. He'd been up all night reading. And one thing was clear—he had to talk to Maria Lindsey immediately.

His phone rang and he picked it up. 'George Harvey speaking.'

As if God had been listening to his thoughts, an elderly woman's voice spoke in his ear. 'Officer Harvey, my name is Maria Lindsey. I received a letter some weeks ago . . .'

'Yes, Ms Lindsey. I know who you are,' he said, stunned.

There was a pause at the end of the line. 'Well, good—ah, it's just that. . .' She hesitated as if searching for words. He waited. 'I intended to come and see you, because I've got something important I have to tell you. I got in my car and turned the key, but nothing happened, and I called the RACQ but they said, well, it's going to be expensive, and the thing is—'

'Where are you?' he interrupted, standing up and searching for his car keys. He didn't have a system for his keys—you'd think at his age he would have it sorted by now—and was forever looking for them, under papers, in the drawer, in his pants pocket.

'I'm just outside Eudlo on the Sunshine Coast. I work at a place called Honeybee Haven. Do you know it?' Her voice was tentative.

'Give me the address. I'll be there in an hour and a half.'

Tansy hadn't slept much last night and found herself awake at dawn. She decided to pick up coffees and croissants and take them around to Jordan and Katarina's place to surprise them. Toby was an early riser so she knew they'd all be up.

They were still in their dressing-gowns, early morning children's television distracting Toby. Jordan welcomed her into the house, both of them smiling sheepishly after the huge outpouring of confessions two days ago, and Katarina clapped her hands at the sight of the pastries.

'I hear congratulations are in order,' Tansy said, passing Katarina the ham and cheese croissant and a warm foaming cappuccino.

'Thanks,' she said, biting tentatively into the flaking pastry, her brow furrowed. 'I'm sorry we didn't tell you earlier. I feel bad about that. But with everything you've had going on with the possible pregnancy and Dougal leaving, it just didn't seem like the right time.'

'Don't be silly. It's your right to keep your secret as long as you like.' Tansy reached into her bag and pulled out a small gift in brown paper, tied with a white bow. 'And this is for the newest member of your family.'

Katarina took it, her eyes welling. 'Thank you.' The bow pulled undone easily and inside the wrapping was a collection of organic cotton singlets and socks in whites and pale yellows. 'They're beautiful,' she said, cooing and holding a wee singlet against her belly, imagining the little person who would come out into it.

'You're due in November, aren't you? I figured it will be so hot then that he or she will be hanging around a lot in a singlet and nappy.'

'Toby was a winter baby,' Jordan said. 'And we were terrified he was going to freeze. Even if he did manage to sleep for a few hours at night we were up every hour checking he wasn't cold or in case we'd overheated him. We were forever wrapping and unwrapping him and turning the heater up or down.'

'A summer baby will be a nice change,' Katarina said, one hand worrying at her hair. 'Gosh, I should probably look in the mirror. I must look a fright with bed hair.'

'You look beautiful,' Jordan said, and touched her face.

'Oh, aren't you the charmer,' Tansy teased.

He went off to get ready for work. The two women sipped their coffees and picked at their croissants and Katarina slowly began to talk about the baby, the tests, the emotional roller-coaster they'd been on, her fears for her baby, her fears for her marriage, her fears for her career, and underlying it all her profound faith that despite all the possible challenges of a Down syndrome diagnosis, this baby was a gift and they were blessed.

Tansy listened, and let her cry, and let her laugh, and let her feel the excitment of a new life coming into their family. She squeezed her hand, and assured her she'd do everything she could to help them.

She'd made the right decision about not having a baby with Dougal. It meant she'd have extra love to share with this new one. She could pour all of her mothering into being the best aunty the world had ever seen. For this one, for Toby, and for baby Hamish too, not to mention Rose's children. Aunties and honorary aunties were so important in the world. She'd grab that role with both hands. It would be great. Better than great. She'd get to do all the fun stuff and pass the babies back when they were screaming. She'd be the one they'd run to when they hated their parents.

Now, back at home, she calculated that it was eight pm in Toronto, the perfect time to phone Dougal and tell him everything.

He answered on the second ring. 'Hello, my darling,' he sang, his voice brimming with delight.

'Well, that's some welcome!' She laughed. 'You've had a good day?'

'Ah, it was fine. But I was just about to call you. I've got something exciting I need to tell you.'

'So do I. But you start.' Her heart swelled with hope. 'Are you coming back to Australia?' She didn't want to leave here. This was her home; she loved it. It might be expected of young people to be willing to simply uproot and move to the other side of the world, but Tansy wasn't like that. Old before her time, possibly. But she was settled here. Happy. And now she wanted to be here for Jordan and Katarina and their baby, and to be more involved with Rose and her children—they would need her now more than ever—and for Belle and Hamish too. She missed Dougal terribly and wanted him back home as soon as possible.

His enthusiasm faltered. 'No, sorry. It's not that.'

'Oh.' Her heart plunged. 'No, sorry, of course. I just . . . that would have been great. But go on, please, tell me your news.'

'Okay.' She heard him breathe in. 'So I've made a decision.'

'Mmm?'

'I want to have a baby with you.'

Tansy did the clichéd movement of the gaping goldfish. 'Why?' she finally managed to say.

'Because . . .' She heard his voice deflate. He'd been so sure that his news would make her happy. 'That's what you want, isn't it?' he said, confused.

'I *did* want that.'

'Did?'

'It's just that I realised it wasn't fair to you and I'd just been struck with momentary baby madness. I think I can be happy without having children, like I always thought I could, and I shouldn't be asking you to completely change now, just because I'm turning thirty and feeling the pressure of the clock running down.' She laughed lightly.

'But I . . .' Dougal murmured, frustrated. 'That's sweet of you, and mature and generous, and I'm touched you would think that. But I don't want to lose you.'

'You won't. It's all good now.'

'I'm not sure it is,' he said. 'I think you've just backflipped because you're afraid that everything we have now will fall apart.'

'Well, what about you? Haven't you done the same?'

'Yes,' he said, and she could hear the smile of hopelessness in his voice. 'I realised that I could have a life with you and a baby, or I might have to have a life without you at all. And the better of those two choices for me is to have you and a baby.'

'Even if you don't want it?'

'Maybe I was wrong.' He sighed. 'Maybe I got too old too soon because I had a child too young. Maybe I made big decisions about not having more children when I was stressed and couldn't see a way to do it better. Maybe I'm at the right age right now, and you and a baby are just what I need to stay young.'

Hope fluttered its wings inside Tansy's chest, but she kept them under wraps. Both she and Dougal had swung dramatically in ideas and emotions and they might swing again. 'Well, this leaves us in even more of a tangle than before you left.'

'Sorry about that,' he said.

'Don't worry; it's not just us. So much has happened here since you left. It's crazy. And this is good. You and me, this is good. We're talking now and thinking more clearly. That's what we need to do.' She heard him open the fridge door and take out a bottle of some sort. 'Are you drinking?' she asked, concerned that she'd pushed him to alcohol.

'Soda water.' He cracked open the metallic top and she heard the fizz of bubbles. 'Tell me everything that's been going on,' he said.

So she did, as thoroughly as she could, given the time constraints of an expensive international call. The only thing she left out was Leo's news about university; that was his information to share.

'I'm completely gobsmacked,' Dougal said, once she'd finished. 'I might have to add some scotch to this soda water after all.'

'Told you there was a lot going on. Can you believe all those confessions just bubbling up like that in our lounge room? Can you believe my mother hit me? I should charge her with assault.'

He swallowed a gulp of his drink loudly. 'I'm still stuck on the fact that Maria is a murderer. You were lucky that day up there with the archbishop. Who knows what these people are capable of?'

'I know you want me to come over as soon as possible, but Maria is determined to confess and I think I need to stay here and help her through this, help her find a lawyer at least, stop her from doing anything stupid.'

'Sounds like the stupid thing was done a long time ago.'

'That's a bit harsh.'

'You think? She killed someone, Tans. I know you've been excited to make contact with her, and I know you still hold hopes of being able to reunite your mother and aunt with Maria—assuming they could get past her crime—but I think you should just stay out of this now. It sounds like something that could turn nasty. You need to protect yourself. *I* need you to protect yourself. Just let justice take its course.'

Tansy bit her lip, but didn't commit.

'And just think about what I said about the baby, okay? We'll work this out, one step at a time.'

30

Chastity, poverty and obedience—the three vows Maria took to serve her faith and God, the same three tenets of a bee's life. A worker bee was there for one thing and one thing only, and that was to obey the order of the industrious hive, serving a higher purpose with unquestioning faith and commitment, keeping no nectar rewards for herself but giving it all to the hive, ensuring the continuation and expansion of her enclosed community, knowing that all her efforts would end for her in one way only—death.

George Harvey would be here soon, and Maria was determined to prepare an overabundance of products for the market stall, not just for this weekend coming, when Petrice had agreed to man the stall, but to carry Maria's replacement through for a few weeks while they found their feet. There wasn't time right now to write down lists of instructions and recipes, but she supposed she might be able to do that from wherever the police took her.

279

Michaela had replied to her email immediately, telling her that she must not confess to the police, that it would do no one any good now and would only cause hurt in so many people's lives, including the orphans'. She was stern, angry that Maria could want to disrupt and endanger the running of the orphanage only to relieve her own conscience.

That wasn't the case; Maria knew she had to confess, in part because Ian could drop her in it at any moment. But she understood that Michaela was panicking. Though she was fond of Maria, Michaela's first concern was for the children in her care, and Maria's departure would disrupt the constant flow of funds to Cambodia.

Tansy had left a message saying she was going to find her a lawyer, which was sweet but too late as far as Maria was concerned. She'd organised for Petrice to arrive later this afternoon and hopefully stay for the duration of the drumming workshop. But Petrice wasn't a manager, and was not even particularly reliable. Maria had decided to ask Tansy to step in temporarily and guide Honeybee Haven through the choppy waters until something more permanent could be arranged. She had great faith in Tansy; her niece had turned up at just the right time in her life. God's plan in action.

Now she had one and a half hours to pour herself into creating beautiful works to leave behind. That wasn't much time—a day would be better, a week ideal. But there was nothing she could do about that. Candles seemed a good place to begin. She'd collected old teacups from op shops for this purpose and stored them in a box under her bed; now she quickly carried them back to the kitchen and washed and dried them.

She set hunks of caramel-coloured rendered beeswax into a steel bowl over a saucepan of water and lit the gas. Wax was slow to melt, and while she waited she gathered up her essential oils, food colouring and cotton wicks. She cut the wicks to length, clamping one end of each in a metal wick sustainer placed in the bottom of each cup. The other end of each wick was suspended to a wooden skewer balanced over each rim. She stirred the hunks of wax over the heat, then drew out four mixing bowls to separate the wax into different colours (pink, orange, yellow and green) and their associated scents (rose geranium, orange, lemon and mint). Finally, the wax was fully melted. She divided it into the four bowls, coloured and scented each one, and then poured the thick liquid quickly and carefully into her eight teacups. She put them aside to set, the wax already changing colour as it cooled, and moved on to the honey butter.

It had been a while since she'd made a batch, but it was a treat to mix up and to lick off the spoon, and today of all days that was just what she fancied doing. The recipe called for equal amounts of honey, sugar and thick cream to add to the butter. Since she wanted to make a lot, and had dozens of empty jars lying around, she dashed to the dining hall's commercial kitchen and took a litre of each from the supplies there, choosing brown sugar for extra richness. Back in her own small kitchen, she heated them together in a large saucepan, stirring with a wooden spoon until the sugar was dissolved. While waiting for the mixture to come to the boil, she put her empty jars into the oven to sterilise them. The aroma of the brown sugar coming from the stove was like a warm balm for her soul. When it was ready, she added the butter and stirred again, essentially making a decadent honeyed caramel sauce.

When all of it had been distributed into the jars, and Honeybee Haven cards attached to the lids with brown string, she licked the spoon, closing her eyes with pleasure as the flavours swam around her mouth. She licked the bowl too, using her finger to scrape up every last drop she could, relishing it as though it was her last meal.

Finally, she put the jars of honey butter into the fridge to chill, quickly washed the dishes, and prepared herself for George's arrival. She showered and dressed in clean clothes—a pale blue pair of trousers, a white collared shirt and knitted cardigan. She tidied the kitchen and wiped down the benches. She zipped up her duffel bag, ready to go.

It was quiet outside, the drumming group having left for a communal bushwalk, so she took out her string of aurora borealis glass rosary beads from the blue velvet case in the top drawer of her bedside table. The lid resisted, its hinges stiff with age, her thumb fitting instantly into the indent on the top and her other fingers into smaller dents around the base. She'd been opening the box the same way since she first received them, back in the mid-sixties. Mother Veronica had brought them back from Rome; Pope Paul VI had blessed them. And the second she seated herself on the sagging floral-patterned couch, a small cushion behind her straight back, the rosary beads in her hand, she felt everything drop away.

She said the Lord's Prayer and then quickly moved on to the first decade of Hail Marys.

Hail Mary, full of grace, the Lord is with thee; blessed art thou amongst women, and blessed is the fruit of thy womb, Jesus. Holy Mary, Mother of God, pray for us sinners, now and at the hour of our death. Amen.

Hail Mary, full of grace, the Lord is with thee . . .

Her hands knew exactly how to hold and fluidly move each bead through her fingers. Her mind was laser-focused, like a bee zooming through the skies with pinpoint accuracy towards the nectar in a garden of flowers, having received the information from a fellow worker who'd communicated the exact geographical distance and location through the inexplicable 'waggle dance'—a vibration in its body. The bees' dance was one of the great mysteries of life, something science couldn't explain.

She'd just finished her fourth decade of the rosary when she heard a car's engine straining as it ascended the steep slope to the small car park near the dining hall. Halting her prayers, she opened her eyes and kissed the rosary beads before replacing them in the velvet box.

The time had come.

George stepped out of his ageing Falcon. He didn't like to take a police car on these sorts of trips: it unnerved people too much and they were usually stressed enough already. He spent a few moments uncurling his body after the drive, arching his back and then doing a few Achilles heel stretches. He got so stiff these days whenever he drove for more than twenty minutes or so.

During the moments it took to loosen up his body, he looked around at the circle of colourful cabins under the trees, with a space where it appeared as though a cabin had recently been removed, and the stretch of lawn in the centre, strewn with folding chairs, drums, a few towels and cast-off shoes. The place was silent and apparently empty. Just some birds and the breeze in the trees. Up here, at this altitude, it was a good few degrees cooler than in the city. A chill skittered up his back. Early June days in Brisbane rarely required much more than a t-shirt—it was July and August that brought the deep cold and bitter winds—and now he wished he'd brought a jacket with him.

A screen door slapped shut and he turned in the direction of the sound to see the former nun Maria Lindsey, he presumed, walking towards him; like Sarah's yesterday, her stride was strong and purposeful. No doubt about it, these old nuns were tough.

'Officer Harvey?' she said, nearing him, tightening her cardigan against a sudden gust of wind that lifted her wavy grey hair.

He stepped forward and held out his hand. 'Maria?' She nodded. 'Please, call me George.'

'Thank you for coming all the way up here.' She gestured towards a yellow Citroen. 'The old girl's going to need some time off.'

'No problem. I'm glad you called. You were on my list to contact next anyway.'

'Yes, I thought I might be.'

They eyed each other for a moment. He motioned around at the buildings. 'This is a lovely spot. Is it yours?'

'I'm the manager. All the profits from this business go to an orphanage in Cambodia.'

George already felt a warm sense of affection for this woman. Like Sarah, she was still living her vows, still serving the people who needed the most help.

'Shall we go inside?' she said, turning and leading him away from the loading bay, past a small hut with a sundial on the wall and a block of wood nailed above the door painted with the words *Meditation Room*, and into a modest cabin, a kit-home granny flat, by the look of it. It was dark and sparse inside, and there were boxes stacked around the floor. He spied a duffel bag near the kitchen.

'Are you going somewhere?' he asked, scratching under his chin.

'I think I might be going to jail,' she said matter-of-factly. 'Would you like some tea?'

31

Maria woke to the sound of a single drum. It was just after dawn, the cold air prompting her to pull her doona up to her chin. And she smiled.

This time yesterday, she'd truly believed she'd be waking up in a sterile, clanging jail cell today. But here she was. She'd confessed everything to George; she didn't leave out a single detail. He'd listened closely, clearly surprised. Eyebrows raised, he rubbed at his moustache, cleared his throat and adjusted his buttocks on the wooden chair. He asked some questions, asked her to repeat sections of the story, took notes, turned the recording device on and off. Accepted a second cup of tea. But he said very little.

After she'd finished her story, she waited. For the lecture, the reading of rights, handcuffs. But he did nothing. He just stared at her and tapped his foot.

'Are you going to arrest me now?' she prompted at last.

George grunted and scratched the back of his neck. 'This has all been a surprise,' he said quietly.

'I should imagine it is,' she agreed.

'To be perfectly honest, what I'm most interested in right now is the archbishop. I'm guessing you're sharing this now because you expect that Ian Tully will turn on you, when push comes to shove?'

She stood up and retrieved Ian's two notes from the cutlery drawer, where she'd stashed them under the tray. 'He most certainly will,' she said, handing them over to George. 'He left me these. I caught him in the act of leaving the second one.' She pointed to the note that said *Murderer*.

George considered her.

'He was in this house,' she said, looking up at the walls and the ceiling of her small abode. 'It was quite frightening to have him appear out of the shadows. My niece was here too . . .' She faltered then, thinking that she shouldn't have mentioned Tansy, she should have kept her out of it. But it was too late. 'Tansy was most alarmed.'

George nodded and slid the notes into his folder of papers. 'Maria, I think we'll need to leave this meeting here for today.'

'But I . . . what do you normally do in these situations?'

George's moustache twitched, as though he was trying not to smile. 'This isn't entirely normal,' he said, packing away his items. 'I would ask you to be available for more discussion, more meetings?'

'Of course,' Maria said, stunned at the lack of consequences.

'And I don't suppose you're planning on going anywhere? Not getting on a plane or anything?'

'No, not at all.'

He'd asked for her passport, which she'd fetched and handed over. He'd popped it in with his notes and nodded again, looking completely unconcerned. And then he'd left, saying he needed to consider everything she'd told him and that he would be in touch shortly.

And now here she was in her own bed, needing to get up and put on a vat of hot porridge for the hungry drummers out on her lawn.

A riot of kookaburras broke into morning laughter high up in the trees outside her cabin. Maria joined in, feeling so free, even if it was for just one more day.

Cramps—big-arsed, bone-crunching, toe-curling cramps in his calves and feet, the kind that made it feel as though his bones were twisting around each other—had seen George leap from his bed in the dark and swear and mutter his way out into the stillness of the house. Since then he'd been pacing the rooms. The torsions had eased, but every time he thought they'd gone and he tried to sit or lie down, they came back with a vengeance. And so he continued to walk, and meanwhile the birds outside had come to life and were talking up the day as if it was the first one they'd ever seen.

Although his body had found relief, his mind remained contorted, turning over everything Maria had said to him yesterday, wondering how he should proceed. Her confession had been unexpected and complicating. He felt real sympathy for her, certainly. But that wasn't what had stopped him from arresting her. More time was what he needed. More time before he had to report to Blaine Campbell. The man was unpredictable at best, and George wasn't sure if his response would be to arrest Maria or sweep the whole thing under the carpet in favour of nailing the person they'd set out to nail—the archbishop.

Hilda came yawning out of the bedroom, tying her pink dressing-gown around her.

'Sorry if I woke you,' he said, passing her on his way through the lounge room.

'Cramps?'

'Yep.'

'I'll get some liniment. You should have woken me.'

'No point in both of us being up, love.'

His wife went to the pantry and fussed around in the medicine box, a pile of prescription drugs three years past their expiry date, miscellaneous plasters for cuts and scrapes, and stiff tubes of antiseptic ointment that should have been thrown away years ago. And liniments—at least six different kinds.

'Sit down,' she ordered, shepherding him to the recliner and perching in front of him on the footstool, rolling up her sleeves.

George winced and screeched and grimaced as he took the weight off his legs and the cramps threatened to resume their vicelike grip, but Hilda's hands were quick and firm, grabbing his calves and wrangling them as if they were thrashing pythons. He groaned, half in pain and half in relief. The liniment smelled of peppermint and aniseed and was starting to warm deep down into the problem areas.

Hilda chewed her lip.

'They're just cramps,' he said, sad that she was worrying about him the second she'd got out of bed.

'I know,' she said, smiling.

'This will all be over soon,' he assured her.

She arched a brow, unconvinced.

'Well, okay, it will take years, of course, for everything to go through the courts, but I think the hardest parts are behind me now. There were interesting developments yesterday and I just have a couple more people of interest to see. Once I've got their testimonies, if it all goes the way I think it will, I'll have enough to lay charges against—' He stopped himself before he could say the name. Even though he knew Hilda had already put the pieces together herself, legally he wasn't supposed to talk about it with her, and that was a good thing, because she was a committed Catholic and this sort of conversation was hard for her.

Tully was the archbishop of her church too. If it was all true, if the archbishop was to be charged, if her faith's structure was to be undone, he knew she'd deal with it then. But it was a lot to process, even for someone as spirited and strong as her.

Even though he had Father Bryce's blessing and encouragement of his work, George couldn't help but feel guilty for being the one to destroy so many people's illusions.

Illusions? Was that really what they were?

And then there was the burden of bringing this huge elephant into the room of their marriage. Perhaps he should have refused early on, asked for a transfer to another department, or even quit. But the time for that had long since passed. He was committed now and he had to see it through.

'Is this feeling better?' Hilda asked, her movements slowing.

'Much, thank you.' He reached out and touched her hair. 'I don't know what I'd do without you.'

She leaned her face into his hands. 'You're my everything,' she said, closing her eyes and soaking up his tenderness.

His heart lurched. 'You're my everything too.' And she was. This whole investigation had been hard on him, but it had been almost as hard on his beautiful wife, who'd put up with his moods and migraines and absences—physical and mental. They needed some time together, to reconnect and rekindle.

She turned her head and kissed his palm perfunctorily, but not unkindly, then resumed her massaging.

'Soon, very soon, let's go on a cruise,' he said, the idea just flying into his head, seemingly from nowhere.

'A cruise? Where's this coming from? You get seasick.'

'I keep hearing about them around the office. Everyone's saying they're good. And affordable. For people prone to seasickness there are berths placed for less movement, there's a doctor on board . . . most people are fine. And we'll leave the kids with . . .' he waved a hand, 'I don't know . . . someone.'

She laughed.

'I'm willing to risk it if you are,' he said, smiling.

'Well, you know me,' she said, visibly cheered. 'I'm up for anything.'

'Then let's do it. How about you go see the travel agent down the road and get some brochures and we'll get it booked in? It's been years since we've been away, just the two of us. We can sleep in late, eat all day long, laze by the pool, drink a few cocktails?'

Hilda stopped massaging, climbed into his lap and kissed him for a long time. Then she nuzzled into his neck and took a long breath. 'I'd love that.'

He squeezed her tight. Everything would be okay. It wasn't long to go now.

The juicer growled and shrieked as Tansy forced ice-cold carrots down its throat, watching the bright orange liquid gush into the jug below. Leo came into the kitchen wearing a ripped t-shirt and long cotton pants, his hair askew, rubbing his eyes. He was studying today, preparing for his last two end-of-semester exams.

'Juice?' she asked over her shoulder, forcing deep red beetroot into the juicer, the motor straining.

He pulled out a stool and sat. 'Yes, please.'

Celery sticks in too, liquefied in seconds, no challenge for the mighty machine.

'You jogging?' Leo asked, taking in her black leggings, fluorescent green shirt and joggers.

'Yep.' She turned off the roar of the juicer with some relief and poured out two glasses of deep purple liquid.

'Can I come too?' he asked, taking his glass. 'Thanks.' He spoke cautiously, aware that she was still angry with him.

Tansy sipped her drink and eyed him over the rim. She wasn't sure she wanted him with her today.

'Or not,' he said, offended, his stubble catching the glow of the downlights in the ceiling.

'You need to tell Dougal about uni—I can't keep this secret whenever I talk to him. It's not fair.'

'It's not a secret.'

'Then why haven't you done it?' She disliked how she sounded right now, like some kind of mother figure, which she wasn't. Or, she didn't want to be, or mean to be. Actually, come to think of it, what was his mother thinking or doing about this? Had he even told Rebecca? Maybe she should give her a call.

But she couldn't meddle. Leo was an adult. Well, kind of, if you considered that the male brain wasn't fully developed until twenty-five years of age. So maybe she *should* be meddling. Parents never stopped parenting. And maybe they were needed more now at Leo's age than ever before. He didn't know what he was doing. He didn't even have a whole brain.

But she wasn't a parent.

Leo glared at her, drained his juice and stood. 'I'll text him now.' He stalked down the hall and into his room.

And now Dougal was saying he wanted a baby, just as she'd talked herself out of it. She was all askew. Ideally, she would call Rose for advice, but her sister probably wasn't in the best state of mind for such marital-themed discussions. Belle would be a better choice. It was only just past seven but she'd be up. She was always up, the poor thing.

So Tansy finished her juice and left the house, shivering as she hit the chilly morning air, walking down the driveway of the unit complex and then up the boardwalk towards the entrance to the national park, warming up her muscles. The sun bounced off the water and sand and made her squint. It was promising to be a lovely day. She put her earbuds in and dialled Belle's number.

Belle's voice was shaky.

'What's happened?' Tansy asked, pushing up her pace to a brisk walk as she joined the coastal track, nodding at other walkers and joggers as each one passed.

'I spent the night in hospital with Hamish.'

'Is he okay?'

'Nothing critical. It's his reflux. It got so bad that he was refusing to eat and crying all the time because he was hungry but he still wouldn't take the bottle, smacking it away and throwing himself backwards.' Her voice cracked. 'He's so light. I can feel how much weight he's lost. I was worried he was dehydrated, so I packed him in the car and drove all the way to Nambour's children's section yesterday afternoon. Took more than two hours to get here. Then I waited so long in emergency, into the night, and they didn't know what to do so they asked if I wanted to stay in with him overnight and see the paediatrician in the morning. So now I'm waiting again.'

'Oh, Belle, that's horrible. How are you coping?'

'Well, they put me on a foldout chair—not a foldout couch, a foldout *chair*—that was so narrow I couldn't roll over and so loud and squeaky that I woke Hamish if I so much as scratched my nose. I'm still in the clothes I had on yesterday and I'm eating from a vending machine. The doctors don't take it seriously. I don't think I'll get any help here.'

She paused, clucking at Hamish, who was making some noise in the background. 'Although, the nurses have been fantastic and one of them said to me straight away last night that we had to get him eating or he'd end up on a drip and that would be awful. She said I needed to ask for a referral to a gastric specialist, which no one's suggested before. So that was probably worth it in itself.'

Tansy began to jog lightly, just enough to elevate her heart rate but not so much that she wouldn't be able to keep talking. 'That sounds like some sort of progress.'

'The same nurse told me they have another little one, about the same age as Hamish, that also has reflux and also refuses to eat and they have to hold him down and force-feed him with a syringe while he screams and screams. Isn't that horrendous?'

Tansy reeled at the thought. 'Sounds like child abuse.'

Belle began to cry.

'How long will you be in Nambour? I can come and see you,' Tansy said. 'I'm not taking on any new work right now, not with everything so up in the air about going to Canada, so I can drive down.'

'I'd love to see you, but you know what the public system is like. I have no idea how long I'll have to wait for the paediatrician, and once I've seen them I just want to get out of here. It's such a long drive home again.'

'Do you want to come and stay with me?'

'I don't have enough supplies and I need to go back home to my GP and get some sort of action. Besides, Hamish'll start screaming again soon and continue until he passes out from exhaustion.' Her voice broke again. 'He's so tired from the lack of food. He'll barely even smile.'

'Keep me up to date. and please let me know if there's anything I can do. If you need to come back to see specialists or whatever, of course you and Raj and Hamish can all come and stay here.'

Tansy ended the call and upped her jogging pace. She felt so helpless for her friend. What a nightmare. She wished she could do something constructive to help, but it seemed that they'd all have to wait to get more information. In the meantime, though, she could help Maria.

She finished her jog and returned home to shower and change just as the cleaner arrived for the week, dragging her vacuum cleaner and bucket of products behind her. Tansy locked herself in her office and went online to look for a lawyer. She narrowed her search down to a couple, called them both to ask a few questions, then made an appointment for that afternoon with Zoe Smart because, well, she sounded *smart*.

Then she phoned Maria and told her she was coming to pick her up and drive her to the appointment and wouldn't hear any argument.

294

32

Maria's protests to Tansy were short-lived, both because her niece had turned out to be fiercely stubborn when she wanted to be and also because she couldn't reasonably argue with what she was suggesting. As she'd expected to be in jail right now, she'd already organised for Petrice to be at the Haven (though hadn't given her much by way of explanation so as not to alarm her) to take care of the drummers, who were so laid-back that they were pretty much self-sufficient anyway. And as she'd put Tansy's name into the mix when talking to George Harvey, she couldn't very well ignore the fact that Tansy might now need some legal advice too. So she bundled herself into Tansy's car and down the mountain they went, Maria feeling unusually free of responsibilities after her unexpected reprieve.

On the journey down, she told Tansy all about George's visit.

'I wish you'd called me straight away,' Tansy said, clearly angry. 'You should have had a lawyer there when you spoke to him. Shit.' She rubbed her forehead. 'Sorry,' she said. 'I shouldn't have sworn.'

Maria shrugged her shoulders. She'd heard worse in her life. Heavens, she'd *done* worse in her life.

'I just want to protect you,' Tansy said. 'I don't want you to go to jail.'

'You're incredibly sweet,' Maria said. 'I'm very lucky you found me.'

Tansy reached across and squeezed Maria's arm.

The lawyer's office was in the heart of Noosa, on the top floor of a menagerie of professional suites. Lots of glass and chrome. A big airy waiting room. A shiny receptionist. Perfect temperature. Quiet.

After a short wait, the receptionist ushered them into a boardroom with a long oval table, a whiteboard, and windows overlooking the street below, tastefully hung with wooden blinds for privacy. A few minutes later, Zoe Smart arrived. She was around Tansy's age, wearing a black corporate suit and black-framed glasses. Her black hair was slicked back into a bun, and she wore neutral lipstick. Maria liked her immediately. She seemed capable and warm—despite being dressed like an undertaker.

They all shook hands and water was poured from a carafe into glasses. Zoe led with some small talk and then lit up with wonder to hear that Maria kept bees. 'I've just installed a native beehive in my courtyard,' she said. 'I researched bees for a long time and the honeybees seemed like too much work for me, but the natives take care of themselves. It's so fascinating to watch them and I love seeing them out there pollinating flowers. I have a cocker spaniel who just loves them too,' she laughed. 'People aren't taking this bee crisis seriously enough. Everyone needs to be keeping bees.'

Maria liked her even more.

Zoe shook herself as if remembering where she was, and opened her notebook. 'Now, how can I help you?'

'Maria is involved with an investigation into the Catholic church,' Tansy began.

'I'm an ex-nun,' Maria said, to clarify.

'And she met with the investigating officer yesterday.'

'George Harvey,' Maria added.

Zoe took notes, nodding.

'I wanted her to wait until we'd seen a lawyer.' Tansy glanced at Maria, sounding more defeated now than angry. 'I'm not sure what harm's been done, if anything.'

'Well, let's see,' Zoe said. 'Maria, why don't you tell me what's happened and everything you told George Harvey?'

So Maria told her story, again. And she knew she'd have to retell it many more times yet before this was over. But it was getting easier. She was stumbling less over her words. In fact, it was almost as though she was retelling someone else's story; so much of the suppressed emotion had gone, along with the sheer effort of keeping it to herself for decades.

Zoe adjusted her glasses in surprise, murmured at the right places, but never once seemed alarmed or horrified. Her expression remained calm throughout.

Finally, she leaned back in her chair and studied Maria. 'Well, everything you've told me certainly makes me feel you could benefit from representation at this time, and I'd be happy to do that if you would like to proceed.'

'Yes.' Tansy jumped in without waiting for Maria. 'We need help right now.'

Zoe nodded. 'I'll need you to sign your consent to engagement of services as well as an agreement to the fees.'

'I'll be taking care of that,' Tansy said.

Maria felt sick then, thinking of all that money. Money that could be better used in Cambodia. 'Surely it's all too late?' she said. 'I've told George Harvey everything and he has it all on tape. There's no going back now.'

'That's precisely why you need a lawyer right now,' Tansy said firmly.

'I agree,' Zoe said. 'Whether or not you choose me to represent you, you have confessed to a very serious crime. More action will follow. Honestly, I'm surprised it hasn't yet. I'd be very keen to talk to Officer Harvey and find out where his motivations lie. It's not the most usual way to proceed. But given your age—forgive me—as well as your voluntary confession and your obviously long track record of community service, combined with a clear record in all other respects, I can certainly appreciate why he would consider you to be a safe bet at this stage.'

'He took my passport,' Maria said.

Tansy gasped. 'Did he?'

Zoe nodded. 'That's standard practice.' She checked her watch. 'As it's now four o'clock on a Friday afternoon, I'm guessing you won't be hearing from Officer Harvey again until Monday.' She slid a business card across the desk to Maria. 'But if you do hear from him, please contact me immediately. You shouldn't be speaking to him again without a lawyer present. In the meantime, I'd like to run all this information past a colleague, just to make sure my thinking is on the right track. Everything remains confidential, of course, but it's standard practice in a matter as serious as this to involve a partner to ensure we're providing the best possible service. Is that okay?'

'Yes, absolutely,' Tansy said.

'Yes, thank you,' Maria agreed, nodding.

Zoe smiled at her. 'I know this is a daunting situation, Maria. But for what it's worth, I'll work hard to see you get the best possible outcome.'

On Saturday morning, Dougal texted: *What the hell is wrong with Leo?*

Tansy didn't know what to say to that—she *didn't* know what was wrong with him—so she simply replied that she was sure it would all work out, and that at least he was deferring and not quitting entirely, so that was something.

Then she texted her dad. *I'm coming down this morning to visit. Should be there around ten. Can you please make sure Mum's home? And can you not tell her I'm coming? I want it to be a surprise xx*

Once again she picked Maria up in her car and drove her down the mountain. Maria was nervous—which was natural, Tansy supposed, given she hadn't seen her sister in almost sixty years—tugging at her collar and shifting in her seat. She sat with her handbag on her lap, clutching it. She was muttering, almost talking to herself, fretting about Petrice alone at the Yandina markets, then reminding herself that it wasn't the first time Petrice had manned the stall and in truth it wasn't a particularly difficult job. Petrice wouldn't actively sell the items to passers-by the way Maria did, but they should still do okay.

'Does your mother know I'm coming?' she asked finally, looking straight ahead at the winding road.

'No,' Tansy confessed. 'It's a bit risky, given how she reacted last time simply to the news that I'd been to see you. But I didn't want to give her any opportunities to back out.'

Maria looked up at the roof of the car. 'Well, this will be interesting.'

Tansy tittered uneasily and shook her wrist to adjust a bracelet that had wedged itself too far up her arm. 'Interesting is one word for it. But it's time, don't you think?'

Maria swallowed audibly, and released her handbag to the floor beneath her legs. She had on a thick cable-knit cardigan that Tansy had seen several times. Maria certainly didn't have many worldly possessions. 'Given that I might be in jail soon, yes. It's time we tried to make amends.'

'Do you want to tell me what happened between you to cause this rift in the first place?' Tansy had been dying to ask. Now, with a couple of hours alone together in the car, and given the pending legal crisis, it seemed as good a time as any.

After their father had died, the Lindsey family struggled. The sorrow left in their home and hearts was one that could never be truly healed. And then there were the practical matters—the family's income was gone, and there was no man around the house to take care of the leak in the roof or fix the wobbly step. It was the fifties; the welfare safety net that Australians would come to rely upon was rudimentary and not sufficient to support a family of four. People had to fall back on their extended families for support, and if that wasn't possible, the church was usually their next port of call. In this respect, the Lindsey family was no different.

Their mother worked, of course, doing whatever she could to bring in an income to buy the necessities of life and pay the electricity bill. The nuns at the girls' school made sure they always had uniforms and books, even if they were second-hand. If more than the most basic maintenance was needed around the home, a member of the church community would come to lend a hand. Elyse felt a great debt to the church, and to the nuns especially. She never sent her three girls off to school without a flower from the garden and a reminder to be humble and thankful towards all the nuns, even the cantankerous ones. 'We couldn't get by without them,' she said often, kissing the girls goodbye at the door.

On her instruction, the girls offered to do extra chores for the nuns—staying back after school to wash the blackboard, carrying piles of books for them, or sweeping the verandah outside the classroom. They gave up time on school holidays to clean classroom windows and pump up the balls in the sporting equipment shed.

Enid, in particular, relished these jobs, humming and skipping as she worked and following the nuns around like a devoted puppy. At home, she would place a handkerchief over her hair when she prayed at night, and wore rosary beads around her neck. Her most prized possession was a statue of the Virgin Mary in her long blue robes, roses at her bare feet, her eyes cast to the heavens. Everyone knew that Enid wanted to be a nun.

For Maria's part, she had great respect for the nuns and was a committed Catholic girl who willingly cleaned the church between services, running the carpet sweeper down the aisles, dusting the holy water fonts and polishing brass. But for Maria, family came first—family, then church. In the end, it was this very order of values that saw her enter the convent.

It began one evening in 1960. Her younger sisters were already in bed, but Maria was studying for her end-of-year exams. She got up from the dimly lit desk in the corner of the lounge room to fetch a glass of water, and found her mother sitting at the dining table. Papers were laid out in front of her, her reading glasses were on her nose, and she was resting her forehead in the palm of her hand.

'Mum?'

Elyse started. 'Oh, I'd forgotten you were still up,' she said quietly, rubbing at her eyes. Dark shadows fell beneath her lower lids. 'What time is it?'

'About eleven. What are those?' Maria tried to see the papers, read what was on them. Elyse gathered them together quickly, but not before Maria spied a red rubber-stamped *Final Notice* warning across one.

'Nothing,' Elyse said, trying to smile. 'Everything's okay. How's your study going?'

'It's fine. I think I'm ready.'

'I'm glad to hear it,' her mother murmured, rising stiffly from the wooden chair. She tucked the papers under her arm and kissed Maria on the cheek. 'I'm off to bed. Don't stay up much longer. You'll need to be wide awake to answer those history questions.'

'Goodnight,' Maria said, watching Elyse walk down the darkened hallway, waiting for the soft close of the door, the turn of the handle and the click of the latch, listening to the squeak of the metal bedframe as her mother sank into the mattress.

With a wave of shame, she realised that she should be doing more to help the family and take some of the pressure off her mother. She made a decision right then that this term of school would be her last. She would finish her exams and then she would find a job to help her mother get the other two girls through school. Her father was already gone. She didn't want to lose her mother too under the strain of being the sole provider.

She went to school the next day lighter of heart now that she had a plan, and flew through her exam. Walking home, she ate an apple, sure that life would be easier for all of them very soon. But when she reached their letterbox, she stopped. A man was standing on the front step, talking to her mother. He held a clipboard in his hand and was pointing at the page on top. Maria couldn't hear his words, but her mother's shoulders were hunched, her arms folded protectively across her body, and she was nodding and apologising, appeasing the man as he continued to lecture her.

Maria knew straight away that he must be a debt collector. She hung back as he trotted down the path and got into his car. Her mother waited until he left and then began to cry, closing the front door quickly to conceal herself from curious neighbours. Maria stood still, watching until the man's car was out of sight, then waited longer still, burning with ignominy, anger, and most of all resolve. But she didn't say anything to her mother of what she'd seen or of her decision to leave school.

Two days later, she was cleaning the church after Sunday morning mass. Needing to burn off the excess energy generated by her anxiety about her mother, she vigorously polished the wooden pews. When she'd finished, there was a smidgen of wax left in the tin. It seemed a shame not to use it up, so she went into the vestry, a place she didn't normally go. She knew the altar boys went in here and she'd seen the wooden shelves through the open doorway. It would be a nice surprise for the priest to come back to the smell of linseed and beeswax polish.

She carefully shifted items to the side, polishing the shelves in sections. As she worked she hummed one of the hymns they'd sung this morning. It had been a huge congregation today, with full voices and earnest attitudes. She moved further along the shelf and there in front of her was a wooden box; she polished it too, and it jingled.

Money. The box held the collection plate money, waiting to be counted and banked. She paused, staring at the lid, noting that it wasn't locked, and wondering how much money was in there. She'd seen quite a number of pound notes go into the plates that morning.

She looked over her shoulder. Listened. All was quiet.

Her heart galloped. It would be an unspeakable sin to steal the money from the collection plate, to take money given in generosity of spirit to the church and to the clergy. That money supported the priest and the nuns. That money probably helped pay for her schooling and the schooling of her sisters.

But family was her highest priority. Her family needed this money now if they were going to keep their heads above water.

She reached out a hand and opened the box and gasped. If this was an indication of what the church collected each week, they wouldn't miss a handful of notes that could change her family's life right now.

With a blinding bolt of adrenaline, she snatched as many notes as she could hold in one hand, shoved them into the pocket of her dress and closed the lid, terrified now and desperate to leave the building. With a quick look over her shoulder, she rearranged a few items on the desk, and fled out through the echoing space.

Over the next several weeks, Maria continued to lighten the clergy's box of pound notes. Every time, her hands trembled, her chest hurt. Still, she forged on, buoyed by the astonished exaltation in her mother's eyes when the debt collectors sent notices of cleared accounts.

'Something miraculous has happened,' she confided in Maria. 'I've not wanted to burden you girls with my problems, but I've been praying so hard and now something has happened that I have to share with you. An anonymous person has been clearing our debts. Praise be to God,' she said, laughing with relief. 'I dare not ask how or why. I only know that my prayers have been answered.'

Maria agreed that it was indeed mysterious but wonderful. Soon, thanks to her thorough cleaning of the church after mass on Sundays, their debts were all but gone.

And then, inevitably, she was caught. Her hand was literally in the collection box, her fist balled around the notes, when a voice spoke behind her. 'What are you doing?'

Maria jumped, dropped the notes, and spun to face Sister Eugene, who carried a basket of washing and must have come to collect the priest's robes. Eugene looked at the box, looked at Maria, turned bright red and thundered, 'You wicked girl! Stealing from the church. What on earth would your good mother say?'

'Please, please, Sister, you can't tell her.'

'You are very mistaken if you think you're getting away with this. Of course your mother must know what a lying, cheating, thieving girl you've become. You've brought shame on your family's name, not to mention the stain on your own soul.'

Eugene dropped the washing basket and lunged for Maria, snared her wrist and dragged her out of the church and all the way home to let her mother know what a shameful sinner her daughter had become.

That night, Elyse sat Maria down in the lounge. Enid and Florrie had been banished to bed early. Elyse's face was drawn, pale. She looked physically sick.

Maria explained why she'd done it, that she was trying to help their family, that she thought the church wouldn't miss a few pounds but that it would change their circumstances so dramatically and that they could make it up to the church in the future when they were better off. She said that she would not be returning to school in the new year and that she would get a job soon—then they would be able to pay back all the money. It was a short-term sin for the long-term good.

But her mother silenced her. 'Maria, I understand that you thought you were doing the right thing, that the end justified the means. And I can forgive you because you are young and I know your heart was in the right place. But we have a very big problem now. The nuns and Father Murphy will see this as a transgression of enormous magnitude. We have been relying on their mercy for many years and will likely need to for many more to come. This is not something we can easily recover from. This story will spread; things like this always do. And the community—especially those who gave money—will want to see recompense.'

Tears welled in Maria's eyes.

'Unless . . .' Elyse held up a finger. 'Unless we can offer an act of contrition so great that all will be forgiven and forgotten. We must act quickly to ensure that this story doesn't spread. *No one* else must know. So here is what I need you to do.'

Maria braced herself, waiting.

'I need you to go to confession tomorrow.'

'Yes, of course I will.'

'And then I will drive you to the convent, where we will meet with Mother Veronica. You will tell her you have no plans to return to school and that you want to join the convent immediately.'

'But, that's—' Maria couldn't understand. 'That doesn't make sense. They won't want a thief in their midst.'

'That's exactly why you will have to explain that you have held a lifelong desire to join the order but that, through a misguided impulse to serve the poor, you took a wrong turn. You will be humble and penitent, and you will ask her to accept you because you've been an exemplary pupil and member of the faithful up until now.'

That was true, she had.

'And you will tell her that you need the guidance of the order to channel your zealous need to serve into appropriate action.'

'But what about you? What about Enid and Florrie? You need me out there working to earn money for the family. That was the whole point.' Maria was panicking now.

'I believe that a sin of this nature, however well intentioned, needs a significant sacrifice in recompense. I believe God, the church, the nuns, will accept your willing service as more than enough compensation. And'—Elyse held up her hand to silence Maria's protests—'and God will provide for our family in return.'

'Mum, no, please.'

'Enid will withdraw from school. She's old enough to find work now.'

'But she's the one who's had the lifelong dream of joining the order, not me. She's the one who should be going to see Mother Veronica.'

'She's not the one who stole from the church.' Elyse let her words hang in the air around them while she recomposed herself, lowering her voice once more. 'Please, Maria, this is not . . . this isn't easy,' she whispered, her voice cracking and her eyes filling with tears. She wiped them away quickly. 'This isn't what I wanted for you.'

'Then don't make me go,' Maria pleaded. 'Enid can go in a couple of years' time.'

'There's no other option.' Elyse was resolute once more. 'We need to fix this now or we'll be ostracised. Enid can join the order after she's helped to support Florrie to the end of school. It's only a short time before they're both working and, perhaps, marrying. It will go quickly. Enid will get her chance to follow her dream, if that's what she still wants. But right now, we need you to repair the family name by demonstrating an unquestionable commitment to the church.'

Maria dropped her head into her hands and cried.

'Do you understand?' Elyse said.

Maria nodded.

Elyse used the armchair to lever herself up and stood there for a moment, clasping Maria's shoulder while she cried. Then she went to bed, leaving her eldest daughter alone in the lounge, preparing to say goodbye to everything she knew.

33

Tansy lifted a hand to her throat. 'It must have broken your heart.'

Her aunt raised her steel-grey brows. 'Not as much as it broke my mother's. Or your mother's, for that matter. Enid couldn't forgive me. She was the one who wanted to join the convent.'

'But she could have joined as well, surely.'

Maria raised a shoulder and let it drop. 'From the little I know, she got a job to help Mum keep the family going and get Florrie through school and, lucky for her, university.' She smiled then, proudly. 'She's the only one of us that got to go.' She suddenly perked up. 'Did you go to uni? Did Rose?'

'Rose studied art history and was a curator at the Queensland Art Gallery for a while, but then she had a baby, and then three more, and now she seems to be pretty happy as a mum.' Tansy paused and bit her lip. 'Well, she *did* seem happy, but things have taken a turn for the worse lately.' Poor Rose. She'd disappeared one day from Tansy's life—too busy with her lover, ashamed, or fearful of being discovered—and now she had a whole new type of life Tansy knew nothing about. She'd have to make a time to go and sit down with her and talk it all through.

'I'm sorry to hear that,' Maria said.

'I'll have to fill you in on that one later. As for me, I started uni but it wasn't for me so I pulled out.'

'But it all worked out? What you wanted to do?'

'Yes, absolutely. I love my job. And I love my life.' And then her enthusiasm was instantly trampled by the knowledge that she'd have to leave it all behind soon to follow Dougal to Canada. 'Dougal says he wants a baby now,' she ventured.

'That's good news, isn't it?' Maria asked gently.

'I guess so. Except I'd decided *I'd* changed my mind, and now it's all confusing.'

Did she just want too much? She had made her choice long ago that she wasn't going to have a baby. Other women had choices made for them by people or circumstance. Like Leo's mum. Rebecca had dropped out of uni to care for Leo while Dougal continued with his studies. And then the marriage ended and things got even tougher for her as a single mother while Dougal's career went from strength to strength. Rebecca had returned to university some years later, embarking on a gruelling eight years of part-time study to qualify with a civil engineering degree. (Both of Leo's parents had engineering degrees; Leo was a lot more like Tansy, interestingly.) Tansy had always admired Rebecca for that and couldn't help but feel a dash of guilt when in her presence, because *she* was now the lifestyle beneficiary of Dougal's career success, while Rebecca had so much ground to make up in her progression. There were years of lost wages and superannuation that Rebecca would never recover. She'd put all the hard work into Leo, too, shaping him into the gentle, compassionate and funny young man he was, and Tansy and Dougal got to enjoy him now because of it. Tansy's life was already so very blessed.

Now, Dougal was offering her exactly what she'd thought she wanted, even though he probably didn't want it himself. It was all very unfair to Dougal, who was wonderful and loving and, okay, always left the top drawer of the bathroom cabinet open and it drove her a little nuts, but otherwise pretty perfect. He always picked up bananas for her whenever he saw them because he knew how many she used to make her smoothies. And he loved romantic comedies just as much as she did (though he was a *Transformers* tragic as well). These things made up for the cabinet drawer. And his offer to have a baby probably made up for a million transgressions in the future.

She mulled this over in silence and Maria left her to her thoughts, perhaps distracted by her own. Before she knew it, she was parking outside her parents' house, under the large leopard tree, its beautifully spotted trunk reaching high above the house. She pulled on the handbrake and cut the engine. 'By the way, just so you know, the last time I saw Mum she slapped me across the face.'

Maria gasped. 'Because of me?'

Tansy grimaced. 'Yes, and also because I lied about seeing you.'

'I never meant to cause such conflict.'

'Do not be sorry. Not for a second. None of this is your fault.'

Maria snorted. 'Except for killing the priest.'

Tansy barked out laughter. 'Yes, except for that.' Then she straightened her shoulders. 'Are you ready? Let's go.'

As soon as they stepped out of the car and onto the ochre-painted concrete driveway, a volley of high-pitched barking assaulted Maria's ears. On either side of the driveway were rose bushes, the leaves starting to look a little bedraggled, as was normal in winter, but still with a few orange and pink blooms bobbing in the sunshine, and a good shape to each bush. Enid must have a green thumb too, Maria thought, and the idea warmed her, that they might have this in common.

Next door, young children ran around the front yard in sports clothes—soccer outfits, perhaps—and paused only briefly to observe Maria and Tansy. The front door of Enid's house opened; inside stood a man, muttering to the cinnamon-coloured flurries at his feet, telling them to be quiet. Finlay. It must be. Maria couldn't stop the smile that sprang to her lips.

He opened the door further, welcoming Tansy, and then stopped and stared at Maria. His jaw, which must once have been set and strong in his youth, seemed unsure of itself as his eyes slid back to Tansy and widened.

Maria's heart sank. 'You didn't know I was coming either,' she said.

'Dad, this is Maria,' Tansy said, and then leaned forward to kiss Finlay's cheek, effectively pushing him back into the house. Maria waited on the bristled doormat that proclaimed *Welcome*.

Finlay found his manners. 'Maria, please, come inside.' He bent down stiffly and swept up one of the dogs, which was still emitting an occasional yap of discontent, stood aside for her to enter. She took a breath, and crossed the threshold.

Tansy looked around the lounge room. 'Where's Mum?'

'She's just in the study, on the phone to Paula. She'll be out in a moment, I'm sure.' He put the dog down; both dogs moved to sniff Maria's feet, and then, deciding she was safe, ran to Tansy to jump at her legs and lick her hands. Eventually, satisfied, they retired to their dog bed—a large tartan-covered oval basket near a glass cabinet—and curled up together.

Maria stood clutching her handbag, watching Tansy for guidance. Her niece headed to the couch and beckoned Maria over too.

'Yes, please make yourself comfortable,' Finlay said, going to the open-plan kitchen nearby. 'Would you both like some tea?'

'Yes, please,' Tansy said.

'Yes, thank you,' Maria said, feeling it was the polite thing to do.

Tansy asked her father a few questions, about his week and about the dogs, while he boiled the kettle and collected mugs.

'Maria, how do you take your tea?' he asked.

'Black's fine.' Then she grappled with the clasp of her handbag. 'I brought you some honey. Do you like honey?'

'Sometimes on toast.'

'Good, because this is wonderful honey. It comes from my own bees. I'm a beekeeper. I love the bees. They work so hard.' She stood and offered the jar of amber-coloured nectar to Finlay. She was nervous, she realised, prattling on about bees. More nervous than she'd been confessing to George. But she couldn't seem to stop herself.

'Most people don't realise that bees ingest the nectar from the flowers and then take it back to the hive, where they regurgitate it and mix it with enzymes in their saliva, and this is the start of honey. But there's such a high water content that it would ferment if left that way, so they have to fan it with their wings to evaporate most of the water.'

Finlay was nodding, murmuring. He seemed interested. Of course he was interested. These were facts and people liked facts. Facts were solid ground. Neutral.

'And they keep the hive at thirty-six degrees. Isn't that amazing? They're insects. Cold-blooded. Yet they know how to regulate temperature. It's astounding.'

Heavens. She should have done a decade or two of the rosary in the car on the way down to calm herself instead of reliving all that history. The past—it caused all sorts of difficulties. As did worrying about the future. That was why the Buddhists were so keen on meditation and training the mind to be nowhere else but in the present.

Let go and let God.

Finlay took the jar from her and thanked her. 'Would you like some now in your tea?'

'That would be lovely, thank you,' she said, not knowing why, since she never had honey in her tea. It just seemed the thing to say. This was dreadful. It was all so stilted and awkward and overly polite and Tansy had just forced her on them and Enid hadn't even made an appearance yet. Her heart began to pound. She clenched her hands together, knotting her fingers. She looked over at Tansy, desperate. But Tansy, with her elegant aqua scarf at her neck and her smooth, clear skin and her youthful optimism, had no idea that coming here had been a colossal error of judgement.

'Tansy, I think maybe this was a mistake . . .'

But it was too late. Enid had entered the room.

Here we go.

Tansy stood and faced Enid, who was on the other side of the couch. 'Mum, hi.'

But her mother didn't respond. Her stocky body was rigid. Her face pale and stiff. Her eyes dark recesses beneath her brow. She was staring across the room at Maria.

The dogs lifted their heads and watched Enid. And there were several full seconds of absolute stillness and silence, except for the rumbling kettle on the bench, nearing boiling point.

Maria, who normally seemed so together and strong, looked small and vulnerable. Yet, seeing them both in the same room together, Tansy couldn't help but notice the similarities between them. Maria was thinner, wiry from so many years of hard physical labour, while Enid had a rounded belly from bearing two babies. But around the eyes, the nose, the mouth, you could tell they were sisters. A mix of emotions swept across her mother's face—apprehension, bewilderment, interest, fear.

'M-Maria?' Enid said, her voice stumbling in confusion. 'Is that really you?'

Maria nodded, and her eyes brightened with sudden emotion. Tansy's heart soared—maybe this would be a beautiful reunion after all.

But her mother hadn't moved. She was still clutching the phone in her hand, and had brought it to her chest.

'Mum, I hope it's okay, I brought Maria down here today to see you because . . .' Tansy trailed off, not knowing how to finish that sentence. 'Come and sit down and have some tea. Please.'

Enid looked at her now, as though she'd only just realised that her daughter was in the room. She nodded dumbly, and Tansy guided her to the couch. Shock was a good thing, perhaps. At least Enid hadn't spontaneously combusted.

'And Maria, please come and sit down too,' Tansy said. Finlay returned to making the tea and Maria crept to the couch opposite.

Tansy's shoulders were stiff, waiting for the yelling. Maybe some more slapping.

But then Enid began to talk, jumping straight to the deepest wound she'd carried for so long. 'Why didn't you come to Mum's funeral?' she asked, her voice thick with all the complex emotions that made up grief.

Maria seemed to search for the right words, unaware that Finlay had placed a mug in front of her. 'I wanted to punish myself,' she said quietly. 'I didn't deserve to go. I'd ruined everything, for you, Mum, Florrie maybe. I'd stolen from the church because I thought I knew best.' She broke down then, and Tansy rushed for a box of tissues and placed them beside her on the couch.

Enid waited a moment, then spoke again. 'What do you mean, you stole from the church?'

Tansy held Maria's hand and spoke for her, filling Enid in as best she could from what Maria had said in the car on the way down.

Maria nodded to confirm the story. 'I'm so sorry.'

'But how could we not know this?'

'I bought silence by giving myself to the church.'

'But that's . . . I don't understand.'

Maria explained their mother's reasoning.

Enid shook her head, confounded. 'I can't believe she thought the church would have abandoned us.'

Maria took a deep breath and nodded. 'I'm saddened to say that I think she was right. The church was a much harsher place then than it is now. It had more power, more control over people's lives. I've seen it do some awful things, firsthand.'

Enid sat still, clearly stunned. Tansy could almost hear her idealistic notions of the church shattering around her. 'But we thought you'd abandoned the family, chosen the convent over us. First when you joined the sisters and then when you didn't come to the funeral. Like you thought you were better than us. That you didn't care.'

Maria shook her head. 'There hasn't been a day in my life I haven't thought of you all.'

Enid leaned back with her hand over her mouth, staring from Maria to Tansy. Then she sprang forward again. 'But you've been out of the convent for years, haven't you? Why didn't you come and find us?'

Maria wiped her nose and took a deep breath, then blew it out steadily. 'I wanted to hide away,' she said slowly. 'I thought I didn't deserve a family. I'd done something bad and needed to . . .' she searched for the right word, 'repent. I needed to show God that I knew what I'd done was very serious and that I was willing to spend the rest of my life atoning for it.'

Enid shook her head, confused and even sceptical. 'I don't understand. Didn't you pay for taking the money with your service to the church?'

'Yes, but there was something else.'

Tansy held her breath, waiting.

'Back in the seventies, I made a choice to help some children. But to do that, I committed a crime.'

Enid laughed, incredulous. 'Another crime? More stealing?' She was getting nervous, Tansy could tell, sensing something bigger and more appalling was to come.

'I got away with this second crime.' Maria's voice was steady now. She'd told this story so many times it almost felt like safe territory. 'But I knew I still needed to pay for my actions. So I stayed on as a sister in order to serve the people who needed me, even though I'd lost all respect for the church. I stayed for another twenty years.' She paused.

'*That's* why you stayed,' Tansy said, satisfied to finally know the answer.

'Twenty years was the term I thought fitting for my crime,' Maria said, continuing to address Enid. 'When that time was up, I left. But I couldn't face you or Florrie. I just wanted to keep helping people until I died, alone.'

'Twenty years?' Enid's face scrunched up in bewilderment. 'But that's ridiculous. The only people who serve twenty years in jail are murderers.' She laughed again, thinly. 'And you're not a murderer, are you?'

Tansy and Maria exchanged a glance. Finlay sat frozen in his chair, watching.

Enid's face fell. '*Are* you?'

'Yes, dear, I'm sorry to say I am.'

They talked late into the evening and ordered home-delivered pizzas and garlic bread. There were tears from everyone, even Finlay, as hundreds of questions were answered and decades of lost time and memories were explained and shared. Enid took the news of the murder better than Tansy had thought she might—but perhaps she was just too overwhelmed to process it fully. They all agreed that they were much too tired to phone Florrie and try to explain, but that it should happen first thing tomorrow. Enid apologised profusely to Tansy for slapping her and begged her forgiveness. And then, when all the words had finally dried up, and everyone was wrung out completely, Enid made up the guest bedroom and insisted that Tansy and Maria stay the night, which they did, gratefully, sleeping side by side in the queen ensemble. Maria snored. And Tansy dreamed, truly peaceful for the first night in weeks.

34

The next morning, Maria tentatively asked if Enid would be going to church.

'I think I might skip it just this once. These are rather extraordinary circumstances,' she said, glancing at Finlay and passing the milk to Maria to pour on her porridge. 'Do you have to get back up the mountain straight away?' she asked, a hint of insecurity in her voice.

'No, for once. I have my assistant, Petrice, looking after the group. And they're all leaving today so I'm sure she can manage to get them fed and out the door. I can help with the washing and cleaning when I get home.'

'Would you like to stay another day?' Enid said. 'I could ask Florrie to come down from the coast, and we could tell her everything—together this time, so it's not as difficult for you.'

Over her cereal bowl, Tansy listened, glowing with pleasure.

'Tansy? Do you need to get going?' her mother asked. 'Because Florrie could always drive Maria home later today.'

Tansy hesitated, unsure whether they were all ready to be left alone together so early in their reunion. They were on their best behaviour now, but what if it all went sour quickly? And what if Florrie didn't take the news as well as Enid had?

'It's okay.' Maria smiled at her as if reading her mind. 'I'd like to stay. I almost never take a day off and, as Enid says, there are rather extraordinary circumstances right now.'

'Alright, if you're sure. But just call me if you need me.'

'Oh, stop fussing,' Enid said. 'She's a grown woman.'

'Okay then,' Tansy agreed, and departed soon after, leaving the women to explore Enid's garden together while continuing to talk about the past.

Belle phoned while she was driving, and Tansy took the call on her hands-free device. 'What's happened? How are you? How's Hamish?'

'It's unbelievable,' Belle said, sounding infinitely more relaxed and happy than Tansy had heard her in a long time. 'I took Hamish back to our doctor and asked for a referral to a specialist, and he gave me the usual rubbish about him eventually growing out of it and so on. But then he weighed him and because Hamish had actually lost weight, he finally took it seriously.'

Tansy *tsk*ed, indicating and moving into the overtaking lane to pass a heavily loaded Kombi van crawling along with its windows down and the long hair of its passengers streaking out into the wind. 'Why do they have to wait until things are so bad before they'll do something?'

'Still, he was reluctant to give me a referral, saying the specialist would want to do an endoscopy with a general anaesthetic and it likely wouldn't show anything anyway. I was crazy mad at this point and just kept firing questions—could we change the reflux medication he was on, could we try another formula, and so on. And then he reached into the cupboard behind him and pulled out a different tin of hypoallergenic formula—the best one you can get; it has to be prescribed by a gastric surgeon. But he had the sample so he said, "Here, try that. But I don't think it will help."

'I took it anyway, and because Hamish had refused everything all morning, I made up a bottle in the car and he refused it of course, because he's just so scared to eat now, but then, I don't know if he could smell it or what, but he tried it, and I swear I didn't breathe for three minutes, but he kept going. He drained the bottle and has been eating like a horse ever since.'

'What a relief. So is that it then? Will he just stay on that?'

'I'll have to go back to the GP tomorrow. I guess we'll still need a referral to the surgeon, because he's the only one that can prescribe it.'

'That's frustrating. But still, what an amazing turnaround.' In the background, Hamish began to kick up a fuss.

'Oh, here we go again,' Belle said, and Tansy could hear the grin in her voice. 'My bubba is hungry.'

Tansy cheered. 'You better go then. And keep me posted.'

She ended the call with a smile; things were on the up for Belle. Not only that, her mother and Maria, somewhat unbeliev-ably, were getting on and rebuilding some sort of relationship. Florrie would be joining them today and, hopefully, the recon-ciliation would continue smoothly.

On top of that, she'd also found Maria a good lawyer, who gave Tansy a sense of hope that somehow it might all be okay. Maybe Maria would only have to go to jail for a short time. Maybe the judge would suspend her sentence due to her age and on account of her lifelong service to the community. There was always hope.

Jordan and Katarina had uncertain times ahead but, fortunately, a strong relationship to fall back on. She was sad to think of Rose and Sam heading for a divorce; Sam had always been a quiet but reliable presence in her family's life and Tansy would miss him. And of course her mother and father still had some things to work through too, but she was feeling optimistic about that now as well. Leo was leaving uni, but at least he had left his options open and could always go back, and Dougal would come to terms with that eventually.

Dougal.

With over an hour to go up the highway, there was a lot of time to reflect on Dougal's offer. She didn't want to lose him. Whatever they chose to do, her marriage was her highest priority.

But she did want a baby. Deep down, she knew it. Yes, she could have a wonderful life without one. But to have the chance? It suddenly struck her, with both dispiriting and amusing clarity, that maybe she'd become a children's bedroom designer because she wanted to live out that fantasy. Huh. Maybe she was getting some wisdom along with turning thirty.

One thing was for sure, it was impossible for her and Dougal to sort this out when they were on opposite sides of the world. And if he was magnanimous enough to make this choice for her, for their marriage, then at the very least she should be booking a flight to Canada as soon as possible. She needed to be with him. She didn't want to go to Toronto, but then she was pretty sure that, despite what he'd said, Dougal didn't want a baby.

When they'd made their vows in St Columba's they'd promised to cherish each other above all else. Everything else had to come second to that—locations, children, her parents, her aunt, and the throes of a legal crisis. Their marriage came first.

So it was decided. As soon as she got home to the apartment, lovely and warm from absorbing the morning's beaming winter sunshine, she booked her flight. She would leave in a week.

Thank you for bringing Maria back into our lives. I'm so sad that we've only just found her now when we'll likely lose her again any day. I'm sorry that I was angry with you. Can you forgive me, Tansy dear? Florrie x

He's still eating! He feels twice as heavy as yesterday. B xx

Hi family, this is just to let you know that Sam moved out today. He'll be staying with his mother for a while. The kids are very upset, of course. I'm sorry I've brought this on our family through all my own doing. I hope you can forgive me. I know you'll continue to support my children, even if you can't support me. Rose xxx

I can't tell you how happy I am that you'll be here in a week. I can't wait to leave this hotel and for us to find a place together. I can't wait to hold my wife in my arms again. I love you.

Sister Veronica was first on George's list for Monday morning, and he drove to her nursing home on the south side of the city. It was a dated Catholic-run home, only minutes from the city centre, red brick, three storeys, on land that must have been outrageously valuable these days to the developers who were always looking to demolish whatever they could to build high-rise unit complexes. He was directed to her room on the second floor, at the west end of the building. His leather shoes squawked on the linoleum flooring, and voices bounced off the walls, with no carpets or soft furnishings to absorb the noise. The hallways were hung with paintings and artefacts from decades ago. The tea trolley wheels yelped as the blue-capped volunteer pushed it along.

He'd been told that Veronica had dementia, but he needed to see for himself. Sometimes the past was still within reach for those with dementia, though it was always difficult to get a testimony admitted to court under those circumstances.

Her room smelled as they always did, of chemicals and ageing plastics, a hint of urine and lost hope. George shuddered as he entered, both at the stuffy oppressiveness and with the desire to never end up in a place like this.

Veronica was in the far corner, and two other women lay in beds nearby. One of them had a tiny television next to her bed, the volume up as far as such a small item would go. The other woman was asleep. Veronica was half sitting, propped up with pillows. She was tiny, with none of the robustness of Maria or Sarah (but of course she was much older than them, he reminded himself), just bones and flapping skin and veins, her short hair looking as though someone had taken to it carelessly with scissors, exposing parts of her scalp. She was knitting—something blue that might eventually be a blanket.

'Sister Veronica?' George said. She looked up and smiled, with no trace of hesitation or suspicion. 'I'm George.'

'Hello,' she said, an Irish accent little worn from the decades of being in Australia. 'Do I know you?' She stopped knitting, seemingly pleased to have a visitor.

He smiled, and pulled over a plastic chair. 'No, we've never met.'

'Are you a nice man?'

'I think I am. My wife and children think so too.'

'Catholic?'

'Yes.'

'We need more parishioners. Dropping like flies, they are,' she said, sucking in her cheeks distastefully.

'I wanted to ask you some questions about your time as a nun at St Lucy's Convent.'

'Do you?' She narrowed her eyes. 'Why?'

Still shrewd.

'I'm a police officer, Sister.' He felt her withdraw the moment he said that, but it would be unethical to ask her questions without disclosing who he was and why he was there.

'Mother,' she corrected him.

'My apologies, Mother. I've been investigating Father Peter Cunningham in his time at your convent.'

Veronica lifted her chin and looked directly at him. 'I don't know who you're talking about.'

He nodded, defeated. 'I thought you might say that.'

George didn't believe Veronica, but there was nothing he could do. If she'd been able or willing to talk, she might have been able to point him in the right direction to look for more information and evidence. But even if she'd delivered him the out-and-out truth, it was unlikely to ever be admissible. The testimony of a ninety-three-year-old woman with dementia was hardly legally convincing.

So it was with some anxiety that he drove back through the city to the north side of Brisbane, to the outer suburbs, and to St Lucy's itself. He parked out on the road, listening to the sounds of teachers lecturing in classrooms up on the second storey of the long college building, and the students talking and laughing. A group of girls in sports gear were out on the oval to the right, playing hockey. The teacher blew a whistle and they cheered.

He walked along the pathway to an annexe with *Office* printed over the door, where he spoke to the enthusiastic receptionist, who gave him a visitor badge and phoned the principal to let her know he was on the grounds, and then pointed him in the direction of the convent proper.

Here in the kitchen he found Sister Celine, a woman of approximately his own age, peeling potatoes. She was thick around the middle, with patches of angry-looking eczema up her arms. Her hair was cut short, like that of all the other sisters he'd met. To get her attention, he knocked on the architrave of the doorway he'd just entered.

She looked up, wary. 'Can I help you?' She glanced around the room, even though they were alone.

'Sister Celine, my name is George Harvey.' He extended a card to her.

'Police?' she squeaked, dropping the potato and wiping her hands on a pink tea towel. Weakening sunlight filtered through the tall windows that overlooked the oval. It must be nearly the end of the school day.

'Yes. I wanted to have a chat with you, if that's okay.' He was treading gently, knowing that Celine was considered delicate. 'May I sit down?'

Sister Celine pulled on an earlobe, a nervous gesture. It was one of those large, meaty, pendulous lobes, and he wondered if a lifetime of pulling at them had contributed. 'I suppose.'

He sat down at the wooden kitchen table and indicated for her to do the same. 'I want to assure you that the principal—Mrs Thatcher—knows I'm here, and why I'm here. I checked into the office.' He showed her his visitor badge. 'So you should feel free to talk to me.'

'Okay,' she said slowly.

'You've been here a long time,' he said, smiling. 'Almost forty years.' She studied his face, his hair, his clothes. But said nothing. 'Can you tell me about your work here, in the kitchen, in the convent?' He gestured around the room.

She spoke with her eyes directed to the ceiling. 'Food prep, mostly. Odd jobs. I do bits and pieces in the school office now too, typing and filing. And I look after one organ in the chapel, and two now retired inside the convent. They're my babies.'

George nodded, remembering Maria saying the same thing. He took notes as she talked, his silver pen rolling quickly over the lined pages. He'd decided against an audio recording today due to Celine's evident wariness of strangers.

'And back in the seventies, when Father Peter Cunningham was around, what did you do then?'

Celine's knee instantly began to jiggle, her fingers worrying at buttons and eczema. 'Same,' she said flatly, her eyes roaming the kitchen, looking anywhere but at him.

His stomach lurched. He'd seen these sorts of behaviours so many times before in the people whose testimonies he'd taken. They wore a haunted look around the eyes; they were reluctant to engage, and when they did they looked at a spot somewhere over his shoulder, back into the past. Maria had mentioned the commonly held beliefs about Celine's background, what little the other nuns knew, and the nervous way Celine had acted around Cunningham.

Had Cunningham hurt Celine too? Had he seen her fragile mind, her damaged psyche, her inability to defend herself? Of course he had. She was exactly the sort he'd prey on. Her mental illness would have been all the better for him—people back then knew so much less about these kinds of conditions and would be quick to dismiss her erratic behaviour.

George swore under his breath: another victim for his file.

The school bell rang, loud and long, like a fire station alarm. Instantly, the air filled with shrieks and chatter as the girls spilled out onto verandahs and ran down stairs. Balls bounced on the footpath and mobile phones trilled. (How times had changed.) Celine's eyes turned towards the window, seeking distraction.

Not wanting to lose her, he changed the subject. 'Tell me about the other sisters and what they did,' he said, adopting a relaxed and open posture, smiling and nodding. To calm her down and salvage this conversation, he needed to pull her mind away from Cunningham, away from the dark place, back to the safety of the sisters. And it was working, her compulsive picking at her eczema notably easing.

'Everyone had their roles. Sister Kathryn, she looked after the plumbing. Her father was a plumber and she was one of five daughters—no sons. He had to teach someone.'

She then seemed to lose her concentration and fall into random nonsense and fragments of nursery rhymes before regaining her clarity.

'Then there was Sister Fiona; she was our spider catcher. Most of the sisters killed normal spiders easy enough, but the big hairy huntsmen . . .' Here, she held up her hands like menacing crawling spiders and walked them up her arm. 'They would make them scream.' She was gleeful about that, and held her hands up by her mouth as if to scream. But then her face fell. 'And we weren't allowed to scream. No screaming. No.'

George swallowed. 'And Mother Veronica? What was her specialty?'

'She was the Mother. What Mother says goes. What Mother hears she pretends not to.' Celine began to chew a nail, or rather a nail bed, her nails so badly gnawed down.

'Tell me more about that,' he said quietly, sitting very still.

'She could see, you know.'

'See what?'

'See, see, see. Everything.' She lowered her voice to a whisper. 'See, see nothing.'

George waited. But she was muttering now, half singing, her eyes unfocused, her mind elsewhere. The hair stood up on the back of his neck. It was just as Maria had said: Veronica knew. She'd always known. And she'd done nothing. And now, because of her dementia, she would never be held to account and might not even by troubled by the knowledge of her culpable failure to protect her students.

'What about Maria?' he ventured.

'Maria, Maria, Maria,' she sang, drumming her short fingers over her lips.

'Sister Maria. She was here when you arrived at the convent. She was the head beekeeper.'

Celine stopped all movement. 'The bees.'

'Yes.'

'She was the only one, you know.'

'The only one?'

'Father Peter. The bees. Maria.' Celine burst into cackles that racked her body and sent tears streaming down her cheeks. She doubled over with uncontrollable laughter. 'Died, died, died, he did,' she wheezed, as the convulsions began to ease. Then she took a deep breath and composed herself, her face stolid once more. 'Died like the rat he was.'

At home that night, George replayed his audio recording of Maria, skipping forwards and backwards to find the parts he wanted. He played these sections again and again, unsure whether or not he was just hearing what he wanted to hear. He returned to the places where she talked of convent life, of the various residents and what they did each day, just as he'd asked Celine to do. And over and over, he listened to her describe the events of that afternoon that led up to her attack on Peter Cunningham.

Then he pulled out the recent test report and read it again.

Lastly, he phoned Blaine Campbell. 'We need to talk.'

35

Belle's name flashed up on Tansy's mobile.

'Hi, I meant to call you yesterday,' Tansy said. It turned out that once she'd booked a flight to Toronto, her to-do list suddenly quadrupled.

'It's fine, totally fine. You've got a life too,' Belle said.

'What's the latest with Hamish?'

'We went back to the doctor yesterday and Hamish has put on a week's worth of weight in just two days.'

'Wow.'

'He's chowing down like there's no tomorrow.' Belle laughed. 'So the doctor thought this was pretty remarkable and hooked us up with a remote Skype appointment with the gastric surgeon to talk about it. And the surgeon says the only difference between this new formula and the one he was on is corn. So he says Hamish might have a corn intolerance. All of that because of bloody—I mean, *flaming* corn syrup.'

'So will he stay on the new formula now?'

'Yep. The surgeon has given authorisation to the doctor to prescribe it. He has to ring some authority centre to clear it each time he writes a script, but hopefully that's it now for quite a while . . . until we hit the minefield of eating solids.'

'What a drama.'

'I know.' Belle took a deep breath and let it out slowly. 'So, enough of me. What's going on with you? Where are you right now?'

'On my way to see Maria. I have some news I need to tell her, and you.'

'What?'

'I've booked my ticket for Canada. I leave Sunday.'

Belle sucked in her breath sharply. 'Sunday?'

'Yep. I just realised I have to get to Dougal as soon as possible. We can't move forward together if we're on opposite sides of the world. This is something . . . a test, a roadblock, a phase . . . I don't know. I hear all marriages go through them,' Tansy said lightly, trying to lift her own mood. 'I have to go.'

'I don't know what to say,' Belle said. 'I know you don't want to go.'

'No, I don't. But, you know, as far as problems in the world go it's a good one to have, hey.'

'You're doing the right thing.'

'You sure?'

'Definitely. Send me the details of when your flight's leaving and I'll come to the airport.'

'No, you don't have to do that. It's a huge drive and effort for you with Hamish and all.'

'Stop it. You're not getting on that plane without a hug from me. I'll leave you to your party on Saturday at Noosa. You're still doing that, aren't you?'

'Yes. It will be my going-away gig now.'

'I won't get enough time with you there, because everyone will want to be spending their last minutes with you.'

'You're probably right. There's been so much family stuff going on I don't even know where to start. I'll give you the Cliff's Notes at the airport.'

'Sounds like a plan. I can't wait to hear all about it and have you all to myself.'

Maria waited. George Harvey was on his way.

A sick bee will abandon a hive, hoping to stop the rot from spreading. A bee has only one aim and that is to build a strong hive. A sick bee could endanger the rest of the hive. So they will leave to die.

Maria wondered if her act of violence made her a sick bee, one who had poisoned the hive she lived in.

She hoped not. She liked to think instead that she was a guard bee. Guard bees ruthlessly killed predators to protect their family. And that was what she'd done.

But for that, now she was to learn her fate.

She heard an engine groaning up the hill and she stepped out into the cold. It was late morning but it still hadn't warmed up here on the mountain, the temperature only twelve degrees. It was quiet, too. No new guests had arrived since the drumming camp had left, and Petrice wasn't due to come in today.

Rubbing her hands together against the chill, she walked to the upper car park just in time to see the nose of George's car peek up over the hill. He swung into an empty space. Seconds later, Tansy's white Barina appeared unexpectedly behind him.

Maria shuffled her feet, both against the cold and with anxiety. She didn't want Tansy here when George delivered his news.

They both got out, Tansy lithely, George awkwardly, and made each other's acquaintance as they came towards her. Tansy's brows knitted together and she folded her arms across her body, as though bracing herself.

'Maria, I need to call Zoe now,' she urged.

'Who's Zoe?' George asked. 'Hello again, Maria,' he said, leaning forward to shake her hand.

'Zoe is Maria's lawyer,' Tansy said. 'She needs to be present for this interview and Maria must not say a word until she arrives.' She was very firm.

'Nonsense,' Maria said. 'It makes no difference, Tansy. It's all over.'

George rubbed his chin, considering. 'Of course you're entitled to have legal representation present,' he said. 'And I don't want to appear flippant about it, but I think you'll be okay for what I have to say today. I'll need to get you down to the station later to make statements and so on, but if you like, to save time and your lawyer making a trip up the mountain, I can simply talk today, and you can listen. How does that sound?'

Maria nodded at Tansy. 'Okay?'

'I don't like it,' Tansy said, still frowning. 'We've no idea what he's going to say.'

'But if I don't say anything at all, will that make you happy?' Maria asked.

Tansy looked unconvinced, but also resigned, perhaps realising that it didn't matter what she tried to do to help her, Maria would do whatever she wanted anyway. 'Lead the way.'

Back in Maria's small house, they all perched uneasily on the sagging couches. It was cold in here too, barely warmer than outside, the tall gum trees casting shade over the cabin and preventing the weak sun from heating it.

'Shall I make tea?' Maria asked.

'Shh!' Tansy practically jumped out of her seat.

'Oh, for goodness' sake, I only asked if the man wanted tea,' Maria said.

'I'm fine, thank you, Maria,' said George.

Tansy looked to the heavens and groaned.

'I'll make this as brief as possible,' he said, cutting into their squabble. 'Maria, I spoke to Mother Veronica and Sister Celine yesterday.'

'Did you?' With her next breath in, Maria's chest froze from the inside. She was guarded, though she didn't know why. It wasn't as if she hadn't confessed everything anyway. But she couldn't help wondering what they'd said.

'I couldn't get a useful testimony out of Veronica, I'm afraid. She's in a nursing home and has dementia.'

'I'm sorry to hear that,' Maria said.

'She claimed she couldn't remember Peter Cunningham.'

Maria wanted to prod him, intrigued by his choice of the word 'claimed'. But she kept her peace and waited for more.

'Sister Celine, on the other hand, was more interesting.'

Maria couldn't help but chuckle gently. 'She was always interesting. You never knew what you'd get in answer to the simplest question.'

'Maria, I'm just going to point out that you're talking,' Tansy said. Maria waved her away.

George gave a half smile. 'Yes. She is quite a character. The thing is, she said something that made me think. She was very down on Peter Cunningham, as you'd expect.'

'She didn't like him one bit,' Maria agreed, compressing her lips. 'What did she say, out of interest? If you're allowed to tell me, of course.'

He tapped his foot. 'She said he died like the rat he was.'

Maria recoiled. It seemed such a harsh thing to say. Her reaction was entirely ridiculous, of course, since she was the one who'd actually killed the man.

'The other thing you should know is that, recently, I organised for Peter's body to be exhumed.'

Beside her, Tansy gasped. Now Maria was silent.

'Science and technology has advanced considerably since the seventies and we discovered something new.'

Maria held her breath.

'We found evidence of strychnine poisoning.'

'Strychnine?' Maria whispered.

'Yes. And putting the pieces together with the sequence of events in your confession, Celine's history, and her job at the convent, about which she was so passionate . . .'

Maria's hands flew to her face. 'The organs?' she mumbled from behind her fingers.

George nodded.

'What? What?' Tansy beseeched.

'The rats.' Maria dropped her hands. 'Oh no, no, no!' She stood up from the couch, propelled by adrenaline.

'*What?!*' Tansy pleaded.

'She hated rats so much,' Maria said, pacing. 'She loved the organs and hated the rats. She used to . . .' her heart fluttered, '. . . she used to poison them.'

'With strychnine,' George said.

'And she'd just fed him his last supper . . .' Maria whispered. She felt hot all over. Her legs turned to jelly and she stumbled, reaching for the couch. George jumped to her aid and helped her back to a seated position.

'In your testimony to me, you explained that Peter had just been to afternoon tea, yes. And that he was burping and sweating and breathing hard. It was the beginning of the poisoning. Strychnine works very quickly. By the time you'd put the bee on him, he was already dying. The swelling in his throat . . .' He rocked his head from side to side. 'Sure, some of that may have been from the bee, but it's unlikely. Anaphylaxis usually takes more than a few seconds, which you say was all the time between the bee sting and the fall into the well. He was going to die anyway.'

Maria shook her head vehemently. 'But I let him fall. And I, I still *tried* to kill him.'

The policeman's eyebrows rose. 'It's certainly unusual to have two people at once try to kill someone,' he said. 'And add an accidental fall to it as well . . .'

'What will happen now?' Tansy asked. 'Is Maria free to go? Or will she still be charged?'

'It's not entirely up to me,' George said. 'My supervisor, Blaine Campbell, ultimately has a big say in how this moves forward from here. But I'm certainly hopeful we can get a much better outcome for your aunt than we were previously looking at.'

'Oh, wow,' Tansy said, taking Maria's hand in hers and patting it repeatedly, as though encouraging herself as much as Maria.

'I also spoke to Sister Sarah,' George said, looking at Maria once more.

'Sarah?' Her hand went to her throat, as she ached with longing to see Sarah once more. She'd had no correspondence with her since she left the convent.

George nodded. 'She told me all about the letters you both exchanged and, fortunately for us, she kept all the ones you'd sent her. There's a lot of evidence there of the cover-up that was going on. I don't suppose—I know it's a long shot, but I don't suppose you still have her original letter? The one warning you about Peter?'

Maria nodded. 'Yes, I do.'

George looked as though he might leap in the air and pump his fist.

'You told me you burned it,' Tansy said, incredulous.

'It's in the bottom of my rosary case, beneath the velvet cushion. I hid it there, thinking I might need it one day, and it's been sitting there all these years.' Maria turned to Tansy. 'I just wanted to protect the letter, knowing how important it was. I should have trusted you. I'm sorry.' She rose and went to the bedroom to retrieve the case from the small bedside table, her heart thumping wildly, her hands shaking.

She carried it back to the lounge room and pried open the lid, her thumb and fingers fitting perfectly into the imprints just as they'd always done; she lifted the cushion and plucked out the letter, folded neatly into many small squares. She opened it, cast her eyes down over Sarah's squashed cursive writing—the kind you didn't see anymore except from other people her age—and handed it to George. He perused it briefly, nodded, folded it again and tucked it into his folder.

'I'm confident that we can lay charges against Ian Tully,' he said. 'And as you say, he'll likely implicate you too.'

'Yes, he will.'

'But he'll be right ticked off when he finds out we already know.' George smiled.

Maria laughed with relief, then burst into tears, her hands supporting her head while Tansy rubbed her back. Everything would be okay now, she knew it. She felt it deep in her bones. Whatever happened, whether or not she went to jail for attempted murder, it would all be okay. What she'd done was terrible. But now she knew she wasn't alone. In truth, she'd never been alone—her fellow sister Celine had been with her in spirit, sharing her burden. And now, thanks to Tansy, she had her family back and she'd never be alone again.

36

Two pelicans, with huge wingspans and long pink beaks, lowered their feet like the wheels of an aeroplane as they touched down onto the rippling surface of the Noosa River. They pulled up effortlessly and began to paddle along side by side. They circled towards the sandy bank of the parkland along Gympie Terrace, the wide green public strip that ran between the water and the road, shops and restaurants on the other side. Tansy loved the pelicans; they looked like a bunch of old men with their nearly bald heads, save for a few spiky wisps on top, and gathered around the jetties, clacking their beaks and deftly catching fish heads thrown to them by fishermen.

'That's what you'll be doing this time tomorrow at Sydney airport to get your connecting flight,' Rose said, pointing to another black and white pelican coming in to land. 'They're so much like planes, aren't they?'

Tansy nodded, smiling. She and Rose were sitting together with Enid and Katarina in one of the wooden picnic pavilions, a colourful *Happy Birthday* sign stretched between the posts, and streamers wrapped around the beams. The park was filled with kids playing with bats and balls, or riding scooters or bicycles. There were dog walkers, Lycra-clad joggers, and women lying on blankets in the warm winter sunshine and reading.

Leo was nearby, being camp counsellor of sorts, entertaining Rose's four children and Toby. They were playing cricket with yellow plastic bats and a soft ball. A woman walked by with a grey and white Old English sheepdog, its silky coat swishing as it trotted, and its hair pinned back from its eyes with a pink clip. Little Amy left her post in outfield and rushed to the dog to *ooh* and *aah*. She had a similar clip in her own hair. Rose smiled, watching her daughter.

'I wonder what it would be like to live on a houseboat,' Enid said, her gaze out towards the water where hire boats were moored to the jetty, bobbing gently in the wake cast by passing vessels—a cruise boat, the Noosa ferry, kayaks, dinghies, an occasional jet boat. She reached across the picnic table for another bread roll, working her way through a tub of butter, preparing the rolls for the sausages and onions that Finlay, Jordan and Alastair were presiding over at the nearby gas barbecue.

'I couldn't do it,' Tansy said. 'I'd be terrified of drowning, and of course of being eaten by sharks.'

'Not in the river, though,' Enid said.

'Bull sharks are common in the river,' Tansy countered.

'But bull sharks don't eat people, do they?' Rose said. '*I* couldn't do it because my kids would drive me crazy in the first twenty minutes all stuck in such a small space.'

'At least you could just pull up on any island or sandbank you wanted to,' Katarina put in, sipping mineral water. 'You could just toss them over the edge and make them swim until they were exhausted. They could catch their own fish for dinner and read books in bed. Sounds lovely.'

Rose glanced down at Katarina's belly. 'That all sounds very idyllic, because it's a fantasy.' She laughed. 'You just wait until you've got two. They gang up on you.'

'It's school holidays soon, isn't it?' Tansy said.

'Yes,' Katarina confirmed cheerfully.

'Well then,' Tansy said, addressing Rose, 'Why don't you bring the kids up here for a week? You can stay at our place. Leo won't mind.' She reached for a cracker and cheese to give herself something to fiddle with while the early onset of homesickness trickled through her.

Rose stopped chopping and looked up from the tomatoes. She was very down on herself now that Sam had left; she put on a brave face for the kids, but became teary when they weren't around. Tansy ached for her, and it also made her that much more determined to cherish Dougal. Now her sister's expression was hesitant. 'Are you serious?' she asked.

'Sure, why not?'

Rose bit her lip. 'Sam has them for a week of the holidays,' she said, the words catching in her throat, revealing her disbelief of this new marital situation. 'But it would be great to get away with them. And it would give them something else to focus on right now. It's been . . . well, of course it's hard on them, with their father gone.' Tears threatened.

Leo arrived at the table then, sweating. He tugged a bottle of lemonade out of the ice and cracked the cap.

'Then again,' Rose said, 'I'm not sure I could handle all the kids on my own in an unfamiliar place. What if one of them drowned?' She was serious, Tansy could see, anxious about solo parenting.

'Who's drowning?' Leo said, reaching for a handful of potato chips and stuffing the lot into his mouth with loud crunching and copious licking of fingers. Tansy filled him in on her offer to Rose.

'I'll help,' he said, pulling off his cap, smoothing his hair back from his forehead and replacing the cap once more. Rose looked doubtful. 'Seriously,' he said. 'It'll be great. I'll take them to the movies too, and we could go to Australia Zoo or something.' He was bouncing on his feet now, energised by the thought. Actually, now Tansy thought about it, he'd been much happier in general since deciding to leave uni.

She encouraged Rose to accept the offer.

'Well, if you're sure,' Rose said, rubbing her nose self-consciously. 'Thank you.'

'No problem,' Leo said, and left the pavilion once more, heading back to the cricket game. 'Hey, kids, guess what?' he shouted.

'What's the latest with him and uni?' Florrie asked, pulling the plastic wrap off the tops of the salad bowls.

Tansy raised her eyebrows. 'He's having six months off, and then who knows? He's going to take some more shifts at the cafe and he wants to do a barista course. Speaking of which,' she looked around the parklands, 'where are our coffees?'

'A barista course? Like you did?' Florrie said.

'Yes. Strange, isn't it?'

Rose disagreed. 'He could travel around the world and pick up work anywhere with those skills. And you loved it.'

'True.'

'And it all worked out for you.'

'You don't think he's making a mistake, not finishing uni?' Given how invested Rose was in her own children's schooling, Tansy was surprised at her attitude.

Rose straightened. 'He's only deferred. He can still go back. Besides, I've made some big mistakes, so I can't sit here in judgement.'

'None of us can,' Enid said definitively. 'I've certainly made my fair share of errors of judgement too.'

A grey-winged noisy miner, with intense yellow-ringed eyes, swooped in under the roof and dive-bombed across Rose's head, darting for a bread roll. She squealed and raised her arms in self-defence, and the miner retreated up to a beam under the roof, cocking its head to the side to better examine the buffet on the table.

'Cheeky bugger,' Katarina said.

The men arrived then with the plate of sausages and onions. 'Right, we're ready to eat,' Finlay said, winking at Tansy for no reason she could imagine other than that he was feeling heavy of heart at her impending departure. She smiled back, her heart lurching. He wedged the plate into a gap on the table, already crowded with salads and dips, crackers and cheese. Rose got up to clap and call for her children to leave their game and come for lunch. And finally Maria returned, carrying the trays of coffees she'd been despatched ages ago to fetch.

Tansy was still getting over the fact that Maria had loosened the reins on her tightly controlled market presence and allowed Trav the handyman to work the stall today. But of course Maria was making plans for the future when she might not be there. And since Petrice wasn't entirely reliable, Trav was a good backup.

'Sorry that took so long,' Maria said, handing Tansy back her credit card and distributing the coffees. She'd stuck with black tea with a tiny splash of milk for herself, Tansy noted. 'It's busy over there. The coffee man makes art in the foam, with little teddy bears and love hearts and cats. People seem to love them, but it does take some time.'

'That's okay,' Tansy said. 'I was starting to think maybe you'd absconded from the law, hired a boat and sailed away into the sunset.' She was only half joking. Nothing would surprise her anymore. If there was one thing she'd come to realise about Maria these past four weeks, it was that she was a woman with many interesting and surprising layers and Tansy might never fully get to know her. Still, she loved the sides of her she'd seen so far and could only wonder what she still had to learn.

They feasted then, the adults taking up the bench spaces and the kids sitting on picnic blankets or fold-out chairs. The sausages were hot and salty and super tasty, the onions dripping with tomato sauce as Tansy brought the roll to her mouth, the drinks cold, ice bumping inside plastic cups, the salad crunchy. They all laughed, sipped coffees, settled squabbles between siblings and had second helpings. And when the kids couldn't bear to look at the beautiful birthday cake any longer, they sang 'Happy Birthday' to Tansy and she cut into Enid's cake, made with honey from Maria's darling bees and topped with butter cream and candles.

Enid and Finlay had managed to call a truce. She'd accepted that there was no point in trying to bully him into going back to church and that she simply had to let him do what he felt was best—although, she'd confided to Tansy, she was still hopeful that one day he'd return. Florrie had convinced Katarina to join her for pregnancy yoga sessions and was sending her to a naturopath to give this pregnancy the best support it could get. Jordan was taking instruction in qi gong from Alastair for stress management, and Toby was helping to decorate the baby's room; the theme they'd chosen, after discussion, was rockets. Tansy would have loved to help them create a nursery, but she'd just have to help from a distance. If Dougal had been here, she thought, it would have been a perfect family reunion, just as she'd wanted.

Sitting beside her, Maria had been silent for most of the feasting, as though she'd retreated emotionally into her cave. Or hive, perhaps.

'You okay?' Tansy asked, while the others were engaged in a heated debate about politics, something Tansy hated to get into. No one could ever be satisfied with the outcome of a political discussion.

Maria wore one of her pairs of grey trousers, sensible dark shoes—the kind you'd see nurses wearing—and the white cardigan Tansy had seen many times. Her short, unfashionable hair was brushed back sensibly. She looked for all the world like a nun. Tansy gave a small smile. Whatever Maria had done in her life, there was no doubting what was in her heart.

'Yes,' Maria said, 'just tired.'

'I'm not surprised,' Tansy said. 'You've been through so much in the past month.'

Her aunt took a deep breath. 'And there's a long way to go yet.'

Tansy winced. 'I'm sorry I won't be here to help you through that. I wanted to be.'

Maria shook her head firmly. 'You can't stay. You have a husband and a life to get on with. You have commitments and exciting new opportunities ahead of you.'

'Bad timing, though.'

'No such thing,' Maria said. 'There is just time, moving on. We all have choices to make. Some of them are good and wise, some are more complicated, but they're still choices. It's important for you now to go and choose your future with Dougal.'

Tansy swallowed a lump in her throat. 'But what if you . . .'

'Go to jail?' Maria shrugged. 'I'll deal with it then. Besides,' she gestured around her, 'thanks to you I have a whole family who might come and visit me.'

'I can always come back, you know that, right? If you need me, I'll be here. It's not a quick flight, but I can do it.'

Maria's eyes went bright and she looked out to the river where several people were larking about, shrieking as they splashed water at each other. Bells from bicycles trilled. A couple of small dogs snarled and snapped at each other in passing on the footpath.

'I don't want to go to jail,' Maria said. She faced Tansy once more. 'I like it out here in the world and I'm just beginning to feel that it might be okay for me to enjoy life, finally. And this,' she nodded again to their family, 'this is such a precious gift at my age. You're a true friend. Thank you.'

Tansy enfolded her in her arms and squeezed her tightly. 'You're welcome.'

Brisbane domestic airport was small by world standards, but bustled with all the usual culprits: zooming taxis; confusing parking and drop-off zones; teary people hugging goodbye; men in suits pulling small cabin luggage; pilots in navy-blue coats and caps; flight attendants also pulling cabin luggage, with flawless makeup and tightly secured hair; confused and lost people; and security guards.

Leo pulled up in the drop-off zone, where he got out and hugged Tansy goodbye.

'Take care of my car,' she said into his shoulder. She could feel him grin against her hair.

'I'll send you photo updates on how she's doing,' he said, then stepped back into the driver's seat and tooted, waving out the window as he drove away.

Dougal sent a perfectly timed message. *I can't wait until you arrive. I need my best friend, lover and wife with me. Thank you for coming. I love you so much.*

Inside, she found Belle, with Hamish strapped into his pram and chewing on a plastic ring. Belle threw her arms around her and they swayed excitedly together, and then fawned over Hamish, before moving into line to check in Tansy's luggage.

At security, Belle was next to Tansy, chatting away as though they'd only seen each other last week, not three months ago. She held baby Hamish in her arms as the pram went through the x-ray machine and they stepped through the metal detectors. Hamish's huge eyes watched the lights flash overhead.

'I'm so glad you're here,' Tansy said, collecting her hand luggage from the x-ray machine and helping Belle get hers. 'You look great, by the way. You should by rights be a ragged, greasy-haired mess.' Belle's skin was clear, her long brown hair was thick and shiny, and she seemed the happiest she'd been since Hamish was born.

'It's amazing what sleep will do.' She laughed. 'Now that he's eating better, he'll sleep for four or five hours. Feels like heaven.'

They made their way up the escalators and found a quiet-ish corner to have coffee and sticky buns. Belle wanted to stay with Tansy right up till the moment she went to the gate.

'Here, before I forget, I made you a care package,' Tansy said, pulling a box wrapped in pink paper out of a shopping bag at her side. 'I'm sorry it's so late. I'm a truly crap friend. Forgive me?' She passed it across the table.

'You are so not a crap friend,' Belle said. 'Thank you.' She started to sniffle and Tansy had to take a quick breath in to stop herself following suit.

'I should have sent it months ago. I hope it's still useful.'

'Doesn't matter if it's not useful,' Belle said, peeking inside the box and smiling. 'It's from you and it's beautiful.' She took out some aromatherapy pulse point perfume and sniffed it, then rubbed it on her wrists. Tansy could smell the rose scent from where she sat.

'I'd say that I'll send you something from Canada, but at the rate I deliver gifts I'll be home before it arrives.'

She squeezed Hamish's fat foot. He was in navy pants and a red and white striped jumper, and kept glancing at Tansy and grinning at her with the sharp edges of soon-to-emerge bottom teeth, drooling. She reached her hands over for him and he came to her happily, smiling as she bounced him and cooed at him and told him he was ridiculously beautiful.

'Look, he knows what I'm saying,' she said, pleased. 'Every time I tell him how handsome he is he gives a big grin.'

Belle watched on, sipping her coffee and smiling, besotted and proud. 'So, have you made a decision about babies? Are you going over there to make a little person? Even if Dougal isn't totally on board? Will you take him up on his offer?'

Tansy kissed Hamish's forehead. He was so warm and so soft. He wobbled around on her lap, bumping his head into her chest, eager hands reaching for her necklace and her hair. 'Honestly, I'm not sure. What do you think I should do?' She played peek-a-boo with Hamish. 'Ah boo, ah boo, aren't you cute, aren't you cute, yes you are, yes you are.'

Belle thought for a while. 'I don't think anyone's ever ready for a baby, you know? Even if you think you're ready, you're not. So, honestly, if the offer's on the table, and when you get there you feel it, and he feels it, and it's all good, then I think you should go for it. I'm not saying rush into it; but make the decision and let it settle. Dream, plan, talk about it. Buy teddy bears. Give him time to truly own the idea in his heart as much as you have.'

Tansy's chest swelled with the idea, and the rabble of butterflies in her belly signalled her excitement. 'You might be right.'

'Trust me, I'm right. You'll never be ready. Dougal will never be ready. But you'll do it. You'll do it anyway and you'll cope. Better than that, you'll thrive. Do you know why?' Belle reached over and took her hand.

Tansy shook her head and leaned to the side as the person next to her got up to the sound of a boarding call and swung his bag into her shoulder.

'Because, my dear friend, you are a creator. You are the type of person who wants to leave the world a better place than you found it. And you will. You and your husband will have a beautiful little baby that will make the world a better place just by being here. And then you will continue to make the world a better place, day after day, taking one challenge at a time and turning it on its head. That's what you do. That's who you are. It's who you've always been.'

Tansy let Belle's words sink in and found they felt right, deep inside her bones. This was what she and Dougal were meant to do. 'What am I going to do without you, Belle?'

'Gosh, what am *I* going to do without *you*?' Belle shook her head. 'I can't even imagine.'

'We'll both survive, I suppose,' Tansy said.

'I guess we will,' Belle agreed.

Then, far too soon, Tansy heard her boarding call. 'It's time.'

Belle reached for Hamish. Tansy stood shakily, checking and double-checking that she had everything with her, tucking her boarding slip into her pocket, and straightening.

'Come on,' Belle said. 'Off you go. Your future is waiting.'

So Tansy walked out of the cafe and joined the throng of people heading to boarding gates, just like her, on their way to new adventures and new horizons, flying into the unknown, but trusting they'd land safely on the other side.

Six months later

Maria knelt in front of her hives. It was a beautiful summer's morning. Blue skies. Bright sun. An abundance of natural beauty all around. The grass was springy beneath her knees. The wide brim of her canary-yellow straw hat cast welcome shade across her shoulders. The hat was a new addition to her wardrobe, picked up at the op shop last week after Sarah's suggestion that she would need a hat every day out in sunstruck Roma. Maria loved the artificial sprig of lavender tucked into its blue ribbon.

She straightened her cotton blouse, suddenly nervous, and knocked on the lid of the hive. Guard bees arrived. A few worker bees sat and took a rest for a moment, waiting for her to speak.

'Hello, my beautiful bees,' she began, emotion thick in her throat. 'I should have told you this news sooner, but I just couldn't bring myself to do it. You've been my salvation, for many years. I don't know how I would have made it without you.' A curious bee, its baskets laden with orange pollen, flew to her and landed on her cotton trousers. She watched it for a moment and her heartache eased.

'I'm leaving you,' she said quietly, and the bees' buzzing lowered in volume as more and more of them settled on the lid of the hive, as if mesmerised by her words. 'I never thought I would leave here, but even at this late stage of my life, God's plan has called me elsewhere.' More bees settled around her, on tree branches, on blades of grass, nestled in flower heads. 'It's still shocking to me that I'm here at all and able to make this choice of my own free will.'

It seemed like a lifetime ago, but in reality it was all still very recent. George Harvey and Blaine Campbell had been good to her. She'd been charged with assault for the deliberate infliction of a sting on Cunningham and sentenced to a hundred hours of community service, which had been waived in view of the service she already gave and under a tsunami of testimonials from sisters, former students and other members of the faithful she hadn't seen in decades, as well as from people she'd met more recently, such as Petrice, Trav and Michaela. There was no historical or medical evidence, as George had explained to her, that Peter Cunningham had been allergic to bees. The only 'proof' was Maria's own memory of him claiming to be allergic, and he might not have been telling the truth. As for her confession, it wasn't enough in its own right to hold up a prosecution for attempted murder.

Poor Celine, on the other hand, was in more trouble. There was enough evidence against her to pull together a case, and when she'd been confronted with it, she'd confessed immediately. She was currently in an institution and her case was being handled through the mental health court. Maria had been to visit her. She'd taken her a pineapple as a gift. 'You remembered,' Celine had said, beaming, and hugged the pineapple to her chest.

Ian Tully had been charged with obstruction of justice. His case had only gone through the preliminary proceedings, but he'd been released on bail and was still serving as the archbishop, although there was growing anger about this from both Catholic and non-Catholic constituents, and an angry media campaign against him. On George's recommendation, Maria had applied for an apprehended violence order against him and been successful. To her great relief, she'd not seen or heard from him since the day she and Tansy had discovered him in her home, and she hoped it stayed that way.

'I'm not leaving you alone,' Maria continued, making eye contact with as many of the magnificent all-seeing eyes of the bees as she could. 'You remember Leo? He's been here with me many times over the past few months, looking after you, looking after your hives. He's quite a competent beekeeper now,' she said proudly. 'And we all know that the world needs more beekeepers.'

If the bees were to survive, it was critical that the old hands educated the new ones. With Leo's encouragement, she'd finally felt confident to put herself out there in the world and share as much of her knowledge as she could before her time was up. Leo had helped her to set up a Facebook page and website on beekeeping and to promote beekeeping courses, which she ran here at the Haven. To her delight, her decades of teaching experience served her well and she'd slipped easily and gladly back into the role. It made her feel alive again in a way she hadn't even realised she'd been missing. Together, she and Leo had educated dozens of new bee enthusiasts in the past few months. His flair for writing was a boon for the Haven. He'd created new marketing campaigns for the orphanage and for the cabin accommodation, and Honeybee Haven was now turning enough profit to build a nest egg for the charity, rather than merely covering costs from week to week.

During this time, it had become clear to Maria that the new leader to take Honeybee Haven to the next level had arrived. Leo had accepted the offer of the role of manager and was officially moving in tomorrow. He thought she'd still be here, but she wanted to slip away quietly, without any fuss. He would be fine without her. Petrice would be here to help him in whatever way she could. Perhaps the change would be good for her too, having someone her own age around to talk to.

But as for Maria, she was leaving her hive.

Good beehives were strong and prolific and multiplied, spreading further and further out across the world, just like education, just like light, and just like faith. A single beehive—maybe even one of her beehives—could quite literally, if it came to it, save the whole world's bee population from extinction. She, too, was leaving to begin a new hive in a town that needed her.

Just as the bush sprouted back with strong new growth after a bushfire, so had her life. Out of all that had happened this year, many blessings had followed, not least of which was her rekindled relationship with her two sisters, who came to visit her often. Enid had even stayed overnight a few times; she'd helped Maria in the garden and baked dozens of honey cakes to freeze for when guests arrived. And once, she'd brought Rose and her four children for the weekend. Having come to terms with Rose's divorce, Enid had thrown herself into the role of supportive grandmother, attempting to fill the spaces the divorce had created, relishing being needed.

Florrie and Alastair were looking at running combined yoga and qi gong retreats up here too. They'd wait another few months, though, right now too busy doting on their newest grandchild, Alice, who had come into the world with no sign of Down syndrome. Jordan and Katarina were deliriously happy, of course.

And sweet little Toby was very protective, Florrie said, not wanting to leave her for a moment. It was a true miracle.

Tansy had phoned last week with news of her own.

'Dougal and I will be coming home in a few months' time. The opportunity came up with his company to relocate back to Australia, so we're taking it.'

'That's great news,' Maria said.

'But after we leave here, first we'd like to take a month's holiday, and, if you and Michaela agree, we'd like to go to your orphanage in Cambodia and help out. I read in the newsletter that Michaela's building a new dormitory and I'd like to go and help decorate it. Do you think that would be okay?'

Maria's heart had swelled. 'I'm sure that would be more than okay.'

'Dougal's got some of his workmates on board too and they're offering to help with engineering or design issues, if they're needed. You'd have to talk to him about that, I don't get all that technical language, but the offer's there.'

'Michaela will be thrilled. I'll run it all past her and we'll get a plan in place for when you're due to arrive. What a generous gift to donate your holiday to helping them.'

'Well, we think we'll get a lot out of it too. And we want to do it now, while we still can, because after we come back to Australia we'll be jumping right into making a baby.'

And then there was Sarah, who had contacted Maria after George had encouraged her, her voice coming down the line from outback Queensland sounding deeper and scratchier with age but still so undeniably *Sarah*, Maria's long-lost friend. Since then they'd been emailing regularly and speaking on the phone, so much to catch up on, so much to heal, so much to celebrate. Sarah had invited Maria to spend Christmas with her on the cattle station, and Maria had crafted dozens of soaps, lotions, oils and candles to take as gifts, and made a special batch of mead. Today she was going to catch the train out to Roma for another new adventure.

And after that? She didn't know yet where she would land. But she had utter faith that it would be clearly shown to her. In her bones she felt that she and Sarah had unfinished business. There was a project out there waiting for them both. Perhaps something to do with helping the victims of the church to make new lives for themselves.

Bees would be there too. Everywhere and anywhere she went, she would be building strong hives and teaching others to do the same, showing them how to care for the bees and how to create food security.

She stood up from the grass and heard something she'd never heard before while working with her bees.

Silence.

Every one of her beloved bees was sitting in silence. Praying for her, she let herself believe. Watching over her. Honouring her.

She bowed her head to them. 'Thank you.'

She walked back down the grassy path, picked up her duffel bag, took one more look around at the coloured Tara cabins, the huts, the grassed area, the dining hall, the trees and the mountains. 'Goodbye,' she whispered. 'God bless.'

She began the descent down the many stairs to the parking lot below where the taxi was coming to meet her and take her to the train. She noted each tread, thanking each step as every footfall landed safely in its embrace. At the midway point she patted the statue of Saint Ambrose, the tears falling down her cheeks and the breeze lifting them up and spiriting them away.

But then, when she was almost down, a small swarm of her bees arrived and surrounded her, the sunlight sparkling off their translucent wings, small rainbows shooting into the air as they moved, embracing her, staying with her as every step took her closer to the bottom of the hill and closer to her new life. Buzzing gently, they swayed and danced, elevating her until she thought she might burst with love.

At the bottom, all one hundred and twenty-four steps done, she paused, smiling at the bees hovering around her. 'We made it. Thank you.'

She lifted her hand and a perfect bee rested on her palm. 'Go on now,' she whispered to her. 'Let's be strong. You have work to do, and so do I. Goodbye, my friend.'

The bee cleaned her wings, washed her face, vibrated, and alighted to the sky, leaving Maria alone again, but filled with wonder.

Author's note

I didn't set out to write this book. I wanted to write about honeybees; that's where it started. (Actually, I wanted to write a family saga set on a coffee farm, but that's another story.) But for some reason, while I was writing scenes and trying to find my story, there were nuns in the background who wouldn't go away, even though they had no place in the plot. Eventually I had to let Maria lead the story and this is where it went.

I want to make it very, very clear that every word in this book is fiction. I made stuff up—lots of stuff. Places, characters, events, legal processes, hierarchies. I did research, sure. But I didn't want technicalities to bog down the spirit of the story that wanted to be told. The only exception to that is any information about bees. To the best of my knowledge and research, all that information is correct, though I am far from a bee expert and apologise in advance for any errors.

And a note about Catholicism. I come from generations of Catholics, was baptised as a baby and made holy sacraments. I went to Catholic schools and studied at Australian Catholic University. I went on to teach in Catholic schools and even taught religion. Some of the nicest people I've known in my life have been Catholics and my memories of Catholicism are overwhelmingly positive.

I had a beautiful nun (Sister Maria, after whom our heroine is named) for a teacher in Year Three; she was kind, loving and fun, and I cried when she left halfway through the year to take up the role of principal in another school. I still find inspiration in words from Peter Kennedy (formerly the long-serving priest of St Mary's church in South Brisbane, but sacked for conducting mass outside of the rules). My uncle Anthony, a sensible, spirited Catholic, is a great humanitarian, backyard theologian and generous wine critic who thoroughly enjoyed helping me write my university theology assignment over a couple of bottles of fantastic red.

My point is that I have great respect for many Catholics. And while today I consider that my spirituality is based in an eclectic mix of many world ideas, philosophies and experiences, the Catholic church and its rituals and teaching will always be a significant spiritual origin in my life.

Acknowledgements

My tremendous gratitude goes to my publishers in Australia and the UK for taking my books on these journeys. So many people work so hard to get these books out into the world. The same goes to my agent, Fiona Inglis, and all at Curtis Brown in Australia and the UK. You are all always on my mind and in my gratitude lists.

Thanks to Gayle Currie, a passionate beekeeper and wonderful woman, for sharing with me so much about bees and allowing me to visit her precious girls.

Chenrezig Institute, situated in Eudlo on the Sunshine Coast, inspired my vision for the location of Honeybee Haven, especially all those steps up the hillside.

I drew inspiration from the wonderful Australian television mini-series *Brides of Christ*; Lesley O'Brien's book, *Mary MacKillop Unveiled*; *Backyard Bees: A guide for the beginner beekeeper* by Doug Purdie; and *Nature's Gifts: Answers to questions about honey, pollen & all things bees* by Athol and Skaidra Craig, with photographs by Glenbo.

Thank you to Simon Groth for inviting me to take part in the Memory Makes Us project at the Brisbane Writers Festival in 2014, and to everyone who contributed memories on my chosen theme of 'soul food'. I found inspiration in your words, and some of them even made the final draft.

The following guinea pigs volunteered to read a much less polished early draft: Amanda Wooding, Kate Smibert, Kathleen Lamarque and Peta Schoenwald. Thank you.

My publisher, Annette Barlow, as always, is completely wonderful and gives the best editorial feedback a writer could hope for.

My copy editor, Clara Finlay, for making me work so very hard and making my words sparkle more than I thought they could.

My family, for everything in between.

My husband, Alwyn, as usual, is the rock and light of my life, as is my adorable cherub, Flynn. I love you guys to the moon and back.